# The Patent

By
Max Garwood
And
Joseph Chamberlain Henry

# Praise for *The Patent*

"When a novel can move readers around the world at breakneck speed, introduce a diverse and fascinating cast of characters, and be a teaching tool about the ins and outs of patents, you know it's a winner. This book's surprises and twists will please readers. Jump on the rollercoaster, the spins are already in motion."

> Dennis E. Hensley
> author of 50 titles including *The Gift*

*The Patent* is sheer genius! It's not only riveting and thought provoking, but it has more twists and turns than a habit trail. An unapologetically modern man's thriller.

> Katie Leigh
> Voice actress

Technological espionage, the race for state-of-the-art weapons, gun smuggling, blackmail, kidnapping, and murder – *The Patent* has everything to keep you saying, "Just one more chapter...just one more."

> Debbie Wilson
> Author of *Tiger in the Shadows*
> Christy Award winning suspense novel

In *The Patent,* co-authors Max Garwood and Joseph Chamberlain Henry, take the reader on wild ride full of intrigue, betrayal, and family turmoil to the brink of World War III. An edge-of-your-seat page-turner that will keep you enthralled to the very last page.

> Henry McLaughlin

Award-winning Author
*Journey to Riverbend*


I love a story that gets to the bones of an idea – and quickly. *The Patent* does exactly that. Civilization as we know it is at stake. If you are a reader who wants strong characters on a complex journey that has you asking "Why?" and "How?" over and over, here's the story for you. Guaranteed: the answers come, but in due time. Garwood and Henry know their craft. Well done!
David Pierce
Author of *Don't Let Me Go* and
*To Kill a Zombie*


As an actor, I live for great stories and this is one! Nothing better than an intriguing spy story and *The Patent* has all the components of a great one. Great story, great characters, all put together by a great writing team!
Gary Moore
Actor


Just finished your new book, *The Patent*! Couldn't put it down! Amazing!
Christine Sacco Williams
Educator and Activist


*The Patent* freakin' rocks! Extremely well written, it is a can't-put-it-down story. Awesome. There is a sequel, right?
Michael Enos
Chief Financial Officer

Published by
Pegwood Publishers

Dedication

To our readers.

And to Max, Barbara,
Marquis and Sarah and Evan,
who have become family.

Joseph C. Henry

# Chapter One

Marc Wayne grabbed a fire extinguisher and doused the greedy flames. His eyes stung and fire erupted a second time. Emptying the contents of the canister, he ignored the chirp of his cell phone.

At last, Marc and the extinguisher prevailed and the flames died. Just to be certain, he stood at the ready, poised to combat another fiery outburst. When nothing happened, he relaxed and set his weapon on the granite kitchen counter next to the television. Movement on the screen caught his attention and he turned to the news channel report.

"In a grab for military superiority, the Chinese have leap-frogged the jet engine technology of the free world. This new Chinese engine powers a superior model fighter plane that according to Howard Vaughan, National Security Advisor to the President, 'poses a serious threat to the safety of our borders.'"

The flat screen showed a gray jet slice through the clouds as seamlessly as a dolphin cutting through the surf.

"Nice."

The CNN report continued while Marc threw open windows

to vent the smoke and fumes. He swept up the disappointing remains of his invention, dumped the ashes into the kitchen sink, and flushed the mess down the disposal.

While the faucet ran, Marc mentally recalculated the interconnecting elements and sequence of steps that led to the now purged ingredients. It was supposed to be an adhesive. He kept one ear tuned to the TV where the morning news predicted overcast skies.

"Weather guessers." He gathered his hair into a ponytail and switched off the television.

The routine bicycle ride downtown was short and pleasant, cycling past welcoming brick homes in the neighborhood where he'd grown up. As he leisurely pedaled, his bike wheels crackled over the early September leaves swirling along the sidewalks and pooling against the curb. He wheeled around a corner and biked down Main Street. Passing the bank, funeral home, and the Veterans of Foreign Wars Post, he braked in front of a narrow brick building that once served as the post office but now was divided vertically into two narrower offices. The sign read *Marcus Wayne, Patents*.

Leaning the bike against the sign, he heard the phone inside. He fished his pocket for the key and unlocked the door. But the ringing had stopped. Recalling the year he was twelve and had worked his first paper route; he picked up the morning newspaper. Today's front-page wire story asserted that rapid advancements in military superiority by governments hostile to the United States could be a precursor to World War III.

"Mornin', Marc." The voice was gravelly. "Did you see the news?"

Marc turned to see Thurmond Yoder peering over his glasses. As long as Marc could remember, Thurmond had been the local veterinarian. The building's landlord, Dr. Thurmond housed his practice in the west section and rented the east side.

"How's business, Dr. Thurmond?"

"Barking along." The wizened old man appeared tall, thin, and angular like the brick office they shared.

"Glad to hear that."

"I'm glad to hear anything at my age."

When Thurmond had an especially mouthy Chihuahua hospitalized for several days, Marc understood why this rental space had been available so often. "And just how old are you, Dr. Thurmond?" This was their customary morning repartee.

"Old enough to remember when you used to come in to get your hair cut."

Marc tossed the key inside where it landed on the receptionist's desk. "I was five."

"Business was slow, so I took up dog grooming. I was clipping your dog and you asked if those clippers worked only on dog's hair."

"And you said, 'Let's see.'"

Thurmond wagged a finger at him. "Looks like you could use another trim."

"Obviously, the experience traumatized me." Marc shook his head. "Haven't been able to face a set of clippers since."

"I might have medication for that."

"I'll keep it in mind." Marc threw a casual salute. He started into his office but his neighbor called him back.

"About the news?"

Marc nodded. "I saw the new Chinese military jet engine."

"Read today's top news story." Dr. Thurmond pointed to the paper in Marc's hand. "During World War II, I served as crew chief aboard the aircraft carrier *USS Monterey*."

Marc knew the story. Well. While a teenager, Dr. Thurmond had lied about his age and enlisted, making him one of the younger veterans of that war. "Along with future president Gerald Ford who helped you fight a fire below decks."

"Fire erupted from colliding aircraft when swells caused by Hurricane Halsey tipped the ship 70 degrees. During that December of 1944, we lost 147 planes and 490 men." Dr. Thurmond removed his glasses and cleaned them with his vet smock. "Do you see the connection?"

Like when he got caught daydreaming in school and the teacher called on him, Marc was unprepared for the question.

"Connection?"

Dr. Thurmond held up his glasses and examined the lenses for smudges. "World War II was a clear case of good versus evil. Enslaving force against republic liberty."

Unsure what to say, Marc shifted his weight.

"My generation fought fiercely with the technology we had." He slipped the clean glasses back on and studied Marc. "What will you do about this new threat?"

"Me?" Marc felt like he wanted to loosen his tie, but he wasn't wearing one. Didn't even own one. "Or my generation?"

"Every generation needs leaders. Especially when the wolf growls at the door."

Dr. Thurmond disappeared into his vet clinic. Marc opened the newspaper across the handlebars. Scanning the disturbing cover story, he pushed his bike inside and kicked the door closed. Marc felt insulated from the world's conflicts in this small Midwest town of Dixon, Indiana. These new political developments had nothing to do with him. Surely someone else would handle the global situation. Someone else always did.

# Chapter Two

Special Agent Mallory Wayne checked the time and mentally rehearsed her argument.

"Relax." Her partner, Fred Ridley joined her at the conference table.

"I'm fine."

"Then stop twirling your hair." He tugged at his own short-cropped crown. "It makes you look like a novice." He snapped his fingers. "Oh yeah, you are the newest member of the task force."

Mallory shifted her twirling into a quick scratch behind her ear. "Welcome back from maternity leave. Have any photos of that new baby?"

"Introducing the reason I was out of the office so you got to be the lead on this project." Fred unfurled the photo section of his wallet like an accordion. "Meet the third Ridley production."

"People keep *albums* on their computer."

"I can show you those, too." He opened his cell phone where the wallpaper was a picture of his wife and children.

Special Agent in Charge Logan Deverell was talking as he entered the FBI conference room. Mid-forties, he sported a deep tan, and a perpetual cup of coffee. "Talk to me, people."

Mallory opened her mouth to open the meeting but nothing came out. Her carefully prepared introduction vanished from her mind.

Fred cleared his throat and indicated the overhead screen. A wide-faced black man reared in Georgia's historic Savannah, Fred had just celebrated his fortieth birthday. The counter-terrorism specialist took the remote from Mallory's hand and pointed it at the overhead screen. "Here's the segment of the CNN special that started this parade." The news clip described a specialized jet engine manufactured by an Asian company, and marketed to governments hostile to the United States.

A decade younger than her supervisor, Hoosier native and Purdue graduate, Mallory specialized in research and analysis. This was her moment to re-engage. To take charge. "According to Department of Defense analysts," Mallory gestured toward the now silent screen, "that engine is an obvious copy of a General Electric engine under development for a new Boeing fighter/bomber."

"That explains why the Defense Department has its underwear in a wad." Deverell unwrapped a stick of cinnamon-flavored gum. "Our directive is to stop the flow of industrial and defense sensitive information to foreign entities."

Mallory passed a file to Deverell. She opened her own copy and began to read. "Going back over the last two decades, Hsu Kai-lo and Chester H. Ho, naturalized citizens were arrested by the FBI in June 1997 and charged with attempting to steal the process for culturing Taxol."

Deverell raised an eyebrow. "Taxol?"

"Used to treat ovarian cancer," Mallory said. "A trace element found in an endangered species of yew tree was used in the formulation of the drug. Bristol-Myers Squibb invested millions to develop the process for culturing commercial quantities of the material from plant cells."

Fred added, "A federal grand jury returned indictments, eleven counts against Hsu, Ho, and a female accomplice, Jessica Chou."

"Hsu, Ho, Chou?" Deverell waved at the stack of files in front of Mallory. "Sounds like verses from *Old MacDonald Had a Farm.* With a ho-ho here and a chou-chou there … What else you got?"

"In August 1997 Harold C. Worden pled guilty to felony interstate transportation of stolen property." She was talking fast. "A 30-year employee of the Eastern Kodak Corporation, Worden was project manager for a processing machine using a secret formula that determines the quality of the photographs." She slid that file to the bottom of the pile and opened the next one. "Kuxuhe Huang sent U.S. trade secrets worth $300 million to China and Germany. Charged under the 1996 Economic Espionage Act, which was passed after the U.S. realized China and other countries were spying on private businesses."

Deverell held up his hands. "Okay. Got it. That stack holds how many such case examples?"

Fred fanned his own stack with his thumb. "I make it to be the size of a D.C. phone book."

"Heavy on the research and evidence, Mallory." He swept his hand in an exaggerated motion indicating the number of files. "What's your point?"

"The point is that we have agents doing a good job tracking down industrial espionage." Mallory tapped the files with a manicured index finger. "The successful development of that jet engine by the Asian company is the result of vital information secured before the engine was tested by the Air Force. Before it ever became another case of industrial espionage."

"Before?"

"General Electric was working on the design, using strict security precautions. The functionality of the GE engine was in foreign hands before GE made the design public." Fred emphasized the word 'before.' "The guts of this engine were disclosed in several patent applications that GE filed to protect the design for later commercial development."

"Meaning?"

"Meaning," Mallory leaned forward. This was the moment to

press her leadership. To display her analysis and deductive reasoning on this case. She spoke each word with overstated slowness. "Somebody had access to the functional design before GE had it tested."

Deverell was quiet, thinking this over.

"Nor was the engine reverse engineered," Fred added, "since there are none on the market."

"Like Americans did to the sturdy and utilitarian German motorcycle during World War II, giving us the Harley Davidson." Deverell smiled. "My personal favorite piece of stolen technology."

Fred smirked. "Yeah, we saw the new model in your parking space."

"Boys and their toys," Mallory noted flatly, eager to get back to her findings.

Deverell tossed his empty coffee cup into the trash. "So, we know what it's not. What do you have for moving forward?"

Quickly, Mallory handed a second file to her boss. "Patent applications are screened upon receipt at the USPTO – "

"Us-pee-toe? Are we back with Old MacDonald's farm? Speak English."

She printed the initials on a legal pad and held up the paper. "United States Patent and Trademark Office. Patent applications that might impact national security are referred to appropriate agencies for consideration of restrictions."

"And then?"

"If the agency concludes that disclosure of the invention would be detrimental to the national security, the Commissioner for Patents issues a Secrecy Order, withholding the publication of the application, of the grant of a patent as long as national interest requires."

"Every pencil pusher has his moments of glory. Okay, so much for the boilerplate. What's your theory?"

Fred nodded to Mallory. There was encouragement in his eyes.

She squared her shoulders. "Secrecy orders were issued for the GE patent applications relating to the fuel delivery and control systems for the engine." To slow the nervous rush of words, Mallory took a deep breath. "The only disclosure of the design outside of the security perimeter was by way of patent applications that revealed the conceptualization."

Deverell looked at his watch. "And the bottom line?"

She set up her theory like setting up a three-point basketball shot. "Our theory is that the information in those applications was compromised in the patenting process."

"Before," Fred emphasized.

"Before General Electric delivered the first engine to the military?" Deverell reached for a pen on the tabletop. "What about leaks at the GE plant?"

Mallory shook her head. "The fuel delivery and control systems were developed by separate teams."

"The plot thickens." He clicked the pen several times. "Meaning?"

"Only the Patent Office had all the applications together in one place." With every click, Mallory's nerves tightened. She glared at his pen.

Deverell followed her gaze and clicked the pen faster. Louder.

"The common denominator is the Patent Office," Fred said.

"Fred and I suggest that we investigate the possibility that the information flow begins at the Patent Office. That's our starting point."

"Is there an echo in here?"

Mallory felt herself flush at the jab and plunged on. "Particularly patent applications stamped with a Secrecy Order."

"Ah – security's weakest link is the individual."

Mallory and Fred nodded.

"Your suggested plan of action?"

Mouth suddenly dry, Mallory wished for a stick of Deverell's gum. "Let's submit our own patent application for an invention desirable for military applications. The goal is to trace the information channels."

Deverell stood and gathered his files. "Find the leaks. Shut them down, and while you're at it – quite frankly – get some good PR." Halfway out the door, he called back. "Eeeny, meany, miny-mo, catch a Hsu, a Chou and Ho. Work out the details, people. Back here in the morning."

# Chapter Three

Shanghai. He hated the place.

Busy and overpopulated, the city offered plentiful opportunities to remain anonymous, a necessary convenience for Colonel Jai Yao's business. China's most populous city and one of the first to adopt the one-child population control policy, Shanghai presented the sadistic illusion of prosperity to countless peasants that immigrated from country villages. It also bore cruel memories that haunted his sleep and confounded his waking hours.

The dirty military vehicle dropped him in front of a tired looking building. The former temple was one of many religious structures confiscated by the government. Owned by the people. The People's Republic.

Most of these historic structures were now Custody and Repatriation Centers. China was "cleaning up her cities," according to the official statement. That meant rounding up beggars, street children, garbage gatherers, prostitutes, the homeless, and any unregistered workers. Anyone authorities opted to bully.

Inside, Yao was processed through a security checkpoint. Under vaulted ceilings, the place smelled of age and centuries of incense burned during religious ceremonies.

Passing an oversized room, sweat broke out on his top lip. Barely lit by narrow windows set far above a man's head, he remembered a similar place years ago jammed with nearly 100 prisoners. Their only crime was that they didn't belong. Yao didn't belong. Insufficient ventilation in the overcrowded space left the inhabitants lethargic, their eyes dulled by hopelessness. Some lay curled on the filthy floor, seeking relief from intestinal complaints. All were plagued by pest infestations and desperate for access to toilets and water for washing.

He shook his head to push away the memory, reminding himself that this was not a Custody and Repatriation Center. This was entirely different.

In a concrete-walled corridor at the building's center, two guards flanked oversized double doors.

Again, Yao flashed his identification and was waved through. What had served as the temple's inner sanctuary currently resembled a laboratory not unlike the one he had studied in on the other side of the world at the Massachusetts Institute of Technology in the United States. Overhead lights were bright and the controlled air was cool and dry. Wearing white lab coats, two-dozen Chinese scientists and technical personnel were busy at workstations.

"Colonel Yao." From the center of the room, one man broke away from what he was doing and came quickly to Yao's side. "We are honored by your presence."

The Colonel barely acknowledged the simpering department supervisor. "Walk with me."

The two passed one workstation after another. Colonel Yao viewed each with a critical eye. "Tell me of your progress."

# Chapter Four

Tim Saad massaged his temples. Maybe some coffee. Someone said caffeine cured headaches. Or was that another American saying. What did they call them? Urban legends?

Stopping at the restroom he checked his sugar level and gave himself an insulin shot. In the break room, he was reaching for a cup when one of the support staff joined him at the coffee pot. His employer, the United States Patent and Trademark Office employed more than 8,000 people at the huge five-building campus headquartered in Alexandria, Virginia. More than half were patent examiners. Fewer than 500 were trademark attorneys. The others were support staff.

"Hi Tim." The pert woman had skin the color of his coffee with just the right amount of cream.

He held his cup under the coffee pot and attempted to fill it. "Hello."

"How are you?"

The pot was empty. "Apparently too late for coffee." Though he couldn't remember her name, he did remember it was Hispanic. Being an agency of the United States Department of Commerce, the patent office resembled the San Francisco airport with half its inhabitants being foreign nationals. He pressed a thumb against his temple. "And this headache is distracting."

"I know what you mean." She stepped closer. "Taking a walk helps. I like to go to the atrium. For the view and some vitamin D."

"Vitamin D?"

"Sunshine." She waved her hand toward the ceiling. "Natural lighting instead of the indoor kind combined with blue computer screens."

"A walk." He was supposed to walk regularly to keep his sugar level balanced.

"I walk every day. Why don't you come with me?" She rested a hand on her slim waist, her fingernails shiny and red tipped to match her lipstick.

In his fifties, Tim guessed the pretty woman was twenty years younger. He looked at his watch. It was lunchtime. He nodded his thanks and they set off in the direction of the atrium.

Once downstairs, she pointed him toward the current display. "You go ahead and take in the new hoopla. I've seen it already. I'll meet you on the other end with coffee."

*Protecting Intellectual Property* was the new exhibit featured in the Patent and Trademark Office Museum housed in the impressive Madison Building atrium. The timeline illustrated the history of patents and trademarks in the United States. "Currently based in Alexandria after a 2006 move from the Crystal City area of Arlington, Virginia," a plaque read, "the office has been fully funded by fees charged for processing patents and trademarks applications since 1991. The move to the new complex was made under the leadership of Under Secretary of Commerce for Intellectual Property, Jon W. Dudas, who was appointed by President George W. Bush in 2004."

Tim considered the modern USPTO campus and marveled at the equally immense revenue generated by intellectual property applications. Awarded in 1421 to Filippo Burnelleschi for an improved method of transporting goods up and down Florence's Arno River in Italy, the first patent encouraged the spread of knowledge while protecting the inventor's legal interests. The unlimited ability of the human mind to create was a constant source of amazement. This building was a credit to minds that had designed a process to amass income from the abstract ideas of others. Developed and maintained by the National Inventors Hall of Fame, the museum and gift shop were favorites of tourists. For Tim, an occasional visit reminded him of the bigger picture, a view of the end product of his efforts.

Born where poverty and starvation shadowed everyday life, Tim grew up with the understanding that doctors and engineers were respected. Government positions carried prestige. Now employed with the United States government, he was respected and admired, at least in his native land. Patent examiners, like him, were generally scientists and engineers. Tim's bachelor's degree in mechanical engineering qualified him for his examiner's position, but his proclivity with electro-mechanical devices placed him in the art unit that examined electrical/mechanical devices.

Further along, the exhibit addressed the Invention Secrecy Act of 1951, "designed to prevent disclosure of new inventions and technologies that, in the opinion of selected federal agencies, present a possible threat to the national security of the United States."

Tim leaned closer. Like a writer finding a review of his latest book, Tim read on to see how the exhibit described his particular responsibilities. "The Department of Defense, military agencies, The National Security Agency, Department of Energy, NASA, and the Justice Department provide a classified list of sensitive technologies that earn an invention a secrecy order."

Reading the same information, a tourist pressed close. Tim moved farther down. "A secrecy order requires that the invention be kept secret, restricts the filing of foreign patents, and specifies procedures to prevent disclosure of ideas contained in the application."

Smelling of spicy kimchi, the tourist bumped against him. Annoyed, Tim moved to the next section. "The types of inventions classified under this Act are a secret. By the end of 2007, there were 5,002 secrecy orders in effect."

He looked sideways to see if the tourist without regard for personal space was bearing down on him, but the man was gone. So was his headache. Looking at his watch, he noted that break time was nearly over. Tim hurried his pace to the end of the exhibit. As promised, his co-worker met him with two coffees.

She smiled as he approached. "Here you go."

"Thank you." Tim sipped the strong brew.

"I took the liberty of adding some sugar." She stirred her own cup and tossed the spoon into a trash. "Low blood sugar can cause annoying headaches."

She remembered a lot about him. Perhaps they had spoke at the Christmas party. Her name still eluded him.

"Feeling better?" They began walking back to their floor.

He nodded.

"A walk," she confided, "can be life-changing."

# Chapter Five

As usual, he was there before his secretary. Marc tossed the newspaper onto Nancy's desk and parked his bike next to the oversized pottery crock that served as an umbrella stand. In colors of clear and turquoise, unmatched porcelain and glass insulators from abandoned power and telegraph poles were mounted on the wall and served as coat pegs.

Down the hall, Marc passed his own office in favor of his workroom at the rear of the building. He dropped his backpack on the worktable, slid open the zipper, and set several objects and a legal pad filled with scrawled notes on the already crowded surface. He snapped on the tabletop light and bent over his project.

That's where Nancy found him later in the morning. He knew she had arrived when the overhead office lights came on. Moments later he recognized the honest fragrance of his favorite Earl Grey tea.

"Did you check your email?" From the kitchenette, he heard the ting of a spoon as it stirred. That would be the honey she laced in the morning's tea.

He didn't bother to look up. "Go ahead. Let me know if

there's anything important."

She came into the room and peered over his shoulder. She smelled of spring lavender. "How's it coming?"

"In the tinkering stage, but looking promising."

Nancy set his John Deere mug near his elbow. "Here, hot and steamy. Cream and honey the way you like it."

"By the way. Could you pick up another fire extinguisher?"

"I sent a new one home with you last night."

"Yes. You did. Good thing, too. And I need another one."

"Hmmm. Perhaps I can arrange a quantity discount." She turned to leave but stopped at the door. "This isn't another ice cream scoop, is it?"

He sighed. "You wound me, Nancy. I patented that while still a teen and sold it to Ronco."

"Or a hairbrush that removes static electricity?"

He glanced at her from under his arm. "And used the static to cause the brush to glow. Very cool." He returned his attention to his project. "I patented that design, too. Which led me from electrostatics to electro-magnetics."

"Magnets."

"Magnetic field sensors and superconductors and the Meissner Effect to be precise."

"I see," she said, and they both knew she didn't. "All these inventions yet you can't work the tea pot."

"That's why I need you, Nancy."

She snorted. "You need me for a lot of things –" The phone interrupted her.

"Including answering the phone." Marc's elbow bumped the mug and sent it crashing to the floor where it shattered, sending ceramic shards scattering, and Earl Grey splashing across the room.

The phone rang again. "That's the phone," Nancy said as they both eyed the damage. "I'd better get it."

# Chapter Six

A letter awaited Yao when he returned to his home. Simple by Western standards, his house was larger and nicer than most. Flanked by tall vases, the mail lay on a lacquered tray in the entryway where the housekeeper had left it. It was from his parents. Their correspondence arrived like clockwork. Pouring a cup of pale colored tea, he scanned the contents.

"The medicine you sent is helpful. It eases the swelling in our joints and the pain the winter cold brings." He recognized his father's careful handwriting. He pictured those old hands that once skillfully nurtured fledgling plants. Now, those same hands were crippled. The previously long and slender fingers were bent and gnarled.

Jai Yao recalled his years growing up as a peasant farmer's son in a poor farming village situated in China's countryside. Each year a traveling preacher arrived. Thin and gentle, the preacher was nameless except that the villagers called him Brother.

"Brother is here," the villagers had whispered as they passed each other in the fields or carried water.

After dark, many neighbors quietly crowded into his parents' home. Yao fell asleep in his mother's lap as Brother spoke late into the night. In the morning, Yao would wake on his own pallet where his father had carried him sometime in the middle of the night. Then it was back to the fields, sleepy, and always hungry. There was rarely enough food to quiet the growing boy's empty stomach.

As he grew older, Yao sensed that the villagers were careful to keep the Brother's brief presence secret from the stern village cadre. It was an unspoken understanding between the common farmers.

When Yao was 15, he and his father were bent over, working side by side in the green rice fields. Smelling dank and promising, the earth had to be coaxed, even seduced to produce enough crops to see them through until the next year's harvest. Suddenly, they heard screaming. Racing from the fields, Yao saw strangers throwing the few household belongings from Yao's simple home. One man held a worn portion of a Bible over his head with one hand and in his other hand was Yao's mother. He clutched her hair by the roots, holding her head at an unnatural angle.

"This is what happens to criminals." Superiority in his voice, he yelled to the neighbors who cringed a fair distance away.

Bolting forward, Yao quickly outdistanced his father. Head down, he barreled into the man who held his mother.

"No, Jai," cried his mother as she was thrown to the ground. The man and the teen rolled and sprawled apart. Yao sprang to his feet, ready to fight. From behind, the cadre and the other stranger grabbed him and pinned his arms. A hand gripped Yao's hair in a tight fist, forcing the boy to look at his parents. Yao's mother and father were being brutally beaten.

"Stop!" Again and again he screamed the same word. Struggling fiercely against the iron grasp that held him, his body was drenched with sweat and his own tears. He wailed until his voice was gone. At last, the attackers exhausted their rage.

Curled in a fetal position on the bloody ground, Yao's mother did not move. The men who held his father released their hold on the battered and bruised man who crumbled to the ground like a pile of broken sticks. As the men yelled something to the horrified villagers gathered around this nightmare spectacle, Yao watched his father crawl to his wife, place a hand against her face, and sag into unconsciousness.

Then Yao was thrown aside. A booted foot cruelly crushed his fingers. He heard and felt the bones snap like dry twigs.

The boy's childhood home was set ablaze along with the family's belongings, heaped into a pile like so much rubbish. And then the strangers were gone.

# Chapter Seven

"The phone is for you." Nancy called back to the workroom.

Marc swept the broken pieces of his cup into the dustpan and tossed the wet mess into the trash.

"It's Mallory."

Marc jogged to his office and picked up the receiver. "Hey, big sis."

"I've been trying to reach you. I tried home early this morning and then your office."

"Yeah? What's happening in the big city?"

"The usual. Stuffed shirts wearing the same hairstyle and trying to run or ruin the country."

Dropping into his swivel chair, he glanced at the familiar words framed on the wall.

*Congress shall have power ... to promote the progress of science and the useful arts by securing for limited times for their authors and inventors the exclusive right to their respective writings and discoveries.*

*– Article 1, Section 8, United*

*States Constitution*

Next to it, hung a second framed quote.

*The question whether there is a patentable invention is as fugitive, impalpable, wayward, and as vague a phantom as exists in the whole paraphernalia of legal concepts.*
*If there be an issue more troublesome, or more apt for litigation than this, we are not aware of it.*
*U.S. Judge Learned Hand*
*Supreme Court*

"Thinking about a trip home to Indiana?" He peered out the window. "The hot summer season is over. An early frost sent Dr. Thurmond scurrying to his garden to harvest his still green tomatoes."

The siblings knew the drill. Tucked inside brown grocery sacks and stored on basement shelves, the tomatoes would emerge rosy red for the Thanksgiving table. In vibrant contrast between the greens and yellows of green bean casserole, and deep-dish macaroni and cheese. It was a Hoosier tradition.

He heard her sigh. "I'd love to see home in the autumn but I've got an assignment."

"Which you can't tell me about," he mimicked in his best James Bond impersonation, "or you'd have to kill me." From the top of his broad wooden desk, he picked up a horseshoe magnet and twirled it around his finger.

Balancing a nine-iron and a collection of coarse fish nets, Nancy came into the room. With creative efficiency she threaded ecru netting onto the golf club and rested the nine-iron in the curtain rod hooks above the window. She fluffed the antique draping into place and stood back to evaluate the look. In the short time she had been working at the office, she had been steadily redecorating.

Marc wondered if it was part of a receptionist's job to add texture to a business. He knew he hadn't talked about it during the interview process. Maybe core classes for university business majors included accounting, marketing, computer skills, and creating tasteful environments for bosses with style deficiencies and no interior designer on the payroll.

He also wondered if there was a term for her style. It certainly wasn't anything he'd seen before. Antique doilies framed the window by Nancy's desk, artfully strung on a Queen Anne piano leg. Turned horizontally, the shapely cherry wood functioned in its second life as a window treatment. Beside the receptionist's desk was a small side table where Nancy kept a collector 8-track player and a stack of Elvis Presley, Lynn Anderson, and Charlie Rich tapes. Across from Nancy's desk and smelling of furniture wax, squatted a wooden church pew for clients while they waited. A hymnal rack held several magazines.

Mallory's tone changed and Marc knew she was getting to the real reason for her call during business hours. The two spoke often but this wasn't just the big sister checking up on her little brother and the usual parrying of sibling witticisms. "Actually, this call is equal parts personal and business. We could use your help."

Nancy adjusted her handiwork and nodded in satisfaction. From his desk she picked up the outgoing mail and left the room.

"My country needs my expertise as a small town patent attorney or one of my world-changing inventions?" He passed the u-shaped magnet over a stack of ferrite magnets. Absently, he observed the attraction of the two elements. Rotating a rectangle magnet, he intuitively measured the distance until he felt them repel.

"A little of both."

He swiveled his chair to look out the window. "The autumn colors are your favorite shade. Grape, orange, and lemonade as you used to name them." Marc did not add that the view looked better with his receptionist's fresh framing. "You can have whatever you need in exchange for a visit home."

"Are you bribing a government official?"

He flipped a ferrite magnet into the air and caught it with the horseshoe magnet. "Negotiating, baby. Negotiating."

# Chapter Eight

In the weeks following their beatings, neighbors gave generously of their limited medical supplies and carefully nursed Yao's parents. Despite kind ministrations of herbs and oils, their injuries were severe and the boy knew they would never be the same. He kept busy doing what he could while his broken hands healed. And he did a lot of thinking.

The Brother came from somewhere else and departed to another destination. The sadistically wicked men who brought destruction were not from any of the nearby villages. They were well dressed and well fed. Yao had heard of other villagers who traveled away from the quiet countryside fields into the large city of Shanghai where jobs and food were rumored to be plentiful. Unable to eke out a living for the three of them here, the boy knew his only option was to venture to the city.

Without a good-bye, because he knew his parents would not want him to go, the teen set out on foot. Days later, he spied Shanghai on the horizon. The throng of humanity crowded together among the immense buildings stunned Yao. But even with all these people in one bustling place, he struggled to find work in this unfriendly setting.

Going from shop to shop in a retail district pungent with odors of food and waste, Yao was offering to do any odd jobs when chaos broke out. Around him people yelled and ran. A group of men dressed like the ones who descended on his village, appeared in front of him. Instinctively, Yao spun around and ran as fast as he could, his feet pounding up and down like pistons. He dodged people and leapt over objects. Glancing back, he was relieved to see he had put plenty of distance between himself and his pursuers. He knew he'd get away.

Until he ran into two policemen.

# Chapter Nine

At his desk, Tim reviewed his progress. All patent examiners were under a strict quota system since the office had received public criticism for customarily taking longer than a year to process patent applications. An accelerated examination procedure had been implemented promising patent applicants a speedy evaluation of their submission. Most patent applications were filed electronically, and filing fees were paid by credit card, putting the patent hopefuls in the queue at a rapid pace.

For several hours he concentrated on a particularly intriguing application, until, feeling his headache return, he decided to purchase a pain reliever at the museum gift shop. He stood and stretched. Reaching for his wallet, he withdrew an envelope. He turned it over, trying to understand what it was and why it was in his pocket. Sliding his thumb under the edge, he tore open the flap.

From inside he removed a white sheet of paper folded around a photo. The clear image showed three men. They were sitting atop a cliff overlooking Israel's Salty Sea – the Dead Sea as the Americans called it. One swarthy Bedouin poured Turkish coffee into the small cup of a second Bedouin. The second man's face was visible and

Tim recognized him from news reports as an arms dealer.

Taller than the other two, the third man in the picture trained a pair of high-powered binoculars toward the distant mountains of Jordan. Tensions between Israel and Jordan were high and unsavory men used this to their advantage. For a bribe, Jordanian border guards didn't object when their border was crossed illegally into Israel's Negev wilderness.

Looking at the tall man, Tim studied the picture closely, gasping for some relief from the panic that surged inside like a storm building on the Mediterranean coast. Suddenly his shirt felt too tight and he wiped his moist palm on his pant leg.

His adult son, his only son.

A second photo lay behind the first. Sweat from his hands made the two stick together. Again, he wiped his hand on his pant leg, and fumbled at the thick corner to pry the first layer off the second. What he saw caused his knees to buckle and he dropped into the office chair. The same three men were gathered around a stack of rectangle boxes. The lid had been crow-barred off the top of a wooden crate to reveal Kalashnikov AK-47 rifles.

The son of a Muslim man and his Jewish wife caught trafficking illegal arms amidst the boiling cauldron of friction in the Holy Land. Action would be swift and public as an example to others – and depending on who got to him first – torturous.

With trembling hands, Tim turned over the photo but there was nothing on the back. Searching the envelope, it was empty. Smoothing the folds of the white paper that had enfolded the picture, he found a lightly penciled message. "I'll be in touch."

# Chapter Ten

Tucking the first of his father's carefully and painfully scribed pages behind the second, Yao paused to pour hot tea from the pot into his half-full cup. The contents had cooled and he detested tepid tea. While always welcome, these letters from his devoted parents occasionally triggered undesirable memories. He lifted the cup to his full lips and drank, his eyes no longer seeing the letter, but a time many years past.

Along with a dozen others who didn't run fast enough, Yao had been transported to an old building that looked out of place among the modern structures that flanked it.

"A temple," one prisoner exclaimed, relief in his eyes.

"It's a temple, all right." A policeman grunted and shoved Yao and the others toward the majestic doorway. "Welcome to the new religion."

Inside, Yao was crammed into an already full cell and the door was locked behind him. In time, the teen learned that he was detained as one of the three no-haves: no papers, no job, and no abode. Detainment was arbitrary. Food was provided once each day and it was low quality and never enough. There was no medical attention for the widespread skin infections, lice, and sickness.

Each day, Yao was escorted to a work center where he and the others were forced to labor to pay for their room and board.

"Eight yuan for daily food." The guard listed on his fingers. "Ten yuan for daily management for three no-haves personnel." He poked Yao in the chest. "If you don't like it here, you can be transported to another Center for 200 yuan."

"I don't have money."

The man gave him a toothless sneer. "Your family can pay what you owe."

Yao stared at the man, trying to make sense of the senseless situation. Then he was pushed back into the vermin infested cell.

Despondency settled over the prisoners in the Confinement and Repatriation Center like a sodden wool blanket, pressing from them hope and life. Several prisoners were taken away. Rumors were murmured that these poor souls went to work prisons. They'd be worked to death, and die in obscurity. Another whisper was that prisoners that disappeared were executed and their organs harvested. Their fate would be a mystery to their families who would never hear from them again.

Yao convinced the work camp's supervisor that he would do the work of two men if the tally would be applied to his account. But after several days, Yao realized his wages were not being doubled. Exhausted and angry, he returned to dragging through a regular day's tasks.

When the work supervisor was berated for the drop in production, a wink told Yao he would receive extra if he worked like two men. But the food rations remained the same.

As Yao's concentrated efforts began to reduce his bill, he encouraged the other detainees to use more effective and efficient methods. Production improved, as did the attitude of his cellmates, though they were still starving.

One day, Yao was brought to a room. A man in a military uniform looked him over and asked questions. Another man in a white lab coat passed endless tests under Yao's nose until his eyes wanted to cross. When he had enough, Yao threw the pencil at the coated man and went for the door. At that moment, the military man uncovered a tray filled with food and told the boy he could have it all in exchange for more tests.

It was the first time Yao could remember having his belly filled. He ate every morsel and found the next wave of tests were far simpler. Pointing to the boy's protruding ribs, the man in the military uniform offered an opportunity to be schooled and trained. And fed. When the man assured Yao that his parents would be provided for as long as he remained loyal, the teen accepted.

Later, in school he realized the second battery of tests were probably no easier than the first batch. The difference was that after eating, his blood sugar was at a level that helped him think and reason with ease. He determined first that he would never be hungry again. And he would find a way to improve his nation so that no one in his country must be hungry as he had been for most of his life.

# Chapter Eleven

The rest of Tim's afternoon was a blur. His emotions darted like a wild bird caught indoors. Who had taken the photos? What did they want? What about his wife? Though years, cultures, and an ocean separated them, he still loved her. Was she in danger?

As he made his way home after work that evening his thoughts chased each other like mice on a wheel. Approaching his front door, he tentatively reached for his keys, afraid of discovering another unwanted surprise in his pocket.

"Hello." The cheerful voice made him jump. The small girl who lived next door appeared at his side. She was nine years old, Tim recalled. Her family had invited him to share birthday cake some months ago. In preparation for the birthday celebration, they had conspiratorially deposited a small kitten into Tim's care that Saturday morning.

"I just picked her up from the pet store." The girl's mother pressed the soft bundle of sleeping fur into his hands. "It's the one she's had her eye on. Could you keep the kitten here while we put the party together? Then bring it over with you. I want to surprise her."

Before he could protest, the young mother had flitted off. "Don't tell," she called back.

Tim had looked dumbly at the kitten dwarfed in his palms. To his relief, the two of them had spent a companionable morning together. He sat on the couch and watched television while the tiny visitor slept in his lap. When the kitten woke, she had followed him, playfully batting at anything that moved while he went about his usual weekend chores of laundry and tossing forgotten leftovers from the refrigerator.

In the afternoon he had picked up his small charge that immediately fell asleep again in his grasp. Making his way next door, he was quickly transformed into a hero when he produced the now purring birthday gift and placed it in the hands of the beaming birthday girl. Since that day, the kitten often met him as he returned home in the evenings, rubbing against his leg as he collected his mail, mostly junk with a sprinkling of monthly bills, and unlocked his door. Then she disappeared back to her own address. On the weekends, the neighbor girl frequently wheeled the kitten past in a baby stroller, the sleepy eyed cat content under a lacey baby bonnet.

"Hello." Tim put out a hand to pat the nearly grown cat purring in its young owner's embrace.

"She has a new collar." His neighbor shifted the cat in her arms so Tim could admire the addition.

Tim fingered the neckline appreciatively. "Looks like she likes it."

"Yep." The little girl bounced on her toes. "See ya' Mr. Tim." And she skipped away.

Tim was jumpy all night, expecting someone to appear at any moment. By midnight he decided the mysterious visitor would choose his own time to make contact. But sleep eluded him as he tossed restlessly on his bed, chasing answers and his blankets.

Certainly the ill-mannered tourist had slipped the envelope into his pocket. The man who pressed too close and smelled of chorizo. How long had someone been lurking, watching, waiting to pass the photo to Tim?

Whether his son was merely exploring the Negev and

stopped for coffee with Bedouins or was involved in smuggling, whether the photo was staged or not, wouldn't matter. The image was enough to inflame zealots to murder.

# Chapter Twelve

Like a drought-ridden field soaks up rain, the young Yao had eagerly absorbed his studies provided by the state. He graduated from the university and was sent to the United States to attend MIT.

In modern Boston, surrounded by a host of the most brilliant minds on the planet, he learned that the population of his homeland was nearing two billion. The population of the relatively newer United States was a mere three hundred million. Yearly in China, 20 million children were born and six million people died for a net increase of 12 million. China's population tripled since the founding of the People's Republic in 1949. Shanghai was home to nearly 13 million of his country's people that congregated there.

On the darker side, each year China arbitrarily detained two million people. A shocking twenty percent of those were children. Over 900 million people in his native land lived in rural locations and made less than one dollar a day. Like he had. Like his parents before him. With his belly full for the first time in his life, he determined to do something about the sparse situation his family lived in and the abysmal conditions he experienced in the C&R.

With an advanced degree in Computer Science and Artificial

Intelligence, the graduate was sent home for a visit with his parents. Though unable to work to provide for themselves, they were once more living in a simple home and for the first time in their lives, had sufficient food.

"You are a fine son," Yao's father had said. "You have honored us by taking good care of us in our old age."

In the village, Yao implemented systems for clean water and improved irrigation for the fields. Until Major Gao's car had arrived to take him to back to the city.

"We have invested a great deal in you," the older man began and Yao knew this was about what he owed his benefactors. What he owed The People's Republic. His service would ensure his parents lived in safety.

Now, finishing his tea, Yao folded the letter. He placed it in a drawer along with the other letters that had come before. Each correspondence reassured him that his parents were cared for. Each letter reminded him of what his government expected from him. And each letter renewed his desire to make his country, and its people, powerful.

# Chapter Thirteen

The next morning, as usual, Tim drove south on Jefferson Davis Highway. At Duke Street he turned right, followed by a left onto Holland Lane, and a right onto Emerson Avenue. He motored into the parking garage. He turned off the engine and reached for the door handle when the passenger door suddenly opened and a man slid onto the passenger seat.

"What do you want?" Tim tried to keep his voice steady.

"You've been expecting me." Small, humorless eyes bore into his. "Good."

"Who are you?"

The man waved away the question. "I will trade the life of your son – your only son – for something of equal value to me."

"But – "

"Quickly. I am not a patient man."

"You can't –" Tim gripped the steering wheel to still his trembling hands. "I have nothing you'd –"

Like a striking snake, the man's hand flew to Tim's throat. The sinister grip tightened, crushing his windpipe. Releasing the steering wheel, Tim clawed at the man's sinewy forearm.

With his free hand the attacker drew a spring-assisted tactical knife and pressed the honed blade against Tim's throat.

Like a frightened bird's, Tim's heart hammered in his chest.

With difficulty he rasped out, "What do you want?"

"Every day you are privy to patent applications that the rest of the world cannot view."

"I can't just –"

Pressing the blade harder against Tim's throat, the intruder brought his face near Tim's. "I want you to give me information protected from common view."

Tim's eyes widened.

The man nodded. "I see you understand which ones I am talking about."

"But – "

Through the thundering of his heart pounding in his ears and the stars that clouded his vision, Tim felt the man's sour breath fill his nostrils and heard his menacing threat. "If you want your son to live, you will bring something my clients will want."

Involuntarily, Tim gave a slight shake of his head and suddenly jerked back from the sting as the knife blade deftly sliced through the skin between his nostrils. Tim's eyes watered violently.

Clutching Tim's throat tightly so that he could no longer breathe, the wiry man positioned his sharp knife above his deadly grip and slowly cut a shallow line across Tim's neck. With a final squeeze against his windpipe, the man slammed Tim's head against the steering wheel and was gone.

Looking to his right, Tim saw the passenger door was open. Into his lap, drops of blood dripped from his nose and neck. Tim opened his own door, leaned over the pavement, and vomited.

# Chapter Fourteen

Mallory had a plan and this morning she would sell it to her boss. Though it was a short trip on public transit from her townhouse to work, Mallory employed the time to prepare for her presentation.

An imposing figure on Pennsylvania Avenue, the J. Edgar Hoover Building came into view. Two days after Hoover's death, on May 4, 1972, President Richard Nixon signed a law naming the structure for the Federal Bureau of Investigation's colorful first director. From its inception in 1908 until 1975, the Bureau had been housed with other offices of the Department of Justice. American entry into World War II postponed the formation of a separate edifice. In 1964, a plan was approved for 2,800,876 square feet to house 7,090 employees. Construction began in 1967. Contrasting with the neighboring marble, granite, or limestone government buildings, the poured concrete exterior contained a unique aggregate of crushed dolomite limestone.

Thirty-eight years after the first proposal for a separate FBI building, and fifteen years after Congress approved construction on the site, employees moved from nine separate locations into the FBI building. A kiosk was added in 1981. In 1991, the sidewalk and trees outside were replaced, and a polished granite wall was adjoined to the courtyard as background for the plaque presented to the FBI by the Judicial Conference of the United States Committee on the

Bicentennial of the U.S. Constitution in honor of the Bill of Rights.

Arriving at work, Mallory was aware the expansive building was starkly bland compared to its neighbors. The single exception in her opinion was the 1989 panels depicting U.S. presidents and important events during their administrations. She liked being part of world events even if it was behind the scenes. It made her feel important. Significant. And she had a plan for stopping the information leak at the Patent Office. She collected her thoughts once more and prepared to meet with her team.

Later that morning, Deverell whistled *Old MacDonald Had a Farm* while his assistant set cups of coffee on the conference table for Mallory, Fred, and their supervisor. She tossed two small plastic creamers to Mallory and disappeared out the door, closing it smartly behind her.

Mallory opened the meeting. "Our directive is to trace the source of sensitive information leaks at the U.S. Patent Office."

"Where are we in the process?" Deverell tapped his pen against his coffee cup.

Fred outlined their progress. "We've contacted inventors to prepare and submit patent applications for inventions that would be desirable for foreign commercial applications. Particularly of interest to foreign military."

"These will be tracked." Mallory emptied a creamer into her coffee. "To trace the information channels, watch for the leaks, and shut them down."

"And," Deverell clicked his pen, "getting some good PR – "

"Wouldn't hurt," Fred finished.

"What technologies are involved?"

Mallory knew the answer to this. She had established specific criteria that would yield pertinent information for their investigation. "We stayed away from current Department of Defense projects." Mallory dumped the contents of the second creamer into her cup. "But we want to sweeten the honey pot to attract our target."

"Submit an application that would be irresistible to a technology thief." Fred looked back to Mallory.

This was where she unveiled her strategy. "We opted to

search for an idea with military potential from an inventor completely separate from any government connection. A real person so no one in the information pipeline would get suspicious. Someone with a plausible idea and a legitimate application."

"Does this prince charming come with a glass slipper?" Deverell tucked the pen behind his ear.

"We found a hobbyist who submits patent applications on a fairly regular basis," Fred began.

Mallory turned to face Fred. "It's not a hobby to him."

Fred put up his hands in surrender. "My apologies, Mallory."

Deverell cleared his throat. "Who does he work for?"

"For himself."

"And he's a patent attorney so he would generate his own applications," Mallory added.

"We're not sure if his freelance patent work for other inventors supports his inventions or if his inventions support his office," Fred noted.

Deverell finished his coffee and tossed the cup at the trashcan. The cup hit the rim and bounced to the floor. "What does this hobbyist have that a foreign entity would be interested in?"

"The invention we're interested in is for a vehicle that is propelled by the generation of a Meissner Field." Mallory held her hand, palm side down and circled it above the tabletop.

"A what? English people, we speak English here."

Mallory handed a computer printout to her boss. "If this could be done, it would have substantial commercial and military ramifications."

Their boss waved the paper. "So how did you technophobes come up with that?"

"It was suggested as being the Holy Grail of magnetic inventions by the hobbyist," replied Fred.

Deverell scanned the sheet of paper. "Wrong fairy tale. No glass slipper, but knights, a round table, Excalibur, and a love triangle. Go on."

"This particular inventor is well known for his inventions centered on – "

The supervisor held up his hand to interrupt her. "You said this guy is a hobbyist."

"Who is known for his work in electro magnetism."

He nodded and looked to Fred. "We'll assure him that the FBI simply needs the application to look realistic. The plan is to get his permission to submit this patent application and track it. We'll dangle the Holy Grail and see which foreign knight comes courting."

Mallory cleared her throat. "We have his permission."

Fred turned to Mallory. "You've already told him what we have in mind?"

"This morning. Before the meeting."

Fred directed his attention back to Deverell. "We already have his permission."

"People," Deverell's voice was low, "who is this guy?"

Fred hooked a thumb in Mallory's direction. "Mallory's brother."

The supervisor's eyebrows shot up. "Brother?"

"Her baby brother."

Deverell looked from Fred to Mallory. "Your brother is an inventor?"

"And patent attorney," Fred listed.

"Well, he's my adopted brother, really."

"That explains everything." Deverell retrieved the pen from behind his ear. The pen clicked.

She closed the file and folded her hands on top of it. "My parents adopted him – "

"I understand that part." He clicked his pen with each word for emphasis. "You're suggesting involving family members. It was disastrous in Camelot."

She straightened. Ever since Marc had come home as a winsome infant, she had been fiercely protective and mother hen in love with her brother. "I recognize that. But Marc really is an inventor. He is a patent attorney known for submitting his own patent applications. This application will appear natural, expected."

Deverell was quiet for a long time, the pen still and forgotten on the tabletop.

"He fits the profile," Fred said.

The boss sighed and rubbed the back of his neck.

Mallory pressed, "And he's really working on a –"

"Meissner Field Generator." Deverell thumbed through the papers in front of him. Finally he closed the folder and stood. "All right. Let's run with it." He left the room whistling, *Camelot*.

# Chapter Fifteen

Bent over his computer, Marc became aware of the scent of lavender. Glancing up, he saw Nancy in the doorway.

"Can I get you something before I leave? Tea?"

Marc stretched. "What time is it?"

"Time to close the office." She came to stand beside his desk. "Working on another patent application?"

He nodded. "Lucky guess, considering it's what I do."

"You do a lot of things. But you most enjoy the applications."

"Really? What evidence do you have to prove that statement?" He rocked back in his desk chair and linked his hands behind his neck.

"Easy. Besides tinkering on your inventions in the workroom, the applications are the only other task that consumes your attention so you forget to eat or notice quitting time." She pointed to the atomic clock on the wall. Last year's Christmas gift from Mallory, the device additionally displayed the current moon phase, temperature, humidity, wind chill, wind speed, wind direction, UV index, barometric pressure, rainfall, and dew point.

He huffed. "Tinkering?"

"A scientific term." She straightened the frames on the wall. "How's this one coming?"

He was deciding how much she would want to hear, how much he should try to explain, when she peered over his shoulder at the computer screen.

"I see you've drafted the claims. And the drawings have your handwritten reference numbers on them." She straightened. "So it's time for you to dictate the specification."

She had picked up the process quickly. "Right you are. As soon as I complete more research into the prior art, I will spew techno-words into this apparatus for your listening and typing enjoyment tomorrow morning."

"Techno prosaic with an ly here and an ing there. For these applications, you make up language by attaching suffixes to harmless words."

"Patentese." Marc rubbed his eyes. "Or do you prefer I use some of that country lyric lingo of Chuck Daniels' you listen to?"

"That's Charlie Daniels." She clucked her tongue at his faux paux. "It wouldn't hurt for you to broaden your cultural horizons to music that includes words." She collected his empty mug and was whistling *Devil Went Down To Georgia* when she stopped at the doorway. "See you tomorrowly morningly."

He heard the front door close and she was gone for the day. Unfolding from his computer-focused slouch, Marc stood and took a deep breath. The scent of lavender lingered. Checking the time and outdoors temperature, he wondered what music Nancy would listen to on her way to where ever she would go after work. Did she sing in the car?

He twisted his back until it cracked, and returned his attention to his prior art research for the Meissner Device application. The dictation was the final aspect and he activated the recorder and began the long and laborious task.

"The prior art indicates that there has been interest in gravity control propulsion research with such terms as anti-gravity, anti-gravitation, baricentric, counterbary, electrogravitics or eGrav, gravitics, G-projects, gravity control, and gravity propulsion, being used in the literature. Such approaches have dealt with the attempted manipulation of gravity or the production of gravity-like fields for propulsion."

He flipped pages on his legal pad to find a set of notes and followed the smell of coffee to the small kitchen. Nancy had set a pot to brew before she left. He carried the pot and a clean cup back to his desk. Since Nancy had begun working, his used and stained cups that had formerly grown into biohazards, appeared miraculously clean and shelved in the kitchenette. "Several Universities have done basic research into the nature of gravity and how it interacts with electro-magnetic fields. The present invention, in contrast to these attempts to block or manipulate gravity, uses the projection of a magnetic field exclusionary barrier or boundary through which an external magnetic field does not extend."

Reaching for a magnet from the stack on his desk, he held it in mid-air. Passing a pencil around the magnet, he described the process into the recorder. "The exclusionary boundary encompasses a three-dimensional space defined by the boundary projected from the Meissner device from within the boundary itself. While the present invention is not truly the exclusion of magnetic fields due to superconductivity as is the case in the Meissner effect, it is convenient to refer to this as a Meissner device."

Dropping the pencil, he balanced the magnet across his index finger. "The Meissner device projects this exclusionary boundary which then allows the device to float in the ambient magnetic fields. Similar, for example, to a submarine that is submerged. The submarine has its own exclusionary boundary, which is the hull of the boat. The controlled volume of air and water contained in the ballast tanks provides buoyancy. The Meissner device becomes buoyant in a sea of magnetic fields. This device is described more fully herein along with methods of controlling the buoyancy and the propulsion control."

Hours of dictation fueled by caffeine, culminated in a digital dictation file that he left on Nancy's desk. Right next to her oft-played recording of Charlie Daniels.

# Chapter Sixteen

Tim had something for the blackmailer. A foreign agent, he was sure. Judging from his skin tones and accent, Tim guessed the man was Asian or from India, though he didn't know what corporation, knowledge broker, or government the stolen information would be pedaled to.

Did the beetle-like man, who scurried unseen in and out of deserts, countries, parking garages, the Patent Office, and Tim's life represent a single government? Or did he twist products from spineless cowards like Tim and market them to the highest bidder in some clandestine auction?

Tim had followed the instructions, delivered the data, and now breathed a deep sigh of relief. It wasn't exactly the prizewinner of invention patents but it had been subject to a secrecy order. Tim had played small in this espionage game, like he did in life, and hoped it would satisfy the blackmailer or at least prove that Tim was not worth his time. Either way the man who reminded him of a cockroach would surely go away.

At home that evening, Tim wrinkled his nose when he entered his apartment. No doubt he'd been so distracted over these past weeks that leftovers in the refrigerator had expired. Tim longed to return to his dull, lonely evenings wallowing in self-pity. He went to the bathroom to check his sugar and administer his customary injection. Swinging open the medicine chest, he glimpsed an image reflected in the mirrored door. Slowly, he swung the vanity mirror back several inches until he saw it. Something was in the bathtub.

Leaving the mirror to swing, he cautiously approached the white porcelain tub. The source of the putrid smell. His neighbor's cat, their beloved pet. Now a ghastly, grisly sight. Horror and fear flooded into his throat and he quickly leaned over the toilet and retched.

Sweaty and trembling, Tim fled from his apartment and into the cool night air. Directionless, he ran past restaurants whose dinner aromas caused his stomach to flip, threaded through yellow taxis gleaming under streetlights while waiting for their next fare, and dodged pedestrians. He ran until he couldn't run anymore. Breathless, he bent and rested his hands on his knees. Guttural moans gurgled in his throat. Straightening, he gulped in great amounts of air. His heart thudded against his ribcage, drowning out the bass music that spilled from a nearby bar and pounded from passing car radios.

He walked, passing familiar streets crowded with businesses, neighborhoods, and streets alight with bobbing headlights. He thought about never going back. Not to his address. Not to his neighbors who would ask if he had seen their missing kitty. Not to work. Surviving by his wits would surely be easier than facing what was back there, waiting for him. Not just the corpse of a cat but the insidious demands of a blackmailer that would never be satisfied. Would always want more. Threatening him. Demanding he do, and be, what he couldn't and wasn't. He raked a hand through his hair and cursed.

Collapsing onto a park bench, he put his head in his hands and sobbed. Huge, shuddering sobs. When he'd cried himself dry, Tim lay on his back on the bench. Staring at the stars, he recognized the physical signs of shock. And knew he needed that injection. How easy it would be to deny himself the insulin. Disappear into a diabetic coma.

It was a coward's escape, he admitted. But he already knew he was a coward. Not bold like his passionate wife. He had made a mess of his dreams because he was too afraid to reach for them. He could go on being a coward. He'd done it so well for so long that it was the only thing he was good at.

Above, the moon was clear in the night sky. When his son was three, father and son had watched a lunar eclipse. In their short time together, he had memories like snapshots that Tim occasionally pulled from the library of his mind and viewed through the lens of time. Tonight the moon shone bright, trailed by the little star that dogs it.

He sighed. If he didn't go back, they would destroy his son. That was the message in the bathtub. What was the worst that would happen? Presently he was contemplating ending his own life. But this wasn't about him. It was about his son. The son he'd already let down. Abandoned to the currents of politics and culture. No. Not this time. If it were the last thing he did, this time, Tim would protect his son.

Reluctantly, his legs feeling equal parts concrete and quivering jello, he set out for what awaited him at home.

# Chapter Seventeen

"Though still in a theoretical stage, the Meissner Field Generator would project a diamagnetic field that would serve to repulse all magnetic fields including the earth's magnetic field. It has unlimited potential for frictionless transportation of everything from people to cargo. Even for planetary exploration." Marc stood at the front of an Advanced Physics class. From the rows of chairs, 150 Indiana University students stared at him.

"Sounds like a magician's trick," smirked a boy slouching in his seat. The girl next to him slapped him on the top of his head.

"Levitated above the ground," Marc picked up a notebook from the closest student's desk and balanced it on his fingertips, "this system would essentially eliminate the static and dynamic friction that the engines in our vehicles primarily are used to overcome."

"How will it improve the environment?" A girl with blonde braids wanted to know.

"If perfected it would be an environmentally clean system and use miniscule amounts of energy." Marc returned the notebook to its owner who asked, "What are the economic ramifications?"

"With the cost of fuel these days," Marc pulled his wallet from his back pocket and waved it, "this will prove a dynamic boost to the economy presently stressed under high fuel costs. Not only will consumers have more money in their pocket, but consider the jobs it would create to retool our infrastructure."

The slouching boy slouched further in his seat and rested his sandaled feet on the back of the chair in front of him. "Aren't you considered a crack pot inventor?"

Several students snickered. From his seat in the front row, the professor jumped up and faced his class. "Mr. Wayne, like many great inventors, is viewed by some as eccentric. But I assure you, his work is well-respected and he is a frequent invited guest lecturer at universities and scientific conferences."

Tucking his wallet back into his jeans, Marc leaned on the lecture stand. "Thank you, Professor, but for a serious inventor, being called a crack-pot merely proves he's in the game."

A geeky-looking guy in the back gave Marc a thumbs up.

The professor pushed his glasses up on his nose and sat down.

"Nikola Tesla." Marc watched the crowd for signs of recognition. Several students nodded their heads. "The Austrian inventor who became an American citizen in 1891, is best known for many revolutionary contributions in the field of electricity and magnetism in the late 19th and early 20th centuries. But due to his eccentric personality, seemingly unbelievable and sometimes bizarre claims about possible scientific and technological developments, Tesla was ultimately ostracized and regarded as a mad scientist."

Along one wall of the classroom were poster-sized photos. Marc pointed to a portrait next to a familiar image of Orville and Wilbur Wright's maiden flight. "Indiana's own Art Smith was called the Smash-Up Kid. At his home in Fort Wayne, Smith studied books and articles about flight. He believed he could improve on the Wright Brothers' design. His parents provided him with nearly $2,000 –"

Someone gave a low whistle.

Marc nodded. "For a business investment, that's small change today. But in 1910, it was a lot of money. His invention reached nearly 50 miles per hour, rose alarmingly, dipped, rose again, and crashed."

"Ouch," came a voice from the back.

"Indeed. Art was thrown onto the frozen ground and severely injured."

Marc crossed over and stood next to Art Smith's picture. "On October 11, 1911, he flew from Fort Wayne to the nearby city of New Haven. That earned him the new nickname, Bird Boy. He went on to become a world-class showman and celebrity, known for dazzling crowds with his daring flying."

Marc shoved his hands into his pants pockets. "Any questions for this crack-pot?"

The students laughed and Marc pointed to a chubby young man with his hand raised.

"Like, how would such an invention benefit our military?"

"The way I see it, there could be significant reductions in the cost and bulk of a weapon delivery system. Presently a warhead on a missile is only a small fraction of the total mass of the missile. The fuel required to move the weight of the entire system to its intended target places constraints on the ability of the missile to avoid countermeasures such as an anti-missile missile." Marc returned to the front of the room as he spoke. "For example, due to its substantial weight, the largest investment for a typical intercontinental ballistic missile is in the delivery system. By developing and employing the Meissner Field Generator, heavy cargo can be transported for a fraction of the cost."

A girl shrugged off the arm the boy with flip-flops had draped around her shoulders. "All this talk of war and blowing things up is so typically male." She fingered her earring. "What are the peaceful applications for this device?"

"Mostly the Meissner Field Generator would change the way we transport everything," Marc answered. "Heavy construction materials will be moved effortlessly. Our roads will look like a Disneyland ride as vehicles hover above the ground. In fact, it would eliminate the need for roads altogether and free up the millions of acres used to support the wheels of commerce. Asphalt roads that can then be used for agriculture, recreation, and living areas."

The girl rolled her eyes. "Sounds like a rerun of the television show *Jetsons*."

"Like Luke Skywalker's Land Speeder in the classic Star Wars films." The redheaded student in the back demonstrated by circling his hand, held flat, in the air.

"Quite," Marc agreed.

"With respect to the females in our class," the chubby boy gave a mock bow to the girl who had asked the question, "how can we use this to gain a military edge?"

"The greatest benefit lies in the ability to be undetected. The Achilles heel of the intercontinental missile is the fact that it has limited steering capability. Its course is predictable. Like anything predictable, the weapon is therefore relatively easy to intercept." Marc pressed a button on his laptop computer and an image appeared on the overhead screen. A video showed the launch of an interceptor missile. The narrative described, "The present system is a method of interception. When an Intercontinental Ballistic Missile is launched and detected by a satellite, an anti-missile missile can be launched to intercept the ICBM. When the anti-missile missile nears the point of interception, its terminal guidance system determines the optimal time to detonate to disable or destroy the ICBM."

On the screen, the darkness of near earth space exploded into vibrant flames as an interceptor missile cleanly connected with an intercontinental missile safely above the earth.

The short video ended and Marc explained. "In contrast to current weapons like the ICBM, a weapon delivery system powered by a Meissner Field Generator could theoretically fly at low altitude, just above the ocean waves, and under the radar. Such a device could be programmed to follow an unpredictable path, or simply join the stream of commerce."

After a quiet pause, the geek in the back shifted. "That makes it nearly invincible."

# Chapter Eighteen

Massaging his temples, Tim once more scanned the troublesome patent application. Like a pinball that ricocheted from obstacle to obstacle, his thoughts bounced from the blackmailer to his work. He wasn't making much progress with either.

He didn't want to betray his integrity and his job by forwarding militarily sensitive information. He'd experienced cultures in conflict. Globally, it erupted into war, killing, and hideous rebar reinforced walls. Literal walls like the one in Israel. Figurative walls like the one between himself and his small family that were harder to break down than concrete ones. Personally, it caused him to see himself for the spineless coward he was. It left him alone, hollowly pining for his wife and son. For family. For community. For relationship.

He didn't want to, couldn't, be a catalyst for more of the same. His eyes went back to the patent application he had been considering for days. Without doubt this required top-secret status. Such a fantastic device. It would revolutionize the world. A few innovations had done just that – submarines, missiles, the Internet. Of course, the military would be the first to develop and use this. The country that implemented this transportation system would be –

Tim rubbed his temples again – that country would be militarily superior. A world power. Invincible.

Rocking back in his office chair, Tim weighed his options. The U.S. had a reputation backed by a long history for aiding nations worldwide. Unlike other conquerors, Americans didn't appropriate the cultures they helped or defeated. He thought again of the Arabs who held Bethlehem and the Temple Mount and still bombed innocent children in Jerusalem schools.

Though his superior frowned on the practice, Tim hit the print button. He couldn't remember the last time he had looked at an application on hard copy. All reviews were conducted over the computer screen. It was more secure that way. But today Tim made an exception, partly because he was having difficulty focusing and partly because he hoped if he spread the entire project in front of him he would be able to put his finger on what kept him from forwarding this to the next step in the process.

# Chapter Nineteen

It was morning in the red light district near the United States capitol. Mr. Spencer had been awake for hours, plotting, while the Asian half-breed he had spent the night with slept curled at his side. He watched as she stirred and stretched, much like a cat waking from a nap. Rolling over, she smiled and traced his chest with a lacquered fingertip.

"You like, Mr. Spencer?"

He caught her wrist in a vice-like grip and fear instantly replaced her smile. "Last night I liked very much. Now I like some breakfast."

He released her and she scrambled from the bed, tossed a housecoat over her slender frame and scurried from the room. Lying back, he laced his fingers behind his head and stared up at the ceiling. In moments, the satisfying aroma of sizzling butter made his stomach growl.

Soon she was back with two plates. His was piled high with eggs and bright chorizo, spicy kimchi, and white toast. He devoured it all and two cups of coffee while she observed him over her own serving of toast and fruit.

Typical for the neighborhood, he heard the sounds of others in the nearby apartments. Dogs barked, a child cried, and the whine of bad water pipes told him someone in the unit upstairs was in the shower. With his belly full, he showered, dressed, and went outside.

Mist colored the outdoors a ghostly gray. Near his car, Spencer glanced back and spied a boy about seven, his gaze hard and unblinking. Spencer continued on his way for several more paces before he looked back. Sure enough, from the shadows the boy was still watching.

Anger surged through the man. He was accustomed to spying on others, not being observed. He climbed into his rental car and drove around the corner. After parking, Spencer stealthily made his way back to the apartment complex. The shadowy area was vacant. Retracing his steps from the night before, he saw movement going into the address where he had spent the night.

Slipping silently inside the door, he heard the water running behind the closed door of the bathroom and knew the girl was in the shower. From the kitchen came the sound of a dish scraping against the table. Drawing his knife, Spencer peered around the corner into the room.

# Chapter Twenty

The tactical room was noisy as employees from different departments gathered. Tangy colognes vied with strong perfumes. Most were dressed in business blue.

"Stuffed shirts all wearing the same hairstyle and trying to run or ruin the country." Mallory took a tall backed chair next to Fred.

He raised an eyebrow. "Pretty cynical considering we represent that."

"Speak for yourself."

Conversations regarding football and Nascar quieted when Deverell burst into the room. He was speaking before he sat down. "Talk to me, people. How is Red Riding Hood leaking information out of the United States Patent Office?"

Resembling an out of shape linebacker, a portly man spoke up. "We're monitoring the phones."

"Grandma, what big ears you have." Deverell pulled a pen from behind his ear and pointed it at the man. "What about cell phones?"

"Not allowed in the workplace, sir, and we're listening for anyone who found a way to get one inside."

Deverell turned to a woman with peroxide blonde hair. "My department is watching for potential methods employees might use to smuggle applications out of the building."

"Grandma, what big hands you have." Deverell tapped the pen on the tabletop. "How is the wolf gaining entry to Granny's house and cherry picking from the cookie jar?"

"Patent applications are submitted by express mail or through the Internet." Mallory held up a printout of a patent application. "They are processed on computer. By hitting a few keystrokes, an application could be diverted to a new destination."

"Grandma, what big eyes you have." Deverell swiveled his chair to the left. "Jimmy?"

With brown eyes behind John Lennon spectacles, the forty-something drummed long fingers against a mug of green chai tea. "Computer forensics is already on it."

"And?"

"And we are in the fun stage. Looking. Searching. Exploring. Considering the options and possibilities."

There was a snort from the portly man. "That's code for doesn't have a clue."

With a middle finger, Jimmy exaggeratedly pushed up his glasses on his nose. "Translation courtesy of the auditory department's ass…," he took a drink from the cup, "sets."

Several people snickered.

Deverell ignored the slight. "Where is our patent application for the Meissner Device in the process now?"

Mallory spoke up. Her plan was progressing precisely as she had calculated. This may be her first time to be the lead on a project, but it was coming together swimmingly. She pushed down a feeling of pride. She was made for this type of leadership. She was a natural. "It is exactly where we wanted it to be – being examined for a secrecy order."

# Chapter Twenty-one

Following a lively question and answer session, Marc collected his computer, used to show the film clip, and slid the laptop into a carrying case. From the lectern at the front of the classroom where Marc had given his guest presentation, the professor assigned homework and dismissed the class.

"As always, thanks for coming, Marc." The professor walked with him to the door.

"The students are refreshing. Their quick wit and probing questions keep me from getting stale in my dusty office and cluttered lab."

The older man ran a hand through his unruly gray hair. "Each year students seem less refined, no respect anymore for social graces and protocol."

"They probably slurp designer coffee drinks in comfortable clothes and talk about us dinosaurs." Marc clapped the weary professor on the shoulder. "Be good to them. They will design your old age living conditions."

Tossing the professor a good-bye salute, Marc headed toward the parking lot. Preparing for the Little 500, a string of collegiate guys and girls pedaled past on bicycles. The clusters of bicyclists around campus resembled the flocks of Canadian geese that were taking to the skies in their yearly migration to winter over in warmer climates. Retired Indiana residents, affectionately called snowbirds, followed the geese to Florida for the cold months and returned in the spring to resume their volunteer work at the library and hospital. While Indiana residents didn't always know their way around the Hoosier state, they had long considered Florida to be a suburb.

In the spirit of the nearby historic Indy 500 in Indianapolis, the Little 500 was a popular attraction on campus and a favorite in the surrounding community. The largest collegiate bike race in the nation, the yearly intramural event drew crowds numbering 25,000 to watch the four-person teams compete around a quarter-mile track. Proceeds funded working student scholarships. The final year Marc had participated as a student, riders in the one-day event brought in $40,000.

For the majority of bicyclists, the Little 500 was their first competition. Marc had agreed to make a three-some into a four-some after he was the recipient of Little 500 monies. Ribbing from the other three who accused him of being so parked in the lab that he was suffering from vitamin D deficit helped his decision to get involved.

"Been an addiction ever since," Marc said to himself.

"Can I carry that for you?"

The voice came from behind. Without waiting for an answer, a wiry student with red hair came alongside and reached for Marc's weighty computer bag. He eagerly stuck out his right hand. "Interesting presentation in class, Mr. Wayne."

Marc accepted the firm handshake, noting the boy's *Li'l Abner* t-shirt. "Chivalry is not completely dead."

"Excuse me?"

"Never mind." Marc squinted at him. "You're the guy in the back of the room." Marc declined to add the geeky-looking guy in the back of the room.

"Aspiring crack pot." The student eagerly fell into step next to Marc. "I'd like to show you something I've been working on."

Marc glanced at his watch.

"It won't take long." The words tumbled out, picking up speed. "And I can talk fast."

"Just calculating." Marc dropped his arm. "When I was a student, I ate every two hours. Class was that long and I'm hungry."

The young man grinned. "I can show you where they serve the biggest and best burgers."

"Lead on, Kimo Sabe."

"Hebron, actually. Hebron Heath." He shifted his backpack to balance the load with the weight of Marc's computer.

Another four-some on bikes pedaled past, the last guy calling encouragements like a goose at the back of a flying vee.

Marc glanced at his new companion. "Do you ride in the Little 500?"

His shoulder drooping with the weight of Marc's bag, Hebron looked sidelong at him. "Do I look like the athletic type?"

"An inventor invented the bicycle."

"And inventors have been modifying the design ever since." Hebron pointed to his oversized feet. "And athletic shoes. Job security."

"Even inventors ride bikes. I'm the visual aid."

Hebron shook his head. "I prefer mental work-outs."

"Same argument I used."

"Huh?"

"Get on a bike. Your body will enjoy the attention and your mind will solve problems in the fresh air. Besides," Marc looked him up and down. "You could use some sun."

Hebron held out his pale arms, Marc's computer bag hanging from his left hand like a ripe fig on a tree. "Do I look like I tan?"

# Chapter Twenty-two

Something niggled at Tim about the patent.

He'd kept it at his desk longer than any other project. He was tempted to pass it to the weasel blackmailer but was terrified to unleash such technology into the wrong hands. Such a unique design, should there be an investigation, it would surely be traced back to his desk.

The man in the parking garage who demanded secrets surely sought to empower an ambitious leader. Tim spread the troublesome application on his desk, studied it until the figures blurred and the words no longer made sense. Then, once more, he set it aside. From his desk drawer he retrieved a bottle of pain medication. He shook two tablets into his palm, considered the size and intensity of his headache and shook out two more. From the same drawer, he added two stomach lozenges. With a mug of yesterday's cold coffee, he downed the tablets. Rolling the lozenges around in his mouth, he stood and began to pace.

In 2005, the USPTO issued U.S. Patent 6,960,975 to Boris Volfson of Huntington, Indiana for his design of an antigravity space vehicle. Designs for perpetual motion machines had been submitted since the turn of the 20<sup>th</sup> century. Patent applications on such devices became so numerous that by 1911 the patent office ruled that perpetual-motion machine concepts had to be accompanied by a model that could run in the office for a period of one year. The rule was later dropped.

Theoretically powered by a superconductor shield that changed the space-time continuum in such a way that it defies gravity, Volfson's patent made the news. Physicists charged it was an impossible device. The USPTO's official response was that mistakes were inevitable. With 5,000 examiners handling a workload of 350,000 applications yearly, patents may be granted to unworkable ideas.

Tim's need to keep his name out of the headlines was as strong as the pressure on him to provide something to the blackmailer. But he didn't dare risk playing small again. He thought of the neighbor's pet.

And his son.

The penalty was too dear. Too costly.

"Hi, Tim."

Startled, Tim stopped pacing and stared at the intruder.

"I brought you something." She came forward and put a cup in his hands. "Fresh brewed." She wore a form fitting black skirt and a bright shirt with a deep V-neck.

"Oh, uh, thank you." *What was her name? The Hispanic woman who had walked with him to the atrium?* He still couldn't remember.

"Are you all right?" She came closer and held his gaze with her brown eyes.

*How did she get in this secured section of the building?*

Tim shrugged. "Fine."

She tilted her head flirtatiously. "Do you always pace in your office?" She glided to his desk and picked up the irksome application.

"I don't think you're cleared –"

"Of course. I was just curious about what was troubling you." She replaced the project on his desk. "Can I help?"

Tim gazed into her upturned face. Slowly he shook his head. "No, I don't believe so."

"But you are worried."

He blinked and stepped back. "No, no, I'm fine."

She tapped his coffee cup with a red fingernail. "Well, drink your coffee while it's still hot." She spun on a stiletto heel and left, her heels echoing down the hallway.

Had he been so lost in thought that he hadn't heard her approach? Or had she come in more quietly than she'd left? He shook his head to clear it. He was suspicious of everyone lately. Best get this blackmailer off his back once and for all.

Dropping into his chair, he picked up the application again. What was it that bothered him about this piece? He went over the USPTO criteria. Was the idea patentable by law? Was it new? Based on the current state of science, was the idea described in a manner to enable someone skilled in that technology to make and use it?

Taking a long drink of his coffee, Tim started back at the top. Moments later he sprang to his feet. Of course. The application appeared complete but now Tim realized a section of the information was theoretical. Theory. But not functional. That was what had rankled him like a blackberry seed in his wisdom tooth. A vital aspect was missing. From a patent perspective, it was non-enabling. Someone skilled in the art of this technology would be prevented from building this device.

Under ordinary circumstances, Tim would have rejected the application and sent a notice of the fact to the inventor. He checked the applicant's name again. Marc Wayne. A legitimate inventor and patent attorney.

For the first time in weeks, Tim smiled. He laughed. This was perfect. He'd give this patent application to the creep. It would satisfy the blackmailer's demand for something important. It appeared complete. Tim doubted anyone but he would recognize the problem. It had taken him a long time to see it even though this was his specialty.

Tim could trick the beetle man and send the hostile government on a pointless chase of time, manpower, and money.

Ironic justice. Anyone who stooped to such devious methods deserved to be outwitted.

He held up the application and squelched an urge to whoop. This was the answer to his dilemma. This Meissner Effect Generator seemed too good to be true. Because it was.

# Chapter Twenty-three

Spencer spied the urchin in the kitchen. With both hands, the boy hungrily stuffed cold leftover eggs and toast into his mouth.

"You little …"

At the sound of Spencer's voice the boy looked up, his mouth agape and crammed with chewed scrambled eggs dotted with orange meat. His eyes widened at the sight of the knife in the man's hand and the toast that was halfway to his mouth dropped to the floor.

Spencer lunged, grabbing for the small intruder.

Pulling the table between them, the boy ran. In a powerful thrust, Spencer snatched the table and shoved it to the far side of the room where it crashed against the wall, scattering eggs and broken dishes. He launched himself at the screaming boy. The jump was perfectly aimed and man and boy tumbled into the living room.

Quickly Spencer pinned the boy. "What are you doing sneaking around …"

The boy spit and bit and kicked and attempted to scratch. Spencer had his hands full trying to subdue the wild child. Suddenly from behind, a wet towel covered his face, pressing heavily upon his nose and mouth, suffocating him. Panicked, Spencer staggered to his feet. Tugging at the weight clinging to his neck and head, he crashed blindly against furniture and walls until he shook it loose. He pulled the towel off his head. Sucking in large gulps of air, he turned to find the girl, naked and bruised in a heap against the wall. The towel that she had held over his head he dropped over her.

He searched the room for the boy. The front door was open and the kid was gone. Spencer went outside, searching for signs indicating which direction his young prey had dashed. But the landscape didn't lend a clue and he was well aware that the street rat was adept at disappearing into his own territory.

Back inside, the girl moaned and rubbed her head. A lump was rapidly rising.

"The thief was stealing – "

She began to shake her head and quickly stopped. "Not a thief." She pressed her palms to her forehead. "My son."

He cursed.

"You go." She spoke the words softly.

He went to the kitchen. Crunching over broken glass from the cheap dishes, he reached into the freezer and pulled out a frozen package of pea pods. He took it back to the woman who had moved to the couch. "Put this on your head."

She did as he told her though she refused to meet his eyes.

"His father?"

She gave a small shake of her head. "No father."

He went to the window and gazed out at the colorless scenery. Lingering fog exaggerated eerie shadows. Somewhere out there was the hungry, fatherless son of a prostitute. Street smart, emotionally undeveloped with hyper-developed survival instincts, he lived in the moment. Without a conscience, he was a high risk-taker.

Spencer had been that kid on the other side of the world. Begging from tourists and picking their pockets to survive, it was a cruel lifestyle characterized by beatings from adults who caught him stealing and beatings from bigger street kids who stole from him what he had stolen.

Ill-fed and small anyway, as a teen Spencer passed himself off as a younger child when it served him. It was a memory he had long ago buried. Unwanted and uninvited, it surfaced now like an infected boil. He cursed again. The toxic memory would have to be lanced and purged. In the past he had tried alcohol and drugs. Not even sex restored his ego from the sudden revisit to his former humiliation. No, he had learned what was required to secure that hard won state of control and security. To reestablish his position of power over his past.

His former information supplier in the patent office had been a willing puppet. Spencer's exchange of money with the employee was simple. Give Spencer something he could sell for a great deal of money, and Spencer would deposit an admirable sum into the marionette's bank account. But the arrangement went awry. Financially secure, the employee retired unannounced and early. Spencer was left holding clipped strings with no one dancing any longer at the other end.

Never one to repeat a mistake, Spencer employed blackmail to motivate a new player. A terrified weakling, the mark was as unstable as a sweating stick of dynamite. Spencer's life depended on keen judgment of character. Like a ticking bomb, it was only a matter of the clock before this situation backfired, and the explosion could take Spencer with it. Diffusing the problem was necessary on a business level. Now it was required on a personal level.

Without a glance at the discarded girl, he strode purposefully into the gray morning.

# Chapter Twenty-four

True to his word, Hebron led Marc to a hamburger diner that promised breakfast all day. Dropping onto chrome stools with red vinyl seats, the two bellied up to the bar and gave their order to the waitress. From their ringside spots, those at the counter could watch the food as it cooked on a grill the size of a flight deck.

The cook slathered the hot grill with margarine. Like a symphony conductor, the white-aproned expert threw eggs and hash browns to sizzle, adding ladles of melt-in-your-mouth flapjack batter to the crackling, popping breakfast serenade. Next he plopped quarter-pound burger patties on top of thick slices of bacon for the bacon burgers the two had ordered. The meat was topped with round slabs of provolone cheese. Marc's stomach growled.

In short order, the short order cook had medium rare patties on oversized buns, dressed with generous sides of potato salad dished from a large plastic tub in the wall-sized refrigerator, and a foot long dill pickle. The special included frosty glasses of fresh lemonade.

"I could pack on the freshman fifteen here." Marc took a large bite of his burger, letting the hot cheese stick to the roof of his mouth.

Like he was strumming guitar strings, Hebron ran his fingers over his ribs. "Hasn't had that affect on me yet, but I keep giving it another try."

"Very sportsmanlike."

Marc was surprised when Hebron finished his platter-sized meal while Marc was only halfway through is own burger. "You got a tapeworm?"

"How old are you?"

"Touché."

The student pushed back his plate. "Now for my invention."

From his jeans pocket, Hebron pulled three guitar picks, a tuning fork, and a harmonica. Frowning, he fished in his other pocket and retrieved a collection of wires and conductors.

"You lost it?"

"Nah, I always have it with me. Somewhere." Reaching into his backpack, he continued his search until his eyes lit up. "Found it."

Seeing the hardware store appearing on the counter, the waitress removed their plates, stacking them loudly. Marc snatched the dill pickle before it was whisked away with the burger drippings.

Hebron proudly set his creation on the counter between them. The size of a dessert dish, the device resembled a softball stitched together with scraps of lightweight metal. Using a wire clasp from his pocket collection, the inventor opened the sphere to reveal layers and a hollow interior.

He looked expectantly at Marc. "Whatcha think?"

"May I?" Marc wiped pickle juice on his napkin and reached for the unusual object. Holding it one way and then another, he inspected the design and materials.

"Well?"

"Tell me about it."

The young man's expression fell. "You can't tell what it does?"

"On the contrary, Hebron. It appears to measure –"

"Precisely! Cut, clarity, and color."

The waitress refilled Marc's glass. "Talking about my best friends?"

Marc looked up. "Diamonds?"

"Of course."

"See, Hebron. Even the waitress knows what you're working on."

Hebron smiled at the collegiate pouring lemonade from the cold pitcher. The girl winked and moved away to seat a loud group of students who had just entered. Marc recognized the bikers he had seen earlier pedaling around campus and knew they would be hungry after their strenuous exercise.

Marc elbowed Hebron. "Focus."

The boy flushed and cleared his throat, talking above the boisterous newcomers. "The receptors analyze a stone for color and clarity." From the depths of his backpack, he pulled a small stone and handed it to Marc. "It produces a three-dimensional enlargement to show inconsistencies in the organic make-up or man-made cut."

Tilting it first this way and then the other, Marc studied the direction of moving parts. "The diamond industry spends a half-million dollars for devices that do what you say this one does." He placed the stone inside. "You've tested it?"

"Works as smooth as the bike you're trying to get me to ride."

"What do you measure with?"

Hebron pulled the straw from his lemonade, sucked it dry, wiped the outside on his shirt, and used it as a pointer. "The acoustical membrane when activated causes light to be reflected. The membrane circles the subject. The receptor analyzes the diamond based on the light received."

"A light CAT scan."

"A poor man's CAT scan for diamonds."

# Chapter Twenty-five

Tim's fingers trembled as he typed on the computer keyboard. Catch-22 was what the Americans called it. If he got caught, he would be prosecuted as a spy against the United States. If he didn't do this, he had no doubt that the threats of the sinister man to take the life of his son would be carried out.

With the cuff of his long sleeve shirt, he wiped the sweat that beaded on his forehead. In a last, though laughably feeble act of defiance, he altered the steganography algorithm of a photo of a cat to carry the information he was trading for the life of his son. He had been reassured that this redistribution of pixel information of a photo was undetectable. He also knew that for every innovative kind of encryption, there was another innovative mind seeking to detect secrets.

Secrets upon secrets had burdened Tim. He was now doing what a few months ago he would have considered unthinkable. Brushing the moisture from his face, Tim studied the screen. It was complete.

With a single finger and a single ridiculously simple movement, he quickly tapped the send key, transmitting the seemingly innocent photo of a cuddly kitten.

The deed was done. The top secret patent information for the Meissner Effect Device was now in the inbox of the foul and brutal man with the swift knife.

# Chapter Twenty-six

Yao was optimistic about the current project.

Gritting back his memories once more, the Colonel arrived at the prototype lab. His military superiors including General Gao, had provided the facility, the scientists, and a short time frame for Yao to develop something to give China military superiority. They expected results. Quickly.

The modern technology in the lab was a stark contrast to the ancient building that housed the hopes for his country's rise to an uncontested world power. It had been Yao's idea to monitor the United States Patent and Trademark Office for fresh technology.

America had enjoyed her position as the superior world power since her victory in World War II. After his time in the U.S., Yao understood that the land of the free allowed – even encouraged – freedom of thought. This freedom produced prosperity through capitalism. Well-fed and uncensored thinkers created technology that paved the way for their continued advancement.

The most efficient means to accomplish his end was for Yao to harvest the next great inventions while the United States bound up the ideas in processes and paperwork spurred by expanding federal government control. While the patent was anchored in the methodical procedures, unfettered by burdensome bureaucracy Yao would develop the invention.

That's where the man known as Mr. Spencer had come in. He knew how to get what Yao wanted. And what he siphoned from the Patent Office was exactly what the Colonel had hoped for. The development of the new jet engine that gave his country superior mobility in the skies had been Yao's first victory. He was hungry for more.

Historically the United States had been slow to realize the value of flight for military superiority. It was three years after the Wright Brothers flew the world's first powered flight at Kitty Hawk in North Carolina that the Army Signal Corps formed an Aeronautical Division on August 1, 1907. Progressing from balloons and dirigibles, the Division accepted their first airplane from the innovative Wright Brothers in 1909. A small band of intrepid flight pioneers including Capt. Benjamin D. Foulois experimented with various aircraft to become the First Aero Squadron. During World War I, President Woodrow Wilson created the Army Air Service that grew to more than 19,000 officers and 178,000 enlisted men piloting 11,754 American-made aircraft, mostly trainers like the JN-4 Jenny.

Despite visionaries like Billy Mitchell, the U.S. lagged behind European nations that created a separate air force. A peacetime establishment with limited funds for advancement, American flight remained a small interest until World War II. The last global scale war proved what air power proponents had championed for decades.

The end of the war paralyzed German and Japanese war economies. The two countries had been dominated by the quality and quantity of aircraft and airmen populating the skies. Yao conceded that air power didn't win the war by itself but he had no doubt this weapon made possible the Allies' total victory over the Axis powers. Victory that was sealed when Super Fortress bomber B-29s Enola Gay and Bockscar dropped atomic bombs on Japan's cities of Hiroshima and Nagasaki.

Yao didn't have sympathy for Japan. He was too aware of

that neighbor's cruelty to China's people. The common people like his parents. Like Yao had been while growing up. The horrors of the Nanking Massacre haunted his country. After committing some of history's worst war atrocities against the Chinese, unparalleled rape and murder, Japan played down or even denied that it occurred. While at the western university, Yao had toured many places in the United States. At Pearl Harbor, he learned about the devastation wreaked by Japan's surprise attack. Japan's air power had decimated that pivotal base in the Pacific. For a week, survivors heard the desperate tapping from sailors trapped in the tangled wreckage of their ships. Futile calls for help that weakened as tortuous days passed and the young sons of proud parents died of wounds and dehydration. Died abandoned and alone. In his opinion, arrogant Japan deserved the atomic bombs.

In one of the most lopsided battlefield victories in military history, the U.S. Air Force deployed halfway around the globe during 1991's Operation Desert Shield. Using sophisticated satellite navigation systems, the advanced F 117 Nighthawk delivered precision-guided munitions that neutralized Iraq's air defenses and command structure in a mere six weeks. Air power allowed coalition ground forces to liberate Kuwait with fewer casualties suffered than a typical week in the Viet Nam conflict.

Yao harbored no animosity towards the United States. He saw them as a rich source of technology and ideas he could harvest for his own purposes. Yao's superiors had been pleased with the new jet engine. The Colonel had confidence he would be successful again. The Meissner Effect Generator would change the face of the world. Beginning with China.

# Chapter Twenty-seven

Exhausted, Tim put his key into the lock on his front door. Inside his apartment, he tossed his briefcase onto the coffee table, loosened his tie, and stood staring out the large window, oblivious of the familiar view before him.

This was the second time in his life that he felt completely out of control. Minds far more cunning and fanatical than his own were manipulating his actions. People he didn't even know were creating situations that escalated and swept him along like a lamb caught in a violent wadi flood. He felt emasculated. Again. All he wanted was a quiet existence, a simple and satisfying life. To do a good day's work and come home to the welcoming arms of his wife, and smiling face of his son who was proud of his father.

He glanced down at his trembling hands. His vision blurred. From long pent up emotion? Or was his sugar level dropping again? On top of his other sorrows, his body mocked him and reflected his weakness with diabetes.

After administering the insulin shot, he pulled a bottle of kefir from the refrigerator. Collapsing on the couch, he lifted the lid of the dusty olivewood box on the coffee table and pulled out the photo. She was beautiful. His wife, holding the hand of their handsome young son. All Jewish people in Israel, males and females, spent a year or more in military service. They had met while she was serving her country. Neither her family nor his were pleased with the union when they married. A Muslim and a Jew. Naively, he was certain love would smooth over the political and religious conflicts between their backgrounds. They would be the beginning of peace between the two warring peoples who began as desert half-brothers – Ishmael and Isaac.

And for a time it worked. They made their home in Bethlehem, a colorful mosaic of peoples and cultures who got along by exercising their wits. Lived, loved, worked, and had their son.

Until the year 2000. Never content to co-exist in peaceable compromise, Palestinian terrorists had slipped into adjacent Jerusalem numerous times with intent to destroy. This time, a bomb exploded on the playground of a Jewish school. Young children were dismembered. Killed. His Esther had raced to the scene. He knew she would, and he had followed to be with his wife.

Desperately threading her way through emergency personnel and others who came to help, she called and called for her sister. And her niece. Amidst terrible dust and destruction, and panicked people, Esther saw through the blood and dropped to her knees beside the young mother cradling her still child. The teacher and the student. Esther's sister and her niece.

Lost in stunned shock, her sister didn't see anything or anyone except the beautiful little girl. As during the months when she rocked and sang while the child was once knit together in her womb, in a futile attempt, the mother murmured comforting words as she tried to put her daughter's torn body back together. Tears streaming down her face, Esther cradled the two until someone came to take away their bodies.

Notified of the horrible news, Esther's brother-in-law flew home from his work as an Israeli ambassador to South America. Reuven's deep grief was dark as he arranged for the funerals of his wife and daughter.

While Jewish families wailed for their terrible loss, back in

Bethlehem the bombers celebrated with obscene hilarity. Tim had followed the raucous noise. He wanted to see who was responsible. Who would rejoice in the slaughter of children? He and Esther were bridging the centuries old schism between Abraham's two sons. Outraged, Tim approached the center of the festivities where participants praised Allah for their victory over the infidels. What triumph, Tim questioned, was there in decimating school children? Teachers? What kind of god would command his followers to represent him in this way? Tight-lipped to hold back the explosive anger roiling inside, Tim faced his brother.

That's where Esther found him. No matter how much he explained to his wife that he was not there with his brother, but to confront him, from that moment her eyes reflected a perpetual sorrow born of unspeakable betrayal.

Tensions between the residents of Bethlehem and the inhabitants of Jerusalem escalated until, to protect her children, Israel erected a wall between the city of the Christian Christ's birth and the city of His death.

"They deserve the wall, every inch of it," his wife said. And the ghastly rebar-reinforced concrete wall divided her from him. As hostilities increased, many Jewish people left Bethlehem. He pleaded with her to stay; she was his wife.

But the next day, when he returned home from work, she and their son were gone. He'd known as soon as he walked in the door. Even before he saw that her toothbrush was no longer in the medicine chest next to his. That her shoes and clothes weren't nestled against his in their closet. The life and light was gone from their home. It had gone with her. With their son, so eager to explore and embrace the world. Instead, what greeted him was a vast nothing. A hollowness that shadowed him like a constant specter. An emptiness that filled his bed where she had once cradled against him.

A dull ache radiated across his chest and left arm. The heartache that never went away. Of course, he had followed her, found that she had returned to her family community who welcomed her and their son, took them in and cared for them.

"I cannot bear that grotesque wall between us, separating you from me, separating people." He reached for her hand.

"Separating wolves from sheep, monsters from peaceful families." She pulled away.

"I'm going to the United States." His eyes pleaded for her. "I'll send for you and our son."

"Who knows but that I am here for such a time as this." She had placed the palm of her hand briefly against his cheek and walked away.

True to his word, he had immigrated to the United States. His letters to her went unanswered as he secured employment and a two-bedroom townhouse with a room for their son. Feeling powerless to bring his family together, he sent monthly checks to provide for their needs. The empty years had piled one on top of another, collecting like fallen leaves one autumn after another.

Reaching again into the box, he removed a second photo. His wife had sent it, taken on the day their son graduated from university. Like a vise crushing his ribs, the pain in his chest increased. It was suddenly difficult to breathe. Water. He probably needed water.

He pushed himself to his feet, took two steps toward the kitchen, and then pitched forward. As he fell, he saw the Bethlehem wall crumble and his young wife and small son running toward him, their faces beaming, their arms open to embrace him.

# Chapter Twenty-eight

Yao was familiar with the scientific theory of the Meissner Effect. The Meissner Device promised to turn theory into world-changing reality. Yao anticipated the praise of his superiors.

Flashing his identification, the Colonel was passed into the lab. Four scientists Yao recognized as the project leads were bent over a table spread with blue prints. One man typed on a computer keyboard and the other three studied the screen.

Looking up, the lead scientist came to Yao.

"Tell me of your progress." The Colonel walked to the cluster gathered at the table.

"We are experiencing difficulty," the scientist demurred.

The Colonel stopped and faced his fidgeting companion. "You have failed." Yao noted the flash of fear in the other man's eyes.

"No, no, Comrade Yao." Moisture glistening on his smooth forehead, the scientist clutched his shaking hands into fists and shoved them into the deep, square pockets of his lab coat. "It is our belief that a portion vital to the success of the construction has been left out of the information provided."

"Something is missing," Yao interpreted. He was familiar with this reaction. Nervous men spoke in vague terms and used more words than necessary.

The man in front of him bobbed his head.

"Surely your staff can figure out what is needed."

The scientist shifted his weight, swallowed, and began. "I, that is, *we* are not altogether convinced we are missing an ingredient." He pulled his trembling hands from his pockets and started to gesture but quickly hid them once more. "Our findings indicate there is something about the process that is not included."

"The process."

He nodded. "It's an oversimplification but perhaps I can offer an illustration."

"Perhaps you can."

"When I attended university, an American professor taught English. My wife was interested in American cooking so the professor gave my wife a recipe for making yeast bread. Every attempt failed – " Realization of the word he had just spoken reflected in the scientist's eyes and he glanced fearfully at his superior. "That is to say, she – my wife – experienced difficulty getting the anticipated results."

Aware of the man's apprehension, Yao stared at him. "Continue."

The man plunged on. "Finally, the American professor came to our home. She made the recipe with my wife."

"And the result?"

"Success."

Yao pondered this information for a moment. He looked at the man's hopeful gaze. "You're asking to complete the project with the inventor."

He lowered his head but nodded affirmatively.

"You're asking me to bring this American inventor to your kitchen."

# Chapter Twenty-nine

Marc tilted the device as he examined it. He peered closely at the delicate hinges. "If you can develop a more efficient manner of opening this …" He closed the object and manipulated the wire clasp. It sprang open. He repeated the process.

The waitress set two plates before them. The dish in front of Marc held homemade blueberry pie. Hebron's plate sported deep-dish apple. "We didn't order…" Marc tried to get the attention of the waitress.

The girl had eyes only for Hebron. "On the house." Then she moved down the counter taking orders from new customers.

Hebron switched the pie plates and inhaled the blueberry slab in a record three bites.

"Why diamonds?" Marc quickly forked a bite of apple pie into his mouth before it too disappeared.

Hebron shrugged. "My dad deals in diamonds."

"He must be thrilled with this. The manufacturers of diamond-grading machines claim progress in rating color and cut. But nearly everyone is working on a clarity unit. It's the final frontier of automated diamond grading." He scooped whipped cream from the top of his pie into his mouth. "But no one has been able to develop a reasonably priced machine that can distinguish between inclusions and their reflections."

The young man grunted and forked half of Marc's pie into his mouth. "You'd think," he mumbled around a mouthful of spiced apples and crust.

Marc stared at the college student who eagerly stuffed the final bite of pie into his mouth. "I don't understand."

Sighing, Hebron sat back on his stool. "When it comes to diamond grading in the labs, the eyes still have it. Every major gem lab employs human graders to color-grade diamonds because machines are easily fooled. According to my dad," he dropped his voice two octaves, "the human eye and color-grading machines sometimes see color differently."

Marc leaned his elbows on the counter. "Surely there are others in the industry who will look at your research."

"Dad's viewpoint is widely shared among gemologists. Lab execs and the gemologists agree the newer models are more accurate than the original Okuda Industries machines. Those were introduced over two decades ago. But they insist the machines can be fooled by a number of variables."

"Such as?"

Hebron ticked off the list on his fingers. "Highly fluorescent diamonds, brown body color, dark inclusions, or stone position."

Feeling his lunch settle, Marc adjusted the waist on his pants. "What about use in labs?"

Hebron picked up the invention and studied it. "Dad insists it can't be used in gemological labs for actual lab work."

"What about you? What do you think?"

For the first time since the hamburgers showed up in front of them, the young man's eyes lit up. "I know this works."

"But?"

The young inventor slumped. "But with the door closed to the diamond industry, it's a moot point."

"There is an old man named Thurman who practically built my community. He says when you hit a wall, find a way around it."

A brief look of hurt flashed in his eyes before the college student masked his expression. "Pop is more than a wall. He's a force in the industry."

Marc mulled this over. After the enthusiastic support he had received from his own dad, Marc mentally replaced that image of a father with the unspoken description of a man who apparently did the opposite for Hebron. He voiced another of Thurman's mottos. "Unless the technology can be proven of value in another realm."

"Exactly why I let you take me to lunch. Got any ideas?"

Hebron's attention was suddenly riveted on something going on behind Marc. He turned to see the waitress exchange her apron for a sweater. She said something to the cook and was on her way out the door when Hebron bolted from his seat at the counter. Before Marc could stop him, the student was running out the door.

"Hey! What about your invention?"

Hot on the trail, Hebron didn't appear to hear.

Marc was on his feet. "Hebron! Your invention."

He turned, his feet still pedaling backwards. "No worries." He waved a hand good-naturedly. "I'll find you."

Then he was out the door and trotting down the sidewalk. Through the large picture windows, Marc saw Hebron catch up to the waitress. She stopped and smiled at him. Then the two made their way back to campus and the classes and life that awaited them there.

Marc rolled the invention around in his palm. What other uses could this piece of brilliance be applied to?

# Chapter Thirty

"Dead?" Deverell looked from Mallory to Fred.

Mallory had sped through the halls to the director's office as soon as she received the report. "Marc!" was her only response before she brushed past Fred who tried to keep up with the woman on a mission. She was relieved to find Deverell in his windowless office where she delivered the news.

"The patent examiner is dead?" Deverell repeated and she could see he was mentally putting the pieces together.

"Last weekend," Mallory said.

"How?" The special agent shrugged off his irritation at being interrupted, came around his desk and perched on the corner.

"Natural causes," Fred said. "Probably a heart attack."

"What did the autopsy reveal?" Deverell reached for a pen and clicked it.

"There wasn't one." Mallory's words came like stilettos.

"Let's get one." The pen clicking increased.

"He's already buried."

Deverell's eyebrows shot up. "So quickly? That's suspicious."

"The whole thing is suspicious." Mallory took the offending pen from her boss and dropped it into his coffee cup.

Fred put a calming hand on her arm. "When we looked into it, we discovered he's Muslim."

"Named Tim?"

"Hatim, actually." Fred nodded to Mallory. She opened a file and read. "Mother's parents are Muslim."

With a hand on her shoulder, Fred steered Mallory to one of the two chairs arranged in front of Deverell's desk for visitors. Agitated, she sat and Fred dropped into the second chair. "The Muslim part explains why he was buried so quickly. Custom."

Deverell grunted, and reached for the file. He scanned the details until something caught his attention. "He has a grown son…"

Mallory was feeling more uncomfortable by the minute, the way she felt during the only horror movie she had ever watched. Goosebumps rose on her arms as if something ominous was creeping close in the dark. She shifted in her seat. Deverell lowered his glasses and peered at her. "Something on your mind, Mallory?"

"I'm concerned about Marc."

Deverell gave the two of them that 'I told you I didn't want to involve family' look. His silence spoke volumes.

"Look," Fred pulled the pen from his boss's cup and tossed it back to Deverell, "involving Marc may not have been our brightest notion."

Mallory met Fred's eyes. He was taking partial responsibility for the decision when they both knew it was completely her idea. She opened her mouth to protest, but he quickly continued.

"However, he was – is – the prime profile for this situation. In light of latest events – "

"He means Saad's untimely or timely demise." No longer able to contain her growing unease, Mallory shot out of her seat and paced.

Fred cocked his head in her direction. "Mallory – we – are concerned about Marc's safety."

Deverell spun his coffee cup in lazy circles, ignoring the dribble that stained a path down one side and pooled at the base.

"The death of this mole –"

"Hatim Saad."

"The death of Hatim seems to be of plausible circumstances."

"Seemingly." Mallory emphasized the word, aware that her tone was dripping sarcasm. "But it's too coincidental for me. Just as we trace some information leaks to him, he dies? C'mon, boss."

Deverell bounced his pen against the table. "You think these guys are smart killers."

"I'm not underestimating them." Mallory faced her co-workers. Hands on hips, she spoke her mind. "I want protection for Marc. Immediately."

Deverell looked to Fred who nodded. "I agree with Mallory."

"Why?"

"Hatim may have been one of the examiners who saw Marc's patent application." Fred spread his hands. "He would have known a secrecy order had been issued."

Their boss scanned the information about Hatim once again while Mallory paced and Fred waited. She was formulating a plan to provide protection for her brother even if her supervisor opted not to grant her request.

At last Deverell dropped the closed file on the desk. "All right, we'll arrange to keep a protective eye on our inventor."

"And patent attorney," Fred corrected.

Getting her request emboldened Mallory. Now she wanted more. She stopped pacing and planted her palms on the broad desk. "I want to go."

Deverell sighed heavily. "Go ahead. Take a couple days. Make sure everything is secure in the Midwest. We'll decide if we need to send agents to protect your inventor based on what you find."

Before her supervisor stopped speaking, Mallory was headed for door. "Thanks, boss." Relief and anxiety warred in her mind. Behind her, she heard Deverell address her partner.

"Fred, search Hatim Saad's workspace, his house, his car. See if there is anything that indicates his death was caused by something other than natural causes."

# Chapter Thirty-one

As the plane began its swift descent, Mallory pressed her forehead against the window to view the scenery below. Farm fields stretched as far as she could see like the patchwork quilts her mother used to make with the other church ladies at their weekly quilting bee. She had one on her bed back east in her upscale apartment. The Methodist women had pieced the small fabric blocks with tiny stitches as a gift when she left to pursue a career in the big city.

Square farm fields were edged by creeks and stands of trees where farmers and their sons, dressed in thick Carharts against the winter cold, hunted deer in November. Large, red barns flanked newer metal pole barns housing oversized green and yellow farm equipment.

Ahead, growing larger, were the tall city buildings of downtown Fort Wayne. Tucked in Indiana's upper east corner, Ft. Wayne was 18 miles west of the Ohio border and 50 miles south of neighboring Michigan. The second largest city in the state, Ft. Wayne was named for President George Washington's fellow soldier, Anthony Wayne. A bold fighter, Wayne distinguished himself during the Revolutionary War by consistently advising a singular strategy.

"Attack."

It was this zeal that earned the exuberant Pennsylvanian the title Mad Anthony Wayne.

Wayne was mad like a fox. When Washington desired to wrest from the enemy the impenetrable Stony Point, tactically perched above the Hudson River, he sent Wayne. In a bayonets-only charge that lasted a mere 30 minutes, Wayne led dedicated Patriots up a treacherous cliff and surprised the overconfident British. Following the war for independence, Washington had dispatched the bold Revolutionary War statesman Brigadier General Wayne to the frontier to protect settlers from hostile Indians. As he had with his Revolutionary tasks, Wayne succeeded in procuring security for those living at the confluence of the Maumee, Saint Mary, and Saint Joseph rivers. Though Mad Anthony's daughter and son grew up with their mother in the Pennsylvania family home, Mallory wondered if her family was somehow related to the adventurous man.

Initially a trading post for Europeans, Fort Wayne was built near the peaceful Miami Indian village of Kekionga. Platted in 1823, the city experienced tremendous growth after the completion of the Erie and Wabash canals. Presidential hopefuls Abraham Lincoln and orator Stephan Douglas debated in the city.

A reproduction of Mad Anthony Wayne's 1794 log and chinking fort stood at the junction of the three rivers in the center of the modern city. Mallory knew the history of the city from her school days. Now as an adult, she was aware that Ft. Wayne derived its subsistence from manufacturing, insurance, and health care. Of particular interest to her were the logistics, defense, and security. Especially the security of one Marc Wayne.

# Chapter Thirty-two

Fred entered the office and dropped heavily into a chair across from Deverell.

Chomping hard on spearmint gum, his boss peered questioningly over his glasses. "You found something."

The counter terrorism specialist nodded.

"Granny, what big teeth you have."

Two vertical lines between his eyebrows indicated Fred's concern. "Initially the scene looked like a heart attack."

"I remember. But?"

"Hatim was diabetic. We found the syringe from the insulin shot he apparently gave himself that evening. Just before he died." Fred paused, thinking.

"And?"

"An analysis of the contents revealed it was potassium."

"Not insulin?"

"Traces of insulin. But mostly potassium."

Deverell scratched the back of his neck. "My doctor prescribed a potassium pill each day when I took up jogging."

"Sounds like a personal problem."

"Thank you, Dr. House. Leg cramps were the medical diagnosis."

Fred nodded. "Not enough potassium, as in your case, has its side effects including cramps. Additional lack causes black-outs."

"And too much?"

"Too much, as Hatim experienced, causes the heart to stop fairly quickly. It goes through the normal dysrhythmia that a heart would go through when it is dying."

From the bottom drawer of his desk, Deverell selected a bottle of vitamins and set it on the desk. The label read potassium. "An overdose of this simulates a heart attack."

"Hatim injected himself. With tampered insulin."

"And Old MacDonald bought the farm." Deverell tossed the vitamin bottle back into the drawer. "Smart killers."

# Chapter Thirty-three

As the plane lined up to touch down on the runway, Mallory recognized the General Motors plant, the new strip mall, and the green oblong of the high school football field. Then the plane bumped to the ground and taxied to the gate. Along the adjacent runway, Mallory heard before she saw the two F-16Cs scream into the sky. Located on the east side of the airport, the 122nd Fighter Wing, Indiana Air National Guard base was home to the Blacksnakes. Marc had learned basic rescue and survival skills, as well as how to fly when he was a young teen in the Civil Air Patrol.

"Hey, Sis." She heard Marc call as she followed the flow of passengers into the terminal. On tiptoes, Marc stood behind a collection of overweight relatives gushing welcomes to a young couple in western boots and oversized belt buckles.

"Go left." Marc gave the direction like he used to when they were kids playing flag football. Grinning, Mallory tucked her head and steered around the small crowd. She ran straight into his familiar hug.

"Touchdown," he declared in her ear.

Laughing, she pulled back to get a better look at him. "Hey, bro."

"Welcome back to smallsville, my big shot sister." He took the handle of her carry-on and with his arm slung casually around her shoulders, steered her toward the exit.

The revolving door spat them out of the controlled airport air and into the Midwest afternoon. She breathed deeply, taking in the familiar smell and feel of seasonally mild humidity as they made the short trek to the parking lot. "What's captured your interest lately in that mad scientist lab of yours?"

Marc pressed a button on his keychain and the trunk of his car popped open. He secured her luggage and opened the passenger door for her. "I've toyed with inventing the barkless dog."

"A toy barkless dog?"

"Toys are mostly barkless. Or you can at least remove the batteries."

"Dr. Thurmond's clients getting on your nerves?"

Marc shrugged. "I don't hear 'em really, except today when I was on the phone with a new client. A Saint Bernard kept going off like a fog horn."

"That's a unique way for new clients to find your office. Just follow the sound of the barking dog."

"Makes me sound like a hick."

"You are."

He tipped back his head. "Ahh. That explains it."

Leaving the airport parking lot, they motored by the day old bakery and the United Methodist church.

"What about your work with magnetics?"

"You mean the Meissner Field generator?"

"Yeah, that."

He glanced at her. "I thought this was a pleasure trip, negotiated for my patriotic cooperation with the government."

"All the more reason to ask."

He rested his right arm across the back of the seat. "So is this trip business or fun?"

"Like everything else in my life," she admitted, "some of both."

"Which is why I'm so vital to your life."

"Of course, you are, my favorite brother."

"I'm your only brother." He merged the Jetta onto the bypass. "And to remind you how to play, I'm taking you to lunch."

"I should freshen up." She smoothed travel wrinkles from her clothes.

"Hicksville, remember? We suffer from an iron deficiency. That's why all our clothes are wrinkled. You're fine."

Marc parked outside a small storefront attached to a BP gas station. The sign board advertised steak and Chinese food. Mallory sighed. "No one cooks a steak like Johnny."

"And you're overdue for one of your overdones."

Inside, the older waitress greeted Mallory with a hug. Her oriental features were highlighted by too much make-up. "Hi, honey. How are you?"

"Well, Kim."

"Just like she likes her steak," Marc put in.

Guiding them to a booth with green vinyl benches, Kim nodded. "I remember." She laid two menus on the table.

Marc pushed the menus back to her. "Menus?" His tone was indignant. "We don't need no stinking menus."

The waitress smiled. "Gotcha'. Two usuals comin' right up." She gathered the ignored menus and disappeared. In moments she was back balancing a pot of familiar jasmine tea, and a plate of pot stickers and egg rolls. While Mallory poured tea, Marc dumped a generous portion of sweet red sauce into the center of the plate and topped it with a yellow dollop of mustard sauce. Like a painter layering his brush, he expertly dipped an eggroll into the bi-color mixture and handed it to his sister.

Mallory bit into the eggroll and closed her eyes appreciatively.

"Great, huh?" Marc put an identical piece in his own mouth.

"A taste of home."

"'Cause no one else would put this menu together," he said around a mouthful. "It wouldn't fly in your fancy D.C."

"Nor would this lack of atmosphere."

Marc swallowed. "Are you kidding? The lack of atmosphere *is* the atmosphere."

"Kimmy," someone yelled from the kitchen.

"See," Marc waved a dipped pot sticker in the direction of the call. "Where else can you eat where the cook hollers to the waitress when your meal is ready?" He bit the pot sticker in half and talked around the food. "That's atmosphere, baby. Real atmosphere."

Kim returned and set in front of them plates heavy with steaming steak filets, fried rice, and mixed vegetables.

They were quiet for several minutes, heartily digging into the hot meal. Marc pointed his steak knife in Mallory's direction. "Is this good or what?"

She loaded her fork with colorful vegetables. "How's that pretty secretary of yours?"

"Nancy?" Marc forked another generous piece of rare steak into his mouth. "Fine, I guess. Why?"

"Just wondering. Is she dating anyone?"

"Dating?"

Mallory looked around, and then leaned forward. "Do you hear an echo?"

"What do you mean?"

"Each question I ask about your secretary, you repeat."

"Do I?"

"See."

Marc wiped his mouth with his napkin. "Well, she's… she's … she's Nancy. She answers my email, the phone, and makes tea."

"While you..?" She waved her fork for him to fill in the rest.

"While I work. That's what I do, remember. Patents and inventions."

Mallory rested her chin on her palm. "You might want to look up occasionally to see what's right in front of you."

Marc harrumphed.

Kim replaced their empty plates with a small dish piled with crisp fortune cookies and crumbly almond cookies.

Mallory selected a cellophane-wrapped fortune cookie. "So tell me about your progress on the Meissner Field."

"I've nearly got it, I think." Marc stuffed a whole almond cookie into his mouth and shopped for a fortune cookie.

"That close?"

"Been that close for awhile, actually. But the part I don't have, you know the part I made up for the patent application, that's the part I really don't have."

She stared at him. "That's about the most unscientific explanation I've ever heard from you."

He shrugged. "Occasionally even this brilliant mind operates like the rest of humanity. Besides, I'm not supposed to talk about it, am I?"

"Except with me."

"I lectured at the university about the Meissner Effect theory – which is common knowledge in the scientific world – but the elements of the invention weren't discussed." He pointed the cellophane-wrapped cookie in her direction. "There was one student who had a natural understanding of the concept. Name's Hebron Heath and he's already an inventor."

Mallory held up her fortune cookie. "Ready?"

Marc nodded. They tore the wrappers from their cookies and cracked them open. Mallory found her fortune first. "Your life is full of surprises." She frowned. "What's yours say?"

Marc studied his small paper. "You will go on a grand adventure."

# Chapter Thirty-four

Their bellies full from the large lunch, Mallory relaxed in the passenger seat while Marc drove them home. Turning down Maple Street, Mallory leaned forward in anticipation of that first glance of their childhood home. After periods away, her first view always evoked an avalanche of memories and their accompanying emotions.

"It looks good, Marc," she said as he pulled into the driveway. "You've kept it up."

"Naturally. It honors Mom and Dad, but my true motivation," he looked at her conspiratorially, "is to tempt you home now and again."

As soon as he parked, she threw open the car door. She was inside, standing in the front room when Marc caught up, tugging her carry-on behind. "It smells like home." She inhaled deeply of her mom's favorite brand of furniture oil. "I can still smell Daddy's pipe."

Taking her by the shoulders, Marc turned her to face the two recliners positioned by the fireplace. "Actually, that's the tobacco on the coffee table next to Dad's easy chair."

She walked to the dish their mom used fill with candy M &

Ms. Vitamin Ms, she called them. Take several each day, hourly if needed. "In the candy dish?"

He closed the front door. "After awhile it still felt like Mom, but not Dad anymore. Then I found his tobacco pouch."

Mallory blinked. "You are amazing."

He grinned. "I know."

"And modest."

"Humble." He tossed his keys in the air and caught them. "You do whatever women do, and grab a nap. I've got a late appointment and then I'll be home to challenge you to some basketball hoops."

As he was getting in the car, Mallory followed him out on the porch. "Tell Nancy hello for me."

"Tell her yourself when you come to the office tomorrow morning."

# Chapter Thirty-five

The oversized lunch with Mallory had tasted terrific but now Marc felt sleepy as he worked at his office computer.

Nancy appeared. "It's after five." She crooked her elbow to study the face on her wristwatch. "Nearly five-thirty."

Marc rubbed his eyes and looked up at his secretary framed in the doorway. Her head tipped to one side, she looked fresh, like a spring day, despite the lateness of the afternoon. He wondered if she did have a date that evening. Certainly someone as pretty and vibrant as Nancy had a life outside these dull walls. "Go on." Why hadn't he wondered about her before? "I'll stay and wait for this last client."

"I can stay until six if you'd like."

"Run along to your real life," he said, fishing. But she didn't take the bait.

"Sure?"

"What could happen?" He made shooing gestures. "I'll see you later." Later? He usually said tomorrow.

She smiled and disappeared down the hall. In a few minutes, he heard the front door close and knew she was gone. The office felt empty. Shaking his head to redirect the curious direction of his thoughts, he got up and went to the lab.

Hebron's invention sat on the bench like a question. Marc had played with different theories for the device. Nearly every invention had multiple applications and was a natural catalyst for additional developments. And how many ideas had seemingly failed only to become genius in a completely unanticipated venue.

To keep his thoughts off Nancy, Marc began a mental list of inventions that had begun with one purpose in mind only to morph into another use altogether. During World War II, rubber imported from Africa was in short supply. The United States government needed rubber for airplane and vehicle tires as well as for boots to shoe soldiers. An engineer at General Electric added boric acid to silicon. Instead of rubber, James Wright invented silly putty, a popular child's toy. It was also the preferred substance for astronauts to anchor floating tools in place during antigravity space travel.

In 1970, Spencer Silver was seeking to develop stronger glue for 3M. Instead, he produced the weakest glue yet. Rather like Marc's own failed attempt at an adhesive. Perhaps he would find a use for the explosive he had accidentally produced. His kitchen fire reminded him of the fire extinguisher and that reminded him of Nancy.

Peering inside Hebron's device, he went back to reviewing his list of redirected inventions. A decade after he created it, Silver's concept became the profitable post-it notes. A favorite office supply of Nancy's. She color-coded post-its with office projects. This list was not working – he was back to thinking about Nancy.

Marc forced himself to picture the freckled Hebron. Marc's own parents had championed whatever interests he and Mallory favored. In contrast, Hebron's father was single focused on his business and even when the energetic son attempted to join in his father's world so the two could connect on common ground, Hebron's father had been anything but inviting. The boy's invention was ridiculed and rejected. Probably like Hebron, Marc expected. Spectacular young man. Brilliant invention. There had to be another application for Hebron's device.

His thoughts drifted back to Nancy. Maybe she was going

out to dinner. With someone handsome and athletic. She would smell like spring lavender and wear a dress that flared about her long legs. He had never before thought about Nancy going out. Or about taking her out. He shook his head. It wouldn't do to date his receptionist. What was he thinking?

Mallory's hints came flashing though his memory.

*"How is Nancy?"*

*"Say hi to Nancy."*

What did his sister know that he didn't? That Nancy was lovely? Did she like him? Grasping a pair of needle nose pliers, he lifted Hebron's diamond from the invention's center cradle. Rough, the stone reflected the evening sun that streamed through the window. What other product or industry could benefit from a clarity grading machine?

If he did ask Nancy out, Marc would take her some place special. A destination very different from the normalness of their quaint Midwest town. He studied the lenses that focused on the cradle. He might take Nancy to the Embassy Theater in downtown Ft. Wayne to hear the philharmonic. And to dinner. At an uptown restaurant to impress her. Good food and a bottle of wine. Red.

Wine.

Of course.

# Chapter Thirty-six

Back at his desk, Marc completed the email to the professor at the university. After Hebron's great escape from their lunch, he anticipated this as the best way to get a message to the budding inventor.

Marc hit the send button and directed his focus to the claims he was drafting for a client's patent application. Small numbers at the top of the computer screen read ten minutes after six when Marc heard the front door open. "Be right with you," he called. Saving his work, he quickly left his office to greet his visitor.

"Marc Wayne," he introduced, extending his hand to the wiry, dark man. "You must be Mr. Spencer."

"I'm pleased to meet you." The man firmly gripped the attorney's hand.

Marc indicated the way to his office. "You can leave your umbrella in the stand by the door."

"I prefer to keep it with me, thank you."

In his office, Marc pointed his guest to a chair. "You've come a long way to see me when we could have done this over the phone."

"You came highly recommended."

"Tell me about the invention you'd like me to file a patent for."

"Perhaps you could show me what you've been working on?"

Marc hesitated.

The man's tone was condescending. "I understand that you have an interest in magnetics. As do I."

"Mr. Spencer, if you are concerned that I might use some of your technical information on my own projects, I assure you – "

"On the contrary," he interrupted. "It would reassure me that you understand my project as you prepare the patent application."

"As a matter of fact," Marc explained, "most patent attorneys and agents are not inventors. An interest in inventing is not a prerequisite to understanding the technology and to craft a patent application anymore than being a musician is a prerequisite to building fiddles."

"I am merely suggesting an exchange of information." His gaze was penetrating. "One inventor to another."

From the front of the building came the sound of the front door opening. "You are expecting another business client." Mr. Spencer rose from his chair.

"Excuse me, please." Marc stood. "I'll be right back."

In the reception area, Marc ran into Nancy. "I saw the lights on. Do you need a good secretary while you meet with your client?"

Marc sighed. "Thanks, this squirrel is nutty."

Nancy peered around Marc to glance down the hall. "What kind of a nut?"

Marc dropped his voice. "I can't put a finger on it."

"How can I help? Want fresh coffee?"

Marc puffed out his cheeks and shook his head. "I don't want to encourage him to stay longer than necessary."

"I can interrupt with an important phone call."

Behind her, the door opened again. A handsome man built like a football linebacker came in. "Nancy?"

She flushed and turned to the newcomer. "Just a minute,

Rob." She turned questioningly back to her boss.

Marc smiled weakly. "Hey, this isn't worth interrupting your plans. I'll handle it."

Rob stepped to Nancy's side and slid a possessive arm around her waist. "If you're sure," she offered.

Looking at Rob, Marc nodded. "Yeah, I'm sure."

"Well, you better catch up with your client." Nancy glanced again behind Marc. "He disappeared down the hall right after I came in."

"Probably not for the bathroom."

"Probably not."

Marc started for his workroom, and then called back to the departing couple. "Thanks for stopping in." He took two more steps before remembering his manners. He turned again, noting that Rob held the door open for Nancy. "Nice to meet you … Rob."

As he walked to the back of the building, the deep, rhythmic bark of an aged Labrador sounded from Dr. Thurmond's office next door. But his workshop was empty.

"Mr. Spencer?" Scanning his notes and workbench, he was sure his visitor had looked the place over. "Mr. Spencer?"

The bolt that usually locked the back door from the inside was unlocked. Marc walked outside. The grassy area behind the building was where Dr. Thurmond walked his quadruped patients. Marc knew to be careful where he stepped. He scanned the shadows cast by the setting sun and listened for footsteps. He didn't see anything. And the only sound was the Labrador.

# Chapter Thirty-seven

Early the next morning, Marc stood outside Mallory's room. Through the closed door he could hear her heavy, rhythmic breathing and knew she was still asleep in her childhood bedroom. No doubt she could use a morning to sleep in and catch up on her rest. Life in the big city was a pressure cooker compared to this country town. And her work often demanded she race the clock to outsmart the criminal mind.

Marc left the car for his slumbering sibling and bicycled the country blocks to work. Arriving downtown, he fished a key from his pocket and unlocked the office door. He bent to pick up the newspaper, and groaned.

"You getting older?"

Marc pressed a hand against his lower back and straightened. He glanced sidelong at Dr. Thurmond who stood in the doorway of his vet clinic adjacent to Marc's narrow office space. "The paper is getting heavier."

Secure in Thurmond's gnarled hands, a beige rabbit wiggled its pink nose. "Weighty news." The vet ran a hand gently down the bunny's back. "In the bottom of the rabbit's cage, it's yellow journalism."

Marc swung his stiff right arm in a wheel. "Mallory challenged me to some one-on-one driveway basketball last night."

At the sound of Mallory's name, Thurmond brightened. "Who won?"

"We didn't keep score," Marc mumbled.

"I thought so." The old man wagged a boney finger. "Be sure she stops in to see me."

"You watch," Marc said. "She'll stop in to see you before she comes here."

A smile lit the man's face and he winked. "She likes me better."

Marc signaled good-bye with a wave of the newspaper.

Dr. Thurmond was suddenly serious. "Keep your eye on the news."

# Chapter Thirty-eight

From a bench outside the local diner, Mr. Spencer adjusted the newspaper he was pretending to read.

Wheeling around the corner, Marc Wayne came into view on his bicycle. Squeezing squeaky handlebar brakes, the inventor stopped in front of his office. As he unlocked the front door, an old man appeared from next door. He carried a rabbit in his arms.

Mr. Spencer watched the two men exchange animated pleasantries. Then each one retreated into his place of business, closing doors behind them. Instinctively, Mr. Spencer remained behind the newspaper for a while longer. Then, he carefully folded the paper and set it on the bench. Grasping his umbrella, he crossed the street and entered the front door of the patent attorney office.

In moments, Marc met him in the entryway. His expression showed a wariness. "Perhaps," Mr. Spencer began, "we can continue from where we left off?"

Marc cleared his throat. "I don't think I can help you."

"On the contrary." Mr. Spencer tilted the umbrella in Marc's direction. "You are exactly the one who can help me."

Marc shifted his weight. "Then you better explain exactly

what it is you want me to do for you, Mr. Spencer."

"Of course."

With a sigh, Marc waved his guest ahead of him toward his office.

Mr. Spencer pointed the umbrella, this time toward the hallway. "After you."

Mr. Wayne shrugged and led the way. Mr. Spencer fell into step behind him. Just as the pony-tailed attorney reached his office, Mr. Spencer aimed the umbrella at the back of Marc's right knee. He pressed a hidden trigger and a small dart shot from the tip and found its target. In seconds, the man in front of him crumbled to the floor.

Perfect. Everything was going according to plan.

# Chapter Thirty-nine

Finding the keys on the kitchen table where Marc had left them, Mallory drove the short distance downtown. She parallel parked in front of the historic brick building. As her brother had predicted, she went first to the vet's office.

The bell over the door jangled as she entered. Bent over a beagle on the examination table, Dr. Thurmond looked up. Spying Mallory, he welcomed her with his throaty chuckle.

"Mallory, my girl. You are a beautiful sight for these old eyes."

"And just how old are you?"

He came around the table and opened his arms. She walked into his grandfatherly embrace. "Old enough to appreciate when an important woman from the big city takes time to stop by."

She inhaled deeply and smiled against his vet coat. He smelled of Old Spice and iodine. "I'm here for one of your hugs." She pulled back to look him in the eye. "I don't get hugs like this on the east coast."

"Don't see why not." He patted her shoulder. "You don't smell bad."

The beagle yipped and thumped its tail on the stainless steel table. "Who's your patient?" Mallory went to the table and scratched behind the floppy ears.

"Barney Beagle here cut a foot while chasing rabbits." The vet lifted a front paw and showed her a row of careful stitches mending a crooked tear in the black pad.

"Looks like he'll be back terrorizing Thumpers faster than a DC politician can break his campaign promises."

Dr. Thurmond nodded. "How about you? You in town long?"

She looped her arm through his and walked toward the door. "Long enough to collect a few more hugs."

He opened the door for her. "I'm counting on it."

Next door, Mallory breezed into Marc's office. Nancy looked up from her desk and smiled. "Mallory." The receptionist came to give her a hug. "How good to see you."

"Nancy, you're as lovely as ever. Why you spend your talents here when you could be a million other places is a mystery to me."

Nancy blushed and looked expectantly toward the door behind Mallory.

"Don't worry." Mallory pushed the door closed. "I already stopped in to see Thurmond."

Nancy's eyebrows came together in a puzzled frown as Mallory turned to go down the hall to Marc's office. "Let's catch up over lunch." She raised her voice and winked at Nancy, "Unless you already have a lunch date."

Mallory rounded the corner into Marc's office. His desk chair was empty. She went further down the hall to his workshop where she stood with her hands on her hips. In the room, several projects were in various stages of development. Not as cluttered as usual, on the long workbench lay an array of common tools and parts. But no brother.

"Marc?" She circled the room, trailing her fingers along the back of his tall stool. Returning to the front of the building, she found Nancy at her desk, her fingers busy on the computer keyboard. "Where's Marc?"

Nancy frowned again. "I thought he was with you."

"When did he leave?"

"He wasn't here when I arrived." Nancy looked at his bicycle leaning against the wall next to the umbrella stand. "Just his bike. I figured the two of you went down the street to the grill for breakfast."

"You're probably right. No doubt swapping ideas with the farmers over plates of biscuits and gravy about ways to make their farm equipment function more productively." Mallory opened the front door. "I'll go join him there."

# Chapter Forty

The ambulance drove across the airport tarmac toward a private jet. A half hour earlier, Yao's man had delivered the unconscious inventor in the ambulance. Now the professional mercenary drove while Colonel Yao watched their progress from the passenger seat, a vantage point that allowed him to observe the doctor and patient in the back. There were four airports in the area.

Situated on 250 acres two miles from Interstate 69, Smith Field was the one Colonel Yao had selected. Though it was Ft. Wayne's first municipal airport, just prior to the outbreak of World War II, the army purchased a site south of the city for development of an airfield. The new site became the Ft. Wayne International Airport and Smith Field was reduced to fodder for continued controversy hashed out in the city's newspapers. From an outsider's view, Yao suspected the media occasionally fanned the fire to create news. Editorials argued that the airport was taxpayer funded as a playground for plane owners. He judged the whole affair trivial compared to his responsibilities. Typical Americans. To have so much and fight over the ridiculous when people in his country lacked indoor plumbing and proper medical care.

His research of the four area airports revealed Smith Field to be the smallest with the least amount of traffic. In addition to hosting a weekly meeting for the Civil Air Patrol – moved out of Blacksnakes headquarters after 9-11 – the airport served as an offsite lab space classroom for several colleges that operated a mechanics certification program for high school and college students. Private pilot lessons were available from a sole proprietorship whose owner scheduled lessons over his cell phone while lounging by the pool at a nearby condominium.

The random coming and going of people was exactly the atmosphere Yao sought. Absorbed in the television, the guy at the airport's small counter was happy to answer questions, and conveniently for Colonel Yao, wasn't inclined to ask any.

The pilot stood in the fixed-wing's doorway, watching the ambulance's approach. Yao studied the man. Noting his graying temples and cropped haircut, Yao suspected he was a retired military pilot.

The driver parked the ambulance next to the plane and moved to the back of the vehicle to help the doctor prepare the patient. Yao approached the pilot who met him on the tarmac.

"Once I have a look-see at the paperwork, we'll get your patient aboard and put this bird in the air."

Yao handed him the required documents. Pushing up his sunglasses to rest on his head, the pilot scanned the forms. Above him, someone appeared in the plane's doorway. Yao looked up and saw his reflection in the dark sunglasses of a woman. She stood unsmiling, her long brunette hair curtained her shoulders.

The pilot slid his sunglasses back over his eyes. "You got a doctor to accompany us and see to the patient?"

From the rear of the ambulance, the doctor appeared and held out his hand to the pilot.

"You the doctor who signed these?" The pilot waved the paperwork.

"And I'll see to the patient throughout the journey."

"Your nurse?"

Yao winced when the doctor clapped him on the back. "My

assistant."

The pilot grinned. "Well then. Everything is in order." He turned to the woman. "Okay, Babe. Get 'er ready to fly."

The woman turned and disappeared inside. The pilot assisted them in getting the patient secured aboard. The jet turbines began to whine. As they taxied down the runway, from the window Yao watched the driver get back into the ambulance.

Working with men who reminded him of a cockroach was a necessary evil. This one was particularly efficient. He had found the doctor. A physician who hired himself out at high rates to abortion clinics. A medical mercenary that did what he was paid to do without asking questions. Medical flights required paperwork signed by a doctor and demanded a doctor and a nurse be aboard the flight. This doctor's job was to keep the patient well and unconscious and not ask questions. For this service he would be paid substantially.

Watching the ambulance turn out of the airport and onto Ludwig Road, Yao was relieved to be free of Mr. Spencer. For now.

# Chapter Forty-one

A purposeful tour of the town including a return home produced no brother.

Back at Marc's office, Mallory pretended to be on her cell phone as she waved apologetically at a worried Nancy, pointed to the phone and went straight back to Marc's office.

His laptop was not on his desk where he always kept it. That wasn't a good sign. While many men typically brought home their computer to work after hours, Marc never did. He knew when to say enough was enough, lock the office door behind him and turn his attention elsewhere. He told her that his best ideas for inventions came during the periods when he gave his brain time off. He carried a notepad and a myriad of pieces and parts home in his backpack where he often played with ideas, but not his computer. Customarily, the laptop remained at the patent attorney office for correspondence and patent applications.

Stuffing down an urge to panic, she hurried to his workroom. Looking carefully, she noticed an empty spot on his usually cluttered workbench. It was where he stacked his papers scribbled with notes, formulas, and math equations. A thin coat of dust covered the tools and materials scattered to the edges of the workbench. The most used area of the tabletop near Marc's chair had been cleared.

She tested the back door. It was unlocked. That was odd. Outside she found two faint lines in the manicured patch of grass leading to the gravel driveway. From her training, she recognized these as the marks heels made when someone was dragged. Where the short trail ended, she could see where accelerating duel rear tires had piled dirt.

Cursing, she dialed her cell phone. Fred answered.

"I think someone took Marc."

Fred spoke slowly. "Mallory, why would anyone take Marc?"

"He's gone, Fred. Gone." She traced the path through the grass once more, and studied the tracks in the gravel.

"Surely you're jumping to conclusions."

"He doesn't just disappear." Despite her struggle at self-control, she felt herself tremble. "People don't just disappear here. There's no place to hide an Easter egg. This town is so small you can't open a car door without hitting someone, let alone –"

"Okay, Mallory." Fred interrupted the escalating soprano in her voice. "Calm down."

"He's gone. His notes are gone. His laptop is gone. And there's signs that someone was dragged from his office."

# Chapter Forty-two

During the six-hour flight to Southern California's John Wayne Airport, the doctor monitored the patient and kept him hydrated and asleep.

The pilot's unsmiling wife came back to offer prepackaged corned beef sandwiches, round-cheeked red apples, individual bags of Seyfert chips made in Ft. Wayne, and pop cans of the Midwest's highly caffeinated drink of choice – Mountain Dew.

After lunch, the pilot spent time in the bathroom before coming back to the cabin.

"How's our patient?"

It was the inquiry Yao dreaded. Before he could answer, the doctor spoke up.

"Resting comfortably thanks to your flying expertise." The doctor flashed the pilot a toothy smile. "Just how long have you been doing medical flights?"

"Well now," the pilot looked to the ceiling while he calculated. "First the military, then some time traveling the country, then I hooked up with a doctor here in Ft. Wayne who needed a pilot to transport diabetes patients to regular therapy in Nashville. Did that run until he retired, then went into business for myself."

"A while then."

"I'm not exactly in diapers if that's what you mean." He reached for another can of Mountain Dew and popped open the tab. He pointed the can toward Yao. "What about you? What's your story?"

The doctor looked at Yao and Yao could see amusement in his eyes. "I got my training in university." Yao's practiced English was free of an Asian accent.

"Saw a lot of guys quit college." The pilot took a long swig from his soda can. "Some can't sit still that long. For me, that degree meant I could travel faster and farther."

Yao steered the conversation back to safer ground. "How is our flight time?"

"Like I promised, we're a bit ahead of schedule." His eyes went back to the patient. "What's his story?"

Yao nodded towards the pilot's drink. "Could we have a couple of those?"

"Where's my manners?" The pilot retrieved two more cold cans and tossed them to Yao and the doctor.

"Thanks." The doctor opened the can and it spit yellow liquid on the front of his shirt. "Stuff looks like horse piss."

The pilot guffawed as the doctor pulled a roll of gauze from his bag. Wiping his shirt, the doctor eyed the pilot. "So is that good lookin' brunette yours or can I ask her out?"

The pilot sobered. "Hands off, mate. She's mine all right. Married her as soon as I met her."

"Smart man." The doctor brushed at his shirt. "She'd make a fine nurse."

"A sight prettier than the one you're working with." The pilot eyed Yao.

"Treat her right," the doctor warned, "or I'll offer her a better job."

The pilot grinned and retreated to his cabin. Without the pilot's probing, Yao relaxed. The doctor smiled smugly at Yao, then settled back and closed his eyes for a nap.

# Chapter Forty-three

Back at her family home, Mallory wore a path in the carpet. At last Fred came on the phone line.

"You're pacing," Fred stated over the speaker.

"Aren't you?" she snapped back.

"Hold your horses, Deverell just walked in."

It was only noon but she was exhausted from keeping her panic at bay.

"We've notified the authorities to be on the look-out for Marc." Deverell sounded in control but she heard the rapid clicking of his pen. "They're watching airports and freeways."

For the millionth time, Mallory raked her fingers through her disheveled hair. "That's all we're doing? Watching airports and freeways?"

Fred was patronizing. "Mallory, you know the drill. We're doing all we can and we're doing it thoroughly."

"This isn't just anybody that falls under policy. This is my brother."

"We're aware of that, Mallory. Too aware." Deverell's tone reminded them that he hadn't thought this was a good idea in the first place.

"This is not about blame." Fred was calm in the highly charged emotional conversation. "This is about gathering information and finding Marc." He paused and Mallory took a deep breath. "Now, Mallory, what else can you tell us?"

"I've told you everything. Several times."

"All right." Deverell began his to-do list. "We need you to let his secretary – "

"Nancy. Her name is Nancy."

"Nancy," Deverell repeated. "Let Nancy, and anyone else who would be interested, know that Marc has been called away."

"Called away for what? To get his nails done? Pass a kidney stone? Make a speech to Congress? I know, I'll tell them he ducked into a phone booth, changed into his superman cape and flew off to save the world."

"Mallory," Fred interrupted. "We understand you are upset. And understandably so. But we need you to set your personal feelings aside and put on your professional hat."

"Your big girl panties," Deverell said.

"You are good at what you do," Fred continued. "Get on the team with us and let's do what we do best. Let's find your brother together."

"Stop pacing and sit down," Deverell ordered.

Mallory dropped onto the couch. "Okay." She pressed the cell phone close to her ear. "I'll let Nancy and Thurmond know –"

"Thurmond?" Mallory could hear Deverell's gum snap through the receiver. "Who's Thurmond?"

"The vet next door."

"What's he got to do with any of this?"

Mallory sighed. "He and Marc talk each morning. He'll notice if Marc is gone."

"Great," Deverell said. "Tell the secretary, the vet, the postman, the gas station owner, Curly, Moe, and Larry, the three little pigs, and the muffin man. Whoever."

# Chapter Forty-four

Colonel Yao was relieved when he felt the plane begin its descent. It had been challenging to stay awake for the majority of the trip. The smooth flight and the drone of the humming engines tempted him to doze, especially since he'd had few hours of sleep for the past several nights. Making tactical arrangements had proved taxing.

From the window he watched the John Wayne airport come into view. Unlike Smith Field, this southern California airport served three million commercial passengers annually through direct flights and easy domestic and international connections. An important aircraft manufacturing and flight-training center, the Santa Ana based airport played host to several large airlines and was among the top five busiest general aviation centers in the world. Frequent fliers included air cargo carriers transporting 50,000 tons of goods yearly, as well as Life Flight donor organ and critical care patient delivery. It was that last feature that interested Yao.

Characteristic for a medical flight, the pilot smoothly executed the flare to let the plane settle on the runway and then taxied to a tarmac beside a hangar.

As planned, a second ambulance met the travelers. The smooth talking doctor handed Yao the IV that fed glucose into the patient's veins and supervised as medics moved the patient.

Once they were settled in the second emergency vehicle and on the road, Yao studied the scenery. Entering Long Beach, the view became a jungle of concrete and industry. Small fast food stores were squeezed between large and colorless industrial structures. Next to an In and Out Burger stood a silver-plating company. The ambulance turned into the alleyway and stopped in front of a large set of metal doors. The driver gave a short blast on his horn and someone on the inside raised the door high enough to admit the vehicle. In a moment the ambulance was inside the gray interior.

Stepping out the passenger door, Yao observed the surroundings. A cement floor with metal walls. Above two waist-high tanks hung cranes built to lift heavy cargo and lower it into the plating tanks. But today the tanks were empty and the rusty cranes were still.

"This was successful in its day." The ambulance driver dug a cigarette pack from his shirt pocket. "But shortly after the environmental groups began watch-dogging the industry, that larger tank sprung a leak. Seeped into the ocean before they found it."

"Unfortunate." Yao refused the cigarette the man offered.

"Not for me." Like a thirsty man needing a drink of water, he took a long pull on the lit cigarette. He waved the pack in the direction of the ambulance before dropping it back in his pocket. "Can't smoke in that. Rules about asthmatics, you know."

Yao frowned as the metal door slid closed once more.

"Don't worry." The man blew a lungful of smoke. "We're a couple minutes ahead of schedule." He kicked the empty tank. "Naturally the place got shut down and the city is trying to figure what to do with it. The current plan is to make it a place for the homeless to bed down."

"Until then, you put it to use."

The man spread his hands in a mock bow. "What can I say? I'm a businessman."

"A real entrepreneur."

Outside, another short horn blast sounded and Yao's portly companion crushed out his cigarette under his heel as he signaled for the door to be raised. On their tracks, the rollers echoed loudly, lifting along the ceiling to reveal a hearse waiting outside. Yao glanced at his watch. Right on time.

The elongated car parked and a solemn man emerged from the driver's side. He approached as the metal door slid back down, trapping inside the smell of exhaust and cigarette smoke.

Efficiently, the doctor and the newcomer positioned the patient inside a satin lined coffin. The doctor checked the patient's vital signs, nodded to Yao, and the coffin was loaded into the shiny hearse, as gray as the building they were in.

The ambulance driver slapped the doctor on the back. "I'll get you back to the airport before I return this buggy."

The door opened again and the hearse pulled out. Once more in the passenger seat, Yao watched the ambulance driver take another cigarette from his pack and offer one to the doctor. Another reason Yao tolerated the vile Mr. Spencer was that he arranged the payments to the people who provided services that facilitated the Colonel's plans. Usually that meant an amount up front, padded with a don't ask, don't tell stipulation. The final payment appeared in their bank account when the job was complete. Hirelings weren't tempted to bargain with, or threaten Yao over something as trivial as money. Careful that the money trail would not lead back to him, Yao never dealt with the sordid financial arrangements. Yao focused on the plan.

The hearse navigated down the alley, turned right on the street and drove toward the Pacific Ocean.

Soon they arrived at the Long Beach pier. They were not out of danger yet, but Yao began to breathe easier. Chinese shipping conglomerates owned sections of the harbor. It was to one of these docks that the hearse steered. Looming ahead was a hulking cargo ship, pulled tight against the dock. On the gangplank, several men were loading cargo. Like a giant praying mantis, a crane hoisted a shipping container aboard and stacked it like a child stacks blocks.

A short, blocky man with a gap between his front teeth, the

Captain greeted Yao. "Colonel, welcome aboard." He studied the hearse. "I'll have my men load your belongings and we'll ship out." The Captain signaled to a uniformed sailor. "This man will take you to your quarters."

Yao waved away the sailor. "After my things are settled."

"As you wish." The Captain watched as four men carried the coffin up the gangplank.

As the hearse departed, Yao turned toward and followed the coffin to his quarters. Conditions, the captain assured as they proceeded, would be sparse but adequate.

As soon as the casket was settled in a room near his own, Yao dismissed the Captain. "And send the ship's doctor here."

# Chapter Forty-five

In the living room, Mallory paced. The smell of her dad's tobacco multiplied her feelings of guilt. The last thing she ever wanted to do was disappoint her loving parents. This time she hadn't wrecked the family car. She had lost her brother. And not just lost him, he had been kidnapped by ruthless enemies. She didn't want to imagine his fate if she didn't find him.

What had she gotten Marc into? What began as a simple information plant to track and trap a spy had exploded and she wasn't sure where to find the pieces.

The enemy had proven to be far more dangerous than she and Fred had predicted while they sat in their comfortable conference room on the East Coast. Underestimating the opponent had resulted in a death and Marc's abduction. As she mentally raced through possible scenarios, she feared he would be tortured and killed and she would never find him.

Her phone chirped and Mallory jumped even though she had been expecting the call.

"Anything new in your neighborhood, Mallory?" Fred's familiar voice was a comfort.

"Nothing, Fred. What have you come up with?"

He cleared his throat. A stalling device, she discerned. "I've been in touch with local law offices in Indiana and they don't have anything, either. They'll let us know if something suspicious shows up."

Mallory kicked the couch. "I can't believe these creeps pulled this off without any trace. Look at the reports again, Fred. You must have missed something."

"I'm telling you, Mallory – "

"And I'm telling you to look again."

"All right." She could hear Fred mumbling as he revisited the reports.

"Something," Mallory pleaded. "Anything to show me where to look next."

Fred chuckled.

"I can't believe you think this is funny, Fred. How can you be so callous –"

"Whoa, Mallory. Calm down, I'm not laughing at the situation. Just a note in the police log."

From the front window, she could see the basketball hoop in the driveway. The hoop where she and Marc had just played one on one. Their games were spirited and underhanded and the score was usually disputed which led to a play-off. That was the thing about Indiana. A house may or may not have appliances but every address had a basketball hoop. Hoosiers had priorities after all. "What does it say?"

"An ambulance was at the mechanic's for a routine maintenance. The mechanic reported it missing from their parking lot but when the police stopped by to take a report, the ambulance was right where it was supposed to be." He laughed again. "In the big city, mechanics smoke their lunch, not their breakfast."

Mallory twisted a strand of hair around her finger. "An ambulance," she whispered.

"What? What did you say, Mallory?"

"That's it. That's how they got him out of town." She spun back to face the room. "They took him in an ambulance."

Fred whistled. "No one would check an ambulance."

Mallory switched the phone to her other ear and reached for a pen and paper. "Where would an ambulance take Marc?"

"A hospital? Paramedic headquarters? Shoot, Mallory, an ambulance can go wherever it wants."

In handwriting shaky with anticipation, Mallory listed the places he said and added several ideas of her own. "Wherever it wants," she echoed. "They'll take him out of the country."

"The quickest way to do that is by air."

"Of course! A medical flight."

"They could move a body without many questions," Fred conceded. "I'll follow up on medical flights out of all the nearby airports."

"Still, no flights from our local airports are international. There has to be a connection."

"Ft. Wayne is an international airport."

She snorted. "A misnomer. Or positive thinking by the city planners that gave the place the name. It's still too small to handle anything that big. Medium sized and commuter connections only." She snapped her fingers. "Indianapolis is two hours away. Detroit or Chicago airports are three to four hours away."

"If I was grabbing a guy, I'd want to get him as far away from the area where people would be looking for him as quickly as possible. My vote, Mallory, is that they got Marc on a plane locally. Besides, the vehicle was back at the mechanic's by the time the police came by. Maybe an hour. Two at most."

She scratched several airports off the list. "That rules out Indianapolis or Detroit or Chicago. It would take all day to get there and back."

"That fits with my theory for a local connection. These guys are flying under the radar, attracting as little attention as possible."

"Getting a guy out of the country by commercial air would be tricky. What about a boat?"

"It would take longer," Fred considered. "From the east coast or from the west coast?"

"No telling. The Great Lakes are only two hours away and

that would get them to Canada."

"We'll have the coast guard inspect outgoing vessels bound for foreign ports."

"Right away, Fred. Don't waste a minute."

"Come on back to the office, Mallory. We'll follow the trail better from here."

"Not until I find a trail here. I know the jumpin' off place began in Dixon."

# Chapter Forty-six

Hebron checked for addresses along the Main Street in the small town of Dixon. At last he found the one that matched his computer search for intellectual property attorney Marc Wayne. It was an elongated brick building with character completely unlike conventional law offices that appeared bland and businesslike. Hebron liked it.

Inside, a pretty lady was at the reception desk. "Can I help you?" If he wasn't imagining things, Elvis Presley was playing from an eight track.

"I'd like to see Mr. Wayne."

She got up and came to him. "He is out of the office right now. Can I take a message?"

Hebron adjusted the backpack slung over his shoulder. "My professor said Mr. Wayne wanted to talk about my invention."

She introduced herself. "Is Mr. Wayne preparing a patent for you?"

"Don't think so. He has my device, a round object about this big." He held out his hands to indicate the size. "Said he found another use for it besides categorizing diamonds."

She brightened. "He had that in his workshop. Come on back and you can identify it."

She led the way to an open room at the rear of the building. The size of his dorm at college, the room's walls were lined with low shelves topped with counters and crowded with grouped materials. In the center of the room, a stool sat in front of a worktable. In addition to the overhead lights, a direct light on a flexible stand was clipped to the edge of the table. Dusty yellow legal pads with sketches and formulas were stacked beside books and computer printouts with information on magnetics, magnetic fields, and propulsion systems.

"Cool." Hebron circled the room. "Very cool."

Resting her hand on the empty place on the table, Nancy frowned. "Marc worked with your project. But I don't see it now."

Hebron took this as an invitation to look through the creative space.

"It was right here," Nancy mumbled and Hebron wondered if she was talking to him or to herself. He decided to believe it was to herself so he didn't have to formulate a hypothesis about a question he didn't have the answer to. Clearly she was puzzled though he didn't understand why.

"Why would this area be cleared?" Nancy continued in the low tone he anticipated was reserved for herself. "Marc collects so much material, I need to rent an extra room from Thurmond for storage."

"What's a Thurmond?"

Now Nancy circled the room, looking over and under shelves, cabinets, and counters. "Who. Who is Thurmond." Back to where she began, she stopped and bent to look under the worktable. "Dr. Thurmond is the landlord."

"Does he have a dog?" Hebron cocked his head toward the common wall that separated Marc's office from the other side of building. From that side came the mournful bay of a hunting dog.

"Depends on the day." She rested her hand on her hips. "Yesterday he had a goat next door."

"Kidding?"

"Not even."

A stack of magnets caught his attention and Hebron flipped through the notes on the legal pad. He recognized symbols relating to the Meissner Effect. He scanned theories about projecting a Meissner field.

"Brilliant."

"What's that?" Nancy peered at the pages.

"Projecting the Meissner field will levitate. Objects will float. Like a submarine in water."

"I didn't think it was an underwater vehicle."

Hebron shook his head. "Theoretically, a Meissner device is a superconductor." He squinted. "Okay, not exactly a superconductor in the traditional way the title is applied. The machine would reject magnetic fields, sort-of an anti-magnetic field." He reached for two magnets and held them so they repelled. "It would repel magnetic fields like a submarine displaces water in its ballast to give it buoyancy in water."

"The way a jet moves through air."

Hebron and Nancy turned to see a professional looking woman in the doorway. The college student grinned. Someone who spoke his language. "Exactly. Magnetic currents flow across the earth's surface similar to the currents in the ocean. Giving it buoyancy on earth, the device will generate an exclusionary field, like a bubble, that excludes the planet's natural magnetic currents."

Nancy stepped between the two and made introductions.

Hebron stuck out his hand but Mallory refused his handshake. Instead she folded her arms. "You have an unusual understanding of Marc's theory."

Feeling awkward, Hebron stuffed his hands into his jeans pockets. "He gave a lecture at the college and we talked more about it over lunch." He motioned to the pads of notes. "Once the foundation of the theory is grasped, the rest unfolds."

"Ah." Mallory unfolded her arms. "Marc told me about you."

Nancy picked up yesterday's mug, still half full of cold Earl Grey. "Did he tell you where Hebron's invention is?"

# Chapter Forty-seven

Marc's head pounded. He'd had a few migraines in his day and this felt like one on steroids. He tried to move but his body wouldn't respond.

At first he thought he was dizzy. But the irregular yet rhythmic sway continued. From the exterior sound of a throaty whistle, he surmised he was aboard a ship. That didn't compute. How many ships were in Indiana? Certainly plenty of ski and pontoon boats dotted the one hundred or so lakes in his Midwest state but none of them had a whistle like that. This one's deep tone resonated in his chest.

Breathing deeply, he inhaled the briny smell of salty ocean water. That meant he was no longer in Indiana. In fact, the ocean was either far to the east or farther still to the west. Or south. Either option caused a wave of panic to flood his veins.

His eyelids were too heavy to lift which was another baffling fact. He squeezed his eyes tight and tried to remember. Why was he in a boat on the ocean? He remembered Mallory had come for a visit. He recalled bicycling to work as usual. He had chatted with Thurmond. Then gone into his office. Nancy wasn't in yet. So far it was all as it was supposed to be.

Another long and deep whistle sounded followed by the indignant shrill of seagulls. He heard the hum of the vessel's engine purr to life beneath him. A fresh wave of alarm made him nauseas. He fought the pounding in his head as he again struggled to recall what brought him to this situation. He had been in his office. At the computer. He remembered that the bell jangled over the front door. Slogging through his sluggish memory felt like trying to run a marathon in a swimming pool. With great effort he determined to take the next step. The front bell had rung. That meant someone had come in. Thurmond? No. Nancy? No. Mallory? No. He took a deep breath and tried to relax. To slow the pounding of his heart fueled by fear. To invite his memory to release its panicked stranglehold on the information he sought.

Someone had come into the office the night before. The same person who came in that morning. Someone who made him uneasy.

*"I don't think I can help you."*

*"On the contrary, you are exactly the one who can help me."*
Mentally, he repeated the conversation several times but still couldn't recall who had said that last line. Turning his head, he felt an arrow of pain zing through his temple. The sensation reminded him of being stung by a bee. Once when he was a kid swimming in a pool. And again in the back of his knee. He had been walking and someone was behind him. *"On the contrary, you are exactly the one who can help me."* An eerie image wavered in his memory.

Mr. Spencer.

But why would Mr. Spencer want him on a ship?

# Chapter Forty-eight

"We are near international waters, Colonel Yao." The Captain flashed a grin that showed the gap between his front teeth.

Yao stood on the bridge near the Captain's elbow. With every passing mile between himself and the California shoreline, he breathed a little easier. Once he knew they were safe from inspection, he planned to retreat to his cabin and celebrate with several shots of tequila. It would take at least that much for his tense muscles to relax. He could use several hours of solid sleep, too.

Confident everything was going according to schedule, Yao left the bridge. Out of sight of the crew, he wearily made his way to his quarters. Inside he undid the top button of his shirt and poured that long anticipated shot of tequila. It was a taste he'd acquired in college and only allowed himself to enjoy on rare occasions. In a single fluid motion, he downed the bitter liquid and was pouring himself a second when there was a frantic knock at the door.

"We're being boarded." The Colonel recognized the breathless crewmember from the bridge.

"Boarded?" Yao hated inane questions and was well aware he'd just asked one. "I understood we were past the limit."

"Almost, sir. We were nearly at the twelve-mile limit. But a coast guard boat from the United States has contacted us that they will board for an inspection in moments."

As if to prove the man's words, the Colonel heard the ship's engines slow.

"Captain thought you'd want to know." The seaman jogged back down the passageway.

Yao hurried into the adjacent cabin where Marc Wayne, deep in a medically induced sleep, rested in a bunk.

# Chapter Forty-nine

Having searched Marc's office for anything she had missed, Mallory was disappointed she hadn't found anything. Brooding, she collected her brother's bike and loaded it into the trunk of Marc's Jetta. As she was doing with the two-wheeler, Mallory wanted to take Marc back home where he belonged. To be in the secure haven of their family homestead, play some driveway basketball, and go out to eat at the restaurant where Johnny would cook her steak to perfection. She would talk about Nancy. Then he could one day marry and make Mallory an aunt.

Anxiety and regret churned her stomach so that she wondered if she would ever be able to eat again. Mallory had concocted a plausible story for Nancy. Always smelling of spring, the receptionist would continue to run the office and Mallory was confident she would do her usual efficient job. Two years behind Marc in school, Nancy was smitten and the only person who was clueless about her feelings was Marc.

Typical, really, for the inventive personality. Living with Marc all her life, Mallory had met his friends. Even in college, Marc and his circle of engineers, computer geeks, and mathematicians were exuberant about their scientific discoveries and content to relate to women in a purely academic setting. Like Jimmy at work, behind their back these guys were called late bloomers when it came to noticing females as potential romantic interests.

Nancy was beautiful and smart. She knew better than to share her feelings with the object of her affection. Marc would be embarrassed and avoid her like the repelling end of one of his magnets. Patient, she unobtrusively orbited him and invested her talents making a reputation in the community as the patent attorney's sunny assistant who got things done. One day, Marc would decide he would like to share his life with someone special. But it would be later than the average single guy. Far from average, Marc existed on a different plane then most. It would take a unique woman to love such an eccentric.

Pulling into the driveway of the home where she and Marc had grown up, Mallory's strained spirits plummeted. The house was dark. No one was home. Mom and Dad were gone. And thanks to her strategy as the lead on her first project, her irresponsible planning had gotten Marc kidnapped. She had robustly underestimated the power and determination of the thieves and spies she sought. Chastising herself for mistaking international black market dealers for computer geeks who had merely hacked into the United States Patent and Trademark Office, Mallory realized in her idealism, she had stereotyped the crime.

She wheeled the bike inside and parked it in the usual spot near the front door. Drawing the drapes, the dark closed in and she wrapped it around her. Everything felt gloomy, heavy, and hopeless. Sitting on the couch, she wondered what to do now? After messing up the situation beyond recognition, she was tempted to surrender to the overwhelming depression that beckoned. To be completely female and have a good cry where no one would see.

Instead, she cursed. Loud, bitter words as she paced through the house. Going from room to room, Mallory recalled family traditions and berated herself for being incompetent as an FBI agent, as a daughter, and as a sister. She was horrified by the power of the faceless foes that had invaded her world and stolen the person who meant the most to her. And she was terrified. Fearful of what could happen to Marc, and frightened to be so utterly out of control.

Breathless and spent, she sagged against the hallway wall and slid to the floor. Resting her head back against the hard surface, she faced the extensive collection of family photos her mom had yearly framed and hung. Her mother had dubbed the expanding collection, the Wall of Fame.

The smiling eyes of her parents looked out at her. "I'm sorry Mom and Dad. Really sorry."

# Chapter Fifty

     Commander Luc Gennett ordered the United States Coast Guard Cutter *Resolute* alongside the cargo ship. She was a medium endurance ship, nicknamed by drug smugglers, El Tiburon Blanco; Spanish for The White Shark.

     A sailor delivered the commander's meal from the galley as Gennett reviewed his orders on the bridge. Inspect foreign ships in U.S. waters, particularly looking for an American passenger named Marc Wayne. Apparently Gennett's superiors believed Mr. Wayne could be aboard against his will. The Coast Guard was practiced at search and rescue but this type of hunt was out of the ordinary.

     Career military, Commander Gennett had enlisted to get as far away as he could from the Iowa pig farm where he grew up. He didn't want his father to think for one nanosecond that his second born son had any intention of joining the family livestock business. That decision had been made the day a piglet fell into the muck under the pig barn and 13-year-old Luc had to dive into the smelly pool of pig poop, slop, and water to retrieve the slippery, squealing baby porker.

     Much to his older brother's delight, Luc emerged gripping

the pig by a back leg and holding his own stomach as he retched uncontrollably for the next several hours. His clothes had to be burned and despite multiple hot showers and thorough scrubbings with enough lye soap to remove the top layer of skin, it was weeks before Gennett was free of the stench. It was months before he no longer gagged every time his brother brought up the topic, usually any time the girls paid more attention to the younger and handsomer Luc than to his tormenting older sibling.

From that day forward, Luc had sworn off pork and never reconsidered, even when the ship's cook served fat sausage links and juicy bacon for breakfast.

"Eat while it's hot." The sailor removed the cover that kept today's meal warm. Next to a helping of scalloped potatoes with bits of bacon were a serving of green beans with pork pieces, and two thick slices of brown sugar ham.

Solemnly, Gennett replaced the cover over the offending plate. "Take it away. I'm not hungry."

"Sir?" The younger man's expression was pained.

"Did you already eat?"

"Yes, sir." Wistfully the sailor eyed the tray.

Swallowing against his childhood memories from the pig farm, Gennett scanned his orders once more. "You would do me a service if you could polish that off as well. Wouldn't want to offend the cook."

"Sir, no, sir." Eagerly the sailor reached for the fork.

Gennett stopped him with a look. "Away from here. Enjoy it somewhere else."

The sailor complied. Though he had quickly left with the meal, the aroma of pork lingered. Gennett pinched closed his nostrils, and exhaled long. Catching the curious sidelong glance of the helmsman, Gennett mumbled something about allergies and refocused on the task at hand.

As the Resolute neared the cargo tanker, coastguardsmen on deck prepared to secure the two boats together. From his post on the bridge, Gennett watched the procedures and recalled his earlier standards. When he decided to enlist as a means to get away from the family farm, not just any branch of the military service would suffice. The pig farmer's son chose the branch that boasted the most action.

"The United States Coast Guard is one of seven uniformed services," the recruiter had told the teenaged Gennett at a career fair. "It's unique in that it is also a maritime law enforcement agency with jurisdiction in domestic and international waters."

"What's that mean?" Gennett wanted to be certain about what he was getting into before he signed. Previous experience had made him cautious before he dove in.

"It means we are a federal regulatory agency, part of the Department of Homeland Security." The recruiter unfolded a colorful brochure. "Though we are the smallest armed service, our mission is to protect the public, the environment, the economic, and security interests of the nation."

"What's that look like?"

The recruiter with cropped salt and pepper hair had pointed to a picture. "It looks like we don't take slackers. While most military services are either at war or training for war, the Coast Guard is deployed every day."

While Luc had meticulously filled out paperwork, the recruiter made small talk. "Have any diving experience?"

"Some."

"Most of our work is in the sea." He glanced at Luc's address. "Being from Iowa, you probably have fresh water experience."

Luc shook his head. "Definitely not fresh water."

# Chapter Fifty-one

Marc felt like he was swimming up through a sea of molasses as he fought for consciousness. Like a bad dream, the harder he worked the more the surface eluded him. The light of awareness danced close for a moment and then reeled far away. Reaching, pulling, kicking, he worked to break through. Finally he grasped the evasive, shimmering objective.

At last, he opened his eyes. His head thundered like a massive hangover. He hadn't drank enough to be hung over since college and then once had been enough to swear off too much alcohol ever again. Why people considered a night of being out of control followed by a bout of illness worse than food poisoning to be fun did not compute with him.

Though his limbs were still drugged, too heavy to move, he could will a response from his neck. Gingerly he turned his head to get his bearings. His heartbeat pounded in his ears as he looked around at the surroundings. It was a small, colorless room with a round nautical window. The droning of large engines reminded him of his earlier impression that he was aboard a ship.

The door opened and he quickly closed his eyes. He didn't

want anyone to know he was awake but helpless until he had a better sense of what was going on and who was involved. He heard the footsteps of two men enter the room.

"Give him another dose," someone commanded.

"He'll be asleep on that last dose for some time yet, I assure you," came a second voice.

"Give it anyway," said the first. "I can't afford for him to be awake when our guests arrive."

# Chapter Fifty-two

Elbows on the kitchen table, Mallory went over her written list of facts. Out of habit, she had brewed a cup of coffee that sat, forgotten and cold, in front of her. The morning news droned from the television. She told herself she had turned it on to stay updated, but the truth was the sounds of voices other than her own helped her feel less lonely.

Unable to add to, or cross off anything on her list of possibilities, Mallory poured a fresh cup and walked outside. The crisp autumn air was sharp and uncomfortable without a jacket but Mallory was glad to feel something rather than the physical and mental numbness she had slipped into last night.

In the backyard was the fire ring for bon fires and roasting marshmallows. It was a well-used circle between family evenings, youth group gatherings, and scouting events. Her mother's garden where her parents spent summers harvesting tomatoes, green beans, and cilantro was under a blanket of leaves. Beyond that was the now empty pole barn where Mallory and Marc had raised various 4-H projects including Nubian goats, Jersey Giant chickens, a llama named Dolly, and a soft-eyed cow that grew into the state champ for its enormous size thanks to Marc's scientifically designed diet. One summer's goose eggs, hatched in Marc's homemade incubator, produced a flock of geese and one goose that followed Marc like a puppy. Calling weep, weep as she shadowed Marc, the goose was referred to as Fido.

In the pond, Marc had floated all manner of boat designs, raised an annoying pair of muskrats her parents referred to Suzie and Sam, and became familiar with the microscopic species that made up the unseen aquatic community.

Mallory stuffed her cold hands into her jeans pockets. Her parents had provided a secure and nurturing environment for their two children to grow and develop. Life had been fairly smooth for Marc and Mallory. Until now. It was an excuse, and she knew it, but Mallory credited underestimating the opponent to lack of personal exposure to truly difficult situations. It gave her an answer to the persistent why that needed to be silenced so she could professionally consider the available information.

Or had her parents sheltered her from their adult worries? The result of his mother's bout with measles when he was in utero, her father was born without legs below his knees. Born to an Amish couple, her dad was never expected to walk. But at age two, like most toddlers, he pulled himself up on his half legs and taught himself to walk. The rest of his life was a series of prosthesis, those that fit and those that did not.

With fresh appreciation, Mallory surveyed the fire ring, garden, barn, and pond. All were designed and built by a man without legs. Back inside, she stood again in front of the Wall of Fame. There was a portrait of the four of them, her father with his cane. Her parents met at the Ft. Wayne Embassy Theater. Her mother recalled their father as looking quite dapper when she first saw him with his gold-topped cane in the ornate lobby of the city's grand landmark.

The newlyweds, their wedding photo in the center of the Wall of Fame, welcomed the birth of Mallory. But two years later, her mother fought for her life when their second child died at birth. His tiny heart was too weak to sustain life outside the womb where his mother's body had tenderly supplied the circulation he needed. The diagnosis was that Mallory's mom had lupus. Grieving the loss of their longed-for infant son, they also grieved that the young woman would carry no more babies.

It was several years before the lupus was managed, dark years for her parents filled with uncertainty of the next day of life together. Then Marc joined their family, adopted and arriving with the unlimited potential that comes with all newborns. For the first time, Mallory considered what it had been like for her parents to succeed in life perpetually challenged by her father's limiting physical handicap and her mother's incurable disease.

But they had thrived. Those two intrepid spirits had faced their trials. Without a path to follow, her parents had set the goal to build a wholesome family and future, and navigated a trail. The final portrait, Mallory had taken. It was her parents standing together next to Dad's heirloom Eiffel tower rose. With the help of Marc's fertilizer recipe, the fragrant pink blossom topped a six-foot-tall stem.

No matter what the setback, or the hindrance, Mr. and Mrs. Wayne refused to be detained. Handicapped, they were not crippled. Standing before the photo tribute to the character of her parents, Mallory determined she would never give up. She would find her brother.

Her phone rang and she knew it was Fred. His voice held excitement. "Mallory, I located a medical flight that left the area right after Marc disappeared."

# Chapter Fifty-three

In a handful of years, Gennett quickly rose through the ranks to captain his own vessel. As an enlisted member, that journey included a stint at Officer Candidate School.

Alexander Hamilton founded the Revenue Cutter Service on August 4, 1790, making the Coast Guard the nation's oldest continuous seagoing service. The Guard's initial mission was to collect taxes from a new nation of patriot smugglers. When at sea, the officers were instructed to crack down on piracy. While they were at it, they might as well rescue anyone in distress.

After the September 11, 2001 terrorist attacks against the United States, the Coast Guard formed The Deployable Operations Group. The DOG brought numerous existing deployable law enforcement, tactical, and response units under a single command headed by a rear admiral. The unit contained several hundred highly trained Coast Guardsmen whose missions include maritime law enforcement, anti-terrorism, and port security.

As captain of his own vessel, Gennett was one of nearly 50,000 active duty members who were supported by another 10,000 reservists, nearly the same number of full time civilian employees, and 30,000 active auxiliary members. The Coast Guard's decentralized organization and readiness for missions made the service highly effective, extremely agile, and adaptable in a wide range of emergencies.

Of French descent, Gennett had a slight build and sandy colored hair. Deep lines were etched around his eyes from years of squinting into the sun. Now he peered through binoculars at the Chinese vessel. The large ship had any number of shadowy places where a man could hide. Or be hidden. The ship was radioed in, much as a traffic cop checks the record of a speeding driver.

Gennett readied his boarding team.

# Chapter Fifty-four

Late afternoon the day after Marc's disappearance, Mallory mashed the accelerator to the floor. Tires squealed as they slipped, then grabbed, and her car shot forward. The pilot she wanted to talk to, the guy who did medical transports, was about to take off. If that plane got airborne, who knew when she would get another chance to question him.

Smashing through the chain link fence between the parking lot and the flight field, she skidded around a Cessna as it landed, fishtailed, corrected, and pressed forward. On the far side of the landing strip, her car flattened a runway light and bounced onto the grassy patch. Her tires throwing dirt and grass, she bore down on the second runway.

Moments ago, above the volume of the television, the lanky grandpa at the airport had informed Mallory, "The medic transport plane has just cleared for take-off."

Glancing out the picture window, she had spotted a fixed-wing rolling into position on the far runway. Now she steered for the middle of the take-off path. She could hear the plane's engines at full throttle. The aircraft began its race down the asphalt, picking up momentum that would aid in the jet's release from gravity's pull. Mallory turned directly into the on-coming airplane's path and jerked the wheel. Wheels squealing, the car slid sideways and slammed to a stop.

The engines whined as the medical transport reversed engines and turned to avoid a collision. Askew on the pavement, the plane came to a stop. Mallory released the breath she had been holding and sprinted to the plane. The hatch flew open.

"Can I help you?" A slender man with a military haircut, the pilot leaned coolly in the doorway, a can of Mountain Dew in his hand. "Or are you some kind of crazy?"

Mallory flashed her identification. "I want to see your flight log."

"Of course you do." The man's agitation was clear behind his sarcasm.

From the cockpit, a woman appeared and handed him the book. She took his place leaning in the doorway, silently watching behind dark sunglasses, while he descended the aluminum steps.

Mallory read through the entries. It was the most recent trip she was interested in. Five souls on board. Travel speed in knots. Weather conditions. Coordinates. "Tell me about your last transport."

"What do you want to know? The paperwork was neat and tidy. We had the required doctor to patient ratio."

"Who was your patient?"

"Not my business. I'm the pilot." He put a hand on the fuselage. "My job is the plane."

"Did he look like this?" She showed him a photo of Marc.

He shrugged. "I had no interaction with the patient. I did not observe him. Pilots don't do patient care." He closed the logbook and tucked it under his arm. "Vital signs, orders for patient care, patient responses – the doctor and nurse do their own charts."

Mallory choked back desperation. She needed some indication of where to search for Marc. She wasn't good at interrogation but as a research analyst, she was trained to scrutinize and follow clues. "The patient arrived by ambulance?"

He chugged the last of his drink. "That's usually how it goes with a medical transport."

"What time?"

He tapped the logbook. "Early morning. We were in the air before most folks were at work."

Mallory glanced up. The silent woman stared back at her. Were these people just doing their job or were they directly connected to Marc's disappearance? If they were involved, it didn't make sense for them to return so quickly to Smith Field. Knowing someone would be looking up his skirt, it would be advantageous to remain unavailable.

"Describe who was with the patient."

"Not anyone I've flown for before. Doctor was a cocky guy. His nurse was ugly." He laughed at his own joke and then held up his palms. "Not that I'm racist."

"Racist?"

"Not me. I've worked with all kinds in the military and out. Don't care what color they are. I do care how they do their job."

"Did the nurse do her job?"

"He. Did *he* do his job." He motioned to the woman who tossed down a fresh can of Mountain Dew. "Saw a lot of corpsmen in the service but not many male nurses in the real world. The ones that are, tend to be a younger group – not concerned with stereotypes. With folks thinking they are wussie."

"The nurse was an older guy. Anything else about him?"

"Quiet. But when he did speak, I expected an accent. But spoke as good as you and me."

"What accent did you expect?"

He pointed the can away from Mallory and popped the top. Like a rooster tail, yellow spray splashed on the black asphalt. "Chinese, Japanese, something Asian."

Mallory felt her heart leap into her throat. Asia was on the other side of the globe. It also lined up with the stolen technology that led to China's new jet engine.

"And you took them to John Wayne airport?"

"They were offloaded in time for the Mrs. and me to have a

late lunch at the beach."

Mallory raked a hand through her hair. "Yesterday."

He took a swig from the drink can.

She studied him, stuffing her emotions in an attempt to think clear enough to ask professional questions. There had to be something to gain from this pilot before he flew to his next destination. "Anything you can remember about the patient? Anything at all?"

The pilot shook his head.

Mallory turned to leave but a voice from the plane stopped her. It was the woman.

From behind her sunglasses she answered the question. "He had a pony tail."

# Chapter Fifty-five

Fighting dread, Yao watched the coast guard ship approach. Her flag snapped spiritedly in the Pacific wind. Consisting of 16 perpendicular stripes of alternating red and white, and the ensign of the arms of the United States in dark blue on a white field, the flag signaled ship captains that this vessel had legal sanction to stop and board. It was the symbol of law enforcement authority.

The coast guard boat came alongside the cargo ship. Several men in crisp white uniforms came aboard.

Yao squelched his rising panic. He had come so far in this audacious plan. He couldn't fail now. His country needed this man and his knowledge. Marc Wayne was the key to getting the Meissner Effect Generator functional. With this technology, Yao envisioned his country becoming rich and powerful, strong and admired. He had to make this work. Falling back on his training, Yao inhaled deeply, grounded himself in the moment and focused his attention on his options.

# Chapter Fifty-six

Gennett's radio operator arrived with a report. The ship his men were inspecting was owned by a Shanghai based electronics firm called DHU Aerocomposites. Interestingly, Boeing owned 30 percent of the Chinese company.

The official statement was that DHU had no ties to the Chinese military but manufactured aircraft parts and materials strictly for commercial use.

*Right.*

"Pass the word," Gennett instructed his Lieutenant Commander. "Tell the search party to be extra thorough."

# Chapter Fifty-seven

The leader of the armed boarding party addressed the ship's captain as his men systematically scattered throughout the vessel. For a cargo boat this large, the opportunity was vast to stash something away from probing eyes. To hide something as diminutive as a man.

Turning down the hallway lined with sleeping quarters, two Coast Guardsmen took opposite sides of the passageway. At the end of the row, Lt. Vince Ford entered a room and was startled to find a casket. His eyes narrowed. This would be an ideal place to hide an American reluctant to leave his homeland.

A baby faced man, Lt. Ford approached the casket and attempted to lift the lid. The top of the box refused to reveal the contents inside.

"Perhaps I can help." The voice came from behind him.

Turning, Lt. Ford saw a Chinese man, slightly gray at the temples. "I want to see inside this casket."

"Certainly." The Chinese man made a slight bow in the direction of the casket. "The casket belongs to a relative of one of the owners of our company. He traveled to the United States in the vain hope of finding a cure for his disease."

"Disease?"

The older man lowered his voice. "A humiliating condition that caused the flesh to rot from his bones."

Lt. Ford felt his belly turn. "Who are you?"

The Chinese man indicated the coffin. "The casket, as you experienced, was sealed to prevent not only dishonor to the dead but to prevent the contagious disease from affecting another."

Ford swallowed. "I have to see inside this casket."

"As you wish." He reached into his breast pocket and produced a paper. "According to your laws, here is the death certificate."

The lieutenant studied it carefully and found everything in order. He handed back the paper and focused once more on the distasteful task at hand.

"You must wear a mask to open the casket," came a second voice, this one with a Chinese accent. Lt. Ford looked up to see a second man enter the small quarters.

"I am ship's doctor." He handed a medical mask and rubber gloves to the Coast Guardsman. "In addition to the unpleasant appearance, and the contagiousness of the disease, you will notice the odor of decay as you get near the body. Though the honorable relative has been properly preserved, the body was not discovered immediately after the demise."

Clenching his teeth, the lieutenant accepted the mask and rubber gloves. As predicted, when he bent close to the casket, the stench made his stomach threaten to turn inside out.

"I can get you a scalpel – a surgical knife to cut through the seal," the ship's doctor offered.

The lieutenant stepped back, blinked, and nodded. "Yes. That would be helpful."

The doctor disappeared. A second later, his Coast Guard teammate poked his head inside the room. "All clear on my side. You ready to move on?"

The lieutenant leaned forward once more and cautiously inhaled. The smell caused him to retch. He stepped back and pulled the mask from his face. "Yeah. I'm done here." He peeled the gloves from his hands and pressed them into the older Chinese man's hands as he quickly exited the room to follow his teammate.

# Chapter Fifty-eight

Mere days after her flight to Indiana, Mallory was aboard another plane. This time the aircraft was pointed east. She had been excited to land in Indiana and have a few days with family and friends. Now she was reversing the trip and was as burdened as the treasury under the national debt.

Beside a miniature package of pretzels on her tray table, the stewardess had left a plastic cup with soda. Mallory didn't remember ordering the drink. Ignored, the ice had melted.

Was she really cut out to be in a predominantly male industry? That she would remain in her position until Marc was found was a given. Surrounded by the resources and experts in the agency, she had the best chance of tracking his journey and retrieving her brother. But then what? After such a colossal bumble, she couldn't stay at the FBI. Certainly everyone had assignments that went awry. Recently Mallory had read the autobiography of the commander of the U.S. military's Delta Force. Several of their missions failed before they had a success.

But this was beyond a plan that had not gone according to specifications. Marc had become entangled like a bear in a honey tree. Her exuberance had endangered a United States citizen she was sworn to protect. Worse, she was responsible for her brother being in an explosive situation and she was struggling to dig up the confidence to assure herself that he would survive. Would he? What had she gotten him into?

She turned her face to the window so no one would see the tears that she was fighting.

Where else could she use her research skills? She didn't ever again want to be in a situation where she risked the lives of those she loved. What was she thinking? If Marc was harmed as a result of her, how could she survive? The guilt of the present situation already left her breathless, as if a horse was parked on her chest.

The FBI had appealed to her because she could be part of a dedicated team that served as a watchdog, a protection for the United States of America. Mallory's parents had been deeply patriotic. Her childhood heroes were Patrick Henry and Joshua Chamberlain. Like those two men, Mallory longed to be involved in work that was significant to the unique liberty of her country.

Rather than championing freedom, she had successfully stripped Marc of his. She closed the window shade so she no longer saw her reflection. Someone had Marc and would force him to make his patent a functioning reality. What motivation would his captors use to secure his cooperation? She shuddered to consider some of the torturous methods she had heard people use to pry what they wanted from another. There were some aspects of her line of work that weren't pleasant. She had been stunned to learn the depth of deprivation, the level of evil human beings were capable of. She chided herself for ignoring that information when she concocted her strategy to plug the leak from the Patent Office.

And Marc's patent for the Meissner Effect device was just a theory. Even if he decided to cooperate, how could Marc build something that was not possible?

He couldn't.

She had to find him.

# Chapter Fifty-nine

Several hours later, the Colonel allowed himself to finally relax his defenses. The Coast Guard ship had gone on her way without incident. An hour later, the captain's errand boy had returned to inform Yao that they were safely in international waters and beyond probing eyes.

The ship's doctor had helped return Marc to a narrow bunk in the room next to Yao's own where the inventor would stay in a medically induced slumber for the rest of the journey.

"Here, this will help, though not much." The doctor had handed him a surgical mask. Yao secured it over his face but the smell that wafted into the room after the casket was opened was enough to make a man swear off eating for life.

With medical tongs, the doctor lifted from the casket a kidney-shaped dish that held a diseased appendix. Quickly, he dumped the offensive item into a biohazard bag and sealed it closed. He opened the cabin door and handed the bag to a waiting ensign. "Dispose of this properly."

"Do I want to know what that was?" The Colonel opened the window to allow the sea air to cleanse the room.

"Just after we left port, a sailor, who had complained of abdominal pain for days, collapsed. I knew what the problem was from an earlier exam but the boy wouldn't believe he needed surgery. Lucky for you, I had not had time to dispose of the infected organ when you summoned me again. The appendix was putrid within his body. Your orders were to make the casket unopenable."

Yao removed his mask and inhaled the biting salty air. "Commendable, doctor."

The ship's doctor bowed slightly and set about settling the patient.

Now, just before he retired for the night, Yao savored a shot of tequila. The first shot was in celebration for making it this far. The second and third shots were to calm his nerves enough to let him sleep.

# Chapter Sixty

In the conference room, Mallory paced behind the chair where she usually sat. Her mind ricocheted from imagining Marc's fate to doing the job she was trained to do. She was a research specialist. She should have found plenty of leads by now.

Fred stirred two creams into a cup of coffee and handed it to his co-worker. She ignored it.

"Where has Helen of Troy been carried off to?" Already talking, Deverell blew into the room. "Fred, what do we have to date?"

"The patent application for the Meissner Effect Device was leaked from the USPTO. We know who was the mole in the Patent Office."

Mallory circled the room. "Now he's dead."

"That's a dead end."

"That's a bad pun," Mallory said.

"Sorry." Deverell tossed a wadded gum wrapper toward the trashcan. The rim shot bounced back onto the floor. "That means the foreign entity will try to cultivate a new contact."

"We have a team working on that." Fred set Mallory's cup at

her empty place.

"Anyone with anything worthy of blackmail is a target." Deverell watched Mallory pace. "What else?"

"We suspect that whoever has received the patent information is having trouble getting the invention to work because our inventor has disappeared."

"Kidnapped," Mallory snapped.

Fred rubbed the top of his head. "Kidnapped," he echoed softly.

"We don't know where to begin looking." Mallory faced her boss. She considered this meeting a colossal waste of time that could be invested finding leads. The sooner she could get out of here, the faster she could be back to following the one sure thing she knew; Marc had been flown to southern California and one of the men with him was probably Chinese.

"Based on the results of previous leaks from the Patent Office," Deverell met her gaze, "the patent and our inventor are probably in Asia."

"Great." Mallory threw up her hands. "That narrows it down to a mere quarter of the globe."

Fred crossed to the map on the wall. "Since the cutting edge jet engine was developed in China, why not begin there?"

"I'll get right on it."

"Whoa." Deverell put a restraining hand on Mallory's arm. "Before you invade the People's Republic, while China developed the engine, based on our information I don't credit them with the ability to directly acquire top secret material."

Mallory pounded the table. "Then where do we begin?"

"If China is the recipient of the information, they probably received the designs from another entity. Someone that pilfers marketable secrets."

"A governmental entity or private entrepreneur?"

"That's the question. Where is Cinderella's slipper hidden? Has Marc been delivered to the highest bidder, or is he making the Meissner Device operational for the marketers?"

"Unless." Fred spun the chair in a slow circle. "We can coax them into showing us where they are."

"How?" Mallory halted Fred's chair with a hand on the arm.

"They are probably working around the clock to get this Holy Grail up and running to position themselves ahead of the rest of the world in military superiority."

"Go on." Deverell loaded a second piece of gum into his mouth.

"What if they believe we are also perfecting the design? What if we make it look like we got it running first?"

Feeling taut as a harp string, Mallory resumed pacing. "How will that lead us to Marc?"

"We make it look like we completed the invention but it's faulty. Then see who is the most interested." Fred became animated as the idea developed. "They will be the only other entity besides us who knows about the Meissner Device patent."

Mallory placed her palms on the table and leaned toward her boss. "How do we keep them from killing Marc?"

Mouth open, Deverell chomped loudly on his gum. "They won't hurt him as long as he is valuable to them. Until we find him, we make them believe he is irreplaceable."

Fred made notes on the paper in front of him. "We leak information that the device had a problem. A deadly problem but the answer was found in a small town inventor's workshop."

Mallory smiled for the first time in days. "That makes Marc too pivotal to dispose of."

"A Trojan horse." Deverell pointed his pen in Fred's direction. "We also leak that now the apparatus is working and that the small town inventor has mysteriously disappeared."

# Chapter Sixty-one

Coming awake, Marc was reluctant to leave the deep slumber. The dreamy sensation of complete relaxation seductively enticed him to stay like a warm bed on a frigid Saturday morning.

Looking around from the single bed where he lay, Marc saw a sparse room. Morning light glowed through narrow windows positioned far above a man's head. Too high to see outside. Opposite the bed was a single door. The only other furniture was a chair and table holding a folded set of clothes, a bottle of water, and two covered dishes.

Where was he? How did he get here? Why was he here? Nothing made sense. There wasn't anything familiar about this place.

Gingerly, Marc stretched and sat up. His head swam and he felt as weak as one of Dr. Thurmond's newborn kittens. His body ached and his stomach grumbled with hunger. The floor was cold under his bare feet and the folding metal chair drawn up to the table was unyielding. Lifting the lids, Marc found a bowl heaped with warm rice. In the second dish was a mystery meat in a dark sauce. He sniffed. This was nothing like the rich Chinese dishes Kimmy brought him at the steak and Chinese food restaurant back home.

Greedily, Marc downed half the water and set to work on the food. After finishing, he felt stronger. Surveying his surroundings, he tried the door. Locked. Stacking the table on the bed and the chair on top of the table, he stood on tiptoe to see out the window. It was too high.

Frustrated, Marc took the clothes to the corner nook that served as a bathroom. A nozzle spit enough water for a shower and he gladly washed off the smell of having gone too long without washing. His beard indicated that enough time had passed to give him that unshaved look that Hollywood actors were sporting. And his facial hair grew slowly.

He was standing the metal bed frame on end in another attempt to see outside when the door opened. Flanked by two armed soldiers, a man entered. His bearing identified him as someone in authority. Recognizing the uniforms, Marc's knees threatened to buckle. Chinese. Was the Chinese military on United States soil? His brain raced to recall what nearby countries were friendly with China.

Or was he on the other side of the globe?

# Chapter Sixty-two

Seeking any clue to Marc's captors and his whereabouts, Mallory read through the reports sent in from the Coast Guard, airports, and boarder patrol. Hearing a light knock on her office door, she looked up. Standing in the open doorway was Fred. She spied the Styrofoam cup in his hand, steam rising through the small hole in the lid.

She shook her head. "Thanks, Fred, but coffee is –"

"Tearing up your stomach." He stepped to her desk. "I know. It probably has something to do with worry. Psychological stress is a contributing factor in the formation of duodenal ulcers or peptic ulcers. This is a small erosion –"

"Hole."

"Or hole in the gastrointestinal tract. Common duodenal ulcers occur in the first 12 inches of the small intestine beyond the stomach."

Mallory leaned her elbows on her desk. "All right, Encyclopedia Fred. How do you know so much about ulcers?"

"In fact, I know a great deal about a great deal of topics."

"'Fess up."

"Been there, done that." He set the cup under her nose where chocolate-scented steam tickled her nostrils. "Which is why I brought you a soothing hot chocolate."

"Thanks."

He indicated the paperwork scattered in loose piles on her desk and the open reports on her computer screen. "Find anything interesting?"

"Not yet. Wanna add your unjaded eye to the hunt?"

"Thought you'd never ask." He plopped down, shuffled a loose pile into a heap and began sorting it on his lap.

"Why are you so eager to help me?"

Not bothering to look up, he continued to scan the reports. "What's on my to do list today is not half as interesting."

"And?"

He was quiet for a moment. When he met her eyes she saw worry there. "And I'm concerned about Marc."

# Chapter Sixty-three

The Chinese man regarded Marc, his gaze measuring, weighing, considering. A slight gesture of his hand sent one of the soldiers to return the bed to its original position.

"Sit."

Marc didn't move.

The soldier moved to enforce the command but a single syllable stopped him. A word Marc didn't recognize. Chinese.

"Who are you?" Marc saw the soldiers stand ready for any instruction from this man. They would do his bidding. They were also uniformed, armed, and obviously militarily trained. Weighing the options, Marc decided at this moment their physical abilities trumped his brains.

"You are here to complete your invention." Shorter than Marc, and older, the man spoke as if this was a perfectly reasonable demand.

"Where is here?"

"This is a research and development facility." His English was without accent.

Marc held his voice level. "Where am I?"

"You will remain here, as our guest of course, until the device is functional." The statement was authoritative.

"What device?"

"The Meissner Device."

Marc swallowed and sat down on the bed. Like tumblers in a combination lock, disjointed impressions quickly fit together. Mallory's request for a tempting patent application, the disconcerting visit from Mr. Spencer, and the strange dream state he had floated in before waking up in this bizarre setting. The people his sister was looking for didn't play nice.

He quickly bit back a nervous urge to either laugh or rapidly explain why this was all a gigantic misunderstanding. *You've got me confused with someone who you really should have kidnapped and dragged to your evil lair in who-knows-where. The Meissner Device is still theoretical. Not yet even a laboratory curiosity. Admittedly close, but not close enough to warrant this type of subterfuge.*

Marc raked his hands through his hair. Yeah, they would be fine with that explanation. Fall all over each other apologizing for the silly mistake and book him a first class seat on a non-stop jet back to Indiana. With real china and linen napkins as opposed to the great treatment he had experienced in the process of arriving here. Where was here, anyhow?

"You begin to understand." The man in authority pulled near the metal chair and sat opposite Marc, staring at him.

*They drugged and dumped me in this upscale place –* he glanced at the dingy room and ancient necessities – *the inventor they need. Certainly the guy who can't get the Meissner Device functional, or happens to mention that it is presently impossible, will quickly and painfully disappear. I'm allergic to pain. And I'm not ready to disappear.*

"I understand all right." Marc showed the man his middle finger.

Again, the soldier with the short fuse moved to strike Marc but the man halted him with a word.

"The international means of communication." Marc smirked at the soldier who plainly wanted to rip Marc's face from his head.

"Now you and your baboons understand *me*."

The man put his hands on his knees and leaned forward. "I will be plain. You will get the Meissner Device operational. Quickly. If you cannot, you are of no use to me. No one knows where you are. There will be no, as you call it, cavalry to the rescue. If you cannot complete the device, I have no need of you." He allowed his words to stand between them. "Do you understand?"

Marc held up both middle fingers.

The man stood to leave. A soldier opened the door and the man turned back to Marc. "I will give you a little time to reconsider your situation. But not long."

Then he was gone. The door was pulled closed behind him and Marc heard the hollow sound of the lock on the outside.

# Chapter Sixty-four

For the next two days, Marc was left alone. Completely alone. No visitors. No food. The water to his small bath area was shut off and the toilet he used smelled. The only consolation, if there was one in this dire situation, was that he was dehydrated and no longer using the toilet.

Marc had gone over the room, searching for any means of escape. Above his reach was a video camera. Someone was keeping an eye on him.

Frustrated, he dropped onto the bed. His hands laced behind his head, he mentally searched for options. Again. Hearing someone at the door, he quickly came to his feet.

As before, two soldiers flanked the Colonel. "Have you decided to cooperate?"

"Have you decided to return me to my home?"

"As soon as the Meissner Device is functional."

Marc shook his head. "Not happening."

The Colonel beckoned a fourth man into the room. Small and soft, he carried a nylon medical bag. A myriad of possibilities ran through Marc's mind and none of them gave him confidence. At a nod from their superior, the soldiers grabbed Marc's arms and pushed him toward the bed. Marc fought like a cat on its way to a bath. His pulse furious, and sweaty from the exertion, Marc was forced onto the thin mattress and pinned there.

The Colonel leaned close so their eyes met. "I will have the Meissner Device. You will make it operational."

Kicking and thrashing, Marc glared back. From the black bag, the fourth man removed a syringe and filled it from a small bottle.

"Succsinacoline." The Colonel narrated the movements of the man with the needle. "An effective paralytic. Administered intramuscularly, it immediately depolarizes the muscles while leaving them flaccid."

He nodded and the man with the loaded syringe approached. "Immediately you will experience facilulation. Like a brief seizure. Then you will be completely paralyzed, unable to even breathe for yourself."

Like the sudden fall through the pond ice back home, shocking fear washed over Marc. With the panic of a drowning man, he renewed his struggle against the powerful arms that held him.

"No," he yelled as the sting of the needle pierced his arm. Just as the Colonel predicted, Marc experienced a sudden and violent twitch that began at his head and rapidly swept to his feet. Immediately Marc lost feeling in his body. Even his lungs forgot to breathe. Within seconds, his body exhaled. No matter how hard Marc concentrated, in his drugged state, he could not force himself to inhale again. Complete powerlessness and dark hopelessness descended. Alarm surged through his awareness like a tsunami as the unfamiliar face who had injected him bent near and fitted a breathing bag over Marc's face.

The Colonel moved into his now paralyzed and narrow line of vision. "Not one muscle of your body can move. Your diaphragm no longer pulls life-giving oxygen into your lungs." The Colonel worked the breathing bag. Mercifully, air entered and exited Marc's body.

"This is me breathing for you." The Colonel's voice was

sinister in his ear.

Marc counted. Every five seconds, he was granted air. For a full minute, the Colonel breathed for him a dozen times.

"And this is me not breathing for you." The breathing bag stopped its function and lay like a deflated balloon against his face. All his life, Marc's lungs had done their job efficiently and effectively without any prodding from him. Yet, now he could not will or convince them to even once do the duty they had faithfully conducted since before his birth. His body was still but far from peaceful. Fear and terror warred within while he fought to remain calm and consider his options. His heartbeat thundered in his ears. Deprived of oxygen, electric dots of light and color danced in his vision, obscuring the cruel and determined face of his oppressor.

Mallory and Nancy. Would he see them again? Was there a chance to return to his quiet Midwest hometown and the life of inventing, writing patents, and guest teaching that he had created for himself? With occasional visits to D.C. to see Mallory's world, punctuated by her trips back home. Did Hebron get his message about supplemental uses of his invention? Would Thurmond Yoder miss their morning conversation?

"The doctor has administered a paralyzing drug." The Colonel moved into Marc's limited vision. "A common prescription for those in serious medical situations."

Even as he was dropping into an oxygen-deprived unconsciousness, air was pushed into Marc's lungs and his chest inflated. After three breaths, Marc could see the Colonel clearly.

"This is me breathing for you again. Your life depends on me. And I will keep you alive to give me what I need." He pressed the bag to send fresh oxygen into Marc's lungs. Releasing the pressure, the bag received the exhaled air. Slowly, the process was repeated. This time much slower. Marc's lungs were hungry for air. The Colonel's stingy slowness was calculated.

He leaned closer. "Now we have an understanding and I will return your body to you."

The bag continued to give him air for the next minutes as the drug released its hold and Marc's lungs gradually returned to doing the task. The breathing bag was removed from his face and Marc sucked in a great amount of air, feeling his traumatized body inflate. He felt like a bulldozer had rolled over him.

Roughly, the two soldiers dragged the Gumby-leg prisoner off the bed and dropped him into the chair at the crude table. Before him, was a computer. On the screen streamed a picture.

"Look closely." The Colonel's voice was near his ear. Too near. The man gave Marc the creeps and he fought an urge to bat him away like an Indiana mosquito on a summer evening. The truth was, Marc didn't think he had the strength.

Marc squinted in an attempt to focus. His eyes were struggling to recover from the recent lack of necessary air. The fuzzy image that danced before his vision began to clear. But what he saw made no sense.

# Chapter Sixty-five

When several hours of search returned no results, Mallory pressed her palms against her temples and sighed.

Fred got up to stretch. "According to the timeline, our window for clues would be in the first three days of his disappearance."

Watching him pace across her office, Mallory stifled a yawn. "We are relatively sure he was removed from the area via ambulance." She reviewed her list of facts scribbled on a pad of paper.

"And we tracked the medical flight leaving Ft. Wayne's Smith Field the same day bound for the west coast. The co-pilot identified Marc's hair."

"The next step," Mallory pushed back from her desk, "would be a flight or ship. Unless they used a train."

"A train would mean he's probably still in the United States."

"Or Canada?"

"Private plane?"

"Or private boat?"

"Possible." He made another track across her office. "Let's

read our reports aloud. What one of us is not noticing, perhaps the other will."

Mallory scrolled back to the top of her computer screen and read through the entries aloud. When that report yielded no results, Fred picked up a page from his stack and read to Mallory. Then it was back to Mallory. A long list of airplanes and ships had been searched.

"Coast Guard boarded and searched a Chinese cargo ship named Shanghai Sumi owned by DHU Aerocomposites."

"Wait." Fred stood behind her chair to read over her shoulder. "We've had dealings with them before. Let me use your computer."

Mallory gave him her seat and he began typing. "Here it is."

Mallory felt herself begin to breathe again. She was desperate for a direction to find her brother.

"DHU Aerocomposites is owned by three entities. Boeing owns 30 percent, and Franklin Fabrics owns 30 percent."

"I know Boeing." Mallory studied the screen over Fred's shoulder. "And Franklin Fabrics is a U.S. based firm with offices worldwide."

"Franklin Fabrics manufactures structural fiber, reinforced fabrics, honeycombed cores, aircraft structures, and composite and complex glues that are vital to aircraft construction."

"Who is the third owner?"

"DHU Aerocomposites. An Asian company that manufacturers commercial airlines."

"Okay. What are you thinking?"

"Spokesmen for both Boeing and Franklin Fabrics said that its use of aircraft parts and materials were strictly for commercial and civilian ends. During investigations, they stated that they were fully confident that DHU had no ties to the Chinese military."

"Why were they investigated?"

Fred rubbed the back of his neck. "As I recall, private studies uncovered several links with the Chinese military establishment involving DHU."

"What kind of links?"

"Let me access my notes." He typed in security codes to bring up his files. While he searched, Mallory paced, the forgotten hot chocolate in her hand.

"Here it is," he said finally. "According to State Department reports, the Chinese government entity that owns a minority share of DHU, also produces fighters, nuclear-capable bombers, and aviation weapons systems for the People's Liberation Army."

Mallory faced him. "And their cargo ship left a Chinese-owned dock space in Long Beach during our target time period."

Fred sighed. "But the Coast Guard searched the ship and found nothing."

"Nothing." Mallory swore. "It seems to be a lead or is it just another dead end?"

# Chapter Sixty-six

On the sparse table, the computer Netbook blinked and glowed. On the screen was a picture of his home. Marc suspected the picture was the result of a Skype connection but the sound must have been turned off.

Marc was looking at his own living room where he had grown up. In the evenings when Marc was a kid, his dad used to smoke a pipe that smelled like roasted cherries while his mom read aloud. Marc and his sister sprawled in front of the fireplace. Mallory painted her nails. The smell of the small bottle of color stung his nostrils. While most boys his age built with Legos, Marc tinkered with erector sets, switches, pulleys, and batteries. Some nights they played the family's favorite game, *Trivial Pursuit*.

Peering closer to the screen, he experienced a wash of homesickness. He longed to be back in Indiana, and not in this filthy cell with powerful men threatening his life.

"Do you recognize the room?" Like a bully on the playground dangling Marc's new puppy over his head, there was cruel taunting in the Colonel's voice.

"It's my house." Then Marc swung on them in rage. "Get out

of my house! Get out of my life!" He charged the Colonel who stepped back and the soldiers instantly filled the space between the two, quickly reigning in the furious captive. The two burly men overcame Marc and held him stretched between them. Calmly, the Colonel swung a fist into Marc's stomach. Again all Marc's air was gone from his lungs. Marc sucked in a deep breath but the Colonel pummeled him until Marc hung limp. Already weak, Marc had expended what little remained of his physical endurance. He didn't have much strength to fight or to resist.

At a nod from their superior, the soldiers dropped Marc once more into the folding metal chair in front of the computer screen. Bent in half, Marc crossed his arms protectively over his bruised and beaten belly. It was difficult to breathe.

"Watch closely." The Colonel spoke Chinese into a satellite phone. In moments, Marc watched in horror as three men dragged a woman to the couch and pinned her down. Though it was difficult to see her face in the commotion, the size was familiar. Straining to be sure, and frantic that it not be true, he recognized her hair. It was the color of cinnamon. Mallory.

Deep, primal anger mixed with fear caught in Marc's throat and surged through his body. And the Colonel anticipated his reaction. Marc was coming off his seat when the soldiers pressed him down. Like a spider does with her prey, the Colonel spun a wide roll of duct tape around the captive and the chair. With more strength than he knew he possessed, Marc fought his captors. But he was dreadfully out-numbered and out-muscled. In moments, he was hopelessly struggling against forces he could not budge.

Teeth tightly clenched, he yelled, "You monster! Let her go!"

The Colonel's voice was oily with confidence. Digging fingers into his chin, he held Marc's face to the screen. "Watch."

"Call off your buffoons!" Marc's panic was out of control. "Don't let them touch her!"

The Colonel chuckled. "No one is going to rape her. Though it was difficult to prevent even such loyal men from enjoying the few privileges of their job." He sighed theatrically. "No, she won't be raped. Not this time." He squeezed Marc's shoulder. "Though that could be arranged. Consider it a trade for your cooperation."

With renewed vigor, Marc struggled against his bonds. But it was useless. Futile.

The Colonel spoke into the cell phone while Marc watched the screen. He needed to protect his sister. His stomach was ill with what he was witnessing. While three men held Mallory on the couch, a fourth moved closer to the camera. He held a syringe in one hand and a small, rubber-topped bottle in the other.

"Perhaps you recognize the bottle and syringe?" The Colonel let the words hang between them.

Marc's breathing was heavy as he recalled the nightmare he had just experienced with the drug. "Don't. Please."

"Succsinacoline." The Colonel narrated. "An effective paralytic. Administered intramuscularly, it immediately depolarizes the muscles while leaving them flaccid."

From somewhere far from his home in Indiana, Marc watched helplessly as the needle was stuck into Mallory's arm.

"You son of a …" Marc's curse was cut off when he saw movement on the screen. The men who had held Mallory moved back.

"Immediately she will experience facilulation. Like a brief seizure. Then she will be completely paralyzed, unable to even breathe for herself."

Beginning at his sister's head, a rapid seizure-like movement quaked through her body. Then she stopped breathing.

"Not one muscle of her body can move." The Colonel's voice was calm, informative, as if he was describing the ordinary removal of a splinter. "Her diaphragm no longer pulls necessary oxygen into her pretty lungs."

The Colonel spoke into the phone.

Marc snarled. "You unfeeling beast."

The man who had given her the deadly injection positioned a mask over her face.

The relief Marc felt as a breathing bag was placed over Mallory's nose was tenuous. Mercifully, air entered and exited his sister's body. And cruelly, it could be taken from her in an instant.

"This is me breathing for her." The Colonel whispered the words in his ear.

Marc counted. Every five seconds, her chest rose with the oxygen that was delivered to her. For a full minute, the man who held the bag breathed for his sister.

"And this is me not breathing for her." The Colonel spoke into the phone. On the screen, a wiry man with dark hair pressed a cell phone to his ear and then said something Marc could not hear to the one who held the breathing bag. The bag stopped its simple yet vital function. It lay like a deflated balloon against his sister's face.

"A human typically experiences brain damage when deprived of air for longer than four minutes."

"Don't hurt her," Marc pleaded.

"Now that I have your attention, let's talk about your cooperation."

"Give her air for God's sake!"

"I will provide what she needs when you give me what I require." He pointed to the time at the top right of the computer screen. "She has been without oxygen for a full minute."

He stood erect, clasping his hands behind his back as if giving a college course lecture. "Hypoxia or hypoxiation is a pathological condition in which the body as a whole is deprived of an adequate supply of oxygen. The brain in your sister's lovely head will suffer cerebral anoxia. Complete lack of oxygen. Initially the body responds to lowered blood oxygen by redirecting blood to the brain and increasing vital cerebral blood flow. However, if circulation cannot be increased or if doubled blood flow does not correct the problem, symptoms of cerebral hypoxia will begin to appear."

"Stop it!" Marc fought against his bonds.

His captor went on as if he didn't hear. "Mild symptoms include difficulties with complex learning tasks and reductions in short-term memory. If oxygen deprivation continues, cognitive disturbances and decreased motor control will result. The skin becomes bluish – termed cyanosis – and heart rate increases. Continued oxygen deprivation as is happening here," he pointed to the screen, "results in coma, seizures, cessation of brain stem reflexes, and," he paused to allow Marc to mentally take the next step, "brain death."

Still unemotional, he indicated the time on the screen. "It has been two full minutes. As you have experienced, these physical malfunctions set in quickly."

Hungrily, Marc's eyes bore into the 12-inch screen for any hint that his sister was really all right. That this was only a wicked nightmare and he would wake any moment. His inventive mind searched for solutions, for some way to oppose these bullies, save Mallory, and refuse the Meissner Device to these men. The device was only theoretical anyway. Even if he agreed to cooperate, it would be a hoax. If they were willing to suffocate Mallory in front of him, what were they capable of doing when they realized he couldn't make the weapon of their ambitions functional? Yet, he could not allow Mallory to die. Not because he refused to bend.

"Okay!" The word burst from Marc's lips and he realized he had been holding his breath. "Give her air!"

"We have reached an understanding?" He slowly drug out the words.

"Yes!" Marc slumped. "Yes, whatever you want. Just let her live."

The Colonel spoke into the cell phone. The air bag remained motionless on Mallory's face.

"Hurry!" Marc heard the anxiety and desperation in his own voice and didn't care.

"Be patient." The Colonel waved the cell phone. "It takes a moment for the signal to reach the satellite orbiting in space and then transfer to the cell phone somewhere in your house in Indiana."

When Marc thought he would explode with panic, at last there was movement on the screen. The dark-haired man, that reminded Marc of an insect, put the cell phone to his ear and then spoke quickly to his partner. The air bag inflated. Mallory's chest rose and fell once more with vital oxygen.

In the end, Marc knew he would give in. He knew it as soon as he recognized the danger his sister was in. He had no idea how he would hide the fact that the Meissner Device was merely theoretical. For now, he had bought time. Time for himself. Time for Mallory.

The Colonel turned off the computer.

"Hey! Turn it on. How do I know she's all right?"

His nemesis crossed his arms across his chest. "She is fine. The drug will wear off in about two minutes."

"And? How do I know she is safe from you and your pet rottweilers?"

"She is safe as long as you give me –"

"The Meissner Device." Marc filled in the rest of the sentence. "I got that part."

"Excellent." He waved toward the guard who cut Marc's duct tape bonds. "I will show you where you will assemble your invention."

# Chapter Sixty-seven

Marc was miserable. How in the world would he get out of here? He had to get to Mallory. Where was she? How were they treating her? What were her co-workers Logan Deverell and Fred Ridley doing to locate her? He had to find a way to get her away from the Colonel and his murderous goons.

The Meissner Device, though more than theoretical, was only partially designed. Even if he could get it up and running, did he want to do that for these people? He doubted they planned to use the technology for the good of mankind. Kidnapping him was his first clue. Now they held Mallory's life suspended over his head like an egg about to drop from the Washington Monument.

They could have just invited him. They could have asked. They could have held a worldwide symposium on travel and propulsion options. They could have done a million other approaches. Kidnapping was at the bottom of the list. The Colonel was desperate. Or maniacal.

And if Marc did make the Meissner Device functional, did he believe for one minute that his captors would pat his head with approval and happily send him back home? Release Mallory so the two could have a family reunion back in the United States? Could he ever return to his comfortable office in the Midwest next door to Dr. Thurmond? Back to his routine mornings biking to the office, developing inventions, and waiting for Nancy to arrive smelling of spring lavender?

These were the questions that kept him awake at night. He had tried a hundred different scenarios, but now as he tinkered with his design, he let the reality of the situation settle over him. His life was forever altered. The immediate question was could he find a way to keep himself and his sister alive?

He glanced around the spacious lab, surprisingly modern in this ancient building. At various workstations, white-coated lab workers concentrated on projects. Most were working on various aspects of the Meissner Device. Using his patent information. How the heck did these people get it?

Certainly this was the landing spot for the patents stolen from the United States Patent and Trademark Office. He was in the center of the thievery Mallory was attempting to trace and shut down. When he got the Meissner Device Generator working, the Colonel would no longer have use for him. Or for Mallory. Especially not Mallory with her connections to the FBI. Nor would he send Marc home. When the device was operational, his captors would keep him here to continue to make new developments. Or, more likely, they would kill him. He would be the disposable crewmember.

He swore under his breath.

"Excuse me?" came a voice near him.

Marc looked over. He'd been so absorbed in his thoughts he had not noticed the young woman working nearby.

"Did you say something?"

Good English with a Chinese accent, he observed. He shook his head. "Just thinking out loud."

She tipped her head and studied him. "I know you," she said softly.

"Haven't I seen you someplace before?" His falsetto was sarcastic.

She was nonplussed. "You spoke at my university."

He was in no mood for anything other than his own self-pity. "Trust me, I've never been here before. Where ever *here* is."

"I studied electro-physics in the United States."

He couldn't keep the edge from his voice. "Nice to see you are putting your education to good use."

She looked puzzled, and then frowned. Tossing her shoulder length hair in the same way Mallory did when she was agitated, the girl moved away.

The following day, Marc was still grappling for a solution to his situation when he noticed the scientist in charge hurry to the large doors. Colonel Yao had just made one of his dramatic entrances. The two had a hushed conversation, the scientist doing most of the talking in that nervous way he had only in the Colonel's presence.

The two walked through the work in process, Yao occasionally asking a question, the scientist overly explaining.

Discreetly Marc kept an eye on Yao. There had to be a chink in the staid man's armor. Dismissing the relieved tour guide, Yao slowly circulated in the room. Coming to the girl who had talked to Marc, Yao stopped and spoke to her. Though Marc couldn't hear their words, he watched carefully.

Then the Colonel was at Marc's elbow. "Your progress is too slow."

*Easy for you to say. All you have to do is threaten to suffocate people.* Marc turned on him. "I didn't exactly bring my notes. I have to recreate years of work here – from memory. You might have thought of that when you started this parade."

"For your sake – for your sister's sake – complete the prototype."

Marc watched the man, his back ramrod straight, exit the lab. Though he tried to shrug off the Colonel's words, the memory of Mallory just moments from suffocation haunted his dreams at night and his work during the day. He knew that was the Colonel's intent and he grudgingly acknowledged that it was effective. Marc could guess at the pressure Yao was under. Probably demands from his superiors. Maybe his career hung in the balance. But none of that compared with the very life and well-being of a beloved family member.

Several hours later, the Colonel returned. He set a carry-all container in front of Marc. Reaching inside, Marc drew out his notebook filled with his equations. Then his laptop.

"The computer's internet capabilities have been disabled, of course."

"Of course."

The Colonel walked away. Marc looked inside the carry-all once more. At the bottom, there was something else inside. Curiously, it was Hebron Heath's diamond evaluating device.

# Chapter Sixty-eight

Mallory popped her head in Deverell's office. Her boss's forehead rested against his palm as he sat at his desk, obviously engrossed in a phone call.

"You gotta come see this." At last she had something concrete in this convoluted case and she could barely contain her excitement.

He waved her away.

"Now!"

When he ignored her, Mallory briskly walked over and hung up the phone.

"Geez Louise, are you crazy?" Deverell picked up the phone to reconnect. "What is wrong with you?"

She hung up the phone again. This was the second time someone had called her crazy in as many days. "We found something."

"Mallory, you can't -"

"I can and I did. Now c'mon."

"It can't be as important as who I was speaking to."

"I don't care if you were talking to the President."

"As a matter of fact –"

She grabbed his elbow and hauled him from his seat, and pushed him out of his office toward the conference room.

Rounding the corner, she found Fred was already there. "We've been studying everything that has gone across Saad's desk, combing through the mail, and his phone records."

Deverell threw up his hands in surrender and dropped into a high backed chair at the head of the oval table. "What do you have for me, people?"

"The most interesting discovery was on the computer's history." Mallory snatched up the remote from the tabletop and pointed it at the screen. A picture of a kitten appeared.

Deverell plucked a pen from his shirt pocket and bounced the end against the table, clicking the point in and out, in and out. "Looks like a Hallmark card of Puss In Boots."

"Exactly what we thought at first glance." Fred nodded to Mallory.

Deverell swung his chair to face the two. "So somebody sent the guy an email greeting card."

"Look closely." Mallory pressed a button on the remote and the picture was magnified. Next she put up another image of the same kitten. But at this magnitude, the side-by-side pictures of the same kitten looked different.

"It's almost like there's background noise, extra strokes to the design." Deverell squinted, leaning forward to better study the examples. "Extra pixels that don't quite belong."

"It's noise, all right." Mallory walked toward the screen, swiping the pen from Deverell's hand mid-click. "The difference between the two pictures is the information."

Deverell stood and approached the screen. "Get Jimmy up here right away from digital forensics. He needs to see this."

Fred winked at Mallory. "Jimmy is on his way."

"What are we looking at, exactly?"

"It's a method of espionage called steganography." They turned to see Jimmy. He stood in the doorway, his gaze locked on the figures.

"Steganography?" Deverell repeated the new term. "It's Greek to me."

"It is Greek, actually." Jimmy pushed his John Lennon glasses higher on the bridge of his nose. He carried a cup of chai tea.

"Greek for covered writing," Mallory noted.

"Using innocuous documents, usually an image file like this cat," Jimmy approached the screen, "steganography encodes the message while at the same time concealing the fact that a message is being sent at all. Greek generals tattooed sensitive information onto the shaved heads of messengers. Once their hair grew back, the messenger traveled without suspicion to the intended recipient who decrypted the message by once again shaving the messenger's head."

Deverell rubbed a meaty hand over his own thinning crown. "Nothing new under the sun."

"Indeed," Fred agreed. "Only today, steganography makes use of email."

"For any disgruntled employee or corporate spy, it's an ideal carrier." Mallory tossed the pen back to her boss and winced when he absently began clicking it again. "Or for foreign espionage."

"Good job, you two. Now we know how the patents are being leaked." Deverell turned to Jimmy. "We need a way of disrupting this ..." he waved his pen in the direction of the representation of the cat that still lit the screen.

"Steganography," Mallory filled in for him.

"This steganography."

# Chapter Sixty-nine

Marc watched the Colonel approach the girl again. It was part of his regular routine when he came through, and Marc was beginning to suspect that this custom was becoming the most important part of the Colonel's day.

At the rear of the expansive lab, the large overhead door opened. Usually when shipments were delivered, Marc was ushered back to his room. Apparently, his captors were reluctant for anyone to see Marc or for Marc to see anyone beyond this carefully guarded environment.

Today, supplies were brought in from a bulky military transport at anchor in the water that ran along the backside of the renovated temple. Uniformed men unloaded and a forklift busily lifted and deposited heavy loads. Marc gazed longingly at the sunshine, then away before anyone could think he was too interested in the outside world and escort him back to his unfriendly cell. He positioned his body so he could observe what lay outside without appearing to do so.

Later, Marc found an excuse to go to the girl's workstation. "What university did you attend?"

This time she was the one who was deep in thought. She glanced up at him questioningly so he repeated his question.

"Indiana," she stated. "Why?"

"I was trying to figure out where our paths had crossed before."

"You didn't believe me."

He shrugged. "I apologize. I was having a bad day."

She nodded and glanced nervously toward the door through which the Colonel did his usual coming and going. Marc had watched him leave not long ago after another conversation with this girl.

He put out his hand. "I'm Marc Wayne."

"I know." She ignored his hand. "You were the guest lecturer at my university."

"Please accept my apology. I was rude."

She glanced at his outstretched hand, and met his gaze. "Yes, you were." She studied him before putting her small palm into his.

He gave her hand a gentle shake, suddenly aware of the comfort of a friendly touch. "And your name, physics major?"

"Lei. Lei Quong. Electro-Physics."

He turned to go and stopped. "What was the topic? Of my lecture?"

She stared at him. "You are being rude again."

She was turning away when Marc quickly stepped toward her. "Humor me. It's an honest question."

Lei waved her hand to encompass the large lab and her tone was sarcastic. "The Meissner Effect; Laboratory Oddity –"

"Or Revolutionary Tool for Mankind," he filled in, feeling like he had been punched in the stomach.

# Chapter Seventy

Foreign satellites picked up a sudden beehive of activity in a formerly quiet hangar at Wright-Patterson Air Force Base in Ohio. Equipment was trucked to the location, and people were seen coming and going.

Several well-known scientists were assigned to the new project and their invitations were carefully sent through channels the FBI knew would be compromised by spies.

Major Rory O'Leary, a blonde, raw-boned man who chewed an unlit cigar was put in charge of the project. "Can I choose my team?"

Deverell sat with the base commander as they briefed O'Leary. "Okay by me."

The general nodded his approval.

O'Leary wrote names. "These guys are smart thinkers and efficient." His cigar bobbed when he spoke. "With them, I can move your invention from patent to reality." He tore the page from his pad and passed it to Deverell.

"Good." Deverell surveyed the list. "We've equipped your laboratory. Let me know if you need additional supplies."

O'Leary moved the cigar from one side of his mouth to the other. "Simple really. I strap enough fuel to the butt of anything, it's gonna go up. Thrust and propulsion. The rest is just math to aim it where we want 'er to go. Heck, with enough flammable material I can launch a Sherman tank into orbit. From space, we can point it directly at the North Koreans."

Deverell broke in. "This isn't a shoot 'em all and let God sort it out assignment. The Meissner Effect Device doesn't even utilize –"

With a hand on his arm, the commander cut off Deverell's speech. "Look over the plans, O'Leary. You'll know what to do."

When the cigar-chewing Irishman went out to the Humvee that waited to take him to the new laboratory, the commander clapped Deverell's shoulder. "You alphabet agency guys need to know when to shut up and let us military guys get the job done."

"But this device doesn't require any flammable fuels."

"He'll figure that out." Reaching for the list O'Leary had made, the older man looked at the short column and grunted. "Good men. They can get a beluga whale in a polka-dot tutu to fly."

# Chapter Seventy-one

The Colonel was as intimidating as always. Careful not to be obvious, Marc watched the man whenever he could. From reading history, he knew that military men who knew their enemy well waged successful campaigns.

No matter what his business at the lab, Yao found time each visit to talk with Lei. Maybe she had something to do with Marc's unscheduled trip to this unknown destination. By her own admission, she had known him in the States, after all. And it appeared that Yao favored her.

At lunch, Marc took a chair across from Lei. "Tease me. Tell me what you miss about the United States."

She looked thoughtful and started to speak, then stopped.

"Come on," he said. "Don't be shy."

"Donuts."

"I miss Mexican food," he listed.

"The malls where everything is in one shopping place."

"Blockbuster movies."

"Endless selections of music."

"Chewing gum," he added.

"Indiana University beating Purdue."

"Playing basketball in the driveway with my…" His voice choked.

"Your girlfriend?"

He swallowed back the lump that formed in his throat. "My sister."

She nodded. "I most miss a boy I met in school."

"A fellow science major?"

She slowly spun a ring on her left hand. "A music major. Music and science have much in common."

"Especially math." Marc nodded at the gold band. "Is that from him?"

"We were engaged."

"Were?"

She shrugged. "Maybe we still are. While I was at college, I received a message that my father was ill so I returned home."

"And your father?"

"He's dead."

"But – "

She quickly stood. "He was dead when I returned."

Watching her leave, her lunch forgotten, Marc felt like he'd drastically overstepped. Not that he was fluent on foreign common courtesies. And this place seemed to have rules of its own. What does a captive say to a fellow lab worker? How's the weather? What's your view on the latest movie? Read any good research lately? Do you know a quick way out of here?

# Chapter Seventy-two

In record time, a laboratory was established and equipped in a bulky hangar on the largest Air Base in the Midwest. Several top electrical and flight engineers, known for their innovative contributions to modern propulsion, were assigned to the new project.

Mr. Spencer reported as much to his dinner partner. "The United States military is building the device from the patent."

Colonel Yao sat across from the distasteful man at a gentlemen's club in London. Great Britain had been chosen as the neutral meeting place. Flights into Heathrow were frequent and easy to procure. A major crossroads for travelers from all over the world, the airport personnel were accustomed to seeing and serving a rainbow of people of varied cultures and ethnic backgrounds. A mere six hour flight for each of them, the two men from opposite sides of the globe could meet and return to their duties after a brief absence.

Yao was there at the insistence of the mercenary. Mr. Spencer had new information he wouldn't send by any method that could be tracked and traced. They must meet in person. "What makes you think it is for that exact design?"

Dressed in European slacks and cuffed shirt, Spencer had draped his herringbone jacket over the back of his chair. Yao noted that the spy flaunted expensive clothes anytime it did not interfere with his usual need to stay invisible. This occasional indulgence flattered his ego and served as a buffer between who the man was now and who he had been as a homeless orphan in a third world country. Through his own investigations, Yao knew this much about the mercenary.

"I studied the supplies and they match."

A waitress served a scotch on the rocks in a squat glass to Mr. Spencer and placed a rum and coke on a napkin in front of the Colonel.

"I'm not worried." The Chinese man leisurely took note of the other patrons around them. He had exchanged the uniform of his country for the double-breasted suit of an international businessman. Though his dinner companion caused him to be tense, Yao schooled himself to appear relaxed in the rich surroundings of heavy dark furniture under polished chandeliers. Oversized paintings depicted red-jacketed riders on white steeds galloping through thick forests beside baying dogs in pursuit of a skittish fox. The collection of large rooms smelled of furniture polish, men's cologne, expensive alcohol, and more expensive cigars. "We have the advantage of time. We began work on the project before their government passed it through the bureaucracy. Fools, they didn't even know what they had."

Spencer took a long drink of his scotch. Swirling the clear liquid in the glass, he smacked his full lips. "Don't underestimate them."

The Colonel lowered his voice. "Are you underestimating me?"

"Merely warning you not to get too impressed with your own press."

A short-skirted woman who circulated among the customers, came to them and offered several different brands of costly cigars. Yao selected one and peeled the cellophane wrapper. "Remember that I have the inventor."

Spencer chose a cigar and let his fingers linger against the woman's hand. Suggestively, Spencer held the cigar to his nose and inhaled slowly. "Rolled on the thighs of brown skinned women."

The Colonel ignored the comment and waved away the woman.

"How long have you had him?" Spencer lit his cigar. "How much progress have you made?"

Yao frowned and blew smoke at his companion. "If it takes us a while to get the device working with the inventor, it will take the competition longer without him."

"If that logic helps you sleep at night, but I've seen surprising events when these brains get together." He signaled to the waiter for a refill of his scotch. "What incentive does your inventor have to complete the project?"

The question was the same one Yao had been asking himself. Seeing the crafty Mr. Spencer study his face, Yao once more masked his emotions behind a placid expression. Spencer's eyes narrowed. He sat back and crossed his legs, an oily smile on his face. Spencer knew he had touched his employer's soft white underbelly and Yao suspected this was the opportunity he was anticipating. This was the set-up for the little man to unveil what he really wanted from this appointment.

"Perhaps your man needs a refresher. A reminder of what his lack of cooperation will cost his sister."

The Colonel thoughtfully spun his glass in a slow circle. "You have the girl?"

"Too messy." He nodded his thanks to the waitress who efficiently removed the empty glass and, ice clinking, set a fresh drink before him. "I have an actress who looks like her and enjoys performing masochistic roles. She was who you saw on the computer screen. If you need another performance to motivate your inventor –" he smiled at the thought – "she makes situations appear real because it is."

Again the Colonel considered how unpleasant was this man. A necessary evil. He was skilled at his job and returned the required results while insulating the Colonel from contact with the virulent side of business.

"You are in a race," Mr. Spencer pressed. "If they get the device operational before you do, all of your efforts are for nothing. And I would not want to consider how your superiors will view your failure."

The Colonel gulped his drink. This man had no concept of social station. In a futile attempt to elevate himself over his employee, he issued an order. "Your job is to keep an eye on developments."

"Precisely why I insisted on this business meeting. As a show of good faith, I have the supply list from the Wright-Patterson facility. This assures that I correctly ascertained the function of the place. You need to know what your competition is doing and I can supply you with that information." He took a long pull on the cigar. "Now let's talk financial terms."

# Chapter Seventy-three

Colonel Yao had made his rounds again this morning. He bent close to Lei, and Marc watched her discreetly move to put distance between herself and the older man. Looking like a slow version of the Texas two-step, the Colonel eased his way close to her, and she politely found an excuse to put space between them. At last she found a plausible reason to move to another part of the lab.

After the Colonel left, Marc made his way to Lei's workstation. She sat with her head in her hands.

"You okay?"

She sighed and turned her attention back to her work.

"Need a break?"

She opened her mouth to say something, then closed it and simply nodded. He led the way to the lunch area and served them both tea. Absently, Marc wondered if he would like tea when he got back to the United States or if it would remind him of too many sour memories as a captive. If he got back to America. The deep longing twisted his gut.

Sitting across from him, Lei's shoulders were hunched and she spun the ring on her left hand.

"Was your father opposed to your engagement?"

Self-conscience, she dropped her hands to her lap.

"You don't have to talk about it if you don't want," he said.

Lei was quiet as they both drank their tea.

"My father visited me at college," she said at last. "My fiancé paid for him to travel so they could meet."

"And?"

"The two men were respectful of one another. It was a good meeting. My father was honored that he asked permission."

"He asked permission to marry you."

She swallowed. "Soon after my father returned home, I was summoned back because he was ill."

"But you were too late."

Her eyes filled with tears.

"I'm sorry. I know you miss him." Attempting to form a bridge, he added. "I miss my father, too."

She looked up, questioningly.

"My mother and father are both dead."

She brushed away the tears before they could fall. "I found a letter in my father's effects. It was hidden where he knew I would find it."

"What did he say?"

"He encouraged me to follow my heart and if that was with the American student, he gave his blessing." She reached for the ring once more and began to spin it around on her finger. "The letter was dated prior to his illness. It was a copy, something he often did with special letters – keeping one for himself."

"I don't understand."

"His original letter he sent to me never arrived in the United States."

"Censored?"

"For the good of the Republic."

"Then you'll return to marry soon?" Marc felt his heart race.

Dropping her eyes, she was silent for a time. "My passport and student visa have been revoked."

Just as quickly, his hopes plummeted into his shoes. "By

who? Why?"

"The government says they need my skills here."

"Yeah." Her dad was probably the only tie her government had to ensure the college student's allegiance, Marc calculated. When Lei's father died, apparently unexpectedly, someone was less than honest with the information forwarded to the United States university in a deliberate strategy to lure her back home and lock the door so she wouldn't leave again. Did the authorities know about her plans to marry an American? Would it matter?

"Have you had contact with your fiancé? Could he come to you?" Marc was grasping for an opportunity in this situation.

"I wrote to him but who knows if he received my letters."

"Phone?"

She shook her head. "The number they say is no longer in service."

That smelled fishy. "Email?"

"Returned as undeliverable."

Marc wondered if Lei's intended had merely relocated or if Lei's communications were being blocked. It appeared that Lei was a captive in this place almost as much as he was. Almost. The difference was she went home to a real home when not working at the lab. She had mobility outside these walls. He was locked in that uninspiring cell.

She met his eyes. "He has graduated by now. I don't know where he is."

# Chapter Seventy-four

Mallory bit the inside of her lip as she waited outside the Indiana University classroom. As Deverell had predicted, accustomed to fuel-powered designs, the Wright-Patterson engineers had hit a snag with Marc's patent.

She was aware that there was a significant aspect that Marc had not worked out, but the lab crew had another goal. Their assignment was to make it look like the Meissner Device Generator was functional but flawed.

Just like she had 30 seconds ago and 20 seconds before that, Mallory checked her cell phone for messages. Mentally she reviewed the list of leads she had already followed to a dead end in her anxious search for her brother.

The classroom door flew open and students poured into the hall. Exchanging snarky witticisms and setting study dates, the young men and women went on to the rest of their day. Remorse ripped through Mallory's gut. Wading through syllabuses and required class work, the students were training for their careers. The work was tough but the future looked promising. She longed to be back in the innocence of academia where the hardest decisions were around establishing a schedule that balanced studies, work, and social time. For them, the world was full of potential. For her, the world had shriveled into a frightening black hole where bad decisions exacted their toll in dire consequences to herself, and more importantly, on those she loved. Where ruthless minds mercilessly stole whatever they wanted and Mallory despaired of outsmarting them.

Inside the lecture hall, poster-sized pictures of inventors wallpapered the wall. At the lectern, a bespectacled professor talked with the college student Mallory had met in Marc's office the day he disappeared.

She held out her hand to the professor who covered it with both of his. "Thank you for arranging this meeting."

"Certainly, my dear." He adjusted his glasses and peered at her. "You look tired. Can I take you to lunch?"

Mallory shook her head. "Thanks, but I want to talk to Mr. Hebron Heath."

"Then I will leave you to it." He collected a worn briefcase. On his way out the door, he called back. "Give my regards to your brother Marc for me."

Mallory bit her cheek to counteract the sudden lump in her throat. The professor disappeared and she turned to the young man.

Wearing a Li'l Abner t-shirt, the student was waiting. His eyes were big in his pale face, and he shifted his weight to one side, and back to the other. "You wanted to see me?"

"Talk with you." She waved him to the first row of seats. "How much do you understand of the Meissner Effect?"

"That's like asking how much I know about gravity, air flow, or ocean currents." He shrugged. "Some."

"About Marc's – Mr. Wayne's theory for a Meissner Effect Generator?"

"His lecture was clear." He frowned, thinking. "We talked more about it after class."

"You appeared to grasp the information on his notes when I met you in Dixon."

"The concept is solid." His knee bounced. "The device would

create buoyancy in magnetic fields in the same fashion as a balloon floats in air. Like a balloon that can lift things, but has no need for traditional explosive fuels."

Mallory stood and paced.

Hebron's stomach growled. "Is there anything else?"

She stopped in front of him. "I'm here to offer you a practicum. An internship. It will meet the requirements for your degree."

"With Mr. Wayne?"

"Not exactly. But with the Meissner Device."

Excitement lit his eyes like a sparkler on the Fourth of July. "When?"

"How quickly can you leave?"

Hebron rifled through his backpack and took fast inventory. "Thirty minutes. But I gotta clear with my professors."

Mallory put a hand on his shoulder and walked him to the door. "I'll take care of your professors." She checked the time on her cell phone. "Be back here in forty. Ready to go."

# Chapter Seventy-five

After intensive work, they were ready for a test run of the prototype. Marc made his final adjustments. By incorporating designs from his earlier inventions, and remixing the components that led to the fire in his kitchen, he expected this to levitate for several minutes, and then explode.

Previously he had built small-scale versions but reluctant to waste the time, Marc had convinced Colonel Yao that this device required a minimum scale to be effective. In truth, Marc didn't want to waste the time doing it twice. Nor was he interested in saving these people money, time, or effort. He was gambling that he could somehow get out of here sooner rather than later.

The explosion might take people with it. He had never killed anyone before, and that part initially bothered him. But as his anger grew along with his worry over Mallory, his concern for the people who held him dissipated. His plan was to be far enough away from the blast that in the ensuing chaos, he would escape.

Marc put his tools onto the wheeled cart and moved it back. The nervous project leader eyed Marc eagerly. "Now?"

"Knock yourself out," Marc invited.

The man scurried to the pilot's seat. Others pushed back equipment and formed an expectant circle about the device. Donning protective helmet and goggles, the project leader signaled he was ready to start. Marc tensed, ready to spring when the timing and opportunity were right.

In that moment, Colonel Yao's voice rang loud and curt with a single command to halt. Everyone looked to the Colonel who crossed the room to stand in front of Marc.

His eyes bore into Marc's. "You will start the machine."

Marc stared back at the man who was shorter than himself but confident in his power. The room was quiet, all eyes were on the two locked in an unspoken challenge.

Marc weighed his options. In the pilot's seat, he could possibly pull some wires to prevent the device from starting. Or he could explode with it, taking as many of them with him as possible. But that wouldn't help him locate Mallory.

At last Marc shrugged, hoping he looked more nonchalant than he felt. "Suit yourself."

He roughly shouldered Yao aside and waved the other man out of the pilot's seat. Buckling the helmet strap under his chin, he stared at Yao, and hoisted himself into the cockpit. He was adjusting the goggles when for the second time, Yao's voice halted progress.

"Come on up," Marc invited. "You can be the first to – "

With a sly smile, Yao waved to two men standing sentry at the double doors. One quickly opened the door, and a soldier escorted someone inside. It was Lei.

# Chapter Seventy-six

With his understanding of the Meissner Device concept, Hebron was delivered to Ohio by Mallory. There was a glitch in the patent and perhaps Hebron could bridge the gap between theory and reality. She ushered him into the facility where the scrawny collegiate took in the scope and magnitude of the lab and froze.

"Come on." Mallory walked briskly ahead. "They're waiting for you."

But Hebron didn't follow.

Mallory returned and waved a palm in front of his face. "Earth to science geek. Anybody home?"

Blinking, Hebron focused on her. "You are building it. The Meissner Device. For real. In my lifetime."

She planted a hand on her hip. "Except for the part these brains can't get to function." She tapped his breastbone. "That's why you're here."

In Birkenstocks, and leading with his belly, a fellow came to greet them. He stuck out a hand to Hebron while twisting the end of his handlebar mustache with the other. "I'm Wilson. You're just in time. We're in the war room slinging ideas."

The young man fell into step behind his host and spoke low to Mallory. "Is that a skunk on his shirt? For real?"

Entering the war room, Hebron felt like he had stepped onto the bridge of the Starship *Enterprise*. Several CAD systems were in use, their drawings displayed on a large screen. One wall was covered with butcher paper peppered with vertical lists of equations and designs in primary colored markers. Another wall was all blackboard with chalk sketches like snowflakes on a winter night. A delicious home-baked aroma caught everyone's attention and Birkenstocks held a platter aloft. It must have been the signal to begin because everyone sat up and focused their attention on Wilson. Or rather on his tray. Like Pavlov's dog.

In moments, the dozen men and women had pulled up chairs and were eating generous slices of banana bread. Kids' toys appeared and were tossed from person to person.

"Wilson used to be an Imagineer." Mallory caught a superball and pressed it into Hebron's hand. "His unconventional methods have a surprising ability to unlock untapped possibilities." She tapped a finger against her temple.

"Think fast," someone called and silly putty landed in Hebron's lap.

Molding the familiar substance, he was instantly transported back to childhood, pressing putty against the Sunday comics. Even then, his favorite strip was *Li'l Abner*. He leaned close to talk to Mallory over the noisy room. "Imagineers are the master planners, the creative development, designers, engineers, and production all rolled in one. The research and development of the worldwide Disney kingdom is cutting edge."

"I know." There was sarcasm in her tone.

Wilson spoke around a mouthful. "The kid is here." Using his chunk of bread as a pointer, he waved Hebron to address the group.

# Chapter Seventy-seven

"She will be the first." Yao waved the young woman to the machine.

Marc bent to pull wires, but the strong hands grabbed his arms and jerked him free of the machine. "Wait," Marc demanded. "There are a few adjustments – "

While two soldiers held Marc's arms, his helmet was unbuckled and the goggles pulled from the would-be pilot's head by the stern Yao. He handed both to Lei. "It is a great honor for you to pilot the maiden flight."

Catching her eye, Marc shook his head. "Don't Lei. Don't!" He turned to Yao. "It's my machine, let me. For heaven's sake, let me. Not her."

Through narrowed eyes, Yao stared at Marc but spoke to Lei. "Start the machine."

Marc struggled to pull free as Lei climbed into the cockpit.

"You monster," Marc accused through gritted teeth.

"Who is the monster? What do you have to worry about, Mr. Wayne?" He moved to the outer circle with the others. Again Marc struggled against the two who held him but it was futile.

"Whenever you are ready," Yao called to Lei.

She leaned forward to begin the startup sequence.

"Stop! Stop Lei!" Marc craned his neck around to get Yao's attention. "Tell her to stop, for God's sake."

Yao put up his hand in a signal for Lei to wait. He came to face him, his nose almost touching Marc's. "You underestimate me. I know about your booby trap. In fact, I expected you to do something this stupid."

He snapped his fingers and someone brought him a file. He flashed several sheets of paper in front of Marc. It was his original patent design. The one he had submitted to the United States Patent Office.

"You maggot." Marc spit the words. "Where did you get those?"

"The fact is that I have them. The second fact is that I know when you deviate from the design." With the unexpected fury of a coiled snake, Yao backhanded Marc. The blow stung and Marc felt his lip split and tasted blood in his mouth. His right eye was blurry and Marc knew it would be a shiner within the hour.

"You are out of time." The Colonel's voice was ominous. His face close to Marc's, he jammed a finger into Marc's chest. "This is your final chance. I will have the Device operational quickly or you will watch your sister be brutalized and die. Just before I kill you."

# Chapter Seventy-eight

Hesitantly, the college student stood. Calculating the immense brainpower in the diverse group, he couldn't think of anything intelligent to say.

"Relax." Peering at him over her glasses and looking like his grandmother, a woman in sensible shoes patted his arm. "We don't bite."

"A few of us don't even have teeth." This from a man with a crow on his chest. The younger crowd thought that was funny.

Adjusting horn-rimmed glasses, a man in a wheelchair rapidly typed on a computer CAD system. "This is where the patent transitions from tangible to theory. The Meissner Device is buoyant in magnetic current but the means of propulsion is not defined." Images flashed across the screen and stopped. "Like oceanic currents, like atmospheric fluxations, the magnetic fields are only partially predictable. Corona discharges and sunspots are magnetic anomalies. The sun's poles reverse every 22 years. The current – pun intended – " he snorted at his own joke – "challenge is to accurately detect and compensate for these spastic variances so the machine floats in space."

Wilson crammed the last of his slice of bread into his mouth. "What do you have for us, kid?"

Stuffing his hands into his jeans pockets to hide their nervous shaking, Hebron addressed the brainstorming group. "In sophomore physics, we learned the exclusionary properties of a superconductor. Theoretically, we can define a device to project an exclusionary boundary that would levitate an object. This should work." He shrugged. "But no one has come up with a device that projects such an exclusionary boundary so that magnetic fields are prevented from entering it."

He cleared his throat and noted the faces of the engineers around him. To his obvious great relief they were not laughing. Or yawning. Or ignoring him. "The Meissner effect is a misnomer in the sense that it works more like a superconductor to levitate a magnet. Mr. Wayne's theory is to loop a superconductor flow like a hoola hoop so it continues."

"No fuel. No explosives." The only attendee in a military uniform, O'Rourke unwrapped a fresh cigar and stuck it between his teeth.

As Hebron focused on the science, his intimidation of the group he was addressing dissipated. "Earth has a magnetic field. The sun is an electro magnetic dynamo. The moon has a magnetic anomaly with molten magnetic core. On the moon, the local magnetic anomaly is caused by the concentration of metals under the moon's surface. Magnetic fields such as these are probably only three dynamic situations that are possible." He ticked off the list on his fingers. "It's a control challenge to compensate for the changing magnetic currents. The same way a submarine must deal with flexing currents and varied properties of water that affect the boat's ability to float and navigate."

"Exactly." Wilson licked his fingers and pointed to the figures on the chalkboard. "That's where we are in the process." Wilson eyed Mallory, then Hebron. "According to our bosses, you are the one who can take this project to the next vital step."

Hebron flushed with excitement. "There is a way to manipulate magnetic poles and control them."

# Chapter Seventy-nine

Blood trailed down his chin and dripped on the design for the Meissner Device. Marc wiped his sleeve across his bleeding lip.

Despair was an ugly, hopeless feeling. Marc was as equally ineffective to disentangle his mind from the life-sucking despondency, as he was to devise an escape. What was happening to Mallory? Did his actions today further endanger her? Would the Colonel set him down again in front of the computer screen, give him popcorn, and say the words over the phone that allowed her to be brutalized?

Suddenly Lei was in front of him with a first-aid kit.

"Go away." His words sounded as fat as his lip. He saw a momentary hesitation in her expression, but she dug antiseptic from her box and splashed a generous amount on a sterile gauze pad. When she looked up and wiped fresh blood with the bitter medicine, she had masked her emotions.

The liquid stung and Marc pulled away like every guy in the movies when a girl cleaned his fight wounds. She waited for him to hold still and pressed the cotton against his lip. He guessed it was alcohol. It smelled like Mallory's nail polish remover and their evenings as a family in the living room when he was growing up. The living room where he had last seen his sister being hurt by Yao's beasts. The memory stung more than the antiseptic and he shivered. That was a strange reaction and he sensed his body was experiencing some level of shock.

Lei noticed his response. "I'm sorry." She threw away the bloody wipe and doused fresh gauze with alcohol. He reached to do the cleaning himself.

"I'll do it." Her tone told him not to argue and he was not feeling up to another confrontation. The last one had not gone well. Since she didn't appear like she was going to slug him or beat him with the first aid kit, he sat quietly under her ministrations.

After bloodying Marc's lip, the Colonel had left, his anger tangible through his usual silence. The tension he brought each time he entered a room had gone out with him.

Lei snapped an instant ice pack, activating the chemicals inside, and handed it to him. "Hold this over your eye."

His bruised eye closed under the cool pack, he glanced sidelong with his good eye at the others in the lab. Similar dramatic events in the States would be talked about, opined, dissected, and verbally processed by employees meeting in small groups. Mixing around the water fountain, in the restrooms, lunchrooms, and parking lots, Americans would exercise their freedom of speech. Harassment charges would be filed. If the issue proved especially theatrical, news would leak to the press. Sensational versions would air on radio, in newspapers, and on the evening news. Television and radio talk show hosts would milk as much ratings as could be squeezed by firing up the event with scandalous questions, completely biased statements, and interviews with non-experts. It was the way of American media.

China didn't extend the same freedom to her populace. The Chinese were practiced at holding their thoughts and questions to themselves, processing occurrences quietly and individually.

"I thought I was the only one kept here." Lei spread ointment on his cut lip.

Marc studied her. Lei's ability to travel to the United States had been put on hold, but he had not fathomed the depth of her reality. What an irony. He was so consumed with his own plight under the control of the Peoples Republic and Colonel Yao that he had not suspected Lei was in a similar predicament. Lei had come to the same conclusion, believing she alone was under government discipline. Suddenly their previous conversations took on a completely new dimension. Both had been reserved and danced around the truth of their situation. No wonder, Marc admitted. How would he or the girl know who to trust in this policed environment where people protected themselves and their families by keeping silent and ratting out their fellows.

She looked up, caught his stare and blushed. Putting the lid on the ointment tube, her fingers fumbled the task. Lid and medicine fell. Trying to catch what she dropped, Lei upended the first aid kit that scattered around her feet.

The noise and movement caused several in the lab to look their way. Their expressions ranged from judgment to apathy. Everyone had extra work to make the Meissner Device functional. No one wanted to be the target of the Colonel's displeasure.

Marc picked up band-aids and individual packets of aspirin and added them to the kit Lei was reassembling. Before she snapped the lid onto the first aid supplies, she gave him another ice pack. "For later. You might need it." She took the cold pack from his eye and inspected the damage. Standing on her tiptoes, Lei looked at him meaningfully. "You may need help."

# Chapter Eighty

Skunk Works. Hebron was part of an esteemed Skunk Works team and he couldn't tell anyone. This would so impress the brainiac college girls with the delicious figures. He imagined the female collegiates clustered around him while he dropped just enough of the story to keep their eyes on him, their hands caressing his neck.

"I said let's launch this puppy." The authoritative voice broke into Hebron's daydream.

Talking around the perpetual cigar when he wasn't chewing on it, Major Rory O'Rourke was in charge of the group that functioned with a high degree of autonomy unhampered by bureaucracy, despite the fact that they were quartered on a military base.

In the short time he had been at the lab, Hebron had encountered men and women with patches depicting skunks and crows. He had heard of these legends. Skunks were the elite engineers. Ravens were the electronics specialists. Old Crows were retired but couldn't keep away. They often showed up for the occasional consult or project.

The official trademark for the Lockheed Martin Advanced

Development Programs, Skunk Works projects were developed by a small, loosely structured group of experts who researched and developed purely for the sake of prototype innovation. The name was influenced by Al Capp's comic strip, *Li'l Abner*. Popular in the 1940s and 1950s, the hillbilly strip featured a dilapidated factory located in backwoods Kentucky on the outskirts of Dogpatch. From skunks and old shoes, Skonk Works brewed and barreled skonk oil.

Similarly, the original Lockheed facility was located next to a malodorous plastics factory. As a gag, one day an engineer showed up at work in a gas mask. The neighboring smell, and the secrecy of the work, inspired workers to name the facility after the comic strip factory. When a Skunk Works team member answered a call from the Department of the Navy with "Skonk Works," the name stuck. In compliance with a request from the Li'l Abner copyright holders, Lockheed changed the name of the advanced development company to Skunk Works.

In 1943, in dire need of a jet to counter the superior German models, the U.S. Army met with Lockheed. Young and brilliant engineer, Clarence "Kelly" L. Johnson and his team delivered the XP-80 one month later. Four months before the formal contract arrived. It was common practice for customers to request a project from this prototype team on a handshake. Working under Kelly's 14 rules and practices, projects were always delivered ahead of schedule and without a contract or official submittal process.

Hebron suspected the absence of ridiculous paperwork freed these geniuses to create. Wisely, Johnson had given his team the liberty to function free from bureaucratic constraints. Today was no exception. Ahead of schedule, the Meissner Device was ready to launch.

Hebron wore his lucky Li'l Abner t-shirt. Everyone who had a role in the project was on hand. Project team members took their places and excited talk quieted. O'Leary pointed his cigar and Hebron began the sequence. Acting as a superconductor, the machine emitted a hum as it generated energy to repel natural magnetic currents. Lab personnel were proud of the sound created by their work. Like parents tuned in to their infant's coos, to hear the device's voice as the project progressed, engineers and designers gradually turned down their personal music sources spouting everything from Wilson's classical orchestras to Hebron's heavy metal.

Slowly, the Meissner Device lifted from its platform. The machine levitated for several minutes and Skunks and Old Crows whooped and gave each other high-fives. With a nod from O'Leary, Hebron pushed the remote controls and the device jerked forward. The momentum caused the invention to wobble like a Friday night drunk.

"She's gonna sun her moccasins." O'Leary wheeled his arm in a circle toward the hangar wall. "Now, Mr. Heath!"

# Chapter Eighty-one

Tonight, like every previous night, Marc lay on his back, fingers laced behind his head. Staring at the high ceiling, he took mental inventory. In his mind, he had two lists. One consisted of materials available to him. Items in the lab. The second catalogued the people in this place of confinement with an emphasis on their strengths and weaknesses. To these details, he added the fact that the Chinese were preparing to celebrate National Day.

With a ceremony at Tiananmen Square, the Peoples Republic of China was founded on October 1, 1949. The annual holiday was celebrated through nationally organized festivities. Representing the Peoples Republic of China, and to keep the populace from getting frisky, the military would make a showing. No doubt, Colonel Yao would attend perfunctory events. Like Fourth of July in the United States, cities decorated in patriotic themes, and orchestras performed extravagant concerts followed by bright fireworks.

Fireworks. He bolted up and sat on the edge of the bed as segments of ideas rapidly connected. Pacing now, Marc outlined a plan. Hours later, feeling at last he had a direction worth pursuing, he collapsed back onto the cot. But sleep eluded him. Instead, he felt something he'd not possessed since his abduction. It was a lightheartedness driven by possibility. Adrenalin springing from a fresh sense of options. He felt hope.

# Chapter Eighty-two

In the small garden at his house, Colonel Yao paced. The offensive Mr. Spencer had been right. The Americans were developing their own Meissner Device. Had apparently even got it airborne. No matter that it had crashed. That was part of the process. Much like the previous race to the moon, the engineers would adjust the necessary figures and launch again.

Spencer had provided additional information that a solution to the misfire had been found in the office of the patent's author. Marc Wayne knew how to make the device work. He was stalling.

Hearing a sound, he turned to see his housekeeper bring an envelope. A single letter. Like clockwork.

Sitting on a garden bench he realized he had scanned the length of the correspondence with his eyes and not paid attention to what it said. His current worries dominated his thoughts. The development of the Meissner machine must be completed in China first.

The housekeeper returned with a tray. Silently she poured tea and left again. Sipping the infusion of flowers and leaves, he harnessed his galloping thoughts and began to read the letter again.

The news in the village was typical. A marriage, two babies, and the condition of the rice fields now that they had water systems. "Our only wish, my son, is for a grandson before we die."

# Chapter Eighty-three

In the lab the next day, Marc bent close to Lei at her workstation. "I have an idea."

She kept solemnly focused on what she was doing, poised to listen.

"It will be dangerous. If you don't want to be involved, just do something."

She froze.

He shook his head. "Okay, that was not effective. Look, if you'd rather not be involved, scratch your nose."

Instead, she inclined her head to hear more.

Now Marc froze. If she was with him, he felt he had a better shot with a partner. She was familiar with this country where he wasn't. She knew the language. Her motivation was a deep longing to be reunited with the man she was engaged to, the one she planned to spend the rest of her life with. But if she was with him, could he guarantee her safety?

Lei dropped a spool of wire. It bounced and rolled. "What?" She retrieved the object and set it in front of him.

He picked up wire cutters, stripped plastic from a length and spliced bare wires onto a connector. "I think that while the big shots are away for the celebration, we can pull it off."

A lab worker stepped over. "What are you doing?"

Marc glanced up absently at the intrusion. "Working. Same as you." Marc kept eye contact until the intruder looked away and returned to his work area. *It was all a game of chicken. Who would flinch first?*

With exaggerated motions for anyone who was watching him, Marc pulled a pencil from behind his ear and reached for paper. He penciled formulas along the margins as he wandered to a desk. Some time later, Colonel Yao leaned over his shoulder.

"Tell me about your work."

Marc didn't bother to look up. He didn't want his eyes to betray him. "I have some new ideas I want to try out." *That was certainly true.*

"Good."

"Allow me access to the laboratory over the next couple days. I believe I can make a breakthrough in the controls to divert and intensify the output field."

Colonel Yao moved beside him and clasped his hands behind his back. He was quiet for several moments. When he didn't get a response Marc stood and faced the man.

"What are you afraid of? That I'll escape?" Frustrated, he gestured to include the large sanctuary that had been transformed from a place of spiritual worship to a gathering that paid homage to technology. "From this fortress? Don't you think I've already considered every possible means of getting out of here?"

The Colonel stared at him.

"Look," Marc reasoned, sounding desperate. "I know the only chance I have of going home is to get this machine to fly. I'd like to be home by Christmas."

The Colonel remained cool. Weighing. Calculating.

Marc flopped back into his seat, his back to the cold Colonel. "Forget it."

The man remained behind Marc. Yao's presence made the hair stand up on the back of Marc's neck. *Creepy.* After a silence so long that Marc truly was getting desperate, the Colonel spoke. "Very well. You work during celebration."

# Chapter Eighty-four

At an all-night diner in Dayton, Ohio, Mr. Spencer drank coffee as dark as the night outside. Beside his cup was a thermos. He checked the time on his cell phone. Thumbing to his email account, he reread the report. Satellites had detected a change in the facility he was watching at Wright-Patterson for Colonel Yao.

Outside the greasy spoon's side windows, a set of headlights marked the arrival of a small pick-up that had been used hard.

Moments later, a man sat across from him in the restaurant booth.

"You're late."

The man pulled a stocking cap from his graying head. "Takes longer to do my job."

"How long does it take to round up and destroy trash?"

"That hangar with the new activity is the trouble."

A thick-waisted waitress brought a second cup. At Spencer's signal, she left the coffee pot on their table.

"It's off-limits so gotta use lengthier procedures. Thar's a hole in the side of the hangar. A big hole. Rumor is that it was a forklift accident." He shook his head. "No way. I drive a forklift.

Nothin' to it after the first time. No, sir. That damage is too large and too high for a forklift."

Spencer draped an arm across the back of the booth. "What does it look like to you?"

"Sounds crazy, but looks like something flew through the metal wall." He picked at something between his teeth. "All this goin's on. Somethin' in there and you keepin' my baby-gal in college for havin' coffee with you regular. Keepin' that thermos supplied with papers I find." He whistled softly between his teeth.

Spencer twisted the lid from the thermos, filled it with coffee from the pot, and slid it to his companion.

The man exchanged it for the look-alike thermos he had brought. "Thanks for the coffee." He tugged on his sock hat and disappeared into early morning darkness in the rattling pick-up.

# Chapter Eighty-five

Mallory turned into Fred's driveway and parked. He had invited her to dinner and to meet the new baby.

Since her brother had disappeared, she was consumed with guilt. Passing homes with families gathered for dinner increased her regret. She knew she would not be good company. She leaned her forehead against the steering wheel. "I was only thinking of myself. I sacrificed him to the wolves. It's my fault. My stupid choices."

A knock on the driver's window made her look up. It was Fred. She waved him away, but he stubbornly stood there. Waiting. In the evening light, she could see concern in his eyes. She didn't deserve his empathy or compassion. She didn't deserve anything.

Fred pointed to the lock on the door. Instead she rolled down the window halfway.

"Are you okay?"

Her jaw tight against embarrassing emotions, Mallory nodded.

"Come on in."

She shook her head. "Not a good idea. Tell your family I'm sorry, but I can't do this."

Fred reached through the window and unlocked the car doors. He walked around the front of her car and seated himself on the passenger side. His voice was gentle. "Talk to me."

"I can't."

"Why not?"

"If I start, I will cry."

He shifted in the seat to face her. "Mallory, you gotta talk. This is more than the case, isn't it?"

She pulled a loose sting from the bottom of her sweater and wound it around her finger, unwound it, and wound it again.

"Okay. What else?"

"I sent my brother into the hands of our enemies. Maybe to his death. What kind of murderer am I? I put work ahead of my family. Ahead of the person who means the most to me."

"What else?"

She bit back the humiliating self-talk that had beat in her brain like a tribal drum. *You sent your brother to his death.* She shook her head to his question.

"What, Mallory? What is it?" His voice was tender, the way she imagined he spoke with his children. The way her Dad, the way Marc would probe her hurt feelings.

She took a chance. Vulnerable and raw, the words exploded out. "I'm an atrocious failure." Angrily, she pressed knuckles to her stinging eyes to stop tears that she refused to allow. "A failure as a research analyst, a failure as a daughter. A failure as a sister."

She waited for him to contradict her.

"I'm certain you feel that way." He fished in the glove box and pulled out a handful of fast-food napkins. "It looks pretty dark right now."

"What if we never find him? Never know what happened to my brother?"

"We'll find him. I know we will."

"So much time has passed. Is he hurt? Maimed? Psychologically damaged beyond repair?"

"Mal, you can't torture yourself like this. It clouds your ability to do your job. To follow the leads to find him."

"I had a thousand options, and I chose to exploit my brother. The sacrificial lamb to bait the thieves. I was thinking of myself. Of the easiest way to make my idea, my plan, work. To solve the case quickly and," she did her best imitation of Deverell, "get some good PR." She landed a fist on the armrest. "Recognition and a promotion. Accolades."

The front door of the house opened. A blanketed bundle in her arms and silhouetted in the yellow light streaming from the living room, a tall woman peered out. Fred gazed at his wife. "You didn't make the decision in a vacuum. I agreed. So did Deverell."

"This is all because of my choice. I chose to put Marc in danger."

Two young children pushed in front of each other, tumbling onto the front porch like puppies. "How is beating yourself up helping you find Marc?" Fred waved the international okay sign to his family. His wife nodded and, with a word, rounded up the children and pointed them inside. She gave a wave to Mallory and Fred in the car and disappeared inside, closing the front door behind her.

Mallory stared unseeing out the windshield. "If Mom and Dad were alive, they would be so disappointed that I jeopardized Marc. Disappointed in me."

Fred stretched his arm across the back of their seats. He touched her shoulder. "It's pretty hard to fight a ghost, Mallory. Let your parents rest in peace."

Noisily, she blew her nose. "I pray that Marc isn't a ghost."

"It's not over till it's over. Keep the faith. Give the process a chance."

"If we do find him – "

"*When* we find him."

She swallowed against the choking lump in her throat. "How will I face him? Look what I've done to our relationship. The two of us are all we have. And I betrayed him."

"I have a large family and I would feel the same way if any one of them were harmed. I know how important Marc is to you."

She went back to winding the string around her finger. "Mom

and Dad were giddy when they brought him home. He was an infant," she waved a hand toward the house, "like your new baby. He brought a heightened sense of life and purpose to our family. He completes us. My parents adored him."

He reached for the door. "Come on in, Mallory. Let my wife feed you a good home cooked meal. Play with the kids and hold the baby. It'll be good medicine."

She nodded. Fred got out of the car. As soon as the passenger door closed, Mallory put the car in reverse. In her rearview mirror, she saw Fred standing in the driveway, watching her drive away.

# Chapter Eighty-six

Marc looked up as Colonel Yao approached the table where he and Lei were eating. Disregarding Marc, Yao spoke to Lei in Chinese.

Ignoring the snub, Marc took advantage of the situation to study his nemesis. He noticed something on Yao's hand he had not noticed before. In fact he was sure it had not been there previously. Why now?

So the Colonel was a graduate of the East Coast's illustrious university for geniuses. MIT's class ring, often called the Brass Rat, is uniquely crafted each year. Though the mascot looks like a rat, the beaver was selected as the engineer of the animal world. Marc knew that in the world, there are three recognizable rings; the West Point ring, the Super Bowl ring, and the MIT Brass Rat. As Marc had suspected, the Colonel was trying to impress the lovely, young Lei. This information had to be useful. Somehow.

Turning his attention back to the conversation, Marc watched surprise cross Lei's face. The Colonel waited. Lei appeared to consider her answer before looking back at the waiting Yao. She demurred for a moment. Then her eyes met Marc's. He noted a flash of inspiration, but it was gone so quickly he wondered if he had imagined it.

She turned a flattered expression to the brooding Colonel. With a gentle smile, she nodded. Looking cautiously pleased, he gave a slight bow and left.

Marc watched her push her food around on her plate. "You okay?"

She met his gaze. "He invited me to accompany him to the formal festivities on National Day."

# Chapter Eighty-seven

In a vehicle across the street from a strip mall, Mallory watched several moms with babies in strollers.

Four moms and three strollers. The fourth mother held a preschooler by the hand. In her other hand she carried a protest sign. *Jesus loves the little children.* The reverse read *It's a child, not a choice.*

It was a Thursday morning. The mothers were patrolling the front of a family planning clinic. A car parked, and a mother intercepted the young girl before she entered the building. There was a brief conversation, accompanied by tears. The preschooler pressed into the girl's hand a palm-sized baby doll, a replica of an eight-week fetus.

From the passenger side of the car, an unkept young man got out. Wresting the sign from the mother's hand, he snapped it in half and threw the pieces. Snatching the pamphlet from the girl, he waved it in her face. She cowered while he shredded it to tiny pieces that scattered around their feet like snowflakes. Over the loud objections of the protesting mother, he twisted the girl's arm behind her back, pried the small doll from her hand, and ground it underfoot on the gritty asphalt. A nurse came from the clinic and elbowing the women away, she escorted the girl inside. With a final glare, the man returned to wait in the car.

The drama saddened Mallory. Somewhere she had read that there were many adoptive parents whose arms remained empty while abortion numbers climbed. Aware that abortion was an option, her parents had prayed daily that Marc's biological mom would carry him to term. She shuddered to consider how close Marc might have come to having his life ended in a place like the one the girl had entered. Wondering what meat grinder he was in now made her want to throw up.

But she was waiting for a different person to arrive. Someone that might have information about her brother. After talking with the pilot of the medical flight, she had followed a sketchy trail to find the doctor who had been aboard the plane with Marc. Finding him was like catching a grasshopper. His spastic schedule mirrored the erratic jobs he did. Mallory had to be certain this was the guy. And that he would be in this location.

An hour later her early morning vigil was rewarded when a black limo pulled up to the clinic's back door. The suited driver trotted to the passenger door and swung it open. Dressed in Dockers and a polo shirt, a long-legged man got out. He tipped back the last of a cocktail and handed the empty glass to the driver.

Mallory glanced at the time. It was early in the day to be getting corked but perhaps that helped him execute what he was going to do. A dozen cars, including the one with the surly man, had delivered young ladies to the address. A middle-aged woman who checked her watch and drove away brought three teenage girls. Mallory suspected she was the campus nurse from the local high school.

Pushing their strollers, the mothers crossed the street and got into their minivans near where Mallory watched. Cradling her sleeping child, the preschooler's mother tapped on Mallory's passenger window. Mallory beckoned her inside.

"Did you see him?"

Mallory nodded.

"The clinic is not licensed to perform abortions. We

pressured the health department for an inspection but that was useless. The inspector warned them when he was coming and ignored the obvious." In her arms, she adjusted the child that snored slightly. "Killing babies is lucrative."

"Why not just use a local doc?"

The mother tilted her head. "We let the word out that some folks' trusted family physicians were cutting little babies to pieces. It was embarrassing and not good for business."

They watched the angry young man get out of the car once again and walk aimlessly. "You demonstrated in front of the doctor's house?"

The youngster passed gas and the mother wrinkled her nose and patted the small bottom. "It was effective for a while. The abortions stopped. Then the clinic started bringing in this guy from out of the area." She rolled down the window and waved good-by to the other women as they drove away.

Across the street, the young man who had chosen not to be a father, lit a cigarette.

"Thank you for your help," Mallory said to her companion.

"Hope the information I gave you will help us stop this." She opened the car door and carefully got out without disturbing her daughter's sleep. "The children who are dying in there are contemporaries of my children. The would-be neighbors, friends, and maybe spouse of my girl." She glared toward the clinic. "The Constitution says everyone – e v e r y o n e – has the right to life. Even preborn babies. The Bible says 'thou shalt not kill.' Those fiends belong in jail with the rest of the criminals and murderers." She planted a kiss on the still sleeping child's forehead and left.

Across the street, the young man lit another cigarette and disappeared into the convenience store next door. Through the window, Mallory watched him purchase a soda and drop coins into the video game machine.

Hunched over, the girl Mallory had seen escorted into the clinic, shuffled stiffly out. No one escorted her on the return trip to her car. Nor was her cantankerous companion waiting there for her. Looking fraught, she searched her surroundings and finally made her way to the convenience store. Playing another game, the young man didn't look up when she entered. He shrugged off the hand she put on his arm. Pleading, she began to cry. Until the game was over, he ignored her. Then, taking her by the arm, he propelled her outside and to their car. Lighting a cigarette, he threw the keys in her direction and got into the passenger seat. As the couple drove off, Mallory prayed the girl would disentangle herself from an obviously toxic relationship.

Using her cell phone, Mallory made arrangements for the visiting doctor's afternoon. The FBI had some questions for him. Someone else would do the asking for her. Others who knew the fine arts of inquiring and obtaining advantageous information from slippery men like him.

For herself, Mallory was eager to hear what the doctor's upcoming and unexpected appointment could tell her about Marc's whereabouts.

# Chapter Eighty-eight

"Smoke and mirrors," Marc explained.

Day after day, night after night, Marc worried about Mallory. Where was she? What were those beasts doing to her? His imaginings were a curse, preventing him from thinking clearly. From developing a plausible plan to escape.

Once he was away from this prison, he needed to find Mallory. When she didn't show up at work, had the FBI been searching? Had the FBI connected the fact that Marc and Mallory were both missing?

Would the Colonel's goons keep Mallory near his house where he had last seen her on Yao's computer screen? When Marc escaped, Yao would doubtless make good his threat and kill Mallory before he reached her. For his sister's best chance, it was crucial that Yao believe Marc was dead rather than escaped. He hoped to buy time to locate his sister.

The gravity of their circumstance paralyzed him from formulating a plan when he most needed to. Other times, it served as a fiery motivation. All the time, his thoughts bounced from escape to proving progress on the Meissner Device to keep Yao from further harming Mallory until he could find her. Marc's usually methodical thoughts now rebounded like hail on a tin barn roof.

Lei looked confused and he knew he sounded as disconnected as he felt. Truth was, Marc had decided to move forward with even a crackpot plan before more time was lost attempting to corral renegade ideas. He would take the next step as it presented itself or as he figured it out. The alternative was to develop the safe, guaranteed workable plan and he no longer believed one existed.

"We make it look like the Meissner Effect Generator works. Like we figured it out and used it to escape."

In her eyes he saw a guarded flicker of hope. "But where will we go?"

Marc sighed. "That's where it gets tricky. We hide."

"Hide where?"

"In plain sight. Sort of. Here in the building. They'll think we're long gone."

"But we're still stuck here."

"They will have the city locked down and we have no idea where to go." Mark ran a hand through his hair. "I'm gambling that if they think we're gone, these goons will ease up on the security precautions around here."

"And we'll slip out."

"Right."

"And go where?"

"That's the other tricky part."

She looked at him quizzically.

He shrugged. "Okay, it's a half-baked idea. But it's all I have."

# Chapter Eighty-nine

He'd be thrown inside before anyone noticed the loss. Escorted to his cell, Marc breathed deep and gathered his courage.

When the door was opened, Marc flew at the guard. He chose the largest of the two in hopes that surprise would level the fighting field. Besides, this was the first guard Marc had met when he had awakened in his cell, the short-fused soldier who had wanted to tear Marc's face from his head as a gift from the welcome wagon. Marc had seen it in the man's dark eyes, and ever since Marc had wanted to slug him.

Head down, he charged the uniformed man, bowled into his solid middle, and the two slammed to the floor. Marc threw a fist into the man's chest and another into his face before the smaller guard grabbed Marc, pulled him up, and pinned his arms. Back on his feet, the bigger guard approached Marc with narrowed eyes. The brute had wanted to punch Marc since he first saw him. Marc could see from the glint in his expression that he had every intention of enjoying this opportunity that had so easily presented itself. He slammed a fist into Marc's face.

The blow snapped back his head. Pain exploded in his brain.

Strong arms tossed Marc onto the floor of his cell and the door locked behind him.

This was the tricky part. Face down on the floor, his hands trapped beneath him, he slyly moved his fingers. It was there. He'd pulled it off. The guards thought he was trying to make a run for it, but he had something else in mind. Cautiously, he slipped the guard's stolen badge into his clothes and away from the video camera monitoring his room.

Rolling to his back, he touched his face. The prize was worth a broken nose.

The following day, Marc's face was a war zone. Throbbing under the extra ice pack Lei had given him the last time his eye was blackened, his swollen nose was twice the normal size, making him sound like he had a severe cold. Blood crusted inside both nostrils. He imagined he looked like something out of a horror movie his mom wouldn't let him watch as a kid. Lei had given him a concerned look. He winked back and instantly regretted it. His face hurt like crazy.

Working through lunch, Marc had a brief time of relative privacy. He'd thought this through to require as little time as possible to execute. The core of Hebron's invention was a three-dimensional optical scanner that allowed Marc to read and duplicate the icon on the guard's badge he had pinched.

Using Hebron's diamond device, he separated the fine layers of the identification part of the badge. Then he reproduced them on a new background. It wasn't a carbon copy of the original, but the important part that got doors open was what he wanted to duplicate. Hebron's brainchild did have more than the single function his father had rejected.

Later he slipped his creation to Lei. "Use this to see what's in the other restricted areas. Maybe our way out."

As he walked away, she made a slight movement to adjust her bra and Marc knew she had hidden the faux badge.

# Chapter Ninety

That afternoon, the doctor left the family planning clinic through the back door and climbed into the waiting limo. Full metal garage music drowned out the sounds of the day as he poured himself a snifter of brandy. The velvet liquid warmed his throat and he commended himself for another lucrative use of his skills.

After his second drink, the limo parked. The driver opened the door, and the doctor stretched his legs and stepped out.

"What the - ?" He was in front of the same back door he'd exited two drinks earlier. "You stupid –" He turned to curse at the inept limo driver, but stopped when he saw the Glock pointed at his head. Two men, one bald and the other over-muscled, appeared seemingly from nowhere, grabbed his arms and roughly propelled him inside.

"What's this about?" The doctor glanced at his watch. "If you are health inspectors, you have the wrong guy. You need to track down the director of this facility. And do it quickly. I have a plane to catch."

"Shut-up." The limo driver locked the clinic door behind them.

The employees that had populated the clinic were gone for the night and the lights were off. Down the narrow hall padded with dated rust-colored carpet, the three expressionless men pushed the doctor. They entered a windowless back room and the bald man closed and blocked the door. The limo driver turned on a single light against the evening shadows.

Smelling of mold and alcohol, the exam room had been adapted for inpatient surgery. The doctor knew this room. He had spent all day performing the same procedure over and over in this dreary place.

The man with the gun waved the weapon in his direction. The doctor sighed and half-heartedly raised his arms. The limo driver patted him down, and examined his license and credit cards. He took particular interest in the large amount of big bills overflowing the alligator skin wallet. "Look boys." The driver waved a wad of hundreds. "Killing babies pays better than what we make for killing guys like him."

"Dang. And babies don't fight back." Shorter than the other two, the guy whose face looked like he made side money in a boxing ring, ran a hand over the powerful suction machine used to pull infants from the security of their mother's womb. "Quiet even when you suck out their eyes." The boxer turned on the suction machine. "Here's lookin' at you, babe."

"Gentlemen, what do you want?" The doctor looked at his watch once more. "I'm sure we can come to a mutually satisfactory agreement."

The man with the suction machine pointed the nozzle in the direction of the doctor. "We know what this does to babies, I wonder what it can do to the doctor who uses it."

Moving toward the well-guarded door, the doctor put out his hands, palms up. "Okay, is this about a girlfriend? A daughter? Look, I don't know who they are, I just – "

"You just help them out like a good boy scout." The boxer dangled a latex glove in front of the nozzle. Like a beast devouring prey, the sound of the machine revved and the glove quickly disappeared, sucked from his hand. "You're just the good doctor doin' everyone a favor."

"Just a law-abidin' citizen." The limo driver shoved the Glock up the doctor's nostril. "What other services do you perform?"

The doctor started to shake his head but winced when the gun held his face in place. "There isn't – "

The driver twisted the gun further into his nose. "Ever been the doctor for a medical flight?"

The pain in his nose made his eyes water. "I don't know what you're talking about."

With a deep growl, the man with the misshapen nose lunged at him. Before he could back-pedal, the doctor was thrown onto the exam table with such force that the air was knocked from his lungs. Tissue paper crackling and tearing, the doctor struggled against the attack. In seconds, the bald man and the limo driver had him strapped to the narrow medical table like a bug on a fifth grade insect display.

The boxer brought the suction tube to hover near the doctor's face and bent close. "You won't be doing any medical procedures, legal or otherwise, if you're blind."

An electric jolt of primal fear pulsed through the doctor's veins and he renewed his desperate attempts to free himself. Squinting to protect his eyes, he fought to turn his face away but could not. The focused black hole of the suction tube, the same one he had wielded all day, loomed near. Above the noise of the machine, he heard the boxer.

"Here's lookin' at you, babe."

# Chapter Ninety-one

As he anticipated, Marc and his room were given a nasty shakedown that evening. Not that there was much to look through.

Marc was returned to his room where the two guards from the previous evening's brawl were inside turning over the thin mattress, the bed frame, the table and chair, and looking for hiding places between the walls and the floor.

"You fellas lost something?" Marc couldn't resist the jab. What were they gonna do? Beat him up some more? It would reach the point where Yao would notice and Marc was certain they would not want to tell the Colonel they were missing an identification badge. One of their identity classifications that got people through locked doors around here.

Nor did Marc want them to find the incriminating I.D. on him after his successful heist the night before. That would trash his whole half-baked escape plan. The more time that passed, the more he felt panicked for Mallory. Earlier, Marc had slipped the badge into the women's restroom. When it was found there, it would create some interesting questions for the uniformed group and hopefully divert suspicion from him.

The big guard's eyes narrowed and he advanced toward Marc, clearly intending to work over Marc the way he had been working over the room. His two escorts held Marc as the big guy began the pat-down when a voice called from behind.

Then Lei was beside him, her tone forceful. The big guy blanched and the others snickered and released their hold on Marc. Small and indignant, she pushed herself between Marc and his would be attacker. Eyes flinty with anger, she spoke fast and not in English. She swung the badge in front of the guard's face and the others stepped back to avoid any connection to what was transpiring between the man and the angry scientist. Finally, she dropped the badge on the floor, spun on her heel to quickly lock eyes with Marc before turning toward the lab.

"If I ever see you anywhere near the women's room again …" her steps were as clipped as her words and Marc knew the last sentence was spoken for his benefit.

Marc whistled through his teeth and wagged a finger in the no-no gesture at the guard who looked confused and humiliated as he retrieved his badge from the floor. The others punched him in the shoulder and made comments Marc did not comprehend but he understood the razzing tone.

In a flash, the guard threw a punch into Marc's gut and tossed him into the room. The door slammed. Lying on the floor, sucking in oxygen like a beached fish, Marc considered it had been a productive day.

# Chapter Ninety-two

Like every previous morning, a soldier escorted Marc from his room to the large double doors of the laboratory. The sentry kept his place outside the lab, while the guard followed Marc and assumed a post inside.

*To keep an eye on me.*

The lab was empty except for Marc and his babysitter. Everyone else was celebrating National Day. Even Lei was away with the Colonel. This was his chance. He had to make a run for it and it had to be today. Progressing through his mental checklist, he worked all day. Preparing.

At last, he was down to the final action points. Nervous, his heart pounded and he stopped frequently to wipe damp palms against his pant leg. He tried to remember brave characters from spy movies as inspiration. They never seemed jittery. *What would Batman do? How would the Green Hornet or Ironman figure a way out and bring down the enemy?*

A commotion at the door caused him to lose his concentration and his balance. His supplies spilled to the floor. The guard started over to see what was happening. Breathless, Marc scooped the scattered pieces, hoping the man with the gun at his hip would not know what he was looking at. But Marc knew there was no chance of that. What military trained personnel didn't have a basic knowledge of things that blew up? They destroyed things for a living, for Pete's sake.

Fumbling to gather the most incriminating evidence before inquiring eyes recognized them for what they were, Marc glanced up to see the narrowing eyes of the approaching soldier.

"Hey," Lei called. Marc and the soldier looked to the open doorway where the guard posted outside stood with a satisfied grin and grubby fingers wrapped around a steaming cup. Lei held out a second cup to the guard who menacingly approached Marc.

The man hesitated. He was the big guy whose badge Marc had pinched. The guy didn't like Marc. He was also the same man Lei had derided when she returned his I.D. He turned simpering whenever she looked at him. Quickly, Marc swept the last explosive element out of sight. When the guard glanced back to Marc, Marc looked longingly at the cup in Lei's hand and inhaled deeply, hoping to turn the man's attention to the proffered coffee. He also hoped the deep breath would calm his own panic.

Lei shrugged and carried the cup in Marc's direction.

"Thanks," he said, and tipped the cup to his lips. His eyes on Lei, he saw her frown.

With a grunt, the guard grabbed the coffee from Marc and took a long drink. With a smirk, he waved Lei aside to her work and returned to the door where both guards downed the contents of their drinks and talked quietly.

"Once they're asleep, we have maybe two hours," she said softly.

Marc brushed sweat from his forehead. "What's in those cups?

She cast a sidelong glance at the men. "Benadryl I brought back from the States."

"How much?"

"A lot."

He glanced at the guards and puffed out his cheeks. "Let's

get to work."

The futuristic-looking vehicle had taken shape under Marc's direction. Now, he worked under his own plan, one outlined not on paper but solely in his mind. Lei reassembled the items that had spilled and Marc set the explosives in strategic places.

"What about the Colonel?"

She glanced at the clock. "He is where he's supposed to be with other dignitaries. The fireworks begin soon."

"Will he be looking for you? His date?"

"I told him I had a headache and had to go home." She held the mixture and he pressed it into place. "What happens after it explodes?"

"That's where it gets dicey. We have to squirrel into a hiding place so the Colonel and his boys think we're gone." He glanced across the room. The door was closed which meant one guard was on post outside while his partner remained inside. After a yawn, the man in view tossed back the final swallow of the tainted coffee before crushing the disposable cup and tossing it into the trash. "What's in the other areas of this facility?"

"There is a heavy amount of security at the far end."

"Did you use the badge? Get a look inside?"

"Briefly. It's full of weapons. And big boxes."

"Weapons." Marc thought this over.

"And boxes."

"Is there an opening for shipping? Like the doors in here that open to the cargo ships?"

Her eyes went to the large doors along the waterside wall. "Yes, there are doors like that in there."

Marc continued his way around the Meissner Device, turning over Lei's information about the cordoned off hallway in hopes of figuring their next step. When everything was set, he approached her. "Look, you can leave now. It would be safer for you."

She shook her head.

"Really, Lei. No one will ask any questions or suspect you of anything. Stay here in your homeland. Have the enviable positioned life as the young wife of the Colonel, for Pete's sake."

She drew herself up and thrust out her chin. "I'm going with you."

Seeing the guard slumped in a chair, asleep by the door, Marc dropped a wrench. The tool clanged loudly to the floor, but the guard merely twitched and slept on. "This is beyond risky, Lei. We may kill ourselves or get killed."

She nodded.

"Are you sure?"

"I'm sure."

"Lei – "

Putting both hands on his shoulders, she shoved him into action. "Let's go before I realize what I just said."

# Chapter Ninety-three

Arnold Taylor admired the woman in front of him. Half his age, she was an actress on New York's Broadway stage; that is when she wasn't entertaining him.

Taylor fancied himself as Aristotle Onassis and she was his Maria Callas. But he never told her of his fantasy. It was too intimate. He had first seen her when he brought his wife to New York. The excitement of the long deferred trip and the show-stopping Broadway performance resulted in a migraine. At their hotel, he tucked her into bed with a cold cloth on her forehead. Then he ventured out into the night for a stroll in the Big Apple and maybe a drink.

His wife was convinced that the visit to New York City was an anniversary celebration. He let her believe that and treat him like a hero. After months of suspense, the first product had been delivered to the sly man who had approached the aging Taylor with a business proposition. A secret bank account proved that this new side job paid better than his career position at the United States Patent and Trademark Office.

On his walk that first night in the big city, he happened upon a party in the hotel's upscale restaurant and bar. High on performance adrenalin, a number of the cast and their friends from the Broadway spectacular he had seen earlier were celebrating their successful opening night. That was when he met his Maria. His financial extravagance brought a seductive light to her eyes that he knew was as superficial as his feelings for her. Neither ever spoke about their real feelings. She didn't ask where he went when he was not with her, nor did he question her about where she invested her time when they were apart. It was enough that she dropped everything when he came to town and gave him her full dark-eyed attention.

The affair proved a potent motivation for Taylor to slip additional top-secret patents to the man who paid immediately and abundantly. While his actress mistress played her roles on Broadway, Taylor played deeper into his fantasy. Onassis had made his fortune through a series of businesses, some of which had hardly been moral or ethical. Heady with his emerging secret life, Taylor was ready to play a big game. One that would free him to devote all his time to the pursuits that pleased him.

His chance came in the form of a patent for a revolutionary new jet engine. Like Onassis, he was tough in his negotiations. The day his secret account received a deposit for more money than he dreamed he would have, Taylor retired. Retired from his job at the USPTO, and retired from his mundane, middle class life.

Under the guise of a consulting business, he frequented New York for the periodic rendezvous with Maria. This evening his wife thought he was away for work. In fact, fully Aristotle, he was on the roof of the New York apartment he provided for his mistress. The evening sky was clear with a view of the harbor. It was that magic span of time between day and night when lights began to twinkle on and the city changed from work clothes to evening attire.

With her dramatic flare, the actress had set the stage on the open-air patio with soft music and a low dining table. Waiting for their favorite chef to send up a meal, he lounged on a Cleopatra-style bed, thick with throws and pillows, watching the sultry actress give him a private showing of her upcoming role. He planned to arrange their next tryst in a new, exotic setting. First Monaco, then Paris. He smiled. The future was inviting with an unlimited variety of places to practice being a wealthy playboy.

With a mechanical hiss, the elevator door opened and the deliveryman arrived carrying carefully packed dishes smelling of coconut and curry. Strapped on his back was a pack that Taylor was certain held their chilled champagne.

The waiter arranged the dishes and placed silverware.

Taylor crossed to the table, reaching for his wallet to give the expected tip.

"Sir, is this to your liking?" The waiter gestured to the table, inviting Taylor to inspect the product.

This was certainly a step up from meatloaf Tuesdays and spaghetti Wednesdays. Taylor lifted the lid of a silver dish, noted the bright vegetables, and breathed in the steamy aroma.

Suddenly, the waiter grabbed him from behind. In a single movement, his arms were pulled behind his back and plastic handcuffs bound his wrists. Muscled to the edge of the patio by the waiter, he heard Maria shriek. A tight cord was quickly wrapped around, pinning Taylor to his abductor. Taylor's back pressed against the man's hard chest.

Over Maria's scream came the whop, whop of a helicopter. As the chopper bore down on them, Taylor's abductor pulled a cord attached to the pack on his back. Instead of the expected bubbly champagne, there was a whiplash jerk and a short high pitch whine as a parachute blew heavenward like it had been shot from a cannon, carrying the two men straight up.

A helicopter banked around and Taylor felt it somehow grab the parachute. Another jerk, stronger than the first, and he swung away from his fantasy and from his Maria. The wind took his breath and his feet kicked the air over the concrete streets and buildings passing rapidly beneath him. In that instant, he was certain nothing like this had ever happened to Aristotle Onassis.

After all the business opportunities, all the money, all the hours with his mistress, he was not the legendary Greek tycoon. He was just Arnold Taylor. And he was in trouble.

# Chapter Ninety-four

Marc grabbed Lei's hand and pulled her to a hiding place near the door. "It's gonna get loud and dangerous. When the guards come looking I want you out of the way." Opening a metal locker, he ushered her inside. "Stay here."

Before he could change his own mind, Marc jogged to the machine and initiated the sequence for simultaneous explosions at the same time the city fireworks would begin. The noise he made inside would not be detected as quickly as it would without everyone's attention on the pyrotechnics. Anything visual from the lab would be camouflaged by the light of the official display aimed over the water outside the building.

It was now or never and Marc chose now. The sound was deafening. The outburst felt like being inside a fourth of July display. Dodging sparks and debris, Marc pressed himself out of sight.

With a start, the sleeping guard jumped to his feet as the second guard groggily stumbled through the door. Both men held their guns, searching for a target. Yelling, the two raced forward into the acrid smoke, searching and calling for Marc and the hidden Lei.

This was his chance. Marc slipped out the door behind them. He turned away from his usual route to and from the lab, knowing there was nothing between the lab and his living quarters that would do him any good. He had no idea what lay at the opposite end except the security men Lei had warned him about.

"There are a lot of weapons," Lei had told him. That sounded promising. Right now he could use the American cavalry or at least a sturdy tank.

Dashing down the wide hall, Marc panicked. Hearing something amiss, two guards were running toward him. Looking back, he saw light flash through the smoke that billowed from the lab. The building shook as more explosions rocked the foundations.

Yelling, the guards drew their guns and rushed upon him. In that moment, Marc began yelling and pointing to the laboratory.

"You think you can kidnap whoever you want," he hollered. "There!" He pointed back where he had come. "There's your new weapon. I hope you all go to hell with it."

From the lab, a guard emerged, staggering and coughing. Choking, he tried to gulp in a great lungful of air. The two soldiers who had just come upon the scene looked from their collapsed comrade to Marc.

"You people are crazy." Marc waved his arms in expansive circles at the noise and smoke pouring toward them. More words tumbled out, hysterical gibberish spewed from his mouth like the panorama bursting forth in the lab.

Large black boots thundered past him. Stunned, Marc watched the soldiers run into the smoking laboratory. Surprised that his captors neither shot nor corralled him back into a locked cell, Marc seized the opportunity and bolted down the hall in the direction the two armed men had just come from.

# Chapter Ninety-five

Mallory watched the video again. Her research had located the former USPTO employee responsible for the initial leaks of patent information with military significance. This interview confirmed her preliminary theory. Patents vital to national security, like the superior jet engine currently propelling Asian military aircraft, were being compromised inside the Patent and Trademark office.

Having her conjecture confirmed was a boost for her tormented self-confidence as a research analyst with the Bureau. The corollary she was searching for, yearned for like an addict for the next hit, was concrete information that would lead her to Marc. Today.

Retired from USPTO, Arnold Taylor had made major changes in his lifestyle, changes that included a large amount of money in a secondary bank account. Follow the money. The money trail was a never-fail source in her research. Especially with criminals that were not astutely shrewd. Manipulated and used, pompous Taylor was self-deceived into thinking he was some sort of brilliant spy that absconded with the Crown Jewels. With Hatim

Saad dead, Mallory investigated past and present employees that would be likely candidates for Saad's predecessor. Taylor had left a trail for her to follow as clear as footprints in the Indiana snow. As project manager, Deverell had fed the lead to field agents who paid a surprise visit to the retiree.

Once she had the video of their interrogation, Mallory sent a text to Deverell. Her supervisor was out of the office on fieldwork. She chose a location that was convenient for both of them. *Meet me. July 30.*

In an empty coliseum, Mallory viewed the video, concentrating on each word. There had to be additional information she could exploit in her desperate search for her brother. Realizing she had the episode memorized, she got up from the plastic folding seat and deposited quarters in a vending machine. A root beer for her and a diet coke for her boss. Maybe that was a mistake. If he took very long in arriving, the coke would be warm. She groaned. She was second-guessing her every decision. Terrified she would make another bad choice that further endangered Marc. Or she might send the investigation in the wrong direction. She could mess this up even more than she already had. Hyper-cautious, she couldn't even decide when to buy a soda.

Walking, she circled the large arena several times. She knew if her thoughts kept ricocheting like a bullet in a submarine, she was no good to anyone. Not to herself. Not to her team. Certainly not to Marc.

In the upper stands, a door opened. Light and Deverell came into the cement corridor. The previous July, their department had busted jewel thieves at the National Barrel Racing Youth World Competition. Under the guise of cowboy bling, stolen diamonds were transported in plain sight at the coliseum through sales vendors that lined the upper floor. From the date she texted, he knew where to find her.

Chomping a wad of gum, her boss took the cold soda she offered. "You found something."

# Chapter Ninety-six

A set of double doors, much like the ones that closed off the lab, stood before Marc. There was no turning back and he had limited time. From his pocket he fished the name badge manufactured with Hebron's ingenuity and pressed it to the scanner. The door opened. In that instant, Marc promised himself if he made it home, he would bring in the random-thinking redhead student inventor as some kind of business partner.

Inside the cavernous room, Marc surveyed a well-organized system. Military weapons were neatly arranged. Shipping boxes sat on saw horses. Half were sealed closed. Lettering was printed in different languages. Others were filled with weapons but topless. One row of crates was empty. The Chinese, Marc observed, were involved in several businesses including packing and shipping illegal arms to foreign entities. What a surprise. It was a hunch, but Marc doubted any of the shipments went to allies of the United States.

From an open crate, Marc quickly lifted a Lightweight Antitank Weapon. Not much more than a strengthened fiberglass tube, the LAW was designed to shoot once and then be discarded. Dr. Thurmond collected World War II militaria. From a gun show, the two had brought home an expended launcher that Marc had converted into an air-soft weapon. Though provided by the Chinese, these copies of a U.S. weapon would appear to be supplied by the United States. Arm America's enemies, and if the illegal shipments were intercepted, the U.S. looked bad. It was a win-win for China.

With this one-shot firearm, Marc would have a single opportunity to use the M72 LAW. At five-and-a-half pounds each, he slung two over his right shoulder to rest against his back. A third he hung over his left shoulder, the canister across his chest. They were cold. Shifting his body weight to accommodate the load, he hoisted a fourth launcher in his hands and raced back to the laboratory.

The guard who had staggered outside of the lab lay in the hall in a fetal position. Marc couldn't tell if he was alive and didn't care as long as he was out of commission. One down. Somewhere in the smoke and debris were three men who would like to find him.

"It's either you or me." Dropping to one knee, he shouldered the weapon he carried, aimed, and pulled the trigger.

The blast was raucous. The ancient structure's far wall erupted and collapsed. As the dust cleared, he tossed away the used LAW. From his right shoulder, he retrieved a second launcher, aimed, and fired again. Satisfied that the hole was large enough for his machine to have flown through, he ran toward the opening he had just created.

Something caught him by the ankle and Marc came down hard, his face smashing into the ground. Powerful hands rolled him over and began to pummel his body. Before he could react, his attacker connected a powerful fist with a missile launcher strung across Marc's middle. There was a scream of pain. With all his might, Marc swung the empty launcher he still grasped and slammed his assailant across the temple. The guard rolled to the floor. Marc rose up on one knee and swung the weapon wild a second time at the rushing attacker. Smashing the man's cheekbone, the blow sent him to the ground, blood pooling around his face.

Scrambling to his feet, Marc hurried to the far side of the building where his two missiles had done their work. A military boot, the foot still inside, lay caught on the jagged edge of the opening. Marc dropped the empty LAW as bile rose in his throat. Catching his breath, he tore his eyes away from the grizzly sight. One guard out of commission in the hall, one bleeding on the ground, and a third had been unfortunate to be in the path of one of his missile shots. Three down.

Outdoors, the fresh air was thrilling to behold. Marc realized he hadn't seen the outside world in a terribly long time. Midwest winters were infamous for weeks of skies in what Mallory termed Indiana-gray. It was a color as defined as Payne's gray and cadmium orange were to a portrait artist, but now seeing the immenseness of the horizon in the twilight was a shock. He blinked several times and squinted to absorb what he was seeing. Before him lay the world's largest cargo port in the emerging global city.

Lei had said they were in Shanghai. The vast body of water that coursed past the ancient temple-turned-military-development-complex would be the mouth of the Yangtze. The tang of salt sea air assured him that the broader body of water beyond was the East China Sea and then the Pacific Ocean. The same Pacific Ocean that caressed the west coast of the United States, half a world away. China had been an exotic destination on the opposite side of the globe. A place Marc had planned to visit.

"Not exactly how I planned to get here." There were a number of sites he had anticipated touring. Modern Pudong with its Oriental Pearl Tower, the historic and renovated Bund, and City God Temple. "Not this trip."

He took in his surroundings and made quick calculations. Charging back to the Meissner Device, he examined it like a pool shark considers the perfect angle for a combo. Drawing a third weapon, Marc fired the missile launcher. As hoped, the explosive tore into his project with enormous force, and propelled the largest part of the machine through the newly blasted outlet. Like a wounded falcon, the Meissner Device convulsed over the opaque Yangtze and slammed into the unforgiving water. Hot from the explosion, the shattered pieces sizzled and groaned, listed sideways, and vanished below the surface.

Turning, Marc saw Lei behind him. Fear showed on her face but she wasn't looking at the water. Following her line of vision, he spotted a guard aiming his sidearm at Marc's head.

"Zhi!" Lei's cry distracted the man for the split second Marc needed. Screaming at the top of his lungs, he ducked and ran straight at the gunman. A gunshot rang out and Marc felt fire along his left shoulder that spun him like a top. The momentum carried him around a second time and he swung the empty launcher like Babe Ruth at bat. The weapon caught the gunman across the chest. Grunting as the air was knocked from his lungs, the guard fired a wild shot from his pistol. Mustering all his strength, Marc swung the launcher again. This time he connected with the man's jaw and heard the sickening sound of crushing bone.

With a nightmarish yell drowned in blood collecting in his throat, the man whirled like a kite without a tail. Teeth falling from his mouth, he slammed into a workstation and slid to the floor.

Breathing hard, Marc dropped the empty launcher tube that also served as a baseball bat. He mounted a forklift and dragged the residual section of his creation through the hole in the building and unceremoniously dumped it into the filthy harbor. In moments, the mangled machinery disappeared under the dark surface, a string of bubbles marking its descent. Beside him, Lei tossed the expended LAWs she had gathered into the Yangtze.

Retrieving the last launcher, he carefully aimed it above the hole with the intent to cause the most structural damage, and fired. The ancient building shuddered and large sections cascaded down. Marc threw the launcher, bloody from his shoulder wound, into the water outside where it quickly disappeared under the swirling current.

In the distance, came the tinny sound of sirens. He figured the fireworks had bought him some time but despite the distraction, the neighbors had noticed the noise, the smoke, strange happenings along the water, or all three. Would Colonel Yao be on his way?

Running back from the destruction, Marc grabbed Lei's wrist. "Come on, we gotta go!"

Urgently, he pulled her back along the hallway and into the

weapons room. He took her to a 42 by 48 box on a footprint pallet that Marc guessed was the next to ship. A drill was nearby where a worker had left it until the next day's work. Quickly, Marc bored breathing holes where they would not be immediately noticed.

Turning to Lei, he saw she was trembling. His hands on her slender shoulders, he steadied her and looked intently into her eyes. "It's okay for you to go back. No one will blame you. You will be safe." He waved an arm at the pallet behind him. "This is a risk you don't have to take. Now go!"

She gritted her teeth to stop their nervous chattering and clenched her fists against the involuntary quaking. "I'm going with you."

There was no more time to argue. Marc lifted Lei into his arms and set her inside an empty crate. "Lay down," he ordered. "Stay still and be quiet. Act like a crateful of missile launchers."

Her eyes large with excitement and fright, she did exactly as she was told. "What about you?"

He hooked a thumb at the nearby crate. "I'm dressing up like a load of AK-47s." Marc reached for the propane driven nail gun and secured the lid into place to resemble the other packed crates.

He double-checked that Lei was safely boxed and climbed into his own wooden box. Pulling the top until it dropped into place, he felt for the nail gun he'd brought inside. In the cramped quarters, he managed to crate himself securely inside what he gambled would be their transport to freedom.

# Chapter Ninety-seven

Yao struggled to appear calm. To maintain control. He was enjoying his second gin and the attention of a lovely woman at a formal celebration event for those of his political station when an aide had discreetly whispered that something unexplained was taking place at the lab.

He had hurried back to the temple. Like countless times before, he entered the main door. But unlike other visits, the ancient building's tang of age and incense had been replaced with an odor of battlefield explosives. Outside the lab, medical personnel were hoisting an unconscious guard onto a stretcher. Inside, the Colonel stepped over the still body of another guard and rudely pushed through the stunned workers blocking his path. His gaze went first to the large hole in the wall, then to the empty area at the room's center.

The bodies of two guards lay in unnatural positions, and someone with a medical bag was bending over the nearest.

Touching the blackened floor, he rubbed the ash between thumb and middle fingers. He circled the perimeter of the large burned mark. Last, he examined the hole through the exterior wall. A hole large enough to fly the device through. The others stood still, waiting.

Had the inventor blasted through the wall to provide an exit for the machine? Where had he gone with it? How far was the Meissner Device capable of traveling? Or was there something else in all the destruction? While working under Yao's observation, Marc Wayne had been able to procure a means of escape. And he took the device with him.

Furiously, he barked orders. The others jumped and scurried from the room. Clenching his fists at his sides, Yao marched back to the door where he turned to slowly survey the large laboratory where he had invested his time and influence in recent years. He swore loudly, the angry words echoing in the hollows of the previously bustling center of new technology.

In the hall, men assembled for his instructions. "Divide into teams. Search the building." He glanced at the river through the opening in the far wall. "Search outside. Search everywhere."

He gave orders to notify other government and military personnel to be on the look out on land and above the ground.

Then he summoned the scientists. They arrived from various points in the city where families were celebrating National Day. Stunned by what they saw, each entered the lab and slowly tip-toed through the debris, trying to make sense of what had happened. Looking like ashamed puppies, they gathered before Yao.

"Study all his notes." Disdain dripping from his words, he wanted them to know how disappointed he was in their lack of achievement. "Find out how he made this work!"

# Chapter Ninety-eight

Mallory motioned Deverell to a row of empty seats and replayed the video on her phone. The spec ops guys had tugged a hood over Taylor's gray head and coptered him to the landing pad on a business building and into the hands of agents who pushed him, whining and tripping over his feet, down an elevator and into a small room. Shoved into a metal chair, he quaked as the hood was removed.

Blowing cigarette smoke, a guy whose face looked like he made side money in a boxing ring, leaned menacingly close to the slouched Taylor. The questioning began and when Taylor shook his head and spat in his captor's face, it was his last defiant act. He was backhanded. As a red welt rose across Taylor's cheekbone, a second guy laid out three rows of photos, and copies of bank and credit card statements. Proof that Taylor had been on the take and indulged himself with the pay-off of his betrayal. Now that Taylor was paying attention, the man with the paperwork waved a badge under the older man's panicked gaze.

Mallory tapped the screen. "This is the traitor that stole and sold the patent for the GE jet engine."

"To the Chinese?" Deverell popped the top and gulped the drink.

"Not directly."

"A middle man?"

She nodded.

"What else did we learn?"

"Shocked at all we knew about him, he began to comprehend the depth of the trouble he was in. The word espionage loosened his tongue. The news that his replacement had been killed, and that he could be next, motivated Taylor. He was all too eager to share what he knew in exchange for protection."

"The emperor's new clothes are a sham and our boys informed the emperor that he is naked." Deverell tipped back his head and finished the last of his diet coke. "What do you have so far?"

"We know Marc was taken by ambulance to Smith Field where he was airlifted to the west coast in a medical flight. We've tracked the pilot, and the accompanying doctor – if you can call him that. He's wearing an eye patch and under investigation with the medical licensing board." She pointed to the man on the video. "Now we've taken into custody the previous USPTO employee leak."

"What did you get from him?"

Mallory pocketed her cell phone. "We got a description of the guy who develops the contacts in the Patent office."

Deverell crushed the empty aluminum can. "Guys like Tim?"

She nodded. "Guys like Hatim Saad."

# Chapter Ninety-nine

His box was being pried open. Marc wasn't certain how long he had been cramped in the small rectangle except to know he was desperately thirsty. He squirmed, trying to encourage blood flow to his numb feet. Cramped, different parts of his body had taken turns screaming in agony during the transport. Mercifully a few areas had eventually lost feeling due to pinched circulation. His neck, shoulders, and hips hadn't been that courteous and the pain was intense.

With a final snap, the wooden lid broke open and Marc squeezed his eyes closed against the sudden rush of blinding sunlight.

"Son of a…" the oath was seamlessly streamed into another language. Marc guessed it was Arabic. He recognized cheekia, slang for guns. And dhimmi, a word meaning Christian set apart for religious tolerance by the Koran.

Someone roughly grabbed his shirtfront and jerked Marc upright. Spasms wracked his legs with searing pain. Dragged out of the box and to his feet, Marc was weak-kneed and aware of an AK-47 pressed into his ribs.

Behind him he heard the top pulled off the second box and the lewd cries of men who found lovely Lei where smuggled weapons should have been. He didn't know the language, but Marc knew the tone in those voices. When he heard Lei cry out in protest, he wheeled and lunged at the swarthy man who had his hands on her breasts.

"Leave her alone." Marc barreled into the handful of men around the standing, but weaving girl. Strong arms grabbed Marc and held him. The circle of men laughed as he struggled against them while their comrade eyed the girl. A large bearded man moved in to stroke the girl's dirty, but smooth cheek.

"Don't touch her." Marc yelled again.

Lei slapped the man's hand. Angered and humiliated in front of the others, the bully quickly grabbed her wrists and spun her around so her back was pressed against his chest. Her eyes wide with fear, Lei struggled. He laughed and pressed his body against hers. As he gyrated against her, the others laughed and joked with words Marc couldn't translate but still understood.

With his free hand, the bully reached down to the front of his pants.

"No!" Marc screamed against the violation of Lei. Lei who had trusted him to get her safely back to the United States and the man she loved. Jerking free from the men who held him, Marc charged Lei's attacker like the Wabash Cannonball. Half the other man's size, Marc's momentum carried him headfirst into the brute's kidney. Off balance, the target toppled off balance, and the two sprawled on the unyielding ground where Marc battered the man's temple in hopes of evening the odds against his superior strength. A thunderous boot to his ribs sent Marc rolling in the dust. He looked up just in time to see the butt of the rifle before it crashed against his head.

# Chapter One hundred

"Yala, yala," demanded a man's voice from somewhere nearby. "What have you found?"

Marc groaned and rubbed his head. He winced when his fingers found a large goose egg that had risen along the side of his face.

"These two crates do not carry the weapons." A heavily accented voice gave the report. "Instead, we found these two stowaways."

For the second time, muscled arms grabbed Marc and jerked him to his feet. His head pounded and his vision swam. Squinting, Marc searched for Lei. She was near. The man with the lustful eyes that Marc had charged held her arms, but she appeared unmolested. Marc sagged with relief and turned his attention on the newcomer who stood in front of him.

Younger than Marc, this olive-skinned man was dressed like the Bedouins around him, only cleaner. Intelligent eyes regarded Marc though his words addressed the others. "So you decided to rape the girl and then see who these people are and what they can tell you about your missing weapons?"

The others shifted uncomfortably.

"Bachir," the man ordered. "Release her."

"But …"

The newcomer spit empty sunflower seeds on the bigger man's shoes. With a look, he silenced the opposition. "Where will she go, my friend? Can she outrun your jeeps in this desert? Even your surefooted donkey?"

Lei was released. Cheeks aflame, she adjusted her clothes and came to Marc's side.

"Forgive us," the man said, "for not extending traditional desert hospitality to our guests." His words generated hurried movement among several men. "I am Adi."

Marc shook off the unwanted grip of his captors. "Marc. And this is Lei."

A breeze blew from behind them and Adi wrinkled his nose. "You have been in these shipments for awhile?"

"We are sorely in need of washing." Marc brushed at his shirt.

"Come." Adi turned and led the way.

Following their long-legged host, Marc eyed their surroundings. They were on a hillside overshadowed by higher hills fringing a canyon. Below, the rocky terrain flowed into a wide, dry wadi bed. Two donkeys, a camel, a rust-fringed Mitsubishi truck, and a dusty jeep were parked in the shadow of the hill they were making their way down. The threesome followed a shallow horizontal groove carved into the thirsty hillside. Gradually angling down, the man-made depression disappeared under the base of a rock-lined well.

Perched on the edge of the well, Adi tossed a bucket into the water below. Hand over hand, he pulled the rope that brought the filled container back to the top. Balancing the bucket on the rim, he removed the fabric tied about his head. He strained the water through his scarf into the trough of hewn rock that sat beside the well. Three times he repeated this process. With a wave of his hand, he indicated they should help themselves.

Marc put a hand on Lei's shoulder. "Go ahead."

She bent to splash water on her face and he saw she was trembling. Adi noticed too, and moved several paces away to allow them some privacy.

"I'm sorry." Marc spoke quietly. "Are you all right?"

She threw another handful of water on her face to camouflage the tears that were streaming down her cheeks. "Apes."

"Ugly apes."

Lei splashed water across her arms, rubbed her hands, and sat heavily on the well where she took deep breaths. Marc washed his own face, neck, and arms, grimacing when the water stung the wound on the side of his face. Noting the hole in his shirt, he cleaned the dried blood that had caked around his shoulder wound,.

Adi approached and they followed him to a colorful carpet someone had spread nearby. He motioned for them to sit. Their host sat cross-leg across from them. Dishes of hummus, flat bread, cheese, olives, and oranges were set between the three, along with bottled water and hot Turkish coffee. Eagerly, Marc and Lei dug into the food.

"Who are you and why are you here?" Adi waited with his question until they had finished eating.

Marc took a long drink of water. "I'd like to ask you the same thing."

Adi regarded them, his expression kind compared to the first men they had encountered. "What is that between you and me? Since you are enjoying my hospitality, I invite you to answer first."

# Chapter One hundred-one

Mallory entered the digital forensics department. The men and women who worked in this division were a breed apart. Actually, they often reminded Mallory of her equally unique brother, Marc. Academically brilliant, this group wasn't prone to invest much time or salary shopping the latest clothing fashions, but they easily wore classic styles of inimitable Birkenstocks, and khaki pants. Ball caps displayed the department's spirited rivalry over sports teams.

At Jimmy's workstation, the hyper computer genius spastically moved back and forth between two computers, typing on each keyboard with a swiftness that sounded like a machine gun with a silencer. At her arrival, Jimmy put up his index finger, indicating he needed another couple minutes to complete what he was working on.

Mallory held a finger to her lips as Deverell burst into the room. Oblivious, her supervisor planted himself in front of the concentrating Jimmy. "What do you have for us, Jimmy?"

The computer forensics expert ignored the interruption, giving a final tap on the keyboard with the flourish of a composer bringing an orchestra concert to a theatric end. He swiveled his chair and acknowledged the two spectators.

"Look at this." Jimmy pulled an earbud from one ear and Mallory heard classic Rolling Stones before he turned off the muted tunes. "Steganography algorithms by definition have a vast variety of applications. So far I've identified over 600."

Deverell whistled through his teeth.

"But they all work on basically the same principle."

Mallory leaned closer. "Which is?"

"To embed a message in an image –"

"An image like a cat?" Mallory was hungry to connect anything to her search for her brother.

"Like the cat." Jimmy pressed a button and the now familiar picture of the kitten filled the nearest computer screen. "A commonly used steganography algorithm called LSB takes advantage of the way computers digitally encode color. The algorithm hides the fugitive file inside the noncritical bits of color pixels."

"Noncritical? I thought they were all necessary." Deverell loaded cinnamon flavored gum into his mouth.

Jimmy shook his head. "Like croutons on a salad, these are the least important information in a pixel."

"I like croutons," Deverell said.

"Fattening." Jimmy circled a finger in front of the picture. "See the gray in the cat's fur?"

Deverell studied the screen. "Ninety percent of the fur is gray."

"Exactly," Jimmy said. "Every pixel is a number. The gray is coded as a number much like 00 10 01 00. But by changing the least significant bits – in this case the last two – the programmer produces a one-millionth of a color change."

Mallory leaned closer. "That's so absurdly subtle that your eye cannot detect it."

"Go on." Deverell tapped his foot.

"The steganography application weaves the secret message into the least significant bits of the image." The digital forensics expert looked at his audience with expectation. "Understand?"

"Doesn't the alteration show up in the process of sending it?" Mallory listed on her fingers, "What about compression? Or different formats?"

Jimmy shook his head. "The image file is unaltered in variables such as size, JPEG, in lossy compression or in lossless compression."

"Okay, that's how Hatim delivered the information. How does the receiver unlock the message," Mallory wanted to know.

"The receiver of the message has the original image and he uses an unlocking algorithm to locate the stowaway bits in the cat image," Jimmy indicated the picture on the second computer's screen, "and uses them to reconstruct the secret message."

Mallory caught herself twirling her hair and covered the nervous tick with a quick scratch on her ear. Jimmy had proven her theory. Patent information vital to national security was indeed being leaked to enemies of the United States. Thanks to the work of this department, now she knew the vehicle used to transfer the information in the patents before they could be developed on American soil. It was reassuring that her analysis of the situation had been right on target.

"Nice work, Jimmy." If only she hadn't used Marc to gain the proof she needed.

Deverell clapped the computer forensics guy on the shoulder. "I need you to find a way to halt this method of transporting our secrets into the hands of enemy governments."

Excitement of the challenge gleamed in Jimmy's eyes. "I'll get right on it."

# Chapter One hundred-two

While the others went about their business at the desert site, Adi drove Marc and Lei out of the wilderness. The man Adi called Reuven sat in the passenger seat and Marc saw that he carried a handgun in his waistband.

Though their driver was calm, Marc found the breakneck speed along cliff edges, plunging into deep dry wadi beds, and climbing steep passes in the dusty vehicle to be unnerving. The few times Adi used the brakes, they piercingly squealed their protest at being coaxed to work.

At last an oasis appeared in the desert and the vehicle sped toward this place. As they drove, the desert gave way to acres of carefully maintained orchards, gardens tented under white plastic, and pasture animals grazing among sparse crops of wild grasses. The jeep parked beside a cluster of well-kept buildings.

"Where are we?" Lei's legs were wobbly after the wild ride. Before Marc could offer, Adi took her hand to steady the girl as she climbed from the jeep.

Their host gave a grand sweep with his free hand. "This is my home, my kibbutz."

"Kibbutz? I don't understand."

Adi looked to Marc who also shook his head.

The rusty truck parked behind them and three armed men took their places strategically positioned as they followed Adi at a distance.

Trailed by the brooding Reuven, Adi led the way. "In my country – "

"I assume we are in Israel," Marc interrupted.

The younger man nodded. "In Israel, some 117,300 people live in kibbutzim."

"How many kibbutz?" Lei was asking questions, which allowed Marc to scope the surroundings and take in whatever information he could gather at their urgent pace. He was assembling two lists in his head, one of possible materials and the other of people who may or may not be helpful in his quest to get to Mallory.

"From the Golan Heights in the north to the Red Sea in the south, there are 268 such communities. Some have less than 100 people, most have several hundred, and in a few cases, there are over 1000 residents in the kibbutz."

Marc surveyed what appeared to be a modern hotel and stylish restaurant. Shops and guest cottages circled an adjacent building and from the people coming and going in swimsuits, he gathered there must be an indoor pool.

He was in a pocket of civilization and that meant phones. The ability to make calls. The thought jolted him. Who should he contact? Who would be able to help him find Mallory? Could he reach the people she worked with at the FBI? Were they already searching for his sister? Their co-worker?

Adi and Lei were still talking, and Marc tuned back in as their host answered her questions. "Most of the kibbutzim, 80 percent, were founded before the establishment of the State of Israel in 1948."

"Who were the founders?"

Adi walked beside Lei as he explained. "A century ago, a group of young Jewish immigrants came here from Eastern Europe. Inspired by a mixture of Zionist and socialist ideals, they established the first kyutza on the shores of the Sea of Galilee."

Marc was half-listening. He needed to know all he could about his new predicament. He also had to help his sister.

"Kyutza?" Lei tried the new word.

"Hebrew for group," their host continued. "As membership grew, the name was changed to kibbutz."

"Which means?"

"Community."

Longing to be back in Indiana, Marc considered how differently the Midwest farms appeared compared to the Middle Eastern crops at this place. "Do you support yourselves through farming?" Was Mallory still in Indiana?

"Initially, yes." Their guide had slowed his long strides to accommodate Lei who still moved stiffly after her time in the crate. "Young Jewish pioneers acquired land by the Jewish National Fund. They reclaimed the soil of their ancient homeland, and forged a new way of life. Inexperienced with physical labor and lacking agricultural knowledge, they faced a desolate land neglected for centuries. Water was scarce. Funds were scarcer. Against these challenges, they worked hard and developed thriving communities that played a dominant role in the establishment and growth of the fledgling state."

They arrived at a building. The entryway smelled of water and humidity. Behind glass walls on the left was a workout room populated with modern exercise equipment. A physical therapist coached a teen through strengthening motions. The girl's bald head told Marc she was recovering from cancer treatment.

On the right, three shallow pools of differing sizes were serene under thin clouds of steam that rose from their surfaces. In the nearest pool, an instructor led a class in cardiovascular training. The chests of several participants bore the tell-tale scar of heart surgery.

"Later generations convinced our parents that farming was not enough in modern society. Each kibbutz established a business as well. One makes shoes that are sold worldwide, another developed a drip irrigation system. One provides seeds and specialized green houses, another telecommunication, another software, and yet another medical equipment."

"Yours is tourism?" Marc noted that of the men that shadowed Adi, only the scowling Reuven followed them inside.

"Very lucrative when our enemies are not raining missiles on us from the sky." He indicated the pools. "Guests from many countries come to rejuvenate in the minerals and waters."

Marc glanced sidelong at Adi's companion. "It didn't look like you were booking tourists in the desert when you found us."

As he expected, his comment generated a reaction. Reuven's hand shot out and gripped Marc around the neck. "You know nothing about what we do." His voice was low and Marc read the threat in the brooding man's eyes.

"Relax, cousin," Adi addressed.

"He asks too many questions." Reuven locked eyes with Marc but spoke to Adi.

"As I would expect you to do in similar situations."

The man sneered a silent warning at Marc before releasing his hold.

Marc rubbed his neck. "Do you cage him at the end of the day? Throw him a hunk of raw meat?"

Adi laughed and slung an arm around his cousin's shoulders. "He's a good man, this one."

His cousin easily shrugged off Adi's arm and glowered at Marc.

# Chapter One hundred-three

Pow. Pow. Despite the earplugs, Mallory could hear the muffled pop of the Glock as she squeezed off each round. Keeping her focus on the target in the firing range, she ignored the group of tourists behind the sound-proof glass. Agent hopefuls and FBI wanna-bes led the tours that included the museum in the lobby.

Prior to 9/11, congressmen and senators provided arrangements for citizens in their constituency to visit the FBI building. Now, those rare opportunities were available only to VIPs. Visitors wanted to do three things at the Hoover Building; ask what the FBI did, view items once belonging to high-profile criminals brought to justice, and watch someone fire rounds at the indoor shooting range.

She could imagine the answer to the first question. "Spies. Terrorists. Hackers. Pedophiles. Mobsters. Gang leaders and serial killers. We investigate them all, and many more besides." In the display room, the group could see John Dillinger's bullet proof vest he was not wearing the lethal night agents waylaid him as he exited a Chicago theater, as well as his death mask molded from his face as he lay in the morgue. Much to her chagrin, she was fulfilling the third expectation.

But Mallory wasn't here for anyone else. Not even to practice her skills. Frustrated, Mallory just wanted to blow something to Mars. It was that or cry. And she wasn't going to cry. Certainly not where anyone would see. With explosive frustration as her companion, she was decimating a paper silhouette.

Parking the Glock on the shelf, she picked up a .45. This piece was a standard for the military spec ops. Resettling the plastic earmuffs that served as hearing protection, she gripped the gun with both hands. Focused on the front sight, she squeezed off two shots in succession – a double tap. She fired until the slide locked back on the pistol. She removed the empty magazine and flipped the wall switch. A wire trolley sped the paper target to her. Slightly low and left of center, seven holes peppered the silhouette.

Reloading, Mallory purposely avoided thinking through the list of leads the agency had gathered in their search for her brother. In their driveway basketball court back home, while playing one on one with her, Marc used to suddenly stop. Annoyed that her brother was not engaged in the game, that was her favorite opportunity to bounce the ball off his head.

"Okay, genius. What bolt of inspiration just hit you?"

He would look at her, that sense of discovery lighting his eyes. Marc had learned that when he reached an impasse in the problem solving process, it was time to do something completely unrelated. Coincidently, while he was resting and refreshing, the solution often appeared. Unbidden. Unforced, and of its own accord, like a child peering out from a hiding place.

She switched from shooting at a stationary target to the faster pace of aiming at a moving target. Her adrenalin kicked in as the target rapidly came to her like an assailant would do. Her reaction had to be jaguar fast. Especially with an audience of tourists watching. She didn't want to miss while being observed by friends and network connections of the D.C. elite.

Network connections. That was it. Now she knew where to look for the next clue as she hunted the trail that would lead her to Marc. DHU Aerocomposites was an Asian company with suspicious dealings. Their cargo ship, Shanghai Sumi was searched during the target window after Marc's disappearance. Searched by the Coast Guard. Though the report said nothing was found, the boarding team may have caught something on their helmet camera that was overlooked or not recognized.

# Chapter One hundred-four

The next morning, Lei rose early. She had enjoyed a solid sleep in fresh clothing, stretched out on crisp sheets until early this morning when nightmares about the lecherous Bachir's hands on her body jarred her awake.

Marc had been in a heated argument with Adi last night. While Marc insisted he had to make contact with the states immediately, Adi calmly repeated that his guest must wait. All would happen in due time. Lei was becoming anxious that they had traded one controlled situation for a new one, and Marc was accusing Adi of exactly that, when a woman named Esther took Lei's arm and led her away from the men who were deciding her fate.

Esther brought Lei to this cottage consisting of a large bath, and an inviting bedroom and sitting area. Lei noted that, while not being obvious, one of Adi's men was always nearby.

An extended soak in a fragrant tub imbued with Salty Sea minerals had been followed by a generous application of luxurious soap and soothing lotions. Clean and sleepy, Lei had come out of the bathroom to find Marc laying on the couch, his back to her. She hoped he was finally getting some much overdue rest. Seeing he was showered, in clean clothes, and his shoulder wound had been properly bandaged, she covered him with a blanket and climbed into bed.

Now, in the moments just after dawn, she stepped outside quietly, so as to not disturb Marc's sleep. She was curious to see more of where she was and put yesterday's fright behind. There was something exotic and ancient in this land. Like an old soul. Despite the dangers they had faced the day before, she felt drawn to know more of this strange place. Close to her own age, Adi captured her imagination. He embodied an authority even those older desert ruffians respected.

Several others were already moving about the kibbutz. Cheerfully calling greetings, men and women made their way to the gardens and greenhouses. Young women with energetic children talked and laughed as they went into the dining hall, the building where she and Marc had eaten their fill of fresh vegetables, succulent beef, and sweet challah bread last night.

In a sitting area among the paths, not far from her room, Lei spotted Adi. Like Adi's gloomy shadow, his cousin was there as well as the stately Esther. Seeing her now from this distance, she shared Adi's handsome features. Or he had hers since she was older. These three were in deep conversation with several older men. Lei turned her steps in the opposite direction.

Swooping among the bushes and branches, birds sang birdsong greetings to the rising sun. Lei heard someone whistle an echo to the song of the birds. She bent to smell a flower. Returning to her path, she was startled to find a man standing in front of her.

"Good morning." Adi plucked a bloom. "If I may?" He gently tucked the flower behind her ear, considered his handiwork and smiled. "You do the flower a great service."

Lei bobbed her head. "Thank you."

"Would you walk with me?"

Feeling shy, she nodded and fell into step beside the graceful man, observing the activity of the kibbutz as the gem in the desert rose with the sun.

"How are you this day?"

"Much improved over yesterday." She felt her face flame as the memory of that horrible man's hands on her body flooded back. Quickly she pushed away the accompanying fear by changing the topic. "Though, I have many questions."

"Perhaps I have some answers."

"The people here appear healthy and happy."

"Our community is based on common ownership of the means of production, consumption, and education." Adi spoke the words like a catechism. "Conferring together, we make decisions by majority vote and each bears responsibility for all."

"Is this communism?"

Adi shook his head. "A kibbutz is a voluntary collective built around self-labor, equality, and cooperation."

"Voluntary?" This didn't make sense when she and Marc were kept here against their desire to immediately return to the United States. Admittedly, this felt different from their treatment under The People's Republic. And she knew Israel to be a free country. But why was liberty withheld from her and from Marc?

"Completely. People often come to a kibbutz to rest, and never leave. Children born here are educated at university –"

"Like you?"

He returned the greeting of a pretty young woman who blushed and hurried on her way. "I attended university sponsored by the kibbutz, but I was not born here. My mother was. She left for awhile. We returned when I was a boy. After graduating university, members may bring their education back for the good of the community or they may go into the world. Like my mother, many return."

Lei considered the simple structures around her. "There is a peace here. A quiet joy."

Adi smiled. "That is what attracts others to kibbutzim. Instead of private wealth, each member is responsible for the needs of the members and their families. All possessions are generally owned."

A jeep drove past and disappeared into the surrounding

wilderness. Lei looked longingly after it. "All possessions are generally owned," she echoed and faced Adi. "Then we can use a vehicle to reach a city and ..."

Adi put up a hand. "As I explained to Marc, that may not be the safest action for you."

Lei's shoulders slumped. "But you said ..." she struggled to make clear her need.

"I said each member is responsible for the needs of the members and their families. You are my guest and I will do the same for you."

"But what does that mean for me? For Marc?" Eager to get to the United States, to a familiar and safe place, she didn't bother to conceal her frustration. "Are we free to go? Is being here voluntary or are Marc and I captives?"

He pointed to a stone bench and reluctantly she sat. Adi straddled the bench so he faced her. "It means I will see to your safety and your well-being. It means you may have to be patient."

She gazed off into the distance, calculating the chances of either stealing a vehicle, or walking out of this place. Adi must have read her thoughts.

"Lei," his voice was like velvet over steel. "We are a long way from a city. This kibbutz is the deepest in the Negev. The desert is the large heart of my country. Our closest neighbor is the Salty Sea."

When she frowned, he clarified. "Outsiders call it the Dead Sea."

She looked toward the rugged cliffs beyond the gently tended fields. He followed her gaze and pointed to a high overhang, distant yet close enough that she could see two wild goats frisking their way to the top. Balanced on tiny hooves, the smallish animals gained the peak by way of the gradual rise on the backside of the half mountain. Now perched on the edge and silhouetted in the morning light, the goats overlooked the vast canyon far below and rimmed on the opposite side by abrupt crags.

Adi turned her attention to a place behind the goats. At first Lei could only see rocks. Then a stealthy movement caught her eye.

A mountain lion was also watching the goats. Slinking swiftly behind cover of boulders, the predator narrowed the distance to its prey.

"They're trapped." Lei shuddered. Perhaps one would escape while the lion took down its companion. "The lion has cut off their route to escape back the way they came."

"So it appears."

Closer, the lion crouched, preparing to spring. Then the two stepped over the edge. But rather than tumbling head over hooves into the abyss, one followed the other down an invisible path. Clinging to the side of the seemingly impassable precipice, the surefooted goats casually wove a zigzag pattern that took them to safety. Cheated from her breakfast, the lion swung a claw over the edge but could only watch the animals disappear from view. With a cry that echoed off the crags, the big cat returned to the hunt.

On their way here, the jeep had bounced over rocky paths invisible to Lei. Like rainwater following the unmarked trail from a mountaintop until it reached the cistern in the low country, Adi had steered the vehicle through dry wadis, around steep turns, and past small hillside patches of grass where wild deer-like creatures grazed. She realized that Adi knew the desert like those cunning goats.

"I would counsel you to have a knowledgeable guide if you left here." He touched her chin and turned her face to his. "The desert is a dangerous and unforgiving place. But worse than that, I believe there are dangerous men looking for you. I am more concerned about them than our wilderness."

# Chapter One hundred-five

Adi led Lei to the dining hall. "Most kibbutzim are similarly laid out." Along the way, he described the buildings they passed. "Communal facilities such as the dining hall, auditorium, offices, and library are at the center, ringed by members' homes and gardens. Sports and educational facilities are beyond these, and industrial buildings and agricultural land make up the perimeter."

Inside the hall, delicious aromas and warmth thawed the early morning chill from Lei's body. Their plates piled with colorful variety, people sat in groups and chatted, some in English, many in Hebrew. A few sat alone with a book as their breakfast partner.

Buffet style fish, cheese, hummus, fruit, and pickled eggs were abundantly heaped on trays. Hot and cold cereal was available next to juice and coffee. Adi handed a warm dish to Lei and stepped aside to allow her to go ahead of him. As she made her selections she was aware of curious glances from those in the hall. Though her hair was dark like theirs, she looked nothing like these Jewish people. At least at college in the states, there were several other Asian students attending. Even a professor or two.

Her plate filled with persimmons, dates, eggs, slices of firm white cheese, and small smoked fish, she allowed Adi to chose their table near a window.

Suddenly, the serene morning was upset by a commotion at the entrance. Everyone's attention was on the unusual scene and Lei's fork froze halfway to her mouth. In a jumble of arms and legs, Marc was pushed into the room.

# Chapter One hundred-six

Yao's superiors were not pleased. They invested time, manpower, and finances in the Colonel and this project. They gave him the moon and expected him to produce the sun in return. But there were no results. No military superiority. The entire episode had turned out disastrously and they blamed him.

The blame was not the issue. That was characteristic. For every debacle there was a scapegoat. Assign fault to another lower on the food chain, mete out humiliating and destructive punishment, and a vacuum opened for the next ambitious comrade to do the impossible – to sell their soul to please the unappeasable.

Yao lit a thin Cuban cigar and poured a second shot of tequila. Night was closing in and he didn't bother to chase it away by turning on a light. Tipping back his head he swallowed the fiery liquid and slammed down the shot glass. It landed on the mail tray, rolled off the table, and clanged to the floor.

The mail. Neglected for days. Yao fingered the stack of envelopes and recognized the familiar thickness of his father's usual communication. Suddenly he yearned for the comfort and innocence of the small village. Shut off from the world, the microcosm of culture felt contained and controlled. Separated from the global playing field, the problems of that community centered around the base concern of staying alive. Their needs were for food, clothing, and shelter. Simple. Easy.

Sighing, he reached for the lamp and turned it on. In the circular glow of the electric bulb, he slid an ivory opener along the envelope's edge.

The shaky penmanship told of seasonal events in the farming village, news about a new baby recently born, and updates on the health of Yao's mother and father. "The medicine you kindly provide has not arrived. Perhaps you can see to this? Not for me, of course, but your mother is in agonizing pain."

Yao swore. Rheumatoid arthritis had anchored itself in his mother's body after her brutal beating. A nasty and debilitating condition that wracked her body, and alienated her from the comfort and loving touch of those most dear to her. The physical dictator caused her to be unable to tolerate soft human touch or even the feel of her bed and blankets against her skin.

Punishing him for the American's escape was predictable. Now Yao understood the depth of his superior's displeasure and how cruel and far reaching was their castigation. His parents would be punished for his failure.

# Chapter One hundred-seven

Two men brought Marc to Adi. Lei recognized them as part of the cluster Adi was talking with earlier this morning. Close behind was an older man. Lei watched Adi for signs of anger. But there were none as he stirred milk into his coffee.

The group reached their table. Adi waved Marc to a seat. "Please join us for breakfast."

Marc stood, defiant.

"Of course. First you must get your meal." He glanced to the older man. "Uncle, help him get his breakfast."

The older man grunted and steered the silent Marc to the buffet.

Fear rose in Lei's throat, making it impossible for her to swallow. What would happen to them now? Marc had done something that displeased the men who surrounded Adi. How would this impact their request for a speedy return to the United States?

At the buffet, Lei noted Marc neither took a plate or filled it. Uncle did the task and the other two men once more guided Marc to their table. Uncle's strong hand to Marc's shoulder dropped Marc into the seat next to Lei and he set the plate onto the table in front of the glowering inventor.

"Thank you, Uncle."

The older man nodded and disappeared out the door with the other two close behind.

Pushing his dish aside, Adi folded his hands on the table. "I take it you were borrowing one of our vehicles."

Marc scowled. "Until your goon stopped me."

"Actually Uncle is one of your countrymen."

"American?" Marc's eyebrows shot up.

"Indeed." Adi sipped his coffee. "He fought in your Viet Nam war. After the horrors he experienced there, he came here to rest and heal his soul."

"But he is still here," Lei said.

"For special reasons." Adi met Lei's eyes. "He fell in love with a beautiful Jewish girl. When he returned home to tell his parents he was converting to Judaism to marry, his mother wept uncontrollably."

"She didn't want to lose her son." Lei thought of the American boy she loved. Her father had been willing to let her follow her heart to the other side of the globe. Knowing he might see his only child rarely, that his grandchildren would be far away, her noble father had defied the control of his government and given her freedom to make her own choices.

"That's what Uncle thought, too, until his mother brought out an aged photo of a young woman holding an infant." He paused and Lei found herself leaning forward. "'Your mother' she said, 'asked me to take good care of you when she put you into my arms in Germany. You're not converting' she explained. 'You're Jewish.'"

"He belongs here." Lei glanced around at the families gathered for breakfast. She didn't have a place where she belonged.

"So Uncle has come home and we are grateful for his talents in our community."

"Some talents." Marc rolled his shoulder. "Gorilla warfare tactics."

"I'm not surprised that you were seeking a way to escape."

"You were expecting as much," Marc groused.

Adi indicated Marc's plate. "You will feel better after you eat."

"I'll feel better when I'm back home."

"Like the harvest, all in due time."

With his fork, Marc poked scrambled eggs. "Where's the ham and bacon?"

"According to scripture, we don't mix the meat of an animal with its milk. Therefore, we serve milk and cheeses with breakfast. In the evening, we have meats without diary products." He leaned back in his chair, at peace in contrast to Marc's agitation. Lei sympathized with Marc's drive to be back in control of his life and future. She wondered if Adi ever wrestled with the same frustration. It was hard to imagine.

Something beyond his desire to get home troubled Marc. His sleep last night had been restless. He had called out to an invisible enemy.

Marc flopped a small fish onto Adi's plate. "This is meat."

"Fish and eggs are neutral, and served with meat or dairy. But miniature cows are a completely different matter."

"Miniature cows are called veal back home." Marc emphasized the last word.

"A scripturally clean animal, cows are legal in Israel," Adi said.

"Pigs are quite legal in the U.S."

"Our national law forbids a pig's foot to touch Israeli soil."

"So no ham or bacon like we have freely in the States," Marc said.

"A sister kibbutz does a large tourist business. In response to the dietary requests of their customers, the kibbutz built an enclosed barn with a wooden floor several feet off the ground. Pigs are raised in that barn without ever touching Israeli soil."

"But they're still pigs," Marc said.

"They're referred to as miniature cows."

"A rose is a rose," Marc quoted, pushing around a persimmon with his fork.

Adi smiled. "And a pig is a pig."

"Does the government crack down on them? Or can they do what they want with their own property?" Stressing the last four words, Marc's eyes challenged the man across the table.

"Some things do not appear expedient at first." Adi met Lei's gaze. "The land in Israel belongs to the government. We rent but cannot own the ground because of what is happening in the United States."

Marc stared at his plate. "Much of the United States land is owned by foreigners, even foreign governments."

Their host finished his coffee. "We are a new nation and a small one. We cannot afford for any piece to belong to foreigners, especially those hostile to Israel. But we are also a people long experienced in negotiation and compromise. If we have miniature cows whose feet never touch Israeli dirt, what is that between us and our government?"

"The letter of the law rather than the spirit of the law," Marc said around a mouthful of cheerios.

Uncle returned and waited near the entrance. Lei considered the gray-haired man who had come to the kibbutz seeking rest for his soul, and had found his history, family, love, and belonging. She hoped her journey would have the same satisfying ending.

"I have work." Adi stood. "Uncle will show you the grounds. Once you have seen the layout, you will understand that it would be foolish, probably deadly for you to attempt again to leave here to find your way on your own through our wilderness." He locked eyes with Marc. "Please understand, the people who seek you are as deadly as our desert. And unlike our desert, they are evil."

# Chapter One hundred-eight

Keeping her expectant anticipation at bay, Mallory viewed the footage of the Coast Guard boarding of Shanghai Sumi. There was the strong possibility that Captain Gennett's report was accurate and there had been nothing suspicious on the boat.

She hoped she could use their eyes to see something they had missed. Gennett was well-respected in the service. Having caught the attention of his superiors, he was on a fast-track to a stellar military career. Gennett's boat currently ranked first in the Coast Guard fleet, with top scores in ship inspections. Personnel consistently placed high in skills. When other boats proved to be poor performers, Gennett's crew often got bumped to take the assignment. That reputation weighed against Mallory finding anything but she was determined to explore any possibility.

Equipped with video cameras on their helmets, the boarding team divided and began a well-rehearsed and systematic inspection of the ship. Mallory watched each video recording captured by these trained servicemen, running the video in slow motion to enable her to observe the ship and the crew within range of the camera lens. It was tedious. Her neck ached and her back hurt. She rolled her shoulders in an attempt to release the pent up emotions that had settled as a chronic case of tense muscles.

Time slipped by and she kept at it. She needed a break in the search for her brother, a breadcrumb to mark the trail. With the coastguardsman, she traveled into the cabin section of the ship. One after another, the cabins were sparse. Until this one.

She sat forward and concentrated on the segment of a cabin with a casket. Marc could be inside, but that wasn't possible or the Coast Guard search team would have found him. As she watched, the lieutenant was unable to open the casket. It was sealed. She debated this fact. It was possible the seal was to protect the contents during the extensive transportation. Maybe to hinder any curious crewmembers. Maybe to hide contraband – like Marc.

# Chapter One hundred-nine

Uncle's tour included the residential area of members' simple homes and colorful gardens, children's classrooms and playgrounds, and communal facilities including an auditorium, library, swimming pool, tennis court, medical clinic, laundry, and grocery.

Adjacent to the living quarters were sheds for dairy cattle and modern chicken coops. A short tractor ride away were agricultural fields, orchards, and fish ponds.

"The desert blooms under your care," Lei said. Marc remained quiet and she suspected he was working on another half-baked plan to get them away from the kibbutz and closer to their destination. Since their arrival here, he appeared sullen and driven. She suspected it had to do with his sister because she heard him call her name in his fitful sleep last night. When they first spoke at the lab, Marc said he missed Mallory. Naturally. But after her own experience, Lei was no longer naïve about the manipulations Yao and his people were capable of to accomplish their ambitions. Using and threatening beloved family relationships proved to be powerful motivations.

Uncle was speaking, pulling her attention away from her

questions about Marc and back to the old man. "For the founders, tilling the soil of their ancient homeland and transforming city dwellers into farmers was an ideology, not just a livelihood. Kibbutz farmers coaxed barren lands to produce crops, orchards, poultry, dairy, and fish farming. Organic agriculture is a mainstay of our economy. A combination of hard work, and advanced farming methods account for a large percentage of Israel's agricultural output to this day."

To get from place to place within the kibbutz, people walked or rode bicycles. The elderly and disabled traveled via electric carts.

"From each according to his ability," Uncle explained. "And to each according to his needs. That is the philosophy we live by."

Beyond the upscale hotel, they entered the large spa. It was separate from the rehabilitation complex they had visited upon their arrival. "When the kibbutzim could no longer support ourselves strictly through agricultural pursuits, each kibbutz developed a supplementary," their guide described. "This is ours."

In the steamy facility, tourists and guests experienced mud baths and a series of pools with varying degrees of heat, minerals, and salt content from the Salty Sea. Lei's attention was captured by an elderly couple that painstakingly helped one another down shallow steps into the nearest pool, undulating with pulsing currents. Settling into the therapeutic water, they rested in submerged seating and massage jets rhythmically soothed stiff joints. She had embarked on this questionable venture so that decades from now, she and her American husband would grow old together.

Passing massage tables, they observed the skilled hands of a trained masseuse as she poured oil onto the scars of a man's back and ministered to the insulted skin. Throughout their walk, Lei noted that Marc was more interested in the physical lay-out than the philosophy Uncle had expounded on. She was certain he was considering his options. A glance at Uncle confirmed that the old man was completely aware of Marc's thoughts. As were the two men who shadowed them. Yet Uncle had shown them all about the place. While Adi anticipated Marc's determination to get back home with or without help from the kibbutz, he treated Marc and Lei like honored guests. His only request was that Marc be patient.

But Lei knew Marc was beyond being patient anymore.

# Chapter One hundred-ten

The girl haunted his dreams. Yao woke in the night, his bedclothes wet with perspiration. Lustful desire? Or did he really care what had become of her? Where had Lei gone? Had she left with that American in that cursed device?

His thoughts went back to the last time he saw her. Young and lovely, she wore a dress the color of emeralds when he picked her up. He saw the approving glances of his contemporaries when they arrived for National Day's formal festivities. Perhaps it would be beneficial to have a beautiful wife.

Partway through the evening, she had become ill. Unable to accompany her home due to his duty, he summoned a taxi. That was the last time he saw the enticing Lei.

He left his bed and went outside to the garden. Pacing in the moonlight, he thought back to the events that led him to this moment. In the place where he was raised, villagers feared the city folks who descended upon their quiet lives, searching, threatening, bullying. Though his parents' letters never said anything about it, Yao was certain the Brother or another much like him, occasionally visited.

From the deep pocket of his robe, he pulled a thin cigar and lighter. He filled his lungs with the biting smoke and blew a cloud toward the stars. The smell reminded him of the times he and his family and neighbors crowded around the hearth fire while Brother spoke to them through the night.

Brother's message had always been the same. To love others as God had proven his love by sending his son as remuneration for the evils of mankind. Grace. Forgiveness. Redemption. As the son had shown when he allowed himself to be crucified in the place of sinful men.

As a teen, Yao had ventured into the unknown to provide for his parents. He used his education to improve village living conditions. The Colonel considered himself a good son. His parents' letters said so.

Yet Brother's message was offensive to The People's Republic. For the remainder of their handicapped lives, his parents lived with the punishment for their faith. And authorities hunted the Brother. If captured, he would be imprisoned. The horrible conditions were designed to punish the prisoner for thinking, believing, outside of the prescribed boundaries. The irony was not lost on Jai Yao. The God his parents and the Brother knew was gentle and inviting, offering relationship and gifts of joy, peace, and kindness. The People's Republic suffocated and controlled her own, punishing even thought and belief, suppressing creativity and individuality.

Marc Wayne had ideas he wanted to pursue. Yao had taken the man against his will and forced – threatened – the American to complete his design for the Colonel's ambitions. The Colonel's motivation was to bring improvement to the village of his family. Yet, he knew his parents would be disappointed in his methods. Yao sat on the garden bench and put his head in his hands.

He pictured Lei. Young, smart, and idealistic. There was something sad about her. Of course, Yao knew she had been prevented from returning to the United States. It was common for the government to manipulate its people. It was for their good. The good of the People's Republic. And he had made advances to her. Hinted that a liaison between the two would be a good choice. It would suit him and give his parents what they longed for. A grandson. They didn't ask for much and he always found a way to provide for them.

Good. That word kept coming up as he turned over and examined his thoughts and feelings in the predawn hours. Back inside the house, he downed a shot of tequila and poured himself a second. Was good even good enough? The People's Republic did whatever they lusted for in the name of the good of the people. Even though the people had no say in what was good for them. That was decided for the population by an elite few whose lives in no fashion resembled the circumstances of the people they made decisions for.

Brutal men had destroyed his home and damaged his family, claiming it was for the good of the country. Yao flexed his fingers. The increasing ache in his joints was a keen reminder of the unnecessary damage that had been perpetrated on his hands as a teen.

He recalled the fear of the villagers as they whispered Brother's name. Their desperation as they helplessly stood by while his parents were beaten nearly to death.

The same fear had been in Marc's eyes. Terror he had imposed, wielding it like an invincible weapon to accomplish his own ambitious goals. For Yao's own good, this time. He recalled Lei's passive compliance as she did what was required. There was no passion. No admiration for him and his position, education, or Brass Rat ring. She could tell his attention was for his own gratification. Her eyes had the same vacancy as the faces of the people he had known in the repatriation center. He would have run, too, if given the opportunity and their positions were reversed.

Shuddering, he poured tequila into a tumbler and carried it to his garden bench. Emptying the alcohol into his body, he gave in to the inebriation. In that state, he dared to admit the truth. He had become just like those men who had stolen the lives of his parents. He had become what he most hated – what Marc had called him – a monster.

# Chapter One hundred-eleven

Uncle returned Lei and Marc to Adi. His office was in a hub of rooms that made up the administration of the kibbutz. A phone sat on the desk and Marc reached for it. Instead of the expected dial tone, the sound told him the line was accessed and controlled by a central switchboard.

At that moment, Reuven entered and strode purposely to Adi's side. He spoke low. "It didn't go well."

"What happened?"

With a suspicious glance toward Marc and Lei, Reuven lapsed into Hebrew.

Adi put up his hand to halt the words. "This concerns them."

"But Adi – "

"Cousin, for these two, it is their life."

"You are too trusting."

"The key," Adi confessed, "is knowing who and when to trust. Now, tell me in English."

"The buyer expected two more boxes. When he put a knife to the family jewels, Bachir told them there were other goods." Reuven frowned at Marc and Lei. "Human goods."

"What is that to him?" Taking a cellophane package from his shirt pocket, Adi put sunflower seeds into his mouth.

"The buyer believes there is value. What was in the shipment he believes belongs to him." He tipped his head toward Marc and Lei.

Adi spit sunflower shells. "What is that to us?"

The cousin leaned closer. "Bachir told him to look here, at the Kibbutz."

"The fat pig. He compromised our families." Adi's eyes narrowed. "Where is Bachir now?"

"Dead. After he gave them their information, they killed him."

Adi drew himself up straight. "Rather harsh penalty. Killing a supplier is not good for business."

"They said he could not be trusted with this information. Therefore, he could not be trusted to keep his mouth shut about them."

Their host received the information thoughtfully.

"What will you do?"

Adi put several more seeds into his mouth, systematically split them apart with his front teeth, and spat out the shells.

"Adi?"

"They have value to us as long as they are ours," he considered.

Marc opened his mouth to protest this wanton deciding of their fate. As he had done with Reuven, Adi put up a hand to halt his words. But Marc was not going to be put off again. He moved closer and Reuven quickly stepped between Marc and Adi. Wordless, the cousin stood facing Marc, his fierce expression daring Marc to give him the opportunity to use the fists he clenched at his sides. Marc no longer cared. He had been punched plenty already and had delivered some of his own. He had reached his limit of bullies stalking and controlling him. Marc was going home and he was going home now. With or without anyone's help.

"They are trouble." Reuven spoke to Adi though his eyes looked directly into Marc's.

Adi put a restraining hand on Reuven's shoulder. "We must hide them until they serve a purpose for us."

Lei reached for Marc but he shook her off. "We are not here to serve a purpose for you or anyone else." Marc held a stance to deliver his most powerful swing. "We are leaving now and if anyone tries to stop us, I will kill them."

An unexpected flicker of respect in Reuven's eyes took Marc by surprise. Reuven kept his protective position between this volatile Marc and Adi who appeared to be calculating, weighing, considering. Marc turned and, taking Lei by the hand, started toward the lot where the jeeps were parked.

"I understand," Adi said to Marc's retreating back. "And you need to understand. I will get you home."

Marc whirled at the last word. "When? When my hair is as gray as Uncle's? I don't have that kind of time. I have to get back immediately before ..." He stopped. The demon that drove him, the awful fear for his sister – it was too fantastic. How could he explain it and who would believe him?

"If you leave here now," Adi paused, waiting until Marc was listening. "The two of you will never make it to the United States."

Angrily, Marc marched back. Reuven moved to place himself between the two as he had moments before but Adi halted him with a word. "Are you threatening me? Gonna send your goons," he pointed to Reuven, "to hold us here like some sort of desert prisoners?"

Adi shook his head. "I am protecting you."

Marc snorted and turned to go. Taking Lei's arm, he could feel her pulse hammering as he gripped her wrist. Any moment Marc expected Reuven's hand on his shoulder and Marc would relish coming to blows, fueled by his fury.

Instead of Reuven slugging at him, Adi fell into step beside Marc. "Ruthless men, far worse than the ones who uncrated you, are looking for you. If you leave here, you leave my protection."

Marc kept walking. Lei struggled to keep pace with his purposeful strides.

"These men are at home in the desert. They will quickly

surmise your value to your previous captors." He dropped his voice. "Can you protect Lei?"

The final question caused Marc to stop. Flashing through his memory, he saw the raw fear in her face as the dirty men attempted to rape her. Had Adi not shown up when he did, Lei would have been horribly hurt. And it would have been his fault. By his flex and go efforts, Marc had whisked them away from Colonel Yao's dominion, but he had delivered her directly in the hands of a baser evil. Marc had been helpless, unable to protect her. Just as he had been powerless to shield Mallory. The reality of the situation was that he was a hopeless failure. Adi was the real hero.

"We made it this far." Lei took his hands in hers. "We can make it the rest of the way."

"No." Sorrowful, Marc shook his head. "I can't risk you again."

Reuven broke in. "Adi, they are coming here. To take what they believe is theirs. We don't have much time."

Defeated, Marc addressed Adi. "What now?"

"We hide you."

Reuven was ready to get on with things. "Hide them where?"

Adi spit shells at their feet. "In plain sight."

# Chapter One hundred-twelve

Mallory tuned up the volume as high as it would go on the Coast Guard video that recorded the boarding and search of Shanghai Sumi. Was Marc in that casket?

"Perhaps I can help." The voice came from behind. The lieutenant turned and through the camera secured to his helmet, Mallory saw a Chinese man, slightly gray at the temples.

"I want to see inside this casket." The voices were woolen, the quality of homemade family videos.

"Certainly." The Chinese man made a slight bow in the direction of the casket. "The dead is a relative of one of the owners of our company. He traveled to the United States in the vain hope of finding a cure for his disease."

"Disease?"

The older man lowered his voice. "A humiliating condition that caused the flesh to rot from his bones."

"Who are you?"

Mallory repeated the lieutenant's question. *Was this the same Asian man the pilot had mentioned? The male nurse aboard the medical transport flight out of Ft. Wayne?*

The man was dressed in civilian clothes. "The casket, as you experienced, was sealed to prevent not only dishonor to the dead but to prevent the contagious disease from affecting another."

There was the briefest hesitation before the sailor replied. "I have to see inside this casket."

"As you wish." He reached into his breast pocket and produced a paper. "According to your laws, here is the death certificate."

The guardsman examined the paperwork. *The pilot said his passengers had the proper paperwork.*

"You must wear a mask to open the casket." A second man entered the cabin. "I am ship's doctor." *If he was the doctor, it made sense that the other man could be a nurse. Or posing as a nurse.*

There was additional conversation. Mallory's hopes fell when she saw the lieutenant don medical gloves and mask, and move to open the casket. The coffer must have held what the doctor said it did, or she would not be painstakingly viewing these reports, still searching for clues leading to Marc.

"I can get you a scalpel – a surgical knife to cut through the seal," the ship's doctor offered.

A second later, his Coast Guard teammate poked his head inside the room. "All clear on my side. You ready to move on?"

The lieutenant leaned forward once more, the camera moving close to the casket. Mallory heard the coastguardsman cautiously inhale. Then the picture bobbed as the man retched. He stepped back and pulled the mask from his face. "Yeah. I'm done here." He peeled the gloves from his hands and pressed them into the Chinese man's hands as he quickly exited the room.

She sat back after watching the event a second and a third time. Mallory was equal parts anger and hope. Furious that the inspection was poorly conducted. That single slip had cost her brother his freedom. Maybe his life. If Marc was in that casket, and it made sense considering the timing and the direction of the medical flight that took him west, then the Coast Guard could have rescued him. They were that close.

Seeing that the inspection had grossly missed an opportune

moment, Mallory had renewed hope that she could track Marc's next destination. She enlarged the picture of the Asian man in the footage. Where did Shanghai Sumi dock? Who was this Asian man?

# Chapter One hundred-thirteen

The kibbutz moved with a quiet urgency. Men and women went about their tasks, children were tenderly tended. Among the usual daily responsibilities, was an air of preparation.

Marc observed leaders in the community carry out Adi's instructions. In a short time, vehicles were readied and nearly simultaneously left the kibbutz. First a tour bus pulled out of the parking lot. Next, a van left for the Ben Gurion Airport, located nine miles southeast of Tel Aviv and named for Israel's first prime minister, David Ben Gurion. Last, a jeep drove in the direction of the previous rendezvous place where Marc and Lei had been discovered.

"We're going on the van to the airport." As the plans were executed, Marc took Lei's hand and started for the motor pool. Whatever deception Adi executed was his affair. More like his business. Taking care of his own business, Marc would hitchhike to the next available flight west.

"No."

"It's not a question. We're going home. Now." Flying out of an international airport with regular and trusted flights to the United States was the fastest way to the Midwest that Marc could think of.

Crammed into a coach seat between linebackers snacking on miniature packages of pretzels would be luxurious compared to Yao's travel accommodations to China and Marc's own recent arrangements that deposited them in Israel.

Reuven had blocked their path. Marc smirked at the bodyguard and realized he was no longer intimidated. Events were in place, and Indiana was appearing closer. "You're getting redundant."

From behind them Adi spoke. "That is exactly where your hunters will look. When they find you, you will never see your home again."

Marc hesitated. He didn't want to further risk Lei. But every moment he could not devote to finding Mallory endangered his sister. He faced the young Israeli. "I have to get to the United States. One way or another, I'm going. And I'm going now."

Adi spit empty sunflower shells. "Today we will shake your pursuers from the trail. Then you will go home."

A short time later, Adi led Marc and Lei to the spa. Smelling of water and earthy minerals, the warm air was heavy with humidity. The place reminded Marc of a YMCA gym, with participants busy on physical therapies from swimming to mud baths. Along one wall, thick towels hung over white paneled doors along a bank of individual dressing rooms with showers to rinse off the minerals and medicinal mud. Balancing a tray of tall glasses filled with chilled orange and pineapple juice, a woman Marc strongly suspected was Adi's mother spoke low to Adi. "The bus was followed, as was the van."

Adi reached for a glass and gave it to Lei. He took one for himself and gestured for Marc to do the same. "And the third vehicle?"

She held the tray to Marc while continuing her report. Marc took a glass. She offered drinks to three others who milled casually nearby and continued. "The last vehicle left moments later. It also was followed."

Two men, trying hard to appear as tourists checking out the kibbutz spa facilities, peered intently at faces. A half dozen men and women lounged in the active pool, reclining against jets that massaged their feet and back. In a shallow pool, families played with young children. In the far spa, three elderly men soaked in hot mineral waters produced only in Israel.

The woman circulated, offering beverages to clients. She came to the two men and held out her tray. The taller of the two irritably brushed her off. With an oily smile, the second took a glass and nudged his companion to do the same. Her tray now empty, Esther engaged the strangers. Boldly, the woman walked them through the facility, explaining how much healthier their skin would be for a reasonable fee. One price included the therapeutic waters, massage, and medicinal mud masks.

Again, the taller man attempted to wave her away. She motioned for two therapists to join her and the three began to sell the wonders of the spa experience in earnest. They herded the two to a counter where towels and a sheet to wrap in were placed in their hands. Talking rapidly and convincingly, one therapist guided the two to dressing rooms and was pressing them inside with the promise of immediate attention from a masseuse when suddenly panic stricken, the two pushed the bundle of towels and draping into her hands and beat a hasty retreat back the way they'd come.

Their bodies and faces completely covered with rich mud mineral masks from the Salty Sea, Adi, Marc, Lei, and two other couples, watched them go.

# Chapter One hundred-fourteen

Mallory's heart beat double time. This was the report she had been waiting for. When the phone rang on a secure line in her office, the caller would provide the long-anticipated update on Shanghai Sumi. Mallory was confident that the ship's destination would lead her to Marc's location.

Professionally she knew better than to allow her emotions to run ahead of the concrete facts. Personally, Mallory fanned her smoldering hope. It was all she had.

The voice on the other end was nasally with a head cold. "She docked in Shanghai."

That fit with the sketchy details Mallory had gathered so far. The Asian man on the medical flight and on the cargo ship was probably Chinese.

Sniff. "Agents learned that the military was developing an advanced technology in an old temple adjacent to the port." Sniff.

Anticipation brought Mallory to her feet. The Meissner Device. The thieves were building the Meissner Device Generator from the stolen patent. Marc's invention from his patent. "Get inside that facility. Find Marc."

The caller blew his nose. Mallory twirled her hair. "We did –
"

"Did you find him? Was he there?" She had given up trying to keep her voice professionally neutral.

"There was an explosion. The project is gone."

The words felt like a sucker punch to her gut. Mallory thought about Marc's early description. *The part I don't have, I really don't have.*

But the next statement was worse.

"At least four men were killed."

Her legs suddenly refused to hold her weight. Mallory slumped onto her desk chair. She rested her forehead in her palm.

"Someone meeting Marc's description had been there. A Caucasian with a ponytail."

Had Marc made a deadly miscalculation in his attempt to bridge the gap of missing science for his invention? "A man meeting that description is one of the dead?"

Sniff. "The four dead were Chinese."

She made him check his facts and repeat the previous statement three times. "Then where is he now?" This was the single question she had been asking since the day Marc disappeared.

He blew his nose. "Based on what we gathered so far, I have no idea."

Mallory fought the urge to throw the phone on the ground and stomp on it. "Okay, there is a lot you don't know. Tell me what you do know."

"One; the military was developing something they were keeping secret in the lab. Two; someone matching Marc Wayne's description had been involved. Third; the guy we believe was Mr. Wayne is either dead, has escaped, or has been taken to a new location. Fourth; if he managed to get away, he didn't leave breadcrumbs for us to follow."

# Chapter One hundred-fifteen

After only a couple hours to rest, Marc and Lei were summoned. The cottage they had been given was comfortable. Marc had considered explaining that they needed separate rooms, and then decided against it. Sleeping on the couch where he could be near Lei was more important than their individual privacy. He suspected she was relieved that he was close.

"It's time." Drinking coffee with his cousin, Adi was sitting at an outside table in a garden courtyard.

"You're sending us home?"

"I'm sending you."

Lei sighed with relief and laid her head against Marc's shoulder.

"Come." Reuven filled two small cups. Having put aside his gruffness, Marc could almost see some personality. Almost. "Have coffee while we speak."

Holding Lei's elbow, Marc guided her to the table and a cup of the steaming Turkish coffee. He sat beside her. Her shoulder length black hair pulled back from her face, Adi's mother brought a platter piled with bright oranges, sliced eggplant, smooth hummus topped with a swirl of olive oil, and warm flat bread. Satisfied that the guests were eating, she set about rearranging the furniture on the patio.

*Our last meal?* Marc was eager to begin their travels. The weight of Mallory's safety felt heavier on his heart with every passing hour. He prayed she was still alive, that he could quickly locate her, that he could get her away from the animals that held her. "Have you contacted the American embassy?"

"I have made contacts," Adi assured. "But not with your Embassy."

Marc noticed the smirk on the cousin's face and wanted to smack it off. Instead he leaned forward. "What's going on?" Lei's trembling hand reached for his under the table. He gave a reassuring squeeze that belied the fear rising in his throat.

Esther came to the cousin's side and said something in Hebrew. Reuven mumbled apologies and got up to help Esther move a heavy table.

"You have a value for us," Adi explained.

"You're a weapons dealer." Frustrated with his perpetual double-talk and vague statements, Marc corralled his anger before he swung a fist at Adi. "Playing all sides for the best deal for yourself."

Adi received the insult. "Things are not always as they appear, my American friend." Resting his elbows on the table, he leaned toward his guests. "You must trust me."

"Trust you for what?" Lei spoke up.

"Will you return us to the United States?" Marc held Adi's gaze. "Will you help us get home?"

Over the meaty dates and sweet persimmons, their host nodded. "As I have said."

"When?" Impatient, Marc felt that Mallory's safety pivoted on this question.

The cousin returned to the them. "It's begun."

Marc jumped to his feet. "When? When do we go home?"

"Soon now. Arrangements have been put into place." Adi looked to Esther and Reuven. "Maybe two days."

Esther nodded to the two men and was gone.

"Two days?" Marc's hands balled into fists.

"Maybe sooner." Adi stood. "But it will not be as you think. Not as you expect."

# Chapter One hundred-sixteen

In the dim light, a slender woman with close-cropped red hair studied satellite images. The much-delayed launch of the Israeli spy satellite had finally occurred the first year Shiva was in the Israeli military. With her quick eye for detail, she had been assigned to the satellite team. Fascinated with the science, Shiva memorized great quantities of information, taking to her job like the satellite took to the sky and when her mandatory military term was over, she had stayed.

Through an agreement with India, TechSAR was put into orbit by the Indian Space Research Organization's workhorse rocket, the Polar Satellite Launch Vehicle or PSLV-10. After several delays due to technical difficulties, the satellite blasted into space from the Satish Dhawan Space Center in Sriharikota. The launch had been spectacular. In a flawless lift-off from the First Launch Pad, the homegrown PSLV-10 carried the 300 kilogram satellite into its intended orbit in just under twenty minutes. Nineteen minutes and 45 seconds to be exact, and Shiva was always exact.

TechSAR's synthetic aperture radar obtained clear images of small targets even in overcast conditions. All weather imaging was provided day and night. The microwaves sent from SAR penetrated thick cloud cover and dust storms, producing sharp photos, and significantly boosting Israel's intelligence gathering capabilities.

The first of its kind developed in Israel, the spy satellite's primary mission was to keep an informed eye on hostile neighbors, tracking Iran's territory and spying on their efforts to develop nuclear arms. Circumnavigating the earth with an orbit of 450 kilometers perigee, meaning at its nearest point, and 580 apogee, its farthest point, the TechSAR ranked among the world's most advanced space systems.

The secondary use of the satellite was to provide information to subscribers. For this unique and individualized service, the department collected significant fees that underwrote the expenses of the satellite and its support personnel. There was additional funding to explore advancing technology.

Shiva had a list of organizations that paid for regular reports about what the eye in the sky saw regarding their particular location of interest. That's what she was about now. She was known for being meticulous and thorough. A nuisance to some, Shiva lived her life noting minutia. Now, studying photos of a patio, she checked the position of the furniture once, twice, three times.

Just as she had first suspected. The furniture had been positioned in the exact pattern noted in the directive. The subscriber for that seemingly trivial detail would be notified. Only the subscriber of course, would know the meaning of the change on the ground.

Shiva would never be privy to what message was being conveyed by that specific layout of furniture in an outdoor courtyard deep in the Negev, but then she knew she was not the only one consumed with particulars in the defense of her beloved Israel.

# Chapter One hundred-seventeen

It was lunchtime, and the restaurant at the kibbutz welcomed guests from three tour busses. Recently back from college, two young women met the groups and explained the options between the buffet and ala carte menu, and pointed the way to the restrooms where travelers could wash up. As usual, the bus drivers, tour guide, and the tour coordinator received complimentary meals. It was good for business.

The Japanese tourists talked fast and snapped photos faster. They moved speedily through the lunch buffet, and were the first to board their bus and be on their way once more.

The other two busses carried visitors from Cape Town, South Africa. Dressed in bright colored, loose fitting clothing, they sang their thanksgiving in rich harmony prior to eating.

Esther smiled and extended a welcome to the guests, her eyes expectant as she glanced toward the door each time it opened. At last, a middle-aged man in a conservative suit confidently entered and strode to the hostess.

"Shalom," Esther greeted.

"You were expecting me, of course," the man replied.

"Of course." She led him to a table near the window, her long, wavy hair swaying in rhythm to her hips.

"My favorite table," he acknowledged with a smile and took his seat. Esther set a menu before him and disappeared into the kitchen. When she returned she placed a basket filled with challahh bread on the table. "Just out of the kitchen ovens."

"You spoil me." He smelled the sweet, golden loaf appreciatively.

"What is that between you and me? We do good business together. You bring people to our kibbutz and we give you our best service."

"Is there also some of my favorite hummus available today? Your homemade?" It was a pivotal inquiry. A yes meant she had indeed summoned him. That she had a vital message for him.

She smiled. "As only we make it, of course."

Once more, the beautiful Jewish woman disappeared into the kitchen. The guest watched tourists line-up for the customary buffet. His waitress was quickly back at his table with a pottery bowl of golden hummus. A sprig of fresh mint leaves rested in the shallow pool of cold pressed olive oil.

He dipped a chunk of challahh bread into to mix. "How is your family?"

"Well. The kibbutz is well." From her tray, she set before him a tall glass of orange and pineapple juice. "And congratulations on your sister's 50th anniversary."

He nodded cordially. "Thank you." Sister and 50. She had information crucial to the United States. This was a patient work. His job was to wait on her timing. And to weave her words correctly to understand her message, necessarily vague to protect her and her sources.

She turned to go, then faced him again. "You should send her something special."

He patted the napkin against his lips to absorb the oil that clung there. "As always, you are correct. I should send her something special." Tucking cloth napkin over his tie, he leaned back. "What do you suggest?"

"Such a rare occasion." Esther rested the tray on her hip and appeared thoughtful. "Some jewelry, perhaps."

"Jewelry?"

"Diamonds."

# Chapter One hundred-eighteen

The next day, Adi invited Marc to the school's science department. Classes had ended for the day and the classrooms were vacant except for a teacher tutoring a student through a chemistry lab. Three rows of horizontal tables faced the front of the room where a long counter with a sink served as the lectern. The set-up indicated the course work was taught in a hands-on fashion. Books filled shelves near the door and the far side of the room held a variety of projects in various stages of experimentation.

When Adi and Marc arrived, shadowed as always by Reuven, the teacher left the student to do her own work.

Adi introduced Marc to the instructor, a man near Marc's own age with a mop of unruly curls and several days of beard growth. "Moshe is connected to the Israel Ministry of Infrastructure. He has something I think you will want to see."

Eagerly, Moshe led Marc to a circular track built of magnets in squares that resembled a chocolate bar. Lifting a disk from dry ice, the instructor set it three inches above the oval track. With a gentle push, the disk glided above the magnets, traveling the circle in a perpetual motion and at a consistent speed.

"By suspending a superconducting disc above –" he caught the circling disc and placed it several inches below the magnets – "or below these permanent magnets, the magnetic field is locked inside the superconductor."

"Quantum trapping." Marc tipped the disc and pushed it along where it remained at an angle, like the leaning tower of Pisa.

"Exactly." From behind his ear, Moshe pulled a pencil and waved it above and below the traveling disc. Passing an object between the disc and the track failed to interrupt or even slow the motion.

"This is your Meissner Effect," Adi said. "The reason you are here?"

Marc nodded. "The phenomenon is the expulsion of a magnetic field from a superconductor. In 1933, German physicist Walther Meissner measured the magnetic field distribution outside superconducting tin and lead samples."

The chemistry student abandoned her studies and approached to watch what was happening. Moshe beckoned her closer. "In the presence of an applied magnetic field, Meissner discovered the samples cooled below their superconducting transition temperature. At the new temperature, the tin and lead cancelled nearly all magnetic fields inside."

Moshe caught the flying disc and placed it in Adi's hand. "It is sapphire coated with a thin layer of porcelain."

Adi turned over the object and tapped on it before passing it to the student. The high-schooler spun it back onto the track. She looked to Moshe. "Do you think we will travel like this in my generation?"

Moshe's eyes reflected his excitement in the same way Hebron's did when he talked about his invention. "It is possible. Perhaps even probable."

"What holds you back?" Marc wondered if Israel would ironically conquer the Meissner Effect before either the United States or Colonel Yao's China. Situated at the crossroads of the world, the small country of Israel had large enemies.

"This is still experimental," Moshe said. "There remain

aspects that have yet to be mastered."

Marc nodded. He was well aware of the unmastered elements. Or at least those aspects that continued to be elusive to him.

Adi dropped a hand on Marc's shoulder. "I have arrangements to make. Perhaps you would like to stay a while with Moshe?" Without waiting for an answer, Adi left.

# Chapter One hundred-nineteen

Hot coffee in hand, Mallory stepped into the elevator. She pressed the button for Jimmy's floor, that place where all the computer techies hung out in the digital forensics department. She leaned her forehead against the cool gray steel of the elevator wall, allowing the vibration to serve as a massage for her pounding headache. This headache had been an unwelcome companion since Marc had disappeared.

Too soon, the elevator stopped and the doors whispered open. Deep in conversation, Deverell and Fred were standing there, waiting for her. Fred smiled when he saw her.

Deverell frowned. "You look like five miles of bad road."

"So do you," she grumbled, "but I wasn't going to bring it up."

"Are you getting any sleep?"

"Based on your description, apparently not enough."

Fred gently took her elbow. "Let's see what Jimmy has for us." He steered her toward Jimmy's workstation. Deverell fell into step behind.

Jimmy was watching for them, rocking forward on his toes.

His face brightened when they arrived. "Watch this." He sat down at his dueling computers.

Deverell bent close. "You have a breakthrough?"

Once again the picture of the cat appeared on the screen. The cat with the secret code embedded into its fur. Mallory was beginning to detest that image. She didn't think she even liked cats anymore.

"The only way I could jam the steganography was to turn the technology back on itself," Jimmy began. "Double stegging."

"How does it work?" Deverell wanted to know.

Jimmy swiveled his chair to address Mallory. "You told me to come up with a technique to protect places like the Patent Office. I can't figure a way to keep people from creating these files with embedded information. But I found that if we can damage at least some part of the file, the hidden encryption becomes garbled and cannot be deciphered."

Mallory rubbed her temples. "In simple terms, Jimmy."

He spun back to his computer screen and his fingers flew over the keyboard. "Double stegging adds noise, scrambling the figure's least-significant bits. If the cat in the picture is just a cat, double stegging doesn't cause any harm."

Fred pushed his hands into his pockets. "But for a hidden file?"

"The addition of double stegging algorithm turns the information to gibberish."

"Every time?"

Jimmy leaned back in his chair and laced his fingers behind his head. "An extremely high percentage of the files we tested were destroyed."

"But it's not 100 percent effective," Deverell filled in.

"Like most things in life, it's 98 percent."

"What about text files," Mallory asked. "Will this work on them as well?"

"I've only tested this on image file carriers," Jimmy said, "but I'm confident this method can be extended to additional formats."

"Like video and audio?" Fred handed stomach lozenges to Mallory. "Can those carry hidden messages?"

Deverell pulled a pen from his shirt pocket and began clicking it. "There are so many holes to plug in the information dikes."

"Relax. I've got you covered." Jimmy took the pen from Deverell, slipped it back into Deverell's pocket, and patted it into place. "Digital steganography relies on the same basic principles to conceal data for any digital carrier."

"Can you make this program available?"

"In my sleep." Jimmy waved his arm in the direction of the other geeks busily at work in their cubicles. "We'll create the software and make it available to any organization. The software will scour all outgoing communication for fiendish content."

"Won't installing the software be a heads up for anyone doing this? The last thing we want to do is give someone involved in espionage a reason to find another avenue," Mallory said.

"This goes at the email server level," Jimmy assured. "Every communication will be automatically filtered through an algorithm. Individual employees will not be aware of the addition of the new software."

"Unless someone tells them." After all this hard work, Mallory didn't want anyone to outsmart Jimmy's technology. Not until she got Marc home where he belonged. She wanted the tediousness of spy-prevention at the USPTO behind her so her full attention, and the concentration of her co-workers, could be centered on locating her brother.

"Will this tell us who fits the glass slipper?"

Jimmy looked quizzically at Deverell.

Mallory translated her supervisor's question. "With this program, can you tell us who is the mole?"

"Sorry, Mallory." Jimmy shrugged. "It's easier to jam the steganography than it is to detect its presence. I can't tell you who is doing it, but I can stop the attack."

# Chapter One hundred-twenty

At 8:00 p.m., a tour bus parked near the entrance to the diamond exchange.

The heart of world events, Israel was a popular vacation destination for peoples of many faiths. Generations came to the cradle of civilization as a pilgrimage. From Egyptian hieroglyphics at the world's largest Roman archeological dig in Beth Shan where the Philistines hung King Saul's body, to the caves at Qumran where the Dead Sea Scrolls long lay hidden; from the aqua ducts and man-made port of Caesarea Philippi to the impenetrable mountaintop fortress of Masada, there was an abundance of places that attracted visitors.

Two of the most popular destinations were the Church of the Nativity and the Church of the Holy Sepulcher. Marking Christ's life from the womb to the tomb by planting these churches, Constantine's mother Helena made her pilgrimage when she was nearly an octogenarian. While Helena's arduous trip was based on discipleship, the Middle Ages would bring a different group of travelers who came for penance. Modern day tourists came, many making consecutive journeys, for religious and intellectual reasons.

Ancient history continued to be unearthed each time new construction was begun.

Diamonds were a favorite item for visitors to take home as a remembrance of their trip. From his parking place, the diplomat watched until the front and rear doors of the bus swung open. Chatting excitedly, a kaleidoscope of tourists disembarked.

Dressed in casual clothes, the diplomat left his car and mixed with the tourists. Sponsored by an interdenominational church from Ft. Wayne, Indiana, this group was a collection of congregants on a two-week tour of the Holy Land.

Inside, the group milled in a bright welcome center, reading informative displays outlining the process that transitioned the diamonds, rough from the earth, into costly precious gems. "Sixty percent of all diamonds in the world are distributed through Israel," began the tour guide. "Of those diamonds, 61 percent go to the United States, 14 percent go to China, eight percent travel to Belgium, five percent to Switzerland, two percent to Japan, and two percent to England."

The guide answered several questions from her audience. "The value of a diamond is based on the four Cs," she continued. "Color, carat, clarity, and cut."

Pointing to a colorful wall display, the cheery guide beckoned the group to move closer. "Here we receive diamonds to cut and polish. Each diamond has 58 facets. The round cut diamond represents love. The square diamond is the second most popular."

Following the flow of the building, the tour was led through a low-ceilinged hallway. Along the left side of the passageway, four small rooms were visible through generous windows. Inside each room stood a waist-high glass case. In the first of these private shopping areas, a high-heeled saleswoman showed a velvet case of similarly cut diamonds to a couple seated in plush chairs.

The guide stopped in the middle of the hallway. "If any of you would like to shop for a special diamond," she indicated the adjacent rooms, "one of our diamond experts will be pleased to help you find the exact one you are looking for."

The hall opened into a glamorous showroom. Their footsteps

muffled in thick turquoise carpet, the tourists walked slowly, admiring one sparkling showcase after another. Each stunning display was a collection of precious stones – blood red rubies, sea green emeralds, autumn topaz, glittery opals, and, of course, diamonds.

The diplomat mingled for several moments, admiring a case of cameos. Casually, he drifted to a case of unusual blue and green mottled stones.

"This is the Eilat Stone." The stunning dark haired beauty had a deep, melodic voice. "It is named for the locality where it is found, at the southern most city of Israel."

The diplomat met her eyes. "It resembles a stone common in my country, the turquoise."

"Turquoise was prized by American Indians." She set a polished stone on a soft cloth. "There is a similarity. Eilat stone is chrysocolla that is intermixed with turquoise and a form of malachite."

A small, elderly woman pulled her tall, thin husband to the case. "Isn't this one pretty?"

Her husband bent for a closer inspection. "Shades of blue and green," he mumbled in a Mid-western accent. "It would match your eyes. But I promised you a diamond for our 50th anniversary."

His wife took his arm and they crossed to the next display featuring pearls.

"The Eilat Stone," the sales woman continued, "is our national stone."

"This broach is striking." He pointed to a free-form piece the size of a half-dollar. In a setting of gold, it was surrounded by tiny diamonds.

Pulling a petite gold key from her pocket, the woman unlocked the door on her side of the jewelry case. "The mines from which the Eilat came are believed to have been the copper mines of King Solomon." She laid the broach in his palm. "The gem, in fact, is often referred to as King Solomon Stone."

Gently turning the piece this way and that, he watched the stone and the diamonds catch the light and make it dance. "The diamonds are interesting."

"They are unique. Natural, untreated, responsibly sourced, these diamonds are cut and polished by a specially selected diamantaire. Called Forevermark, these diamonds have an icon and identification number inscribed on the table facet."

He peered closer at one of the clear stones that ringed the Eilat. "I don't see any marks."

"To preserve the beauty of the diamond and not detract, the inscription is 1/500 of the depth of a human hair."

"Incredible."

"Are you shopping for something particular? Does this piece please your eye?"

He held her gaze. "I'm looking for something special for my sister. She is celebrating her 50th anniversary."

The woman nodded slightly. "I'll wrap this for you. You'll be pleased to know it comes with a certificate."

"A certificate?"

"A certificate of authenticity. This certificate tells you everything you want to know."

# Chapter

# One hundred-twenty-one

"Come, your journey is about to begin." In the predawn hours, Adi and Reuven came to the cottage door.

Outside, the two led Marc and Lei to a long, low building on the outskirts of the kibbutz. Made of corrugated steal, the structure resembled a metal pig barn in the Midwest, but without the stink. Fans mounted along the walls circulated air. They ducked into a smaller barn. Inside, under luminous lights, were a half dozen men and several rows of automatic weapons. In the center, balanced on sturdy tables, stood four crates. Two were sealed. Two were empty.

Lei backed toward the door and turned to bolt outside but the cousin blocked her escape. Her shoulders began to shake and tears spilled down her smooth cheeks. When Marc put a protective hand on her back, she turned and buried her face into his chest.

He wrapped his arms tightly around her. "I won't let anything happen to you," he whispered in her ear.

Adi brought bottles of water to Marc and Lei. "I want you hydrated." From a prescription bottle in his pocket, he produced several tablets. "Take four of these. It will make this trip far more comfortable than your previous one."

Marc nodded toward the crates. "Is this necessary? Can't we just go to the Embassy?"

Adi deposited the pills into Marc's hand. "It is necessary."

Marc surveyed his options. He wanted to run, to barrel through the men standing around them and find his own way to the Embassy. Or the airport. Or something. Anything. They could hitchhike. Lasso a couple of camels. He pictured himself pulling Lei by the hand as they rushed the group who stood poised to prevent their escape. Adi's cousin adjusted his position so Marc could see the gun stuck in his waistband. That was merely for intimidation. Marc knew Reuven wouldn't shoot them.

"Liar!" hissed Lei.

Adi again received the insult. He stepped closer. Lei recoiled against Marc.

"Lei, you are a brave woman." Adi spoke softly. "I won't lie to you."

Marc glared defiantly. "You said we're going home." He tried to manipulate some sort of guarantee and felt foolish doing it. These guys owed him nothing. They were arms dealers who blatantly told him they were using him to their gain.

"I told you to trust me." Once more Adi proffered the medication. "For your comfort." When Marc hesitated, the cousin stepped forward menacingly. "We are running out of time. Take the pills and get in the crates, or I will help you."

Adi put a calming hand on his cousin's arm while he kept his gaze on Marc. "A man has to make his own decision."

Lei looked questioningly from Adi to Marc. Marc tightened his hold on the small woman who depended on him while his thoughts raced with the possible options. He and Lei had outsmarted some of the most brilliant minds in China to get this far. Of course, he hadn't been too bright to get into China in the first place.

Adi's steady voice broke into his thoughts. "Have you been harmed here?"

"No," Marc admitted.

"Has anything been required of you?"

Marc shook his head.

"Do you have reason to mistrust me?"

Marc looked at the crates.

Adi shrugged. "So it doesn't look like you think it should."

Still Marc hesitated. He wanted details. Reassurance. Promises. But he knew he wouldn't get that from the quiet man who stood in front of him. This young leader who was surrounded by loyal supporters in a country laced with multiple cultures and manifold points of friction.

"Adi," growled his cousin urgently. "We are running out of time."

Adi waved an inviting hand at the crates. "Your journey begins as soon as you are ready."

Lei looked questioningly to Marc.

"Let's go." The decision was made. Hoping it was the best choice, he pressed the pills into her hand and urged her swallow them. He swallowed his own and escorted the tentative Lei to a crate. Unlike their previous experience, the interior of these boxes had been padded for their comfort.

Marc pulled Lei into his arms to lift her, but swayed as the medication swept through his limbs. Immediately Adi was beside him and steadied Marc. With an assuring look, Adi lifted Lei into his own strong arms. Her eyelids were heavy and she fluttered them in a vain attempt to remain awake. Adi looked long at the girl's pretty face before gently settling her in the open crate.

Feeling woozy, Marc barely kept his balance as he lowered himself into the second container. Marc was aware that the others were speaking but they did not immediately seal the tops. "Are you okay, Lei?" he called to her.

"Yes," came the reply, though he heard the quaver in her voice.

Moments later, he jerked awake and called again. "Lei, are you all right?"

There was no response.

"Lei?" he called again.

Adi came to his side. "Your wife is sleeping now. You may allow yourself to rest."

Marc tried to shake his head. "Not my wife." Each word was an effort. He focused on Adi and saw the confidant man look confused. It was so out of sorts for Adi that Marc grinned, his face only half cooperating like a drunkard's. "She's my friend," he slurred.

"But she wears your ring."

Marc couldn't resist. "Things are not always as they appear."

Adi studied his face, and Marc knew his quick mind was considering all the options. He swallowed, summoning moisture for his thickening tongue. "Not my ring," was all he could get out through lips that refused to cooperate.

Marc's vision clouded but before he permitted himself to sink into the seductive darkness of sleep, he forced his eyes to open once more. Adi was gone. Rising slightly, Marc saw him bent over Lei's crate. The tall Israeli lightly kissed the sleeping girl on the forehead. Or maybe Marc was already dreaming.

Movement prodded Marc to open his eyes again. It was a herculean effort. He had one last vision of Adi, slipping a small package into Marc's pocket. From somewhere far away he heard, "Yala yala!"

# Chapter

# One hundred-twenty-two

"Holy Buckets! Hey, Major, look at this!"

A thunderous crack and loud voices woke Marc. He opened his eyes and shaded his face from the sudden brash light.

"Our bosses back home ain't gonna believe this," came another voice. "Check out those other crates."

As he heard the tops being wrenched from the other boxes, Marc's eyes began to adjust and he opened them. He struggled to orient himself. Where was he? Who were these guys? Feeling hung over, he grabbed at the side and hoisted himself into a sitting position.

"Whoa, easy there partner," said a distinctly southern accent. Marc blinked and squinted at the man who stood over him. His heart jumped when he recognized the American military uniform.

"American?"

"Yes sir. Sergeant Cooper, sir."

His voice choked with emotion, Marc suppressed an urge to hug the soldier. Instead he stretched out his hand. "You have no idea how glad I am to see you."

The soldier clasped his hand in a bone-breaking handshake. "Yes, sir."

"There's a girl ..." Marc began groggily. From somewhere outside his box a voice exclaimed, "Major, there's a girl in this one."

"No way." Cooper trotted away from Marc.

Stretching out the kinks in his cramped muscles, Marc stiffly crawled over the side and out of his coffin-like bed. Israeli soldiers were prying open similar boxes and examining the weapons inside. Four men who looked a lot like the first guys Marc had met in Israel had their backs to him. They were on their knees with their hands clasped behind their heads. An Israeli stood over them with a beretta.

As a second Israeli secured the wrists of the prisoners with plastic handcuffs, a kneeling man twisted and grabbed the throat of his captor. Before the other prisoners could react, the Israeli broke his attacker's hold and crushed the Arab's windpipe. For the next four minutes, the three prisoners watched their companion writhe and struggle for oxygen. At last, the man's eyes glazed over and his form went lax. The sight of his suffering proved a deterrent to any further aggression.

Marc stumbled over to the other container where three men in American uniforms were gathered, a Sergeant, a Major, and Cooper.

"She looks Chinese," said Cooper. "That doesn't fit with any intel."

"We knew we would find weapons. And a special package people in suits have been looking for." The major pierced Marc with his gaze. "But nothing about a second special package."

Marc pushed his way to Lei's side, relieved that he had arrived before she woke and panicked. "Lei." Gently he shook her. "Wake up. The cavalry has arrived."

# Chapter

# One hundred-twenty-three

With astonishing efficiency, the four desert rats – one in a body bag – were loaded at gunpoint into an Israeli military truck. The four Israeli military men, including the one who broke the neck of his prisoner with the ease of answering his phone – prepared to leave.

Marc knew they must be spec ops. One spoke briefly with the American Major. The American and the Israeli soldiers shook hands and the Israelis, with their prisoners and shipments of arms, were gone.

His arm around Lei's shoulder as an assurance for her, Marc took in the scenery. They were still in the desert though in a much different place than they had known with Adi. Marc looked down at Lei. "He did it."

Lei's smile was wistful. "Adi got us to the Americans."

The American sergeant jogged to the helicopter that rested on the ground like an oversized insect. Marc could see the pilot was beginning the sequence for take-off.

"Major, we can't take the girl." Cooper's voice was low, but Marc heard him.

Motioning for Lei to remain where she was, Marc moved closer. "You're not leaving her here. She's coming with me."

The Major shouldered his weapon. "At ease, Sergeant. Major Northington once brought home four girls who weren't part of the mission."

Cooper wasn't easily swayed. "Begging your pardon, Sir. I thought that was a legend."

"Legendary."

"Our orders, sir…" Cooper reminded through clenched teeth.

His nose near Cooper's, the Major was authoritative. "I'm well aware of our orders."

"We're still gonna get our butts chewed."

"That's customary." The Major motioned for the group to move out. "The girl goes with us. Now, everyone in the heli."

# Chapter

# One hundred-twenty-four

Deverell was already in the conference room when Mallory entered. Fred was close behind. Frustrated to have her investigative nose at a dead end, she had voiced as much to her boss. He agreed it was time for another pow-wow.

Papers surrounded his laptop, a map lay to his left, and reading glasses were perched low on Deverell's nose.

"What's all this?" Fred picked up the map.

"More surface space." Deverell mumbled without bothering to look up.

Mallory combed through the top layer of papers. "Anything in here that tells us something about Marc?" Having trailed her brother to Shanghai, she was at an impasse to know where to search next. Had he been hurt in the explosion at the lab? Carted off to another high security facility? If Marc had gotten away, why had he not made contact?

Deverell snatched a handful from Mallory's hands and patted them back into their previous pile. "You know I'll tell you as soon as I have anything new." He pulled off his glasses. "You two sit down and cool your jets. The purpose of this meeting is an exchange of information. To catch each of us up on what we have to date."

Fred sat down. Mallory paced.

"Mallory," Deverell said wearily. "Will you please sit?"

"No."

"Your incessant pacing is distracting to say the least."

She eyed him fiercely. "So is your incessant pen clicking."

"Touché," Fred pronounced. "Now – "

The door flew open and Jimmy bounced inside. Wearing a Hawaiian shirt and Birkenstocks, he looked more like a hippy than a computer genius. "Here it is." He spun a computer disk between the pointer fingers on each hand.

"Here what is?" Deverell indicated a chair.

"What you asked for." Jimmy's tone was impatient like he was talking to a forgetful child. "The double-stegging software, though the guys in computer forensics call it steggo-stomping, they even put a dance to it –"

"Jimmy." Mallory snapped her fingers. "Focus."

He froze, looked again at what was in his hand and started fresh. "This server-level technology will filter outgoing email."

"This will mitigate major espionage?" With his foot, Fred pushed out the chair Jimmy had so far ignored, and waved Jimmy into it.

"The problem in the past," Jimmy accepted the chair, "is that as soon as security personnel figured out how to circumvent one algorithm, the spies easily developed ten more. This," he waved the disk, "is double-stegging. It provides a stop-gap."

Fred leaned forward. "How effective is your program?"

"No matter how sophisticated steganography methods become, those technology advances could be used against them." Jimmy pushed his John Lennon glasses up on his nose.

Deverell frowned in confusion. "Them?"

"Malefactors," Jimmy clarified.

"You mean the big bad wolves."

"How does it work?" Fred asked.

"By attacking the applications using the applications themselves, the algorithms become their own worst enemy."

"The wolf huffed and puffed but could not blow the brick house down." Deverell held out his hand and Jimmy dropped the disk into his outstretched palm.

"What about tracking down the mole?" Mallory stopped pacing and planted her hands on her hips.

Jimmy shook his head. "Sorry, Mal. While this application runs quietly on the email server, that allows time for an agent to seek out the intruder while remaining confident that no out-going mail is exporting hidden files."

Fred frowned. "What does that mean?"

"Thieves use this technique to make uses of static carriers like JPEG or MP3 files." Jimmy held out his left hand. "That's the bad side. The good side," he held out his right hand like the second tray of a weight scale, "is that steganography is a moving target. Now, exfiltrators are making use of streaming data technologies like VoIP –

Deverell waved him to a stop. "English. We speak English here."

"Voice over Internet Protocol."

"You mean phones?" Fred asked.

Jimmy nodded. "That's what I said."

"Right," Fred conceded.

"As I was saying," Jimmy eyed each of them over his glasses to be certain they were listening, "Disrupting or detecting hidden transmissions inside real-time phone calls is the next challenge for digital forensics. And considerably more complicated."

"Job security," Fred noted.

The door burst open for a second time and Deverell's assistant rushed to his side where she bent and said something close to his ear. His eyes grew wide and he looked immediately to Mallory.

Mallory stepped closer. A second later the assistant was gone again, the door closing smartly behind her.

"What?" Mallory held her breath, feeling hope beat an anxious rhythm in her pulse.

"We found him." Deverell grinned. "We found Marc."

# Chapter

# One hundred-twenty-five

Showered and freshly clothed, thanks to the U.S. military hospitality, Marc and Lei were ushered aboard a military transport.

"It's not exactly the airlines so don't expect pretty stewardesses with pretzels and peanuts," the Major had quipped. "But you don't exactly have passports."

Marc glanced appreciatively at the bare interior. "For the record, I didn't exactly have a passport to get to China."

"Israel?"

Marc shook his head. "No stamps in my passport for any of these international stops."

The Major shouldered his way to where they would sit. "I heard that about your initial trip east. Well, this may not be first class seating, but it's a step up from the transportation mode you were using when we found you."

Buckled into seats, the passengers consisted of Marc and Lei, and the men who had uncrated them from the journey Adi had set into motion. Lei finally relaxed after the big plane settled into a westward course and she dropped into a deep sleep. While most of the passengers slept, Marc chafed. Whether it was excitement to be headed home, residual adrenalin, or exultant relief that his escape plan had come together even with the unexpected added, he couldn't be sure. Maybe a combination of all of those. Plus a healthy serving of anxiety about Mallory.

*I'm going home.* After the seemingly endless days of frustration, what he had most desired was finally reality. Marc took in the military plane, the rough yet trained men who had abandoned their own safe environments stateside to rescue him and Lei in dicey surroundings, and allowed a tidal wave of gratitude wash away the persistent fear. Closing his eyes, he pictured home that smelled of cherry pipe tobacco, riding his bicycle to his aged brick office where he heard Dr. Thurmond's noisy patients, and basketball with Mallory.

Surely Yao had no reason to kill her. Perhaps, after their escape, Mallory was no longer leverage and he ordered his bullies to leave her sleeping on the living room couch. Marc grew tentatively optimistic about his sister's well-being. Picturing Nancy's blue eyes, he fell at last into a deep sleep.

Later, turbulence shook Marc awake. Feeling the plane descend below the rough air, Marc swallowed to release the pressure in his ears. As quickly as it had come, the disturbance was over. Shifting positions, he sought sleep once again but when it eluded him, he got out of his seat to stretch. It felt good to walk. The others were dozing with one exception. He stopped beside the Major who was reading.

"Good book?"

"Therapy." The Major rested the paperback upside down to hold his place. "It takes me longer than the others to relax after a mission."

"A perk of being in charge?"

"You should know. You just commanded your own mission." He gestured to an empty seat.

"I gladly leave that to you trained professionals." Marc shook his head. "Those Israeli guys with you were intense."

Taking off his reading glasses, the Major cleaned them on his shirt and peered at Marc though the lenses, much like Dr. Thurmond did. "The Mossad are probably the world's most sophisticated, law-approved killers."

"Israeli special forces?"

"Skilled in poisons, long and short-blade knives, and explosives the size of a cough drop that can blow off a man's head. Use an arsenal of guns from short-barrel pistols to sniper rifles with a mile long killing range. Knew a guy who used piano wire to strangle." He tucked his glasses into his pocket. "They can take out a target without leaving a mark."

"They wanted the arms dealers."

"The Mossad invited us along."

Marc shifted his weight and digested this information. Adi's connections were at his nation's highest level. He had delivered them to the contacts that were certain to get Marc and Lei safely home. "I would be interested in the story about your Commander. The guy you mentioned when we met. Northington, was it? It seems to have made a difference about bringing Lei back with us."

The Major rubbed the stubble on his chin. "I could trade you that yarn for your story about how you got yourself packed into an illegal arms box like a canned Vienna sausage."

Nearby, Marc noticed Cooper stir and lean their way while working hard to appear that he wasn't listening. Marc sat down. "Deal."

"I'll bet an MRE that your tale beats this fiction the pilot loaned me." The Major closed his book.

Marc recognized the author's name as a popular Korean War veteran turned novelist who crafted bestselling adventure suspense novels. He also acknowledged that this book probably released while Marc was holed up as the Colonel's unappreciative guest. He wondered what else had happened while he was out of touch. While a captive of the Colonel's, the few conversations Marc had shared with fellow scientists in the Shanghai lab had shocked him. The People's Republic strictly censored the information provided to their citizens. He guessed that even this educated segment was about two decades behind the modern world in their awareness of global events and technology.

The Major began his story first. "In the late 80's, Major Michael Northington was assigned to bring home a Senator's daughter. He found her in Asia, but she wouldn't leave without a bevy of orphan girls."

"She wanted to adopt them?" Marc knew his own adoption was not international, though many people his parents had socialized with had adopted their children from other nations.

"She wanted to keep them alive. They were on their way to having their organs harvested for the black market."

Cooper leaned in, no longer pretending that he wasn't listening.

"I'd heard rumors, but ..." Marc swallowed. "I guess you guys see all kinds of nasty business." During law school, Marc had learned the basics of many types of law including criminal law. He quickly realized he had not the stomach for dealing with people's vile treatment of others, nor the desire to engage in a battle of wits over degrees of evilness and the rights of those who preyed on others. He neither thrived in such drama nor found it appealing. It was the reason he specialized in intellectual property law. And it came in handy for his own tinkering, as Nancy referred to his inventions.

"There's no lack of bad guys in the world." The Major crossed his arms over a muscled chest. "Northington obeyed orders. Strictly. Like a good soldier is trained to do. Right up until he saw the remains of one of the girls."

Marc grimaced at the idea that someone would take the life of a young girl as if she were nothing more than a car to be parted out. "How many girls did he bring home?"

"Four. Plus the senator's daughter, of course. But he always regretted not making his decision before the fifth was killed. It still haunts him."

"And we're still gonna get our rear ends chewed." Cooper rubbed a hand over his military issue haircut that was due for a buzz. "Geez, that guy has some colorful insults and he never repeats any."

Marc looked puzzled.

"The former Major Michael Northington," the Major explained, "is now our commanding officer."

# Chapter One hundred-twenty-six

"China?" Mallory faced Deverell. "Or Israel?"

After the hours, days, and weeks of panicked suspense, she wanted details before she allowed herself to celebrate. What was Marc's condition? How much had her decisions harmed and affected her brother? She knew the repercussions would be long term. Right now she needed to know what damage control was required immediately.

"This little piggy went to market, this little piggy stayed home." Deverell was already on his way out the door. "Both, actually."

"That makes sense." Fred trailed the other two.

Mallory was hard on the heels of her retreating boss. "Where is he? Is Marc all right?"

Fred tagged behind, shadowing the fast walking supervisor and the power-walking analyst demanding information. "Those two countries began trade relations long before the actual establishment of diplomatic relations in 1992. No doubt conservative, current figures indicate the bilateral trade between them is in excess of five billion."

Mallory waved an arm behind her to silence Fred. "Will you shut up! I can't hear Deverell." Rounding the corner into his office, Deverell picked up his phone. Behind him, Mallory and Fred followed like ducklings. "Is he safe?"

Deverell motioned for her to back away and be quiet.

Pressing near to overhear his phone conversation, she ignored his gestures. "Well? Where is Marc?"

Deverell snapped his fingers to get Fred's attention. He pointed to Mallory and to the door. With a slight nod, Fred took Mallory's elbow and guided her back into the hall.

"I want to know what is going on!" She jerked her arm free.

Quickly, Fred took her arm once again and steered her out of the office, closing the door tightly behind them. "Let him do his job, Mal. You'll know soon enough." Positioning himself between his anxious partner and the door, Fred stood sentry while he continued connecting information. "The Israeli Ministry of Industry and Trade defined China as an export target country and went fishing. China was an easy catch."

Mallory was only half listening to his constant blathering. "What are their primary fields of trade?" Mallory placed her hands on her hips. "Stolen U.S. patents?"

"The Israeli's main exports to the Chinese are telecommunication, high tech, agro-technology, security, and environment and info-structures."

Mallory began to pace. "If anyone hurt him …."

Fred paced right to left, passing Mallory who paced left to right. "The Israeli Minister of Industry, Trade, and Labor made an official visit in 2008 to promote trade ties and cooperation between the two countries."

"Apparently the two are quite chummy." Mallory faced her partner. "Where is Marc?"

"It's more than that, Mallory." Fred spoke gently. "Israel is exposing local Chinese industries to Israeli companies in their fields. Each year business delegations are conducted to various provinces such as Guangdong, Sichuan, Yannan, Hainan, and Heilongjiang. A trade representative office is established in southern China's city of

Shenzhen and in the northeast city of Dalain."

The door opened and Deverell beckoned them into his office. "To market, to market to buy a fat pig." Deverell parroted in sing-song. "Kosher, of course."

"China imports from Israel and exports to them as well." Mallory waved for her boss to hurry with his explanation. "I know the drill."

"Home again, home again, jiggity-jig. Israel also knows that China arms Israel's enemies. Trade agreements allow Israel to have a better finger on the pulse of what is being supplied. And to who."

Mallory pointed to Deverell and then to Fred. "What does any of this have to do with Marc's current location? What are you two hiding from me?"

Deverell stuck a piece of gum in his mouth. "It is through one of these situations that we were able to track Marc."

"You tracked him?" Mallory's voice rose an octave. "You tracked him. You knew something, and didn't tell me." She drew herself up and pushed her face close to his. "How dare you not tell me – " From his desk, she grabbed a stained Harley Davidson coffee mug and flung it at the wall. The cup flew into pieces and large chunks of glass dropped onto the carpet.

Deverell put up his palms. "Bad choice of words. Sorry. And in my defense, this information came through fast. It was through one of those channels," he held up the phone receiver, "that we were notified of Marc's location."

Through gritted teeth she repeated her question. "How is he?"

Deverell shook his head. "I don't know."

# Chapter

# One hundred-twenty-seven

Marc felt the plane begin its descent. Gazing out the window, he recognized farm fields stretched as far as he could see like the patchwork quilts his mother used to make with the other church ladies at their weekly quilting bee. There was one on his bed back home. The women had pieced the colorful fabric squares with tiny stitches as a gift when he became a patent attorney.

Creeks and stands of trees edged square farm fields where farmers and their sons hunted deer in November. Flanking traditional red barns, newer pole barns housed oversized green and yellow farming equipment, beef cattle, and a variety of 4-H projects the country kids would display in the summer at the State Fair.

A flash caught his eye. Like lightening, three F-16s streaked past, white exhaust marking their trail. The sight of them brought a lump to Marc's throat.

Then, coming into view below, was an expansive military base. Huge hangers, box shaped dorms, and oversized buildings adjacent to the runways.

"Look familiar?"

Marc looked up to see the Major leaning over him to look out the window. "Definitely Midwest." Marc craned his neck to survey the size of the runways. "Wright-Patterson Air Base?"

"Yep."

Marc called Lei to the window.

"It looks like a city," she said.

"That base is the size of a medium community," the Major agreed. "It has everything a city has – shopping, a movie theater, and child care centers. At last count, some 25,000 military and civilian employees work there. Wright-Patt is the largest employer in Ohio and one of the largest Air Force bases in the world. The current economic impact to the Dayton, Ohio region is $4.4 billion."

"Billion with a B?" Marc whistled.

"Your tax dollars at work."

"Trust me, I won't complain about taxes ever again." Suddenly Marc even looked forward to filing the previously grievous forms. If that was how these guys got paid, he wanted to add a significant tip.

"Wright-Patt has a rich aviation heritage," the Major continued. "In 1904 and '05, on Huffman Prairie Flying Field, the Wright Brothers flew the first turn, circle, and figure eight. From 1910 to 1916 the brothers operated a flying school. Among their 119 students was Henry 'Hap' Arnold."

"The guy who commanded the Army Air Forces in World War II?"

The major nodded. "And H. Roy Brown, the Canadian ace."

"He shot down the Red Baron in World War I." Cooper stretched as he joined the group by the window.

"Just off the end of Runway 23 is a replica of the Wright Brothers 1905 hanger and catapult launcher." The Major pointed to the site. "That's the exact location of their early aviation accomplishments."

The sound of the engines increased an octave as the plane aligned itself over the tarmac. With a swift drop and a bounce, they were back on terra firma. Cooper swore. "Where'd that pilot get his license?"

As the soldiers shouldered their gear and made their way toward the door, Lei came to Marc's side. "Welcome back to the United States," he said.

"Truly?"

"Yes, ma'am," the Major assured. "Smack dab in the center of the country."

Tears filled her eyes and Marc put a comforting arm around her shoulders. "You can relax, now, Lei. You're safe."

The Major addressed Marc. "What about you? How are you feeling about landing back in the U S of A?"

Marc took a deep breath and considered. "Strangely, I feel nervous about meeting people I already know."

"Re-entry." Cooper shook his head.

"There's a term for this feeling?"

"That's the technical term." The Major jerked a thumb in Cooper's direction. "Cooper has a slang word for it if you are interested."

# Chapter

# One hundred-twenty-eight

Their rescuers stood aside to allow the Major to lead Marc and Lei off the plane first. The aircraft's pilot and co-pilot stepped from the cockpit in time to say their good-byes.

Behind him Marc heard Cooper's drawl. "Did we land or were we shot down?"

"You wanna try it?" the pilot shot back.

"A monkey could do it better."

"Then you're certainly qualified," the pilot responded.

Stepping into the Ohio afternoon, the first thing Marc saw was Mallory, bouncing on tip-toes and waving a cellophane wrapped bouquet of flowers. *Mallory!* His knees buckled under the wave of shock and relief. His last sight of her on the computer screen had given him nightmares ever since. Mallory! She was safe.

And here.

All his anxiety about locating her and getting her away from Yao's hired brutes suddenly dissolved. The intense shift felt like an emotional whiplash.

She ran straight into his familiar hug, the rustle of tissue and smell of flowers all part of their embrace. "You're okay." His voice choked. "You're all right." He repeated the words over and over, drinking in the reality of his sister's unexpected presence.

She held him tightly and he must have held her even tighter because after a long moment she squirmed and exclaimed, "Hey bro, sissy can't breathe."

He pulled back and looked at her. "That's why your eyes are wet."

Quickly she brushed her palm across her eyes. "Allergic to the flowers." She pushed them at him.

He blinked back powerful feelings of relief and joy at seeing her. "Me, too." He held her shoulders and studied her face. "Are you hurt? Did those fiendish ogres hurt you?" He shook his head at the stupidity of the question. "Of course you were hurt. And traumatized. I saw what they did to you – "

"Marc," she put a palm against his cheek. He saw worry and fear in her eyes. "Marc, I'm fine. Aside from horrible worry about you, I've always been fine."

A shudder went through him. "But they had you, I saw them inject...."

Stubbornly swallowing back tears, she shook her head. Gently and slowly, like she was speaking to a confused child, each word was carefully chosen. "No one had me. No one injected me with anything. I've always been right here, either at home or at work. Looking for you."

Marc searched her eyes. She was telling the truth. Now he wrestled to exchange what he thought had been reality. To trade out what Colonel Yao had shown on the computer screen with the new information Mallory just provided. He dropped his hands from her shoulders.

Mallory seemed to sense his turmoil. "Breathe," she coached. "Just breathe."

Obediently, he sucked in a lungful of clean Midwest air. Like one of his physics equations, he sorted through the sequence of events, reconciling this puzzle. Mallory had nothing to gain by lying.

On the other hand, Yao had everything to lose if he couldn't make Marc believe Mallory was in danger. Once Marc had convinced the Colonel he would die before giving in to his captor's demands, Mallory was the only motivation that ensured Marc would complete the Meissner Device. His hatred of the man seethed anew and he cursed. Smoke and mirrors. Somehow the Colonel had staged a scene that convinced Marc that Mallory's life was at stake, dependant solely on Marc's cooperation and contribution.

"Marc?" Mallory put a hand on his arm.

He met her concerned gaze and grinned, the movement stretching facial muscles that had not been used in a long time. When was the last time that he had grinned? Smiled because he was happy? "That's the best news, sis. The very best news."

Relief showed in her eyes.

Marc put the flowers in Lei's arms and pulled her forward. "Lei, this is my sister. I suspect she had something to do with our meeting in China."

Mallory shook Lei's hand and cast an apologetic glance at her brother. "Guilty as charged. Marc has a lifetime of leverage over family vacations." She linked arms with Marc and Lei, and steered them toward a waiting car.

"Wait," Marc told her. He turned back to see the Major and his men, heavy 72-hour packs thrown over their shoulders, striding to the terminal. "Major!" Marc called.

The small squad halted. Marc jogged over to them. "Major," he began. "Thank you …" He flushed at his frustrating inability to find the right words. To express deep gratitude. These guys had given Marc back his life.

"Next time you decide to run your own spec ops mission, call me. I'll be your support." The Major saluted.

Marc stood speechless and the Major turned and walked away. The others nodded at Marc and followed their Major. Cooper stood a second longer to give Marc a thumbs up, then he too was gone.

# Chapter

# One hundred-twenty-nine

Marc and Lei were taken straight to Wright-Patterson's 88th Wing Medical center. "Maybe a little worse for wear." Marc tipped his head to each side to stretch neck muscles. "But I'm sure nothing a few days of great food and some rest won't cure."

"You don't have a say." Mallory was nearly exuberant with the quick change of events that placed her back in her comfortable position of being in control. "The military will check you thoroughly and let you know how you are."

Lei looked nervous, and Mallory patted her arm. "Don't worry. We arranged for a kindly female doctor for you. You've had plenty of excitement and this lady is like a grandmother to all of her patients."

The hospital came into view through the military vehicle's front window. "You're in good hands." Mallory knew she was chatting nonstop, but tossing information was a means of connecting to Marc. It was their common language. And therapy for her nervous happiness. Marc was back. Her first project as lead agent hadn't ended as a complete disaster. The most important factor was her brother's safe return. "This Air Force medical facility is the third largest and handles 300,000 outpatient visits annually. From here they deploy trained medical personnel to support global exercises and operations."

"Is that all?" Marc whistled appreciatively. "This whole base is impressive."

"This wing," she added, "oversees the largest service division in the U.S. by providing fitness, food, library, recreation, and youth programs for past and present base personnel and their families."

"What do they do for fun?"

"They are famous for hosting the annual U.S. Air Force Marathon each September, attracting thousands of the nation's top long distance runners," Mallory said.

"Darn," Marc lamented. "Missed it by that much."

"Maybe next year," Mallory quipped.

The driver stopped at the hospital entrance.

"Only if you run it with me," he returned.

"I'd rather beat you at driveway basketball."

# Chapter One hundred-thirty

As Mallory promised, a grandmotherly physician took Lei under her care and gave the girl her full attention. Marc winked an assurance to Lei and turned to see what Mallory had lined up for him. A large black doctor who looked like he just came off the playing field from sacking a Colts' quarterback stuck out a meaty hand and introduced himself to Marc as Dr. Williams.

"How come she gets the nice, knit-you-a-sweater doctor and I get John Henry who can out-hammer a machine," Marc complained quietly to his sister.

Mallory clapped her brother on the back. "Just do what the good doctor says and you won't get hurt."

His voice still low, Marc pressed the point. "Do you cage him after hours? Throw him raw meat?"

"I get extra days out when they need me to help Air Force beat Army." Dr. Williams folded his arms across his beefy chest. "I disassemble 'em on the field and bring 'em back in here to put the poor suckers back together again. It's a package deal."

"Sorry." Marc gave Mallory a 'didn't know he could hear me' look.

Williams cleared his throat. "You comin' or what?"

"I'd rather 'what,' actually." Casting a last sheepish glance to his sister, Marc entered the exam room Williams indicated.

In the course of a few hours, Marc was prodded and poked in places he didn't previously know he had. Blood was taken and tests were run including a full body x-ray. He was lying in a hospital bed enjoying the stiff, clean sheets when Mallory entered with two tall cups smelling strongly of rich coffee.

She eyed the IV bag plugged into his left arm. "Do you want to drink this or just have it fed to you intravenously?"

"Don't deprive my deprived taste buds of American coffee," he begged.

She handed him a cup. "Made the military way."

"How's that?" He held the cup under his nose and breathed deeply, the fragrant steam warming his face.

"They put a bullet in the pot and when it dissolves, the coffee is ready."

"Just the way I like it – bulletproof." He took a sip and closed his eyes, tasting the rich liquid.

"What are you thinking?"

He opened his eyes and saw Mallory's concerned look. He waved her into the nearby chair. The vinyl cushion squeaked as she sat.

"Just remembering the taste of Turkish coffee. It has a spicy, sweet flavor and grounds at the bottom that you either have to be careful to leave or chew when they swish around your teeth." He swirled the coffee and watched the miniature vortex in the cup. "It's a different color, too, sis. More orange."

"How are you?"

He looked up at her. "Nervous about a lot of things. It's a strange feeling. I wish I could blend in but I feel like I'm being noticed. Stared at."

"We see this a lot, Marc. It's a normal part of adjustment."

"Not permanent?"

"I promise. And gives you an appreciation for what our soldiers – our military – experience with reentry."

"Those guys who brought me home?"

"It's their job. And they go through a debrief and reentry. It is hard on marriages. The ones who seem to do the best spend the first few days in a neutral place with loved ones before going to their civilian address."

Marc downed the last of his coffee. "What did Dr. Grandma say about Lei?"

His sister nodded toward the nearly empty IV bag. "Much like you, she's getting a large bag of fluids and supplements. Overall she's in good shape considering her adventures, which you can fill me in on tonight." She cocked her head. "Now spill. Who is this pretty girl you brought all the way home from China? My future sister-in-law?"

Marc's eyebrows shot up. "Whoa. Down girl. I just got back into the states and you're marrying me off. One shock at a time, please." Last time they were together, Mallory had been talking about Nancy.

She crossed her arms. "Got it. You need time to date."

"It's not like that." He adjusted the hospital bed so he was eye level with his interrogator. "We're not dating. She's," he fished for the right words, "she's like a student. Well, she was a student, but graduated now." He fumbled forward. "Lei is a friend who needed to get out too, so we got out together."

"She likes you."

Annoyed, Marc shifted. "That's what Adi thought, too. Escape from a barbaric situation, and suddenly everyone links your names together."

"I'm a research and analysis specialist. I just call 'em as I see 'em."

"She is brave and terrified at the same time. I tried to protect her, though I doubt I did a very good job. I'm weak on my super hero skills."

"You did something right. You're here."

He was thoughtful. "She is in love, actually. Lei took the risk to return and find her boyfriend. She's engaged to a boy from college."

Mallory considered this. "Okay. I wondered if you were as clueless about Lei as you've been about Nancy."

He frowned. "Nancy? What does Nancy have to do with this? She's all right, isn't she? And the office?" Fresh panic washed over him. Had Colonel Yao and his goons threatened Nancy?

His sister rolled her eyes. "Nancy and your office are fine."

He sighed his relief. "So what about Lei? Medically?"

"The doctor said she is shell-shocked and exhausted. Post-traumatic stress syndrome. She's prescribing several weeks of rest, refreshment, and excellent nutrition."

"I hope I get the same prescription."

"Doubtless, Dr. Williams will offer something similar, but I'm ordering R and R and some great meals."

Marc settled back on his pillow. "Ah, steak, pizza, brats and sauerkraut, Amish-made pies, and good ole' American burgers. Lots of 'em."

"You'll die of scurvy if you don't get something green on that menu."

"Of course, what was I thinking? Plenty of mint ice cream."

# Chapter One hundred-thirty-one

Released by the medical facility doctors the following day, Marc and Lei were escorted into a waiting Humvee. Much to Marc's relief, Lei looked much perkier. Mallory was safe and well. Marc told himself he could relax but the doctor had warned him the process wasn't always immediate. Cooper and the Major called it reentry.

"Where are we going?" Feeling better, Lei was more talkative today.

"There's something we want to show the two of you," Mallory said mysteriously.

After several turns, the driver stopped in front of a building. Lei tensed at the sight of the armed guards.

"We're home, remember?" Marc looped his arm about her shoulder and gave her a squeeze. "These are the good guys." He smiled and held her gaze until she relaxed and smiled back.

Through several checkpoints, Mallory ushered them inside where they were joined by two others.

"Fred!" Marc exclaimed. "What are you doing so far from your D.C. office?"

"They let me out for special occasions." Heartily, Mallory's co-worker pumped Marc's hand.

A tall man with tanned face and glasses stepped forward. "This is my boss," Mallory introduced. "Logan Deverell."

"So this is your little brother." The man clasped Marc's hand. "Well done. You checked out worn and weary, but healthy."

Marc looked about. "What is this place?"

"It's our lab for the development of the Meissner Effect Vehicle," Deverell announced proudly.

Lei turned and started for the door.

"Hey," Deverell called. He looked at Marc. "Was it something I said?"

"As a matter of fact." Marc jogged after Lei. Catching up he walked in step beside her. "Could be fun to compare," he offered. "Strictly on a scientific basis, of course."

Mallory came up on Lei's other side. Her voice was gentle. "You okay?"

Lei stopped and put her face in her hands. Marc drew her into his arms and tenderly cradled her against his chest. "Trust me?" he asked into her hair.

She nodded.

"Just breathe," he coached.

In a moment, she took her hands from her face and slid them around his waist. Mallory's eyes met his questioningly. Marc winked his okay.

"These people are our friends. Maybe not smart," he smiled over Lei's head as Mallory wrinkled her nose at his jab, "but you are free here to make your own choices. You are free to come and go, to choose what you want." He tightened his arms around her. "I think they just want to show us something."

Lei pulled back to study his face. Marc brushed a couple tears from her cheek. "Wanna take a peek? I bet they don't let just anybody in here."

Mallory stepped closer. "Only VIPs, Lei. And that's what you are. A very important person."

Lei nodded and the three made their way back to Deverell

and Fred.

"Right this way." Fred pushed the confused Deverell into the lead. "We settled on this location for a variety of reasons. Wright-Patt is one of the largest, most diverse, and organizationally complex Air Force installations. From the pioneering flights of the Wright brothers to the development of today's most advanced aircraft and aerial systems, it's all here. Missions for the base's units vary from research and development, to advanced education, and flight operations."

"This base," Mallory added, "is headquarters for a vast, worldwide logistics system, a world-class laboratory research facility, and is the Air Force's foremost acquisition and development center. There are some 60 associate organizations contracted with the Department of Defense activities."

Deverell took his cue and jumped easily into the conversation that kept pace with their footsteps. "Wright-Patterson Airbase is the birthplace, home, and future of aerospace. Their legendary past attracts aerospace specialists, scientists, engineers, and trainers to keep 'em flying faster, higher, farther, and safer than man has ever flown before. That made this the logical and perfect place for a faux laboratory."

"A false laboratory?" Marc spun in a slow circle, taking it all in. It looked pretty authentic to him. He glanced at Lei and could see she was puzzled, too. "I don't understand."

"When we couldn't find you," Mallory explained, "we created a laboratory and leaked that the U.S. was working on the final elements to make the Meissner Device reality."

"Why?"

"The plan," Fred put in, "was that as long as your captors felt there was value to your life, they would keep you alive. That bought us more time to track you down."

"Which you never did," Marc noted.

Mallory sighed. "No one knows that better than me."

"Yet," Fred said, "every day we discovered new information related to the mole, the information leak, and your whereabouts."

Deverell opened an inner door and ushered the group into a

highly technical facility. A half dozen men and women populated the space. In the center, under construction, was a larger model of the machine Marc had assembled in China.

"You put all this together for me?"

"We wanted to keep you alive until you could be located and brought home," Mallory said.

"A facade laboratory for a fake device," Marc said.

"Will you close this now?" Lei wanted to know.

Fred shook his head. "As long as the Chinese and other foreign governments think we are working on this, they will continue to try to beat us to the formula."

"Those Chinese will spend billions getting this going."

Lei looked sidelong at Marc. "They probably already have."

"Which deflects their funds from other pursuits of military interest," Mallory said.

Deverell unwrapped a stick of gum and shoved it into his mouth. "Truth is, our government saw real potential in your design. Enough to assemble this facility for the development of the Meissner Device." He led them to a side room. Above the doorway was a sign that read, "Designgineering."

Inside, a heavy metal band played from one CAD system, fighting with classical music coming from a vinyl record player hooked up to a set of woofers and tweeters. Toys from the 50s, 60s, and 70s overflowed a toolbox. A slinky and an etch-a-sketch rested with dry erase markers in the white board tray. The whiteboard and adjacent chalkboard wall were filled with equations and theorems. The place smelled of homemade banana bread.

Looking up from a set of blueprints, a man in Birkenstocks came to meet them, his body led by his belly. "You just missed the daily brainstorm session but there is banana bread left." He indicated a tray that held slices topped with cream cheese, and one remaining poppy seed muffin.

"This is Wilson," Mallory introduced. "He is the design engineer for the project."

"Designgineer," he corrected, shaking Marc's hand. Marc's eyes widened at the small patch on Wilson's shirt. Sitting up on its back legs, it was a skunk.

Mallory went to the CAD, and over the heavy metal screams, tapped the user on the shoulder. He turned and when he saw her, quickly turned down the music. Looking past Mallory, he locked eyes with Marc.

"Hebron?" Marc tried to take in the shock of seeing the redhead college student in this setting.

Then the boy was shaking his hand, a grin displaying a blue-black poppy seed stuck between his front teeth. "Mr. Wayne, good to see you."

"You're looking good, Hebron. Stronger." Marc flexed his fingers after Hebron's enthusiastic handshake and took in the boy's frame. "And you've filled out. I don't see those ribs anymore. Got rid of that tapeworm?"

"Had to let out my belt. This place has unlimited food and this guy," he jerked a thumb to Wilson, "knows how to fill in during the between-meal lows."

"Made it myself." Wilson passed the plate to Marc.

To avoid a poppy seed in his teeth, Marc took a piece of bread. "What are you doing here?"

"Thought you knew." Hebron shrugged, his long arms still needing some sun. "Bringing your patent to reality."

From his pocket, Marc retrieved Hebron's diamond device. The boy brightened and Marc returned the object to its owner. "I found another use —"

"For clarity of fine wine." Hebron opened his invention and peered inside. "I got your message from my professor."

Lei came to Marc's side, watching the exchange. Marc shook his head. "Something else, Hebron. Your device has another use."

Lei put out her hand and shook Hebron's. "Thank you."

# Chapter One hundred-thirty-two

Following a tour of the rest of the facility, Deverell brought the group back to the Designgineering room. "Everything is state-of-the art."

"Except for Wilson," Mallory observed.

He folded another stick of gum into his mouth. "Would you consider working with them on the blueprints?"

Marc took Lei's hand. "Is that an invitation, or a demand?"

Deverell grinned. "Hey, this is the United States of America. Land of the free, remember?"

"You choose if, and when, you visit," Fred assured. "Maybe more importantly, you choose when you leave. We'll take you anytime we can get you and strictly on your terms."

Marc shook his head. "I'm really not interested."

"Everything is supplied," Fred pressed. "You can have anything you want for your work. The most exciting aspect is that your patent for the Meissner Device is nearly operational."

"Except that troublesome spot," Deverell said. "Sir Galahad is still searching for the Holy Grail."

Again Marc shook his head.

Mallory put a hand on his arm. "Don't make a decision now," she said gently. "Take your time. Think about it."

"Look," Deverell checked his watch, "let's get you both a good meal." He led the way back through security and outside where the Humvee they had arrived in was gone. In its place stood a bus usually designated to shuttle tourists from the main Wright-Patterson Air Museum to exhibits in outlying hangars. Climbing aboard, Marc was surprised to see they were the only passengers.

Once the party was seated, the driver swung the bus onto a main road. Passing the entrance, Marc noted the visitors making their way from the patriotic museum to the parking lot. Several stood for photos while others viewed the outdoor memorial. Open year round, the museum closed at 5:00 p.m. It was nearly 6:00 p.m.

Behind the Air Base's perimeter fence and west of the museum, the bus passed the Research and Development Flight Test Hangar and parked at the next structure.

Fred led the group inside. Lined up in the quiet hangar like soldiers in formation, were row upon row of stately jets. Though they were different shapes and sizes, they all bore the Presidential Seal.

"Where are we?" Lei asked.

"I remember this. I came here for a school fieldtrip." Marc inhaled deeply. "But it sure didn't smell this delicious."

The informal tour of the retired presidential aircraft gave Marc a renewed sense of security. He suspected that was the goal. Planes used by Franklin D. Roosevelt, Harry Truman, and Dwight D. Eisenhower sat like the sphinx, silent and proud. The centerpiece of the one-of-a-kind collection was a SAM 26000, used regularly by Presidents John F. Kennedy through Richard Nixon. During Nixon's shortened second term, the super plane served as the back-up aircraft for the commander-in-chief. This was the plane that had winged President and Mrs. Kennedy to Dallas, Texas on November 22, 1963, the day an assassin's bullet took the life of John F. Kennedy as Jacqueline Kennedy struggled in vain to hold her husband's brains inside his broken skull. Shortly after the assassination, Vice President Lyndon B. Johnson was sworn in as president of the

United States aboard the aircraft. The modified Boeing 707 carried the body of the slain president back to Washington.

Deverell ran a hand over the sleek surface. "She's seen a lot, this plane."

"She wears it well," Fred said. "A grand dame."

"The old girl got a face lift – a new paint job back in 2009," Deverell added. "Mirror, mirror on the wall, who's the fairest of them all?"

At the bottom of the jet's stairs stood a man smartly dressed in a black tux. He bowed slightly. "Welcome aboard. I will be your maitre 'd."

As they followed him up the gangplank, Mallory whispered to Marc. "He's one of ours."

The aroma of fine food grew stronger as the group entered the dining area of the luxurious plane that had once served the most influential men on the planet. An oval table was set for a seven-course meal. The smell of succulent roast prime rib came from the galley and Marc's stomach growled.

"Lei, Marc, have a seat," Deverell said. "I've been looking forward to hearing your side of this crazy story."

While a waiter filled their goblets with ice water and topped each glass with a tangy slice of lemon, Mallory reached across and squeezed Marc's hand. "It's such a relief to have you here."

Marc lifted his glass in a toast. "To you heroes who got Lei and me back home."

"We're the same guys who got you into this adventure." Deverell flashed his I-told-you-so look to Fred and Mallory.

Mallory looked sheepish. "I wasn't going to bring that up."

"It seemed like a good idea at the time." Fred reached for a crab cake from the plate of appetizers.

Their server poured a red wine and Marc thought of Hebron and his clarity invention.

"If the whole episode hadn't happened, I would still be back under Colonel Yao's control," Lei said. "Being here is freedom for me."

"Here, here." Fred lifted his wine glass in salute. "To

freedom."

Tucking into a Caesar salad, topped with croutons and anchovies, Deverell turned the conversation. "Your Adi is an interesting character."

"His real life reads like something out of an action adventure novel," Fred put in.

"Maybe more like a contemporary suspense," Mallory said. "Or a mystery spy story."

Marc nodded. "He's something all right."

Lei leaned forward. "What do you know about him?"

Marc raised an eyebrow. "I thought you hated him."

Lei flushed. "I'm just curious."

Mallory put a gentle hand on Lei's arm. "Of course you are curious after all you experienced in Israel." She gave Marc the look she used to tell him he was once again being a clueless male.

Deverell forked the last of his salad and pointed the dangling lettuce at Marc and Lei. "For Adi's safety, and the protection of his people and his work, everything about Adi must be kept secret."

"Just a kibbutz specializing in mud baths for tourists," Marc said.

"Adi works with illegal arms shipments."

"I figured that out myself," Marc told his sister.

Fred dipped parmesan bread into herbed oil. "He receives and sends arms, then tips off the authorities about particular shipments that are dangerous to Israel or her allies. When the authorities bust those transports and pick up some nasty criminals, it looks like they were sloppy with their arrangements."

"Adi's work allows Israel to know who is doing what in their country," Deverell said. "And Israel is pivotal in world events."

"He was doing something to a shipment that went out just before he sent us," Marc recalled. "I'm no arms specialist, but from my shooting course in 4-H, it looked like he was tampering with the bullets."

The main course of honey-glazed carrots, steaming baked potatoes, and tender prime rib arrived. The last time Marc had tasted such a full-bodied American meal was his lunch with Mallory the day she flew into Indiana. A great deal had taken place since then.

"Brilliant actually," Fred credited. "It's a trick borrowed from Viet Nam. When American forces came across stockpiles of the enemy's weapons, they couldn't carry them out and certainly didn't want to leave the artillery for the enemy to use to kill Americans. They jimmied with some of the ammo so the weapon would explode when fired by the first sorry fella who used it."

Deverell added horseradish sauce to his plate. "The same end will happen to the terrorists who fire the weapons in that shipment. The beauty of the plan is that the buyers assume the weapons are faulty from the factory."

Lei looked puzzled. "Adi is a good man pretending to be a bad man?"

"Exactly," Fred said.

"It is a dangerous work that Adi does," Lei murmured.

"Very treacherous." Mallory smiled her thanks to the waiter who cleared the table.

"Certain foreign governments are committed to obtaining the American trade secrets that can advance the development of their military capabilities," Deverell stated. "Foreign spying remains a serious threat."

"Adi is young to be making such world-impacting decisions," Marc mused.

"There's more." Mallory stirred cream into her coffee. "Adi is the son of the man who leaked your patent design for the Meissner Effect."

# Chapter

# One hundred-thirty-three

"His father?" Lei deeply missed her father since his death. They shared a close and supportive father/daughter relationship, completely polarized from the absent father Adi had experienced. "Does Adi know?"

"Probably not," Deverell said. "They haven't been in contact for many years, not since Hatim Saad emigrated to the U.S. From the photo we found in Saad's apartment, he may have been blackmailed into trading information for his son's life."

The efficient waiter returned with a tray and placed before each diner a dish of chocolate mouse topped with blueberries and cream.

"Who are the blackmailers?" Marc stirred cream into his coffee. He leaned to Lei. "Look, beef and milk at the same meal."

Lei passed on the cream he offered. "Don't think I can mix the two anymore."

"We rounded up the woman inside the patent office," Fred said. "She was a sleeper."

"Sleeper?" Lei frowned at the unfamiliar phrase.

"Previously planted in a strategic position to be called into active service when needed at a later date." Fred shook his head. "They can be a red herring for us. We've encountered spies who were adopted into the country and groomed for espionage. Others who are born here and cultivated for the same purpose."

"If the blackmailers used a photo of Adi to manipulate his father, that means someone knows about Adi," Marc said. "He's in danger."

Fred spoke up. "Our conclusion is that whoever was blackmailing Saad knew Adi was involved in illegal arms shipments. Even the Israeli government knows that. The blackmail worked as long as the blackmailers believed Adi is who he pretends to be – a smuggler of illegal weapons."

"Or the blackmailers were threatening to share Adi's true motives with terrorists who buy from him," Marc said.

Their movements practiced and quiet, two waiters cleared the table. Balancing dishes stacked in precarious towers, one man carried out the plates while the second poured another round of coffee.

"We saw some of them. The terrorists." Lei shivered. "That may be worse for Adi and his people."

Marc recalled the brutes attempting to rape Lei. The man who swung his gun into Marc's head hadn't cared whether the blow knocked Marc out or killed him.

"We've considered that option," Deverell assured. "Mossad has special agents keeping an eye on Adi for awhile."

Bellies overfull, the guests lingered in the cushioned chairs around the presidential table. Long taut muscles in Marc's shoulders and neck were beginning to relax. There was still much to talk about, and, he reminded himself, they were safe at home.

"Mossad?" Lei looked questioningly around the table.

"Those no-nonsense men that had helped the American spec ops team find us," Marc told her. "The American major had said they were Mossad."

"Israel's Institute for Intelligence and Special Operations."

Fred held up three fingers. "Mossad is one of three main entities in the Israeli Intelligence Community, along with Aman which is their military intelligence, and Shin Bet, which is internal security."

"And the kibbutz and his mother?" Lei asked.

Deverell nodded. "Yes. Keeping a protective shield on all of them."

"His mother is quiet and stays in the background, but she's a spit-fire," Marc said. "I can see where Adi gets his passion."

"Some things run in the family." Deverell stood and stretched. "Speaking of which, its time to get you all back where you belong."

Mallory looped her arm around her brother's waist. "Now, you get home where you can rest over the weekend and return to work on Monday."

"Business as usual," Fred added.

Marc rubbed his temples. "This adventure has all the elements of a classic espionage novel: the world teeters on the verge of World War Three, a foreign government focused on accessing our military secrets; foreign operatives who effectively use stealth and guile to gain that access; and an American government official who is willing to betray both her public office and the duty of loyalty expected from every American citizen."

"Don't forget the Holy Grail of weapons world powers are in a race to develop for military superiority." Fred swept a hand toward Marc and Lei. "That's where you two come in."

"A contemporary suspense or mystery spy story," Mallory said.

"Or an action adventure novel," Fred put in.

"The hard part about saving my country and the American way of life as we know it, is not being able to brag about it to women," Marc moaned.

Fred nodded knowingly. "Certainly a drawback to the job."

"Hebron complained of the same ailment." Mallory put her hands on her hips. "Would you really want a woman to love you for that?"

"Or for my superhero good looks." Marc winked at his sister.

"And you." Mallory looked to Lei.

Marc saw hope spring into the young scientist's eyes. She had braved uncertainty, hardship, and danger to return to the United States.

"We've arranged for you to return to your college town so you can look up that young man of yours."

# Chapter One hundred-thirty-four

Marc Wayne pulled his gray streaked hair into a ponytail. He tugged on a jacket, and threw a backpack over his shoulder. The ride downtown was short and chilly, past familiar brick houses in the neighborhood where he'd grown up. As he leisurely pedaled along the Midwest streets of Dixon, it felt good to be home. Secure. He didn't think he would ever again take that feeling for granted.

Wheeling around a corner, he biked down Main Street. Passing the bank, funeral home, and the Veterans of Foreign Wars Hall, he stopped in front of the former post office that now served as his patent office with his workshop in the back. Next to the door, the sign read *Marcus Wayne, Patent Attorney*. He unlocked the door and bent to pick up the newspaper.

"Mornin' Marc," came a gravelly voice.

Marc turned to see Dr. Thurmond standing outside his office door, peering at him over his glasses.

"Good morning yourself, Dr. Thurmond." He clasped the town vet's gnarled hand.

"It wasn't the same around here without you." Thurmond covered their handshake with his left hand. From the adjoining office space, Marc heard the insistent high-pitched yip of a small dog.

"How's business, Dr. Thurmond?"

"Barking along," the wizened old man quipped.

"Glad to hear that," Marc returned.

"I'm glad to hear anything at my age."

Marc smiled. "And just how old are you, Dr. Thurmond?"

"Old enough to remember when you used to come in here on your way home from school to play a game of checkers."

Marc tossed the newspaper inside where it landed on the receptionist's desk. "I was six."

Thurmond wagged a finger at him. "Looks like you're due for a round."

"An accurate diagnosis. What do you prescribe?"

The aged World War II veteran's eyes sparkled. "You be red. You always liked that color best. Best two outta three after work."

A raucous squawk emanated from the vet's open door. It sounded like the worn brakes on Adi's rusted four-wheel drive jeep. Marc recalled the day he and Lei met the Israeli man. After rescuing the illegal arms stowaways in the desert, Adi had driven them in his jeep. The jeep with the ear-splitting brakes.

"That doesn't sound good." Marc had commented diplomatically, clutching the grip above the passenger door handle while Adi careened along a steep hillside and dipped bumpily into a dry wadi bed.

"It's the desert." Adi shrugged. "No need for brakes."

The worn jeep had delivered Marc and Lei from the Negev to the safety of the kibbutz. The same vehicle that made its last, explosive desert trip as a decoy for the black market weapons dealer intent on finding Marc and Lei and offering them back to Colonel Yao for a fine price.

Two more grinding squawks, more insistent than the first, brought Marc back to the present. "That doesn't sound like a dog."

"A parrot." Dr. Thurmond stuffed a fist into his pocket and retrieved something. Opening his palm, he exhibited a handful of sunflower seeds. In the shell. "Calling for more of these."

Marc stared at the small black and white striped shells lying loose in the old man's hand. "No kidding," he said, his voice dry.

"What's that?" The man cupped a hand behind his ear.

Marc cleared his throat. "I said, no kidding."

Tossing a seed into the air, Dr. Thurmond caught it in his mouth. With his front teeth, he split the hull, and spit out the shell. "That bird has me trained. Got me eating these too."

"It's easy to develop a taste for sunflower seeds." Marc was physically in Indiana, but his thoughts were back in Israel.

More insistent, the bird called again. "Stop in." The vet waved toward his clinic. "This bird is not something you see everyday."

Marc fingered the package of sunflower seeds in his own pocket. "I'll do that."

He tossed a casual salute to his neighbor. In his office, he parked his bike next to the oversized pottery crock that served as an umbrella stand. That's when it hit him. The umbrella that Mr. Spencer would not leave behind. Marc had read of several designs that transformed umbrellas into shooting devices. From behind, Marc must have been injected with a sleeping agent. Colonel Yao seemed to be versed on such drugs. Putting the past behind, Marc looked around his patent attorney office.

As usual, he was there before Nancy. Beside the receptionist's desk and under the window was a small table. The 8-track, and stack of Elvis Presley, Lynn Anderson, and Charlie Daniel tapes, had been replaced by a CD player. He thumbed through the short stack of CDs. Neil Diamond. Over 40 years old, a classic album of *Hot August Night* Live at the Greek. The sound tracks from *Fiddler on the Roof* and *Top Gun*. Nancy had gotten adventuresome with her music.

He started down the hall, then turned back to pick up the newspaper from where he had thrown it on Nancy's desk. Under the rubber band, the word China had caught his eye. He shook out the newsprint and scanned the front page.

"China Accused of Being Intellectual Vacuum Cleaner," the headline declared. "China deployed a diverse network of professional spies, students, and scientists according to a long-range plan to collect defense and industrial secrets," reported the head of counterintelligence for the Office of the Director of National Intelligence.

"This week, authorities arrested Kathleen Dongfan on espionage charges for passing classified information to China, and blackmailing employees in the United States Patent Office to supply designs classified Top Secret to foreign agents."

This must be the sleeper Deverell had mentioned over dinner. The USPTO employee that was involved in blackmailing Adi's father.

"A Cuban raised in Hawaii where her parents still live, Dongfan is one of a dozen investigations of Chinese espionage that have yielded guilty pleas in past months. The Immigration and Customs Enforcement officials have launched more than 540 investigations of aggressive illegal technology exports to China."

"Aggressive," Mark murmured. "That's an obscene understatement. Especially for those of us who wake up on the other side of the globe where someone sinister steals my ability to breathe."

"Recent prosecutions indicate that Chinese agents have infiltrated sensitive military programs pertaining to nuclear missiles, submarine propulsion technology, night-vision capabilities, and fighter pilot training. The critical information facilitates China's attempts to modernize its programs while developing countermeasures against advanced weapons systems used by the United States."

He thought of Mallory, Fred, and the hyperactive, hyper thinking Deverell and realized that Mallory and her team had a big challenge ahead of them. "Today's prosecution demonstrates that foreign spy networks pose a grave danger to national security," said the assistant attorney general for national security. "We should all thank the investigators and prosecutors for effectively penetrating and dismantling this network before more sensitive information was compromised."

Rolling the paper, Marc snapped the rubber band back into place. Flipping the newspaper into the air, he caught it, flipped it higher and caught it again before leaving it on Nancy's desk. Whistling, he started down the hall.

The phone rang and Marc picked it up.

"Marc? This is Lei."

He dropped into his desk chair. "Lei. I didn't expect to hear from you so soon. How are you?"

"I wanted to thank you."

"Surely not for the splendid travel arrangements." Her light laughter delighted him, especially after previously seeing the stark fear in her eyes. "How's your Romeo?"

"Married and expecting his first baby."

The memory of her college co-ed had kept her hopeful for a new future while she was stuck in China. "I'm sorry, Lei. That must have been a shock." He thought back over her hardships to return to the man she loved. To the man she thought cared about her. The spunky electro-physics engineer conned powerful military minds on the opposite side of the globe, dodged despicable desert criminals, and concealed herself as contraband weapons to return to this man who once promised her his love. His loss. He obviously wasn't worthy of such a woman. "Are you all right?"

After a long silence, he asked again, "Lei, are you all right?"

He heard a wobbly sigh. "That's a comparative question. All right compared to the conditions in the lab. Free from Colonel Yao's attentions. Liberated from the manipulations and stringencies of The People's Republic."

"What will you do now?" He drew a question mark in the dust on his desk.

"I've come up with my own, as you say in America, half-baked idea."

"Go on."

"I'm thinking about applying to teach science at a university."

He grinned. "Of course. You'd be a natural. Will you invite me to guest lecture?"

"Is your passport valid?"

"Passport? Where are you applying?"

"Israel."

Marc rocked back in his chair. "Of all the places in the world, why Israel?"

"The more I think about our serendipitous encounter there… well… maybe I can –" Excitement topped her voice.

He stared out the window where his hometown was coming awake for the day. Two town councilmen followed an elderly farmer clad in overalls and a Carhart jacket inside the greasy spoon diner where the chef's special changed with the seasons and the coffee was all you could drink. "Sounds like you developed a taste for sunflower seeds."

She laughed. "In the shell."

"And hummus and eggplant."

"Dates and flat bread."

"Turkish coffee." Just the name made him check his teeth for coffee grounds.

"And an occasional mud bath."

"And maybe a zealous young man who introduced you to mud baths?"

Lei's reply was tenuous. And hopeful. "Maybe."

"Certainly intrigued. He is rather the superhero type of guy."

"Intrigued, yes."

"You'll be back in the center of action," he warned.

"If they can use me."

"I'd bet lunch that a university connection will come in handy. You'll let me know, won't you?"

"You'll be the first." He heard her take a breath and hesitantly begin. "Marc?"

"Mmmmm?"

"Would you think I'm crazy if I told you I had a dream that Adi kissed me?"

Marc gave a low whistle. "Funny you should ask."

"Why?"

"Because I had the same dream."

# Chapter One hundred-thirty-five

It was the middle of a clear night when Yao coasted off the unpaved road and parked. He sat for a moment and surveyed the surrounding area. Purposefully, he breathed slowly to steady the beat of his heart. Confident he was alone on the landscape, he picked up a package on the passenger seat and folded it into his pocket.

On foot, Yao traced a direction that had once been familiar to him as a boy. Both he and the countryside had altered since he had farmed alongside his father, and twice he lost his way and had to double-back. In the cooling air, the warm earth smelled musky. A night creature skittered through the undergrowth, startling him.

At last he spied the village. A collection of modest dwellings surrounded by fields that made up the whole of his childhood memories. Stealthily, he crept behind the finer home of the cadre, the man who enjoyed a higher level of living in exchange for being the probing, suspicious eyes of the People's Republic in this remote village.

Yao smirked his derision. The arrogant poppycock strutted his power among these placid families whose largest concern was to keep their bellies full. The cadre was no more than the fattest goldfish in a bowl, unaware of the great oceans teaming with rapacious predators.

Clouds blotted the starlight and Yao stumbled. The noise disturbed the cadre's sleeping mutt who set up a racket and came running. From his pocket, Yao pulled a dead rat and pitched it to the mongrel. Like everyone else in the village except the fat cadre, even the dog never enjoyed the satisfaction of a satiated stomach. The unexpected meal consumed the animal's attention as the former resident knew it would.

The dog whined warning growls to two other canines that approached, their noses high as they sniffed the air. Quickly, the three were circling each other, snapping, and tearing the rat between them.

With the noise of the dogs behind him, Yao stuck to the shadows but was less careful about being completely silent. Someone yelled at the dogs to be quiet and Yao froze. The suspicious cadre peered into the darkness, looking for a long time in Yao's direction. Memories of the village cadre participating in the destruction of his home and the beating of his parents flashed through his mind. Yao flexed into fists the fingers the cruel men had crushed under their boots.

Fighting erupted anew between the curs and the cadre snapped at them to be quiet. Cursing, he kicked the mongrels apart and stomped back inside to his sleep.

A breeze blew, cooling the nervous sweat from his face and the clouds moved, unveiling a gibbous moon. He had chosen tonight, gambling that the moon's glow had guided another to the same destination only hours earlier.

At the rear of his parents' modest home, he tapped lightly on the door. As he had hoped, someone had been waiting. Listening. The door opened immediately. His father's craggy face appeared, the old eyes squinted, and blinked.

"Is it you?" The old man spoke like a dreamer not certain if he is awake or asleep.

Yao pressed the package into his father's hands. "I brought you medicine. For you and for mother's arthritis."

Then his father's bird-like arms were around Yao's neck, hugging him and drawing him inside. "My son. You are medicine enough."

Yao could smell the hearth fire and anxiety beat in his breast. He listened hard and thought he could hear murmuring. "Is he here?"

"Who, my son? Is who here?"

Yao took a deep breath. "The Brother."

# Chapter One hundred-thirty-six

In his workroom, Marc absorbed this new turn of events. He pictured Lei back in Israel, teaching students at the university. He knew she would be an unexpected and brave connection for Adi in his delicate balance between patriotism and the enemies of freedom.

Beside the stool at his workbench was a sealed carton. He dropped the backpack and pulled out a pocketknife. With a slick slice from the blade, the carton sprung open to reveal a dozen bright red fire extinguishers. He grinned. The fire in his kitchen that had cost him the contents of a new fire extinguisher seemed years past. Definitely an event from a different, simpler life. The ill-fated experimental adhesive mixture had proved instrumental as an explosive. Recalling that early morning flushing ashes down the sink while the news kept him company, his world had been innocent. In a short time, his life had been altered. He didn't think there was any going back now.

From his pocket, he retrieved the package of sunflower seeds and studied the rumpled cellophane label with Hebrew words.

"Well done, Adi," he said aloud. He propped the souvenir against his toolbox, snapped on the overhead light, and blew dust off the yellow legal pad that sat where he had left it. Well, almost where he had left it. Someone had turned pages and written fresh calculations. Hebron, no doubt. Who else in Indiana, maybe in the world, had a grasp on the fantastic theory of the Meissner Effect.

That's where Nancy found him later in the morning. Bent over new sketches and equations, reconciling Hebron's scribblings with what Marc had developed in China. Adding what he had picked up from Moshe in Israel. He knew she had arrived when the overhead lights came on. She must have seen his bicycle because he heard her surprised intake of breath all the way down the hall.

"Marc?"

He liked the way she said his name. He didn't bother to look up, suddenly aware of how hard his heart was pounding at the sound of her voice. He tried to call back to her, but there was a surprising telltale catch in his voice.

She hurried to the workroom. "Marc!" There was warmth and joy in that single syllable. His name, spoken with deep affection.

He turned then and swallowed against the knot in his throat that told him volumes about his feelings for her. "How are you, Nancy?"

Her smile was radiant. "I have a list of calls that came in while you were away. I've been docketing the due dates of communications from the patent office –"

He stood and put a finger to her lips. "But how are you?"

Her cheeks flushed. "Fine. Now that you're back." She smelled of spring lavender. "Where were you?"

He shook his head. "I would tell you if I could." She frowned and he wanted to touch her forehead, to smooth away her confused emotions.

Nancy stepped closer. "How are you?"

"Good to be back. Glad to see you."

She flushed deeper. "I'll make you some tea." She disappeared back down the hall.

He watched her go, heard her familiar movements in the small kitchen as she filled the pot with water and spooned fragrant leaves. In moments, the honest smell of Earl Grey teased his nose.

He thought of sweet Turkish coffee prepared by his Israeli hosts that he had quickly developed a taste for though he never felt comfortable with the thick layer of sediment at the bottom of each tiny cup. Grounds that if he wasn't careful to leave in the cup, managed to stick in his teeth like Hebron's poppy seed and make him look like he needed dental work.

Steaming mug in hand, Nancy returned and peered over his shoulder. "How's it coming?"

"In the tinkering stage, but looking promising."

She set the cup near his elbow. "I see," she said and they both knew she didn't. "All these inventions and you can't work the tea pot."

Marc smiled. "That's why I need you, Nancy."

She regarded him. "Really?"

"Really." He looked intently at her.

"For making tea?"

He stood and cupped her chin in his hand. "For a lot more than making the perfect cup of tea."

Suddenly self-conscience, Marc dropped his hand. "Tell me how things are going with – what's his name – Hoss? Tom? Bob?"

"Rob."

"Right. I remembered that."

She tipped her head. "I can tell."

"What does he do, anyway? Lawyer? Doctor? Politician?"

"He builds and drives monster trucks."

Marc blinked. "Monster trucks."

"You know, the ones that show at ticketed events at the Ft. Wayne Coliseum." She gestured to indicate something large. "The ones that make a lot of noise driving over the top of a long line of cars."

Unable to suppress it, Marc laughed heartily.

"Are you making fun of him?" Nancy's hand was on her hip like Mallory often did.

He put up his palms in surrender. "Quite the opposite. Living in a country where a guy can make a living driving monster trucks in public demolition demonstrations makes me want to salute something." He gently placed his hands on her shoulders. "I'm happy for you. Really."

Nancy shook her head. "Rob and I are friends, Marc."

"Friends?"

She nodded. "That's all."

"That's wonderful." Butterflies suddenly danced in his belly.

"Wonderful?" The question was reflected in her eyes.

"Really wonderful. Really, really wonderful." He bent and tenderly kissed her. He was lost in the surprising softness of her mouth when the phone rang. He felt her stiffen, knowing she thought she should answer the untimely interruption.

"That's the phone," she murmured, her breath sweet against his mouth. "I better get that."

"Who cares." He pulled her against him for a deeper kiss. As his arm moved to wrap around her waist, they both heard him bump the full mug. Instinctively, she pulled back to see the damage. Then she turned wide eyes back to his smiling ones.

Rather than crashing to the floor, the cup was suspended in the air, as Marc would explain in due course, floating in a sea of magnetic fields.

# Author Biography

Max Garwood has a Bachelors and a Masters degree in Electrical Engineering from Purdue University, a Juris Doctorate degree from the Indiana University School of Law in Indianapolis, and is licensed in Indiana as an Attorney and a Professional Engineer. He additionally is licensed as a Patent Attorney and earns a living by pursuing patent protection for clients of the law firm of Taylor, IP, PC.

Joseph Chamberlain Henry is the pen name for a writer and author of over a dozen titles. Including an audio finalist, these books have been published nationally, internationally, and translated into several languages.

Made in the USA
Lexington, KY
14 July 2013